THE LEWIS LEGACY SERIES

by
JoAnn Durgin

Awakening
Second Time Around
Twin Hearts
Daydreams
Moonbeams
Enchantment
(Coming in 2015)

Stay tuned for more to come
in the continuing series!

Moonbeams

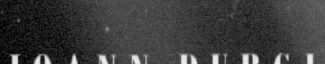

JOANN DURGIN

ISBN: 978-0-9912252-9-3

All Scripture contained within is from the New American Standard Bible.

Text set in Garamond
Printed and Bound in the USA
COVER DESIGN BY Dino Piccinini

From the Author

This fifth contemporary romantic adventure in the **Lewis Legacy Series** is dedicated to my faithful readers. Your prayers, notes of encouragement and emails are precious for my heart.

This book is also dedicated to the victims, survivors, and families so profoundly touched by the World Trade Center tragedy of September 11, 2001, and Hurricane Katrina in late August 2005.

May we never forget.

And may we remember that our God is mighty and He is always in control.

Blessings,

JoAnn Durgin
Matthew 5:16

1 Samuel 16:7

But the LORD said to Samuel, "Do not look at his appearance or at the height of his stature, because I have rejected him; for God sees not as man sees, for man looks at the outward appearance, but the LORD looks at the heart."

Romans 12:21

Do not be overcome by evil, but overcome evil with good.

James 2:14-17

What use is it, my brethren, if someone says he has faith but he has no works? Can that faith save him? If a brother or sister is without clothing and in need of daily food, and one of you says to them, "Go in peace, be warmed and be filled," and yet you do not give them what is necessary for their body, what use is that? Even so faith, if it has no works, is dead, being by itself.

2 Timothy 1:7

For God has not given us a spirit of timidity, but of power and love and discipline.

Ephesians 4:25

Therefore, laying aside falsehood, speak truth each one of you with his neighbor, for we are members of one another. Be angry, and yet do not sin; do not let the sun go down on your anger, and do not give the devil an opportunity. He who steals must steal no longer; but rather he must labor, performing with his own hands what is good, so that he will have something to share with one who has need. Let no unwholesome word proceed from your mouth, but only such a word as is good for edification according to the need of the moment, so that it will give grace to those who hear.

Chapter 1

Friday, February 13, 2004

IS THIS WHAT a panic attack feels like?

Mitch Jacobsen's stomach lurched as the plane hiccupped through the latest air pocket. The perks of flying in a private plane aside, why hadn't he followed his instincts and flown commercial? He'd never felt so queasy and on the verge of losing it.

Curling his fingers around both arms of the seat, his jaw tightened as he stared in disbelief at his sister. With one jeans-clad leg crossed over the other, Amy slowly swung her black high-heeled boot as she flipped through the glossy pages of a magazine. How could she remain so calm when they could imminently plummet to their deaths? Not that he was superstitious in any sense of the word, but did it have to be Friday the 13th?

Amy tossed her magazine on the adjacent seat and then grabbed an airbag. "Here, take this. You look like you might need it." She handed the bag across the aisle with a frown. "You're all pale and clammy. If I didn't know better, I'd think you'd never been on a small plane before. What's up? You used to love to fly." A frown creased her forehead. "Is this about Brad—?"

"Not at all." *Liar.* More than two years later, the mention of his closest friend seared straight through his gut and pierced his soul, the wound still gaping, raw and fresh. Snatching the airbag from Amy's hands, Mitch mumbled his thanks and hoped he wouldn't need to use it. "I've never experienced so much turbulence before. And how do I look clammy?" He shook his head. "Never mind. Don't answer that one."

His dress shirt was damp and strangling him at the collar. After loosening his tie, Mitch unfastened the top button of the shirt. He should have changed into jeans and a T-shirt before boarding the flight, but he'd rushed straight from the office to get to the airstrip on time. He'd definitely need to change his clothes after their arrival in Houston. *If* they arrived.

He'd probably lost five pounds of sweat on this flight, more than during the grueling racquetball match earlier in the week against his brother-in-law, Landon Warnick. The man in the cockpit now. He needed to chill. Landon would get them there safely. Even so, as soon as this metal trap landed, he resolved to drop to his knees and kiss the ground. At least Texas asphalt should be warmer than the pavement in New York.

"You sure you're okay? You'd tell me if you're having a medical emergency, right?"

If one of his former patients presented with identical symptoms, he'd have pegged the case as classic hyperventilation brought on by anxiety.

"I'll be fine," he said. "I need to relax. And hope we don't run into more heavy turbulence." Moving one hand over his abdomen, Mitch deep breathed. In and out, in and out. "Keep talking," he said. "It helps if I focus on something else."

"Not a problem. That I can do." Amy eased back in her seat. "Landon's a great pilot, and there's nothing to worry about. Sorry about the turbulence although it's beyond his control."

In terms of her husband's ability to pilot his beloved Cessna, Amy was right. Landon was experienced and steady. The man led a charmed life. No way God would allow this guy to go down in flames. Straightening his shoulders, Mitch reached above him to adjust the vent. The blast of cool air felt good on his face. "I'm not questioning your husband's skill as a pilot, but sometimes nature can be an indomitable force."

Amy stared at him like a horn had suddenly sprouted from his forehead. "I think you missed your calling. I won't give you the whole *trust in the Lord* versus the *forces of nature* speech because you know it as well as I do. Maybe you should have trained to be an actor like Grandpa Carlisle. Play up those dramatic tendencies of yours and put them to good use."

"Not in this lifetime. I wouldn't want to ruin Grandpa's good name."

Tilting her head, Amy eyed him as she tucked a section of shoulder-length dark hair behind one ear. "The older you get, the more you're the spitting image of him. Only more muscular and a couple of inches taller. Did you know Grandpa was voted one of the most handsome Broadway actors for ten years running? I always knew he was popular and well-respected, but Mom told me he was an honest-to-goodness heartthrob. I think she used the term matinee idol."

"You don't say." Considering ego strokes were few and far between as of late, he'd take what he could get no matter the source. Since their Hollywood-turned-Broadway stage actor grandfather died years ago, it was weird enough when older women swarmed him at random times, most often at the theater. They'd request his autograph, touch his sleeve, gush and call him Eric Carlisle. On the other hand, it was also sweet and sentimental. Depending on the circumstances, he'd either tell them he was Eric's grandson or let it go, allowing the ladies to believe in the fantasy. Not that he was proud of it, but he'd rather tell a half-truth than disappoint them.

Amy shook her head. "Okay, I can see that little bit of flattery does nothing for you."

"While it does feed my ego, you also implied I'm getting older as we speak. It's a backhanded compliment if ever I've heard one."

"I'm not trying to *feed your ego*, but let's approach it from another angle. Think about the fact you might be meeting the woman of your dreams this afternoon." A small smile curved Amy's lips and she narrowed her chameleon-like eyes, currently more green than gray. That stubborn tilt of her chin and sly *I've got a secret* expression spelled t-r-o-u-b-l-e and then some.

A hundred comebacks came to mind, but none Mitch wanted to voice. "That's over the top, even for you." He chuckled, thankful this discussion at least served as a distraction. "I think you're the one who inherited the family acting gene, not me. Why don't you try a little subtlety sometime?"

Of course, Amy referred to Cassie Thorenson, her co-volunteer in TeamWork Missions. Long, gorgeous auburn hair, sweet southern accent—Alabama?—and luminous blue eyes that held no hint of guile. Technically, he'd made her acquaintance at Amy and Landon's wedding reception. To his discredit, he'd assumed Cassie was as naïve as she appeared. During their brief conversation, she'd blown him away with her insightful response to some offhand comment he'd made. Then his unfortunate choice of a date—a woman he preferred not to remember—hauled him off to the dance floor.

Thoughts of Cassie lingered in his mind long after the wedding, but admitting as much to Amy would be a regrettable mistake. If he gave her the slightest hint he might be interested, she'd book the chapel and minister faster than he could say *think again*.

As it was, Amy had dropped broad hints about Cassie with alarming regularity during the past year. How many times had he heard about the woman's quick wit and seemingly unending acts of kindness? In offhand moments, she'd slip in some casual reference. Last week, she'd gone so far as to hum the tune of "Sweet Home Alabama" as they'd waited for a table at their weekly dinner.

Sure, he was intrigued, but what would be the point? The logistics—geographically speaking—were impossible. Bottom line, he lived in Manhattan and Cassie lived in Houston. As he'd gotten older, for various reasons, he wasn't especially fond of flying. When Amy first married Landon, he'd enjoyed the idea of a private plane at his disposal every now and then. Now, not so much. Except for the occasional business trip, he generally stayed close to home. That fact alone should nix a long distance romance, no matter how charming the woman.

"You were thinking about Cassie just now, weren't you?" Amy's smug smile tugged him back to reality.

In order to avoid her piercing gaze, Mitch glanced out the window. Light, fluffy white clouds floated across the horizon in his range of vision. Pretty things could also be deceptive and play with his mind. Any minute they'd probably hit another nasty air pocket, more of a hard burp than a minor hiccup.

"Okay, fine. I'll humor you," he said. "Tell me why you believe a relationship with Cassie could possibly ever work."

~

Cassie Thorenson eyed her reflection in the full-length mirror. She had to admit, the vision staring back at her didn't look half-bad. Secretly, she loved the opportunity to wear this elegant, emerald brocade gown. For a few hours, in the backyard of Sam and Lexa Lewis's Houston home, she could pretend to be a princess in a fairy tale. Of course, her story boasted no castle and no white horse. Not even a moat or a fire-breathing dragon. And certainly no handsome prince. Not that she needed any of those things to find her own happily ever after.

She met Rebekah Moore's green-eyed gaze in the mirror. "Tell me the truth, Beck. Do I look like a displaced Shakespearean player or maybe Renaissance Barbie?"

"Hush. You're gorgeous." Rebekah anchored one hand on her shoulder. "Stand still so I can finish putting this baby's breath in your hair."

Cassie obeyed as her friend added the delicate flower sprays to her braid. Running her finger over the gold filigree pattern stitched into the skirt of the gown, she sighed. "Can you imagine wearing a dress like this all the time, especially in this heat and humidity?"

"You have to admit it's a lot of fun." Rebekah secured one last pin in Cassie's hair. "It reminds me of playing dress-up when I was little."

"You're right. This gives us the chance to indulge our inner child."

Rebekah stepped back and appraised her handiwork. "Here," she said, grabbing a small mirror from the nearby dresser and handing it to her. "Turn around and let me know what you think."

Doing as she instructed, Cassie held up the mirror and followed the length of the elaborate braid halfway down her back. "Very impressive. Thanks. The braid's perfect and the flowers look positively whimsical. Wasn't that your word?"

"I think I said romantic, but whimsical works fine, too. Glad you approve."

After handing back the mirror, Cassie adjusted the bodice, lifting the sturdy fabric to settle more squarely on her shoulders. "I'd better be careful not to bend over too far if I do the dip and curtsy thing. Now I have a theory why the necklines on these gowns are scooped so low."

"What's that?" Rebekah tucked a strand of long blonde hair under a pink beaded headband that matched her gown. She was statuesque, blonde and effortlessly beautiful. The fact that she seemed oblivious to it, or simply didn't care, made her even lovelier. Otherwise, it'd be incredibly annoying.

"Think about it," Cassie said. "Women weren't allowed to show off their ankles, knees or elbows. That would be an abomination or whatever, so they had to make the effort of wearing a cumbersome gown like this worth the trouble. Not that I'm promoting dressing provocatively, mind you. Not at all, but I find it amusing. Seriously, am I showing anything I shouldn't?"

Rebekah shook her head with a small smile. "Stop worrying. Take your own advice about not bending over too far, and you'll be fine. With your sense of humor, and how beautiful you look, you're guaranteed to turn a guy's head."

Cassie ignored that comment. As far as she knew, no single men would be in attendance at the party. Only married fathers with tots in tow. Hardly a breeding ground for a potential husband, but that suited her fine.

Thank goodness, her friends never made her—or any of the other single, female members of TeamWork—feel like the odd woman out. Not that they didn't introduce her to eligible men at any given opportunity. No matter how many times she protested and told them she didn't want or need a man, they still kept trying. In a way, it was sweet, but—depending on her mood—their matchmaking ways sometimes irritated her. As if having a man in her life would somehow complete her. If the Lord wanted her to have a man, then He'd good and well bring one in His own perfect timing.

"I just don't want to wilt." Fanning her face with one hand, Cassie squirmed as a trickle of sweat snaked its way down her back. "Who could have guessed it'd be almost eighty degrees the day before Valentine's Day?" Taking the tissue Rebekah handed to her, she blotted it across her forehead.

"I know, but remember we had an ice storm a few weeks ago. Anything can happen," Rebekah said. "Leave it to Lexa to plan such a great event for her twin girls."

Cassie laughed and tossed the tissue in a corner trash can. "Hannah and Leah are only a year old. They won't remember a thing."

"But everyone else will, and that's reason enough. The first birthday is always a good reason for a big party. Besides, it's also a great excuse to get the TeamWork crew together for a long weekend and mini-reunion. We haven't all been together as a group since—"

"Amy and Landon's wedding eight months ago," Cassie said. How she knew that off the top of her head was anyone's guess.

"Right. Speaking of Amy and Landon's wedding, did you get to meet her brother, by any chance?" Rebekah's question seemed too pointed to be random, and she avoided her gaze.

"Only in passing. I think we exchanged all of two sentences between the rehearsal dinner and the reception. I can't even remember his name. Matthew? Michael?"

"Mitchell, and he goes by Mitch." Rebekah retrieved a plastic bag and pulled out tennis shoes. After crossing the room, she dropped onto the bed. For a woman of her height—five foot ten in her stocking feet—athletic shoes were a sensible choice. At five foot seven, Cassie still needed the added height, and she wore her high-heeled, gold silk pumps—the fanciest shoes she'd ever owned—beneath her gown.

"He has an important job on Wall Street. Stockbroker, I think. Kevin talked with him at the reception and said he's funny, personable and not at all snooty. Winnie's gotten to know him from her visits with Amy and says he's a great catch—great guy, I mean."

Seeing Rebekah's frown, Cassie moved over to the bed. "Wait. Let me help you." Kneeling on the floor, she made quick work of looping and tying the laces.

"Thanks. I didn't think about how difficult it would be to bend over and reach my feet. Wearing this dress gives me newfound respect for our female ancestors."

"Keep that in mind when you're expecting." Cassie grinned when she glimpsed Rebekah's smirk. "All I'm suggesting is that you wear slip on shoes. . .when the time comes."

"Not that I plan on wearing a dress like this when I'm pregnant. Trust me, Kevin and I will jump on the baby brigade soon enough." Rising to her feet, Rebekah offered her hand to help Cassie do the same. "My husband hints about it almost every day, and if he doesn't, then Mom does. For now, my brother and Winnie are doing a fine job of populating our family all on their own." She smoothed one hand down the front of her gown. "Now, back to Mitch."

Cassie arched a brow. "Why are we talking about a man we'll probably never see again? Please don't tell me you're suggesting I do some *populating* with Amy's brother?" She batted her eyelids in an exaggerated manner. "I mean, how nice for Mitch with his fancy credentials and pedigree, but for one thing, I can't imagine your husband ever using the word snooty."

Rebekah pulled a tube of lip gloss from her handbag. "So maybe that's my interpretation. Entitled, then. Just sharing some observations." She slicked the gloss over her lips and smiled. "And never is an awfully long time, my friend."

Chapter 2

THE EAGERNESS IN Amy's expression disgruntled Mitch.

Here we go.

"Let's start with how you and Cassie both operate outside the box. You're independent thinkers who will do almost anything to help someone in need. Add compassion into the mix. And while you're book smart, Cassie's intuitive and a great interpreter of human nature."

"I'm not sure that last statement bodes well either for me or the lovely Cassie. In addition to telling me I'm getting older by the minute, you implied I'm intelligent but have little to no common sense. You also insinuated Cassie might possess the uncanny ability to read me like the proverbial book. No, thanks. Not sure I can—nor do I want—to go there. Besides, the whole *sen-son* thing with our last names doesn't work. Doesn't sound right." Ridiculous thing to say, but—short of hyperventilating—he was willing to try anything to thwart her. He pinned her with his gaze. "In spite of your valiant and admirable efforts, I'm going to disappoint you."

"And you just demonstrated one of your most annoying yet strangely endearing traits—your sometimes unrelenting sarcasm." Although Amy's tone teased, Mitch detected her underlying seriousness. Sparring with Amy had made his life interesting and fun from the time they were kids growing up in suburban Philadelphia.

He'd never been as close with their younger sister, Celeste. Happily engaged and working in Philly, Celeste was content with their bi-weekly phone chats, oblivious to how he struggled to find common ground for a conversation lasting more than five minutes. They'd never shared similar pursuits and his younger sister didn't *get* him the way Amy always had. Only eighteen months separated them in age, and Amy kept him centered and straight.

"If you and Cassie marry, she'd probably take your last name and not hyphenate it."

"Not a modern woman?"

"Not a feminist."

He laughed. "Just because a woman—"

"Cassie's beautiful, she's smart and she's better for you than any of the other women you've dated the past ten years." Amy also never minced words, a quality he begrudgingly appreciated.

"Against my better judgment, I'm listening," he said. "It's not like I can get up and walk away from this discussion."

"You're feeling better now, right?"

"I think I'll survive. Thanks for your concern."

"Here's the thing, Mitch. Your previous choices in women haven't worked out, so why not give Cassie a chance?"

"Welcome to the modern age, Amy. An arranged marriage isn't in the plan book for my life, no matter how attractive, intelligent, compassionate and generous a woman may be." Try as he might to prevent it, a hint of sarcasm managed to seep into his words. "Surely you understand the harder you push, the faster I'm going to run in the opposite direction."

"In other things, maybe, but where Cassie is concerned? Admit it. You're interested."

He shook his head. "You're delusional. No wonder the TeamWork crew nicknamed you Daydreamer."

"You're looking forward to this weekend. Don't deny it."

"You're a hopeless romantic," he shot back.

"And you're lonely, Mitch the Itch."

That barb silenced him as Amy knew it would. His sister was deliriously happy and that's what mattered most. On the flip side, her own state of marital bliss seemed to fuel her insatiable desire to find *him* a mate. While he couldn't be more thrilled for her, keeping her from meddling in his love life had become a top priority, especially in the past year.

And as much as he hated to acknowledge it, Amy was—admittedly, regrettably and completely—right.

~

The mention of Mitch Jacobsen brought him front and center in Cassie's mind. His physical resemblance to Amy was striking. Both Amy and her brother were well-educated, attractive trust fund babies who didn't put on airs although their good breeding was stamped on their Ivy League foreheads. Mitch had walked Amy down the aisle at her wedding since their dad passed away a number of years ago. When he'd stepped aside for Landon to take his place beside Amy, Mitch had kissed his sister's cheek with such tenderness it'd brought tears to her eyes.

How she missed a close sibling relationship. The sting of loss pierced Cassie at the thought of Tagg, as it always did. Fourteen years hadn't removed that heartache, but the passage of time had eased it somewhat. Now she could smile without breaking down in tears whenever she thought of her brother.

Her conversation with Mitch had been cut short at the wedding reception when his date—a willowy brunette who'd clung to him closer than a leech—corralled him and monopolized his attention. Busy for the rest of the evening, Cassie hadn't given Mitch another thought. Until Amy tossed the wedding bouquet and it landed right in front of her, as in directly on top of her feet. She'd purposely refused to grab it even though she'd been the catcher of her high school girls' softball team. So, there she stood, staring at the bouquet while the other girls scrambled for it. Silly tradition.

Snapping back to reality, Cassie opened the small jewelry box she'd brought and carefully removed one of the vintage gold earrings.

"My turn. Let me help you with those," Rebekah said, tossing the lip gloss back in her purse.

Cassie held up the gold, dangly earring and admired its intricate pattern. "I know you're trying your best to pair me off with someone, but you must be desperate to consider a man who lives in Manhattan, of all places. Just because Mitch is single doesn't necessarily mean he's unattached. Besides, I'm perfectly happy with my life as it is."

Great. Why'd she say that? It sounded like something a woman in denial, or one who wished for a mate, would say. "I mean, why complicate anything? Based on the woman I saw him with at Amy's wedding, I got the impression Mitch prefers professional career women. Or waif-thin model types," she mumbled under her breath.

"No snap judgments allowed." Taking one of the earrings, Rebekah carefully helped her put them in. "These are exquisite. Where'd you find them?"

"From the same friend who loaned us the costumes. The design is very similar to the gold pattern in the dress, don't you think?" Having a friend who worked as the wardrobe mistress for a local theatre company—and owed her a favor—had its perks.

"Yes, you have a very good sense for things that match perfectly," Rebekah said with a coy smile. "All I'm saying is, you never know when the right man might walk around the corner and straight into your heart. It *is* Valentine's Day weekend, after all."

"Today is also Friday the thirteenth," Cassie said. "Not that I pay any attention to silly superstition, but I'm still not sure I want to meet the man of my dreams today of all days."

Rebekah darted one last glance in the mirror. "Promise me you'll keep your possibilities open this weekend. That's all."

"Fine. If the Lord decides to plant a candidate for husbandhood—is that even a word?—directly in my path, then maybe I'll pay attention. But no promises."

Chapter 3

*M*ITCH FIGURED HE might as well let Amy have her say. Then he might be able to get a little shut-eye. He could tell her he needed to rest so he'd look his best for Cassie, but he doubted even that plan of counter-attack would stop her. When his sister set her mind on something, she could be as relentless as a tigress. On the flip side, she could also be as fiercely protective, which sometimes worked to his advantage. Being forced to examine his deepest insecurities might actually prove to be a positive exercise.

Turning in her seat to face him, Amy wore that all too familiar *I'm going to win this debate at all costs* expression. "First, let's look at the facts. In the past year alone, there's been quite a parade of women in your life. Starting with Monique the lawyer who apparently takes perverse satisfaction in draining the bank accounts of her clients. Then she tried to drain your financial resources by having you squire her to all those fancy places and donate to her numerous pet causes. Then there's the librarian with the mermaid-sounding name. I have to give you credit for that relationship. She wasn't as sleek and sophisticated as the women you normally date, but she was—"

"A closet klepto," Mitch said. Unfortunately, Arielle lifted more than books from the townhouse. He was still hunting for the Lee Lawrie sculpture inherited from Grandpa Carlisle that had gone missing. The same housekeeping service had worked for Amy when she'd lived there. Since Arielle was the last woman in the place, she had to be the culprit. If she found out, Mom would kill him. So would Amy, so he'd best keep it to himself.

Things meant nothing except when it was a valuable heirloom. Maybe he should have reported it to the police, but he didn't want to see Arielle thrown in jail. He'd tried to figure out a way to get into her apartment, but her building security was tighter than Ft. Knox. Yeah, he'd been clueless. No wonder Arielle could afford to rent such an expensive apartment on a junior librarian's budget. She also dressed well, and could obviously spot things of great value. A visit to a pawn shop or two nearest her apartment might be in order upon his return to New York.

"Oh. Didn't know that. Sorry. Then came—" Amy shot him a curious expression—"help me out here."

Mitch exhaled. "Must we get into this now?"

"No time like the present. Okay, was it Katie the nurse? Or, wait a minute, Southern Belle, or how about Jenny, the cologne-spritzing girl from Saks?" She snapped her fingers. "I know. That cat-eyed, exotic looking Nordic blonde from Café Eduardo? What was her name—Ingrid? The hostess you flirted with shamelessly the night I met Landon?"

"I'm surprised you even noticed. Like you didn't do some heavy flirting of your own. The way you said, 'Thank you, Mr. Warnick,' in that breathy voice when he came over to our table practically channeled Marilyn Monroe and dripped with the innuendo of *I want to marry you and have your children.*"

Although her lips twisted, Amy surprisingly let that one go. "Moving on."

"Fine. Next would be Lorelei," Mitch said, wondering why he was indulging this line of questioning. "Daddy's girl from Georgia. Sausage empire heiress."

"Ah, right. How could I forget? You met her at an art gallery opening and nicknamed her the Macon Bacon Girl. Or was it the other way around?"

He shook his head and allowed the hint of a grin. The release felt good. "I get your point."

"You know, I'm not really sure you do." Amy's smile sobered as she stared him down. "Here's the thing. It's time to grow up, Mitch."

"Thanks for that." Mitch glanced out the window. At least the turbulence wasn't so bad at the moment. "Forcing a confrontation about my love life isn't part of what I bargained for when I agreed to come on this trip." Returning his gaze to his sister, he sighed. "To borrow your phrase, you just demonstrated one of your most annoying yet strangely endearing traits—your sometimes unrelenting bluntness."

"Well, someone's got to do it. I prefer to call it blatant honesty." Amy settled back in her seat, closing her eyes. It was too much to hope for that she'd ease up on him for long. Most likely, she was only refueling. Even their mother wasn't on his case as much as Amy, although he'd sensed her frequent disapproval of his choices for female companionship. For the most part, the women he'd dated displayed a negligible faith, if they had any belief system whatsoever. He'd finally reached the saturation point with aimless relationships, but Amy didn't know it yet. If she did, she'd push Cassie on him with even more fervor. So, he'd kept silent.

Opening her eyes, Amy focused on him again. "I know you've wanted to get to know Sam and Lexa better for a while now. This weekend is the perfect opportunity. Other than the birthday party today, we don't have any major plans except to be together and have fun." Her lips upturned. "It'll also give me a chance to brag on the great work you've done with the inner-city TeamWork projects in New York. I guarantee Cassie will be impressed."

"No one likes a braggart, but thanks for the thought." He purposely ignored the reference to Cassie. "TeamWork's a terrific organization. I admire how you all rally around each other, and I know how much you respect Sam and Lexa." He chuckled. "I guess I should say y'all since we're headed to the Lone Star State."

"Once you get to know Sam, you'll understand." Amy's smile grew brighter. "The man's pretty persuasive. With a Texas-sized heart for the Lord."

"Right. As long as y'all don't start drinking Kool-Aid at the Lewis compound and make a pact to—"

Based on her scowl, she didn't take kindly to that one. Perhaps he'd crossed a line. "If you know what's good for you, you won't finish that sentence, Mitchell Ainsworth."

"Down, Amelia Madelyn," Mitch said, laughing. "I'll be good. Don't take it personally. You led yourself right into that one. I couldn't resist."

"Promise me you'll be on your best behavior when we get to Houston."

"If you're afraid I'll embarrass you, then why'd you bring me along?"

"It's not like I had to twist your arm."

"Unfortunately, I had no valid excuse to get out of coming. Which says a lot about the sorry state of my current social life. Momentary slump." He ducked when she tossed another balled-up airbag his way.

"Truce," he said, raising his hands. "I've witnessed how you and Landon pour your hearts and souls into TeamWork." He shifted in his seat, thankful for the new direction in conversation. "Seriously, it's a beautiful thing. Case in point: taking a girl you met in a no-name Texas town under your wing and bringing her to Queens. Tam's a natural leader and works incredibly well with those girls. I'm sure you'd say she's found her calling."

"You're as much a part of that project as we are, so don't discount your own involvement," Amy said. "And you didn't promise."

"Never."

"I hope you know Tam's got a huge crush on you."

"I love that kid of hers. He's cute as anything. Who'd have thought a girl like that would name her son Henry James?"

Amy sniffed. "A girl like that? What's that supposed to mean? Harvard sheepskin does not give you the right to be a snob."

His smile sobered. *Did* he sound like a snob? That was one four-letter word he never wanted to be called. Heaven forbid. "I wouldn't expect Henry James to be in her reading repertoire, that's all."

"Let's not get off topic."

"Let's do," he said, disgruntled.

"You claim to fall in love on a semi-regular basis yet you can't seem to hold onto a relationship more than a few months. What's the problem, Mitch?"

He'd been expecting this interrogation. Difference was, he was usually on the phone and could make a convenient excuse and escape. No such luck here, currently suspended in a metal cocoon in the sky. "Not the best time for this discussion."

"Why not?" Amy's grin was irritatingly smug. "I don't think there's any better time. If we die, at least we'll clear the air and can plunge to our deaths knowing we're at peace with each other."

"Comforting." He stifled the groan trapped in his throat when the plane hit yet another blasted air pocket. Would this flight never end?

"I'm taking us to a higher altitude. These winds are killer," Landon called from the cockpit.

Mitch gripped the arms of his seat so hard his knuckles turned white.

"Watch your language," Amy said, elevating her voice. "No references to death and dying, please. Mitch is on the verge of hyperventilating as it is."

"Am not. I'm fine." Great. Now he sounded whiny.

"Next time I'll bring along a pacifier. Maybe that'll soothe you."

He shot her a pointed look. "The only reason to have one of those handy is if you give me a niece or nephew to spoil. How'd I ever let you talk me into this trip? I should be getting ready to spend Friday evening on the sofa in the townhouse, feet up, watching a movie or reading some classic Twain."

"I was right. You *are* a snob."

"I beg to differ. Snobs don't have serious brawn. Take a look." He raised his arm and flexed. "I beat your husband in racquetball twice this week alone. Handily."

"Impressive, but anyone who uses the word brawn is a snob," Amy said, laughing.

"And that last game you won by default," Landon said, his tone laced with amusement. "I got summoned into an important meeting."

"With your wife, Warnick, so it doesn't count. Man up and admit you lost that game and fly the plane already." Glancing out the window, he chuckled.

"I'd like to hear what Mr. Twain would say about your love life," Amy said. "No doubt he'd have some pithy advice."

"You journalists and your fancy words." Relief slowly began to seep through his senses. "See, that's exactly why I like Twain. He's uses plain and simple language, but he's funny and ironic as anything."

"Agreed, but he could also be acerbic. Sour, bitter, critical," she added when he gave her a look. "I'm sure the two of you would be fast friends if he were alive today and living in New York. But in terms of your love life? Fine. Let me make it plain and simple for you. You make poor dating choices, never mind trying to have any kind of ongoing, lasting relationship. You choose women who are beautiful on the outside but empty on the inside. You're tired of being alone and—deep down—you desperately want a woman to share your life. But for whatever reason, you steer clear of the type of woman you need. More than that, you know they're wrong for you, and I suspect that's exactly why you choose them."

"Is that a fact?" He tried to find a rebuttal but came up short. She had him pegged. "I'm not desperate," he finally said. "And the women I date aren't empty. They're just. . ." For once, words failed him. Vapid. That was certainly an appropriate word, but one he would not say. Pretentious was another, but maybe he should stop there.

"They might not be empty in some respects, but in the ways that matter, or at least the way they should matter? Yes, they are, and you know it," Amy said. "I'm sorry if that sounds heartless, but do you need me to spell it out?"

Mitch raised his hands. "I think you just did. I surrender. I'm your captive here, so you might as well lay it all on the line. Have at it."

"Honey, I know you're still hurting about Brad." At least Amy's tone had softened. "I don't mean to sound insensitive, but ever since he died, you've erected this shell around your emotions and your heart. You choose relationships you consider safe where there's no real danger of giving away your heart, including that dalliance with Brad's widow."

"Felicity—"

"Sure, you were a huge help, an important lifeline for her," Amy said. "That was a great thing. You fixed things around the house. You held her hand through the rounds of insurance claims and 9/11 memorial services. Basically, you helped her adjust to life without a husband. I can only imagine how much your strength and support meant to her. You helped her find a well-paying job in Manhattan even though she had little experience. But I suspect your feelings for Felicity—genuine though they might be—were based on mutual grief."

"Sometimes grief draws people together, Amy. It doesn't mean it's necessarily a bad thing, and I've already conceded on that point. I'll never regret being there for Felicity as a friend. Okay, you want the truth? We never kissed or anything else, and it was never any kind of dalliance. Give me a little credit. I only let you think it was to get a rise out of you. Anything romantic with her would have felt like a betrayal to Brad." Shifting in his seat, he stared her down. "Nothing happened that shouldn't have."

Amy sat back with a puzzled expression. "You don't say. Glad to hear it, and I'm proud of you. You know what it is, Mitch? I think you're afraid of losing someone you care about again. You choose women you know you can't possibly fall in love with for the long term. I mean, it's understandable after what happened to Brad, but that's coasting." Her gaze zeroed in on him. "You're meant for better things than simply coasting through life."

Coasting? Hardly. Interesting she'd said better things as opposed to bigger. Amy always chose her words carefully, so that was no random off-the-cuff statement. After his once promising medical career crumbled, he'd somehow managed to build a successful and respected career as a broker. His life consisted of trading by day for high-profile clients and schmoozing them by evening.

As Brad's death illustrated, you don't always get what you want. His friend would never have the opportunity to grow old and raise children with his bride of only a few years. Because sometimes terrorists hijack planes and slam them into office towers full of people doing their jobs in order to provide for their families.

Not that he'd ever fully resolve the loss of his best friend, but he'd finally stopped blaming God. As a volunteer at the remains of the World Trade Towers, he'd cried buckets with the sheer magnitude of the horror. As it always did, the thought of it made Mitch shudder. Dusting off the remnants of unfulfilled hopes and sacrificed lives, he'd finally gotten on with his own life as a tribute to Brad. Not much more he could do or he'd get sucked into the pit of self-despair. He'd been there, and no way would he scrape and crawl his way out of that hole again.

"What are you thinking?"

Amy's question startled Mitch back to reality. He'd really zoned out on her, but there was no sense in wallowing in the sadness. "How I've expressed my undying affection to a number of women, but sadly, they haven't reciprocated. Shocker."

"My guess is they can tell your heart's not in it." Her gaze bore into him. "That's not fair to you or any woman you date."

Perhaps subconsciously, he'd led himself into that one. "I do believe Mom and Dad lied to us all these years."

One brow shot upward. "Explain."

"It seems you can read my mind. You tell me."

"Haven't a clue."

"I'm thinking you and Landon lead the charmed life."

"Not charmed. Blessed." She picked up the magazine again. "Lest you accuse me of being holier than thou, you're blessed, too, but you're too blind to see it. When you find the right woman, you'll understand. You just need to know where to look and then open your eyes and mind to the possibilities. I'm still holding out hope."

"Keep holding, please," he said, his voice quiet. "And praying."

Her eyes softened and she appeared to hover on the verge of tears. "You know it. I'm always praying for you. I don't want to swell your head with compliments, but beneath all your sarcasm, deep down, you have one of the softest, kindest and most giving hearts I know. When you find it, love's going to grab hold of you, and I guarantee it'll be a beautiful thing to watch. You're going to make some woman a terrific husband one day." Amy's gaze met his over the top of her magazine. "I can hardly wait to see what might develop in Houston."

Lost in thought, Mitch closed his eyes when Amy returned her attention to her magazine. His sister had planted a seed of hope in his mind whether he liked it or not. As much as he tried to deny it both to himself and Amy, he looked forward to the weekend even though he'd be in for some fancy tap dancing around Cassie. He seriously doubted she was the type of woman to indulge in a weekend of no-strings romance followed by a *have a nice life* parting, never to see one another again. As it was, he'd participated in more of that kind of behavior than he wanted to admit.

He was tired of pointless flirtations. The aimless relationships were all in the past. He'd made a personal vow—to himself, but more importantly, to the Lord. Sure, it'd taken him a few years to come around, but he was back. He could almost envision his dad's smile when he'd made that vow and sensed his approval.

Thank you, Dad, for always being an example of how to live for the Lord. You proved you can have it all—a career you loved and a faithful wife and mother of your children by your side. I hope you're enjoying all the riches Heaven has to offer. You deserve them. Still, I miss you every day. I'm doing the best I can to watch over Mom, Amy and Celeste, but it's not the same without you.

Amy was wrong about one thing. He was finally growing up. Now, he had to act like it.

Chapter 4

REBEKAH GAVE CASSIE an approving smile. "I think we're as ready as we're ever going to be. Time to go downstairs, grab some snacks and greet the little lords and ladies in the Lewis kingdom."

"Lead the way." Relieved for the change of subject, Cassie gathered the voluminous skirt of her gown in both hands as she started down the front steps behind Rebekah. "I can hardly wait to see the guys dressed in their costumes. How you bribed your husbands to wear them, I'll never understand. That's quite an impressive feat."

"It's called the power of persuasion," Rebekah said as they carefully descended the staircase. "Goes to show you what these guys will do for their kids. And their wives."

"As long as you don't call us wimps." Rebekah's twin brother, Josh, passed them on the first floor landing, carrying his six-month-old sleeping son over one shoulder. Cassie hid her grin at his court jester costume and elaborate face paint.

"Never," Rebekah said, running a hand over her nephew's blond hair. "Luke couldn't handle all the excitement, huh?"

"Guess not. I'm going to put him down for a late nap and hope we don't regret it later tonight." Josh paused on the bottom step so Rebekah could plant a kiss on her nephew's flushed-with-sleep rosy cheek. "Hey, Cass. You look great. Are you excited about Mitch coming?"

Cassie's pulse sputtered. "Excited about Mitch. . .what?" Narrowing her eyes, she stared at Rebekah and resisted moving her hands to her hips. "Right. I should have known better."

"My job here is done. I'll see you later. Have fun!" Josh bounded up the stairs two at a time with a tight hold on Luke.

"Chicken!" Rebekah called after him. Turning to Cassie, she shrugged her shoulders but had the grace to offer a sheepish smile. "What can I say? Amy and Landon are bringing Mitch for the weekend."

Cassie resisted crossing her arms. "You could have told me he's coming without resorting to that whole *Mitch is so great* discussion upstairs. Is that why you took such pains to braid my hair and add the fresh flowers? To get me all gussied up so you could parade me in front of some man who could probably care less?"

"Guilty to the *gussied up* part." Rebekah said. "Sweetie, you look absolutely spectacular in this gown. If a certain Wall Street broker doesn't take notice and fall madly in love with you, then he doesn't deserve you."

"Not helping. Who says I want a man to fall madly in love with me? Do I have a say in this. . .this fantasy romance or whatever you have planned in the mind of Rebekah? Why not Marta or Gayle? Why am I the chosen one?"

Rebekah slid one arm around her, squeezing her shoulder. "You know how Amy's always thought you and her brother would make a fabulous couple. Her instincts are very good, so I have no reason to doubt her. We're all kind of hoping you two will. . .click."

Cassie groaned. "All? You're *all* in on it? Wonderful. Don't even plant a kiss on my cheek, Judas."

She couldn't be mad at Rebekah. Not really. Irritated, yes, but never mad.

"Fine. To humor you, I'll play nice with Mitch this weekend, but please give up hope for anything more, okay? You can tell everyone to forget about it. Like you said, the man works on Wall Street. I could care less about anything to do with money or corporate greed."

Her mother's words from years ago floated through her mind. "God doesn't look at status in life or how much money or power someone has, Cassie. He looks at what's in a man's heart, his soul. Whether it's pure or corrupted. Seek His will first in your life, and you won't ever go wrong." Mama had curled her fingers over her heart as she'd quoted from her beloved scriptures, "*But the Lord said to Samuel, 'Do not consider his appearance or his height, for I have rejected him. The Lord does not look at the things people look at. People look at the outward appearance, but the Lord looks at the heart.'*"

Rebekah frowned. "Mitch works in the financial industry, but from what Winnie says, he's a genuine guy. I mean, look at Amy. She might come from money, but she's as giving and unpretentious as they come. Money doesn't necessarily have to be a bad thing."

"True," Cassie said, headed for the kitchen. "There's also more than a thousand miles separating us. I'm not only talking geography." She'd raised her voice when it appeared as though Rebekah might interrupt. "Harbor illusions if you must, but anything more than friendship with Mitch is impossible."

"Ah, but God is the God—"

"Of the impossible, I know. Look, believe in your fairy tale if you must, but please leave me out of it. Not going to happen. End of story." Moving as fast as she could in the floor-length gown, Cassie pushed the swinging door and walked into the kitchen with Rebekah close behind.

"You both have hearts of gold. He's incredibly witty with a hint of sarcasm. Not the stinging, put down kind, but the intelligent, amusing kind."

Cassie swallowed her frustration. Rebekah wasn't giving up on the whole *let's get Cassie fixed up with Mitch* campaign anytime soon. Maybe she should revisit the subject of babies.

"Who's witty?" Winnie worked at the butcher block island in the middle of the kitchen, putting the finishing touches on dozens of cupcakes. "There, that should do it." She grabbed a dishtowel from the counter and wiped her hands, appearing pleased with her efforts.

"Mitch Jacobsen," Rebekah said, dabbing her finger in a paper liner with pink frosting. "Your husband let it slip that he's coming with Amy and Landon." She glanced at the clock on the far wall. "Their plane should be landing any time now."

"Amy's supposed to call when they're on the way to the house," Winnie said.

Following Rebekah's lead, Cassie sampled the lavender frosting, savoring the homemade buttercream taste. She licked her lips. "Yum. This tastes great."

"Thanks." Winnie waved her hand at the cupcake-covered table. "I know it looks like a rainbow exploded in here, and these ridiculous sleeves are going to be the end of me." Pushing them to her elbows, she blew a long strand of blonde hair away from her eyes. "I should have dressed like a cook or scullery maid—whatever they're called—instead of a lady in waiting. It'd be a whole lot easier to work in the kitchen."

Cassie retrieved the dishrag from the sink. She'd always admired Winnie's devotion in making her culinary creations a work of art, especially since they were devoured in seconds. Holding Winnie's sleeve out of the way, she wiped frosting from the countertop. "Tell us what else you need."

"Right. Put us to work," Rebekah echoed. "What's next?"

"If you want, you can fill the bowls over there"—Winnie angled her head toward the back counter—"with pretzels and chips. The bags are on the kitchen table. Sorry Josh spoiled the surprise, Cass. And Mitch is adorable although he'd probably hate that description. He's a terrific big brother for Amy. In a lot of ways, he used to remind me of an overgrown kid, but I've noticed some pretty significant changes in him in the last year alone."

Cassie couldn't resist. "How so?"

"He's more serious and settled, more focused on his career." Winnie shrugged. "Poor guy. I can't begin to imagine losing his best friend in such a tragic way."

Cassie's heart skipped a few beats. "What happened?"

"He died on 9/11." Rebekah's voice was quiet. "His office was in one of the Twin Towers."

"Oh, no. How awful," Cassie said, lowering her gaze.

Winnie began adding blue rosettes on cupcakes. "After his friend died, Mitch wanted nothing to do with the church or ministry. Amy and Mitch's dad died of a stroke a few years before that, and both losses were really hard for him. A couple of months after Amy and Landon's wedding, Mitch started volunteering with some inner-city TeamWork projects. I guess he had to work his way through the tragedy and come back to the Lord in his own way and time."

Finished with one tray of cupcakes, Winnie started on another. "Mitch is one of the smartest men I've ever met, but he also has a great sense of humor. From what Amy says, he's every bit as handy with a hammer as he is trading stocks. He pours his heart and soul into a project and loves kids. You've got to admire a guy like that." Pausing in her task, she glanced up at Cassie with a grin. "Wouldn't you say?"

"Of course," Cassie said. "I'd be a fool not to fall madly in love with the man. I'll try to be at my wittiest even though I know less about a hedge fund than I do a hedge*hog*. Which isn't saying much."

Rebekah laughed. "Maybe that should be your opening line."

They chatted about the party and plans for the weekend as they worked together. Cassie volunteered to make a salad and a peach pie for the picnic the next day. Those were two things she could prepare easily enough without ruining them.

They all turned as Lexa rushed into the kitchen, face flushed. "Sam! Oh," she said, putting one hand over her heart. Her royal blue gown was fit for a queen and she wore a jeweled crown. "Sorry. I didn't know you all were in here." Sam came into the kitchen so close behind his wife that he bumped into her when she abruptly stopped. Lexa dipped her head, unsuccessful in hiding her grin, and dislodged her crown.

After catching the falling crown, Sam repositioned it for his petite wife. "Forgive us our youthful folly, ladies." His smile lines deepened as he tugged on Lexa's long braid.

Goodness, Sam even *sounded* like a royal. Their tall, dark-haired TeamWork leader wore a king's costume complete with black tights and a maroon, faux-fur trimmed cape. Not many men could pull off such a costume with dignity nor deign to wear it in the first place. Sam managed it with aplomb and looked as handsome and masculine as ever. The touches of silver at his temples only made him more distinguished. Judging by the adoration in Lexa's expression, Sam would be duly rewarded. Cassie suspected that was a huge reason he agreed to wear the costume in the first place.

"Far be it from us to interrupt you," Winnie said, winking at Lexa. "I can only imagine the fun you two must have when you don't have a Renaissance Faire going on in your backyard. Give us a minute and we'll clear out and give you lovebirds some privacy since it's your kitchen."

"No need." Sam planted a quick kiss on Lexa's forehead. "I'll have time with my queen later on in our private chambers."

Rebekah coughed. "Well, okay then."

Cassie chewed the inside of her cheek, tempted to curtsy and address them as *my liege.*

Nothing seemed to embarrass Sam, and the unabashed affection he showered on his lovely wife was a beautiful thing. Equally sweet was how Lexa still blushed like a newlywed at her husband's touch, his tender words. All the marriages of her TeamWork friends were solid. Divorce might happen on average in one of every two marriages, but these people were blessed beyond measure. They worked hard on their relationships and it showed. Tears stung the back of Cassie's eyes. Her emotions were on such a roller coaster today.

Rebekah leaned against the counter and surveyed their hosts, a wide grin upturning her lips. "After three kids and going on six years of marriage, you're quite the inspiration."

"Let's not forget two bestselling marriage books," Cassie added. If anyone was qualified to write a book on how to keep the spark alive in a marriage, it was Sam.

"Keep this up, and my crown won't fit my swelled head, but I appreciate the sentiments." Selecting a chocolate cupcake with blue frosting, Sam gave a thumbs-up after he consumed it in a few quick bites. "Excellent as always, Winnie. Thanks."

"We had to escape the madness outside for a few minutes," Lexa said as Cassie worked with Rebekah to arrange gluten-free cupcakes on a serving platter. "Marc's on Sam's case about wearing tights, and he's running around taking photos. I wouldn't doubt he's conjuring up some crazy blackmail scheme."

Cassie giggled. "Too bad I didn't know Marc and Natalie were coming earlier or I'd have borrowed costumes for them, too. Complete with tights for Marc. And a micro-mini tunic. In pink."

"No worries. Marc's having fun at my expense, as usual." Reaching into an upper cabinet, Sam retrieved the punch bowl while Lexa grabbed sherbet from the freezer and then pulled a bottle of ginger ale from the pantry.

"I'm so happy they were able to make the trip," Lexa said. "And boys will be boys. That's why we love them."

"Amen to that." Winnie grinned. "I'm going home tonight with the most handsome court jester in all the kingdom."

They all laughed as they headed to the side door. Carrying the punch bowl, Sam moved ahead of them and held the side door open as Winnie led the ladies outside. Rebekah slid a large tray of cupcakes from the counter and Cassie grabbed the snack bowls and bags for refills.

Sam touched Cassie's sleeve as she brought up the rear. "You okay, Little One?"

"Yep," she said with a pasted-on smile and perhaps too much forced enthusiasm. As it always did, Sam's special nickname swelled her heart. She'd never told him it was also Tagg's nickname for her.

"If you need us, we're here. Say the word."

"I know, and I appreciate it." How could he always tell? Was she that transparent? She shifted from one foot to the other. "I understand Amy's bringing her brother this weekend."

"Is that a problem?"

"No, it's not a problem. It's just that some of the TeamWork crew seem to hold high hopes or expectations for some kind of. . .connection between us. A *romantic* connection." As soon as the words slipped from her mouth, Cassie felt silly for saying such a thing to Sam, of all people. When he didn't immediately respond, she blew out a sigh. "Please don't tell me you're in on it, too?"

His blue eyes were kind as they met hers. "I'm not in on anything other than praying for you."

"Yes, and I appreciate it, but my happiness doesn't revolve around having a man in my life. After all, I have you, Papa Bear. What more could I possibly need?"

Sam smiled. "Different and you know it. Keep your mind open to the possibilities."

Two of her friends had said the same thing in a very short time span. Cassie lifted her chin to meet his gaze again. "My mind or my heart, Sam?"

"Both. The lines of separation are sometimes indistinguishable. If the Lord wants you and Mitch to share anything other than friendship, He'll make it known. In His time."

"That's exactly what I'd expect to hear from you," she said. "Not that I want anything romantic to happen. With Mitch. So we're clear."

"Loud and clear."

Ducking under Sam's arm, Cassie heard his low chuckle as she headed outside, thankful for the slight breeze which caressed her heated cheeks.

Chapter 5

*M*ITCH OPENED HIS eyes. What was that weird noise? Did that come from Amy? She tossed down her magazine and gripped the arms of her seat. The fear written in her expression frightened him, and her eyes looked a little wild, reminding him of her ashen face when they'd first learned their father had died.

"What's going on?" His voice wavered, betraying his already shaky nerves.

Amy gestured for him to be quiet and hunched forward, apparently trying to hear Landon. From what Mitch could tell, Landon was radioing air traffic controllers, presumably in Houston. His usually unflappable brother-in-law's tone sounded bothered and hurried. They should be starting their descent soon. What could be wrong? When Amy slumped back in her seat and closed her eyes—her face pale and drawn—Mitch's heart pounded.

After another minute passed, he could endure it no longer. He might die today, but he'd like to know what would kill him, morbid as it was.

"What's happening?" Mitch hissed across the aisle. He'd been unsettled about this flight from the point of takeoff. Not a good time to mention it. Thinking it was bad enough.

A telltale flush spread from Amy's neck into her cheeks and quickly traveled up to her hairline. Panic wasn't in her normal repertoire of reactions, but the stare Amy gave him sent deep shivers crawling down his spine.

"Speak to me. Now." It came out more a command.

"I'm sure it's. . .nothing," she said, her voice quiet. "Everything's under control."

"And I'm heir to the throne. Everything's not all right. You're scaring me with that Stepford wife, glassy-eyed thing you've got going on."

"Stay in your seat, Mitch." Her voice sounded strange, eerily calm. He didn't like it.

His stomach roiled with the jerk of the plane and a rumble beneath them as the private jet finally began its descent. Glancing out the window, Mitch inhaled a deep breath, thankful to see suburban neighborhoods.

"Make sure you're strapped in," Landon said over his shoulder. "It's going to be a rough landing, but I'll bring us down the best I can."

What did *that* mean? They hadn't lost power and they weren't rocking back and forth. Mitch's pulse throbbed. Something was definitely wrong. *Dangerously* wrong. Shouldn't the landing gear be engaging by now?

"Dear Lord, help us," he whispered as he felt a surge of speed and the worst patch of turbulence yet. *Breathe.* He refused to allow anxiety to control him.

Landon flipped a succession of overhead switches before returning his attention to the control panel in front of him. All the blinking lights and beeping drove Mitch crazy. He trusted Landon, apparently with his life, but he'd never have guessed it would ultimately come to this.

When his brother-in-law spoke again, Mitch's worst fears were confirmed when he overheard the words "malfunction in the landing gear." Not good. Still, a plane could conceivably land without tires from what little he knew. . .which wasn't much.

"We've got some rough turbulence ahead," Landon said, elevating his voice. "Use the masks if you need them."

The pressure in the cabin changed as the private jet rapidly descended. Sputtering, Mitch gasped in an attempt to catch his breath. From the corner of his eye, he saw Landon motion to Amy. Oxygen masks dropped down in front of them, dangling from overhead compartments. Grabbing hold of her mask, Amy positioned it over her face, deep breathing into it and gesturing for him to do the same. How many times had he seen this demonstrated on commercial jets but never paid attention? Seizing the straps, Mitch mimicked her actions. A few seconds later, the plane leveled and the pressure stabilized.

When Amy leaned forward and reached for his hand, he squeezed and held on tight. Shoving his mask aside, he managed between raspy breaths, "It'll be okay." His words came out hoarse and labored, his attempt to give her a measure of comfort falling miserably flat.

She gripped his hand tighter and began to pray aloud. "Heavenly Father, we ask You to be with us. Keep Landon steady behind the controls and help us land safely in Houston. Or anywhere."

Mitch unstrapped his seatbelt and bridged the distance between them. Dropping into the seat beside Amy, he gathered her close and leaned his head against hers. "I'm here, Amy. Always." Smoothing one hand over her hair, he kissed the top of her head. If today was his time to exit this life, he hated to think he'd take Amy and Landon down with him. That kind of thinking wasn't doing any of them any good. *Be strong for her.*

"Here," Amy said, sniffling and disengaging from his embrace. "Put this on." He watched as she reached across him and secured his seatbelt. She clicked the lock and settled her gaze on him, her eyes softening. "I love you, Mitch. God's not done with you yet, you know."

"Love you, too." He squeezed her hand again. "You've got to give me some nieces and nephews before either one of us is kicking off." As much as he wanted to reassure Amy that everything would be okay and they'd make it safely to Houston…he couldn't.

The one thing Mitch did know? If he died protecting his little sister, it'd be the best, most honorable thing he'd ever done.

"We'll be touching down in a few seconds," Landon said. "Brace yourselves."

Amy clutched his arms, holding on tight. Strong as ever, she didn't whimper, didn't cry. With her eyes closed, she bowed her head.

Mitch followed suit. He'd already lost too many important people in his life.

Lord, do whatever You want with me, but keep Amy and Landon safe.

Chapter 6

"I GOT A number three, Cassie. See?" Chloe deposited a dripping wet, yellow plastic fish on Cassie's palm with a look of triumph. Winnie and Josh's daughter's delight in winning a small prize was infectious. "What did I win?"

"That's the fun part. You get to pick what you want. Let's go see what we can find." Cassie smiled at the little girl's enthusiasm as Chloe skipped across the yard to where Kevin and Rebekah handed out prizes beneath a large tree.

"Princess Chloe, you're looking lovely today indeed." Kevin removed his feathered hat with a flourish and bowed low. Cassie withheld her sigh. This man would make such an awesome father, and she hoped he'd get his wish soon enough.

Chloe eyed him up and down as Kevin returned to his upright position. "You're funny. Indeed," she said, shaking her head, her blonde curls bouncing.

"Thank you, your Highness," Kevin said, "but your dad's the funniest subject in all the land."

"Yes, my brother is the best court jester in the kingdom," Rebekah said. "Chloe, you can take your pick of any of the prizes in this basket." She helped the little girl pick through the basket and smiled as Chloe squealed when she found a pink plastic ring with a sparkly fake diamond.

At least thirty children gathered in different areas of the spacious backyard, engaged in various activities, and groups of adults chatted and waved to their offspring. Hannah and Leah, the birthday girls, giggled as Marta Holcomb and Gayle Ferrari, two TeamWork volunteers—also dressed in medieval gowns—carried them around the yard so their guests could greet the miniature princesses.

Squeals came from children bouncing inside a large, inflatable castle in the middle of the yard. Teenage volunteers manned the station and helped the kids climb in and out. Next to it, some of the youngest guests played in a ball pit. Cassie smiled as she surveyed the scene. What a fun day, probably as much for the adults as the kids.

For the next half-hour, she watched over the snack table. She helped Chloe and two of her friends settle beneath a tree with plates of kid-sized peanut butter and jelly sandwiches cut into castle and crown shapes. She gave them a bowl of apples and bananas to share and fruit punch in juice boxes. During a lull in the action, Cassie sampled a peanut butter and jelly castle. Oh, it tasted sooo good. She was hungrier than she'd thought.

"Hi, Cass," Kevin said, stepping beside her. "Are you having a good time?"

"Sure am," she said, finishing her bite. "Stand by the food, and you see the world go by. That's my motto." She waved her hand to the table laden with a variety of kid-friendly snacks. "Just sampling the food to make sure it's edible. You never know with these caterers. Won't you join me?"

"Don't mind if I do. I wanted to thank you again for helping put the finishing touches on the cottage for Leah and Hannah," he said. "It looks great." He chose a pimento cheese sandwich—shaped like a dragon—and accepted the cup of punch she offered him.

"Always glad to help," she said. "Are you still planning to deliver it in the morning?"

Kevin nodded. "Sam, Josh and Marc are coming over about ten to help me load it into the back of my truck. It's supposed to rain, but I'm hoping it'll hold off until we can get it here." After taking a drink of his punch, he nodded to the girls. "I hope they'll have as much fun playing in it as we did making it for them."

"What little girl wouldn't? A beautiful yellow cottage with flower boxes beneath the windows and real working lights inside? Matter of fact, I love it so much, I think I'll move in." Cassie nibbled on another sandwich. "I'm definitely inviting myself over for playdates. The twins can barely walk and they've already got a great place to play. Not too shabby. From gazebos to cottages, you do great work, Kevin."

"Thanks." She was rewarded with one of Kevin's shy smiles. No wonder Rebekah fell for this guy.

"So, your wife tells me you've applied for a patent for the Rebekah's Heart design on that fabulous gazebo you made for her once upon a time. I hope you get it. Then you can apply for a patent on this cottage design. I think you've got yourself a second career, Lumber Man."

Kevin laughed and finished his punch. "We'll see about that."

Marc stopped in front of the snack table and held up his camera. "Okay, you two. Smile like you mean it. Say Frienaissance."

They complied and Marc darted off again. "Later!"

Two little boys approached the table, and Cassie helped them fill their plates with food. When she turned back to Kevin a minute later, he frowned and a shadow passed over his face. "Kevin? Is something wrong?" Usually calm natured, he seemed agitated.

He shook his head slowly. "Mayday." Then he repeated it.

Cassie scooted closer, keeping her tone low so as not to alarm anyone around them. "What did you say?"

"Something's wrong. I can't explain it, but we need to pray. *Now.*" A line between his brows surfaced and the set of his jaw tightened. "I'm getting Sam and Lexa." He nodded to where his wife helped a little girl choose a prize. "See if you can get coverage for our stations and bring Rebekah to the kitchen as soon as you can. If you see any of the other TeamWork crew, signal to them."

"Sure thing." Cassie beckoned to a small group of the young mothers from their church. After being assured they'd help, she heard Kevin call to Sam and

Lexa. Excusing themselves from their guests, they headed hand-in-hand toward the house.

Rebekah caught up to her, slightly out of breath. "What's going on, Cass?"

"I don't know. Kevin and I were talking and all of a sudden he said the word *mayday*. He said he couldn't explain it, but he knows we need to pray. No time to waste."

"Mayday?" Rebekah frowned. "I've never heard Kevin use that word before. He has a direct pipeline to these things sometimes, though. Like Sam."

"Right. From what little I know, it's used primarily for emergencies related to boats and. . ." Stopping, Cassie moved one hand over her chest. She stared at the ground, her heart racing, her mind spinning with unwelcome thoughts. "Oh, no. No, no. Please, Lord, no."

"What is it?" Rebekah put a hand on her arm.

"Planes." The word was barely more than a whisper. "Beck, Kevin must sense something's wrong with Landon's plane." She tried to tamp down her rising trepidation.

Rebekah called to Marta and Gayle while Cassie caught the attention of Marc's wife, Natalie, where she played a game with their daughter, Gracie, and several other children. "Come to the kitchen!"

As she was about to go inside the house, Cassie felt a tug on her gown. Turning around, she looked into Chloe's big green eyes.

"Cassie? Where are you going? You look sad."

Biting her lip, Cassie hesitated. "We're going inside to pray together, sweetie."

"Why?"

This child's sweet compassion seared straight into her heart. "We're not sure, but sometimes we get a little nudge that lets us know we need to pray." So nervous she couldn't stop trembling, Cassie hoped her attempt at an explanation made some kind of sense to the little girl.

"The Holy Spirit, right?"

Cassie could only nod, amazed. Chloe wasn't even quite six years old.

"Then I'm going to pray, too." Marching ahead of her, Chloe opened the side door and scooted inside.

"Let the little children come to Me." Humbled by this child's deep faith, Cassie followed her into the kitchen. *When I grow up, Lord, I want to be bold like Chloe.* Josh walked toward his daughter and took her hand as the others moved to make way for Chloe in their prayer circle. Joe Lewis, the toddler version of his dad at only a little over two years old, stood between Sam and Lexa, holding his mama's hand. Marc carried Gracie and Natalie followed him into the house, and the group made room for them.

A lump rose in Cassie's throat and tears formed in her eyes. She glanced around the circle as they all clasped hands. When Sam began to pray, she lowered her head and closed her eyes, trying to concentrate.

"Lord, hear our prayer," Sam said. "We ask for Your watch care now over Landon, Amy and Mitch. We don't know what's happening, but You do. Keep them safe, Father. Wrap Your special hedge of protection around them and the plane bringing them to Houston. We pray for Landon's skill at the controls, and help calm their hearts. Above all, help them to know that whatever happens, You are always in complete control. You are sovereign."

A tear squeezed out from the corner of Cassie's eye and slipped down her cheek. She brushed it away while beside her, Rebekah slipped her hand from hers so she could do the same. Sniffles came from a few of the women and more than one of the men grunted or cleared his throat as one by one, they lifted their prayers.

This was TeamWork. Being there for each other, no matter what. In the best of times, and the worst.

Lord, hear our prayer.

Chapter 7

$\mathcal{M}$ITCH THOUGHT THE rumbling and shaking would never stop, but the aircraft finally came to a shuddering halt. A quick glance confirmed they'd touched down on a remote airstrip and then skidded off the runway. Even though it had only been a few seconds, it seemed as if everything happened in slow motion. Almost like a dream. Lifting his head from his knees, Mitch groaned and then unfolded his stiff limbs from their hunched-over position.

Landon dashed through the plane, straight to Amy. After unhooking her seatbelt, he scooped her in his arms and rushed to the door. He unlatched and then kicked it open with one foot while hollering over his shoulder for Mitch to follow. "Hurry up, in case we blow."

That's all Mitch needed to hear. Grabbing his suit jacket, he jumped out of his seat. He'd never bolted anywhere so fast, and that included his hundred meter winning sprint at a Pennsylvania statewide track meet in high school. The silence was eerie and dust swirled around the plane as he bounded down the metal steps and jumped to the ground from the fourth step. Made his workouts in his overpriced Manhattan club worth the cost.

Giving Amy a quick kiss and hugging her tight, Landon turned his attention to him. "You okay?"

He nodded. "I think so. Do what you need to do. I'll take care of Amy."

"Thanks." Landon dug his phone from the inner pocket of his leather jacket. "I need to call the FAA and report the incident. They'll have to come out and investigate. There's bound to be a lot of paperwork." He stepped a few feet away to make the call.

Mitch turned to Amy and they stared at one another.

"Are you in shock?" she said, appearing dazed.

"Don't think so." He raked his hand through his hair. "A little shook up. You okay?"

Tears welled in her eyes and her lower lip trembled. "I'm not sure." She tugged down the sleeves of her sweater and crossed her arms. "All I know is, I'm so cold I'm shaking."

"We made it. We're fine." Enfolding her in his embrace, Mitch pulled her close. He figured he needed it as much as she did. "I'll hold on as long as you need me and Landon can take over."

"Thanks." Leaning into him, Amy sniffled. "In spite of my lecturing, you're a great guy." She patted his chest. "The best. Thanks for putting up with me."

"I wouldn't let just anyone harass me, you realize. You're special that way."

"He couldn't land at an airport. It wasn't safe for us or any of the other aircraft. That's why we're here." Easing out of his arms, Amy narrowed her gaze and surveyed the rural landscape.

"Makes sense. You don't owe me any explanations. I'm incredibly. . .grateful."

"Me, too. I guess I'd better call Sam and Lexa and tell them what happened."

"That's a good idea." A hint of a grin escaped, and it felt good. "You might ask them to send the TeamWork posse to come and get us. Wherever we are. Landon might be able to give Sam the coordinates."

Amy reached into the outside pocket of her purse—she'd grabbed it when Landon hauled her from her seat—and pulled out her cell phone. Bless her heart, her hand shook as she made the call. When she glanced his way, he gave her what he hoped was a reassuring wink.

Glancing down at his once crisp white dress shirt and suit pants, Mitch grimaced. He started to smooth the shirt but dropped his hand. Lost cause. Stretching his neck right and left to ease out the kinks, he massaged his aching muscles. He'd be sore tonight and probably worse in the morning, but—focusing on the positive—they were alive.

~

The sound of a ringing phone broke the silence at the exact moment Josh ended their time of prayer. Cassie exchanged stunned looks with the other ladies. Startled into action, Sam ran one hand across the front of his tunic. "Where are the pockets in this thing?" His tone was gruff and impatient.

"It's not your cell. It's the home phone." Lexa darted across the room and peered at the ID screen. "Amy's cell phone number." Grabbing the phone, she ran back to Sam within seconds, and he wrapped his hand around his wife's much smaller one.

Cassie's heart stuck in her throat. Unable to move, she could barely breathe. Lexa pushed the button on the phone. "Amy Warnick, please tell me it's you and that you're safe and sound in Houston."

~

Mitch stood shoulder-to-shoulder with Landon and stared at the remains of the downed plane. Judging by the visible damage, its flying days were over. Nothing was smoldering and—to his untrained eye—a fire seemed unlikely. Not that the absence of a fire was any comfort to Landon. Poor guy must be hurting. He'd always found it amusing how Landon spoke about his plane with such affection, to the point of naming it Madelyn, both his mother's name and

Amy's middle name, curiously enough. Now, seeing the worry and exhaustion in the other man's expression, he rested his hand on his shoulder.

"I'm sorry about Madelyn, buddy. I know how important your Cessna is—was—to you. I guess this means I'm indebted to you for the rest of my natural born days. You missed your chance to do me in. A less-skilled pilot would have killed me for sure." His attempt at humor once again fell flat, and Mitch fought the surge of deep emotion. "Thanks, man."

"That's a compliment I never thought I'd hear, but I'll take it," Landon said. "The damage to her underbelly is too extensive. I don't think she can be repaired this time." Running a hand through his thick dark hair, he blew out a breath. "I don't have the heart to look. I need to wait until the FAA arrives, anyway. I hope you didn't have anything important in your luggage. Sorry about that, but I'm thankful we made it without any major damage to any of us. One of God's miracles."

Mitch glanced his way. "Need a hug?"

"Yes, but not from you. No offense."

"None taken."

Landon nodded in Amy's direction. "Look at her. We crash landed and the first thing she does is call Sam and Lexa to let them know we're going to be a little late to the party."

"Amy's always been the micro-organizer in the family. God love her."

"He does, Mitch. And so do I." Slapping him on the shoulder, Landon strode toward his wife. Extracting the cell phone from her hand, he spoke a few words to the person on the other end before hauling Amy into his arms. He pulled her as close as humanly possible and kissed her with such passionate abandon that Mitch turned his head. Current circumstances warranted the desire for that touch, that intimate connection. For a few fleeting seconds, Mitch wished he had a woman beside him to kiss like that. If nothing else, his dating experiences of the last few years had taught him that he didn't want just any woman beside him, but the *right* woman.

Brushing his leather shoe across the hard dirt, Mitch recalled his earlier thought. With firm resolution, he dropped to his knees and kissed the ground. Oh, man. Bad idea. Spitting out a pebble, he swiped the back of his hand across his mouth. Maybe he *was* in shock. He sat back, the heels of his shoes digging into his backside, and raised his eyes heavenward.

"Thanks again for sparing us. I owe You a big one, if that's even the right thing to say. Look, Lord, I know I haven't exactly been a faithful servant the last few years. I hope You understand. Part of the whole *mind is willing but the spirit is weak* thing. An excuse, yes, but it is what it is. You know me and my heart better than anyone. If You're trying to reinforce Amy's point about me coasting in life, I get Your point. Trust me. You've got my attention. But, as You are my witness, I'm never getting on another plane—large or small, commercial or private—for the rest of my life."

Chapter 8

Two Hours Later

*H*EADED UPSTAIRS TO change, Cassie hesitated. From the raised, animated voices coming from the kitchen, she knew Amy and Mitch had finally arrived. Based on Amy's report, the plane was a total loss, but by God's providence, they'd been spared physical harm.

Sam and Kevin had darted off—not bothering to change out of their costumes—to retrieve the weary travelers. In one way, that mental image was amusing and helped lighten the situation. Lexa mentioned that Sam planned on staying with Landon to meet with FAA officials to file the formal, written report. Kevin's mission was to bring Mitch and Amy back to the house, maybe with a stop to the ER to get them checked out first.

Cassie started back down the stairs. After all the earlier talk about Mitch, she was nervous about seeing him again. Had Amy been talking to Mitch about *her*? She couldn't imagine the emotions he must be experiencing after surviving a crash landing. Inhaling a deep breath, she wound around the stair landing and through the living room. She paused outside the swinging door for a few seconds before giving it a light push.

Winnie, Natalie and Lexa had their arms wrapped around Amy as tears streamed down their faces. Marc and Kevin stood to one side talking in low tones with Mitch. Taller than she remembered, Mitch's dark hair was mussed, his white dress shirt was wrinkled and his slacks were smudged, especially on the knees. Still, for having survived a crash landing, both Amy and Mitch appeared to be in good spirits.

As Cassie watched, Amy moved over to Marc and the ladies turned to Mitch with open arms. After only a moment's hesitation, he walked into the circle of their embrace. As he hugged each of the women in turn, Mitch's gaze fell on hers. Her breath hitched when she glimpsed the deep emotion in those gray-green eyes, uncannily similar to Amy's.

Lowering her gaze, Cassie waited as Amy finished her conversation with Marc and then she wrapped her in a tight embrace. "God kept you in the palm of His hand today, my friend," she whispered. "Love you, and I'm so thankful you're okay. This hug is from Gayle and Marta, too. They had to leave, but they said they'll see you tomorrow for the picnic."

"Love you, too, Cass." Amy smiled through her tears. "The whole thing's so unreal. I thought the plane would never stop, but you should have seen Landon. He managed to bring us down safely without landing gear. Then my big strong hero jumped out of the cockpit and swooped me up in his arms. I was so proud of how calm he was under pressure."

Cassie plucked a tissue from a box on the counter and dabbed it lightly over her friend's cheeks, absorbing the dampness. "Landon was your hero a long time before today."

"You're right," Amy said, sniffling, her gaze encompassing Cassie from her hairline down to her shoes. She wiped away a few remaining tears and her countenance brightened. "I'm sorry we missed the party, but aren't you the most fetching wench in the land? I was hoping it'd be a surprise that Mitch was coming with us for the weekend." She shrugged. "Guess that's kind of a moot point now."

"A well-intentioned court jester tipped me off, but his sister also did a fine job of dropping hints. Speaking of which, Josh and Beck are upstairs with the kids, and they'll be down in a few minutes."

Cassie inhaled another quick breath. "Amy, I'm sure your brother is a great guy, but. . ." Was it insensitive to bring up the topic now? She didn't want to hurt her friend's feelings, but neither did she want to give her false hope. "I'm happy with my life, but I get the feeling everyone's trying to fix me up with Mitch. I don't need a man to make me feel complete or whatever, and especially not one who works with money in New York. No offense, but I'm not overly fond—"

"Of money? Or maybe New York?" an amused male voice said from behind her. "Surely not. . .men?"

Cassie's gaze fell to the floor. *Mitch.* Did he have to be standing right behind her? She bit her lower lip, unsure whether to be appalled, offended or charmed. Heat warmed her cheeks as she slowly turned around. So much for feeling sorry for him after what he'd endured. Seemed his purported sarcasm had returned full-force. His comment about men didn't sit well. Determined to shake it off and give him the benefit of the doubt, she raised her chin and met his gaze head-on.

Don't rush to judgment.

"Mitch, stop it or you're going to be in trouble from the start," Amy said. "Cassie, you might remember my wayward brother from the wedding. He's actually a nice guy if you can get past the sarcasm."

One thing Cassie wasn't prepared for was how the man's smile made her traitorous pulse jump. Talk about roller coaster emotions. Fine, she'd play along. For now. Placing one hand across the bodice of her dress, she dipped in a low curtsy. "I beg your pardon, my lord. I spoke out of turn."

Taking her hand, Mitch waited as she rose to her full height. He stood at least a half-foot taller than her, even in her heels. Mitch's eyes crinkled at the corners. "Forgive me. Almost coming face-to-face with Jesus must make me punchy. It's good to see you again, Cassie." His gaze quickly swept over her. "You look terrific, but I'm afraid I left my knight gear at home. My sister didn't mention a medieval theme for the weekend."

"Only for the party this afternoon. Knight gear is otherwise optional."

"I'll let you two get acquainted," Amy said before slipping away.

Not thinking about what she was doing, Cassie leaned closer to Mitch. A few faint freckles were sprinkled across the bridge of his nose. For some reason, it surprised her but also hinted of the little boy he'd once been. Made him more approachable somehow. "You've got them, too."

"What?" A generous grin tipped the corners of his mouth. "Cooties?"

"Freckles," she said.

"Yeah, I've always had them. You?"

"No, I just paint them on for effect."

A gorgeous smile framed perfectly aligned white teeth. "I say if God gave them to you, might as well accept and make the most of them. At least on you they're pretty cute."

This man was fun. Cassie didn't want him to be fun. She didn't want to be attracted to him, but he was much more handsome than she'd remembered. Seemed a near brush with death hadn't dampened his flirting skills either. Charisma practically oozed from him. In an odd way, the rumpled look really worked. At least it worked on *her*. No, this couldn't be good.

Cassie broke out of her musing. "My sentiments exactly…about the accepting them part. If you don't mind the observation, you don't seem the type to stand on a trading floor staring at a wall of stock quotes all day. You seem too. . .well, you're certainly not stuffy." She swallowed, ruing how unsophisticated he must find her. Compared to most of the professional women he knew, she must seem like a plain country bumpkin.

"That's because I don't. It's only a very small part of my day. Making money—for myself or others—isn't what I'm about. Sure, it's my job, but it's not about greed or making the rich even richer. It's more about helping people secure their future through sound investments."

"I didn't mean to imply otherwise." Lowering her gaze, embarrassed, she turned to go. "If you'll excuse me—"

"Cassie, wait. Please."

She experienced the odd sensation of being touched although he hadn't laid a finger on her.

Mitch stepped closer, lowering his voice for her ears only. "Based on what you said to Amy, you're aware these fine people are hoping to pair us off this weekend."

Cassie noted a few covert glances directed their way from across the kitchen. "I'm aware."

"How do you feel about that? Are you interested in getting to know each other better this weekend? As anything more than TeamWork friends?"

"Are you always so forward and brash?"

"Usually, especially after—"

"The plane crash. Right." She shook her head. "The truth is, I can't imagine you'd be interested in getting to know *me* better. We come from completely different worlds. You live in a world of sophistication and"—she grasped for words—"stocks, bonds and mutual funds." It took everything in her not to roll her eyes. She didn't even know how to speak this man's language. If she said much more, he'd definitely know she was nothing more than an uneducated hick from the sticks. Certainly nothing about hedgehogs—or any other kind of hog—would come out of her mouth.

"All a state of mind." Walking around her in a slow circle, his gaze encompassed her gown and long braid.

"Please stop." She could feel her cheeks pinking from his appraisal. "I'm not a doll on display, and what you're doing is making me dizzy. It's like an Alfred Hitchcock camera trick."

Stopping, Mitch crossed his arms over his chest. "Listen to you. And you don't think you're sophisticated."

"Who said I don't think I'm sophisticated?"

"You did." He shrugged, drawing attention to his broad shoulders. "More or less."

"No, I said you live in a sophisticated world. There's a difference." Could he read her mind?

"Tell you one thing. Guaranteed, few—if any—of the women I've dated would understand your Hitchcock comment."

Cassie leveled her gaze on him. How nice of him to bring up his love life. Based on looks alone, Mitch must have a ton of experience in the dating department, but did he have to throw it in her face? "Something tells me your qualifications for a woman don't include a working knowledge of classic Hitchcock films." Okay, maybe that was a bit presumptuous.

Although he barely blinked, a veil lowered over Mitch's eyes. "I'm also very aware you're not a doll on display, as you put it. In fact, you're a fascinating woman who looks like she stepped through a door from the past." His gaze found hers. "In some ways, I wish I could go back through that door with her. With you," he added quickly.

"Why? So you can change the past?" Not sure where that question came from, Cassie shook her head. "Sorry. I'm apparently projecting my own wishful thinking on you." He found her fascinating? That fact alone made *him* fascinating.

Mitch nodded slowly. "It seems we have a few things in common, you and me. We might understand one another better than you think. Maybe we shouldn't write off a relationship without first exploring the possibilities. I'm game."

She stared at him, unsure of how to respond. "Are you for real?"

Laughing, he held out his arm. "Pinch me. As far as I know, I'm alive and well."

Yes, he certainly was that. No pinching required.

"Hey, you two." Lexa approached them, carrying a tall glass of ice water in each hand. "Why don't you go talk on the back patio where it's quieter?"

"Commotion is underrated. A good thing." Cassie's protests were cut short when Mitch propped open the side door and cocked a brow, daring her to join him.

Thanking Lexa, Cassie took the glasses of water. She paused beside him. "Don't you want to change your clothes first?"

"Why? Am I offensive?" He lowered his head and sniffed beneath one arm. "I did sweat bullets on the plane, and that was *before* the landing. I'll definitely shower and change before dinner."

If she wasn't holding the glasses, she would have swatted him. "You're not offensive, but you must be exhausted. Mentally, as well as physically."

"You'd think so, but I'm really not. I'm going to ignore your insinuations that I stink and look terrible. I'm sure it'll hit me later and I'll cr—" He shook his head. "What happened gives the word crash a whole new meaning." Following her outside, Mitch dropped onto the floral cushion on the black, wrought iron loveseat. He stretched out his long legs, lifted his face to the sky and closed his eyes.

Was he praying? Taking a seat in a nearby chair, Cassie quietly set their water glasses on a small table. Not sure what to do, she busied herself arranging the folds of her gown. The image of a prim and proper schoolmarm popped into her mind. One who was keeping company with a handsome suitor and didn't know what to do with herself. Stilling her hands, she waited, his nearness making her a bit lightheaded. No, not his nearness. That couldn't be why because. . .well, that would be ridiculous. Wearing such a heavy gown in the warm temperatures had to be the culprit. She should have changed her clothes when she had the chance. If Mitch kept his eyes closed much longer, she might as well leave and let him relax. Any minute, she fully expected to hear him snore.

"You can come sit by me, if you want. I don't bite."

Thankful he didn't pat the cushion beside him, Cassie twisted her lips in an effort not to grin. "I think you just might. I also suspect I could get whiplash trying to keep up with you. By the way, did Kevin take you to the ER or a medical clinic?"

That made him laugh. "Don't worry. I'm still in possession of my mental faculties. I stuck out my tongue like a good little boy for the doctor. Then he listened to make sure my heartbeat wasn't erratic and poked around my dignity before pronouncing me fit. None the worse for wear. Although I did have a close encounter with hyperventilation on the plane."

"Really? That can be scary. My grandpa hyperventilated sometimes. Said anxiety caused it. The first time it happened, I was scared to death since it was only the two of us in the house. I took his hand and he asked me to tell him stories. So I made up something silly, anything to keep talking. He said it helped calm him down so he could breathe easier again."

You're rambling now. Stop talking.

"Exactly. I'm sure your grandpa appreciated those stories." After taking a long drink of his water, Mitch swirled the ice in the glass, staring at it. "Sorry I zoned out on you. I needed a moment to regroup. For one thing, the plane ate our suitcases, but at least they were the only casualties. However, if I don't want to look like a little boy playing in his daddy's clothes, I'd better not borrow anything from my giant of a host."

"Not many men are as tall as Sam," Cassie said with a small smile. "I'm sorry about your suitcase. You're about the same height as Marc. He's staying here at the house, too, and I'm sure he can lend you some clothes until you can get to a store."

"I'll check with him. Thanks. To think I came all the way to Houston to go shopping. Definitely not what I had in mind." Turning to face her, Mitch propped one elbow on the back of the loveseat. "Answer something for me, Cassie. Do you love your family?"

What a random question. "Without question." He didn't need to know her father was all she had left, and even then she rarely saw him. Reaching for her glass, Cassie took a long drink of water, avoiding the intensity of those eyes.

"And do you want to be the best person you can be—the woman God wants you to be—while helping others and putting their needs before your own?" He raised a hand. "Sorry, that question is pointless. Of course, you do. I mean, you're a member of TeamWork. That's what they're all about, right?"

She was thankful he didn't sound flippant about TeamWork. "Yes, that's a big part of it. I understand you've worked on some TeamWork projects, too. In New York."

A slow grin creased his features. "Asked about me, did you?"

She blew out a breath. "No, of course not. More like some well-intentioned but misguided people—in the kitchen at this very moment—volunteered the information. Freely. Without my asking."

"Fair enough. Another question for you: do you sometimes get sentimental at emotional stories involving kids, animals and selflessness? Get all sappy, maybe even weepy, by TV ads, books or romantic movies?"

"Sometimes, yes. Do you?" She wasn't sure how she hoped he'd answer.

"I've been known—on rare occasions—to get a little misty eyed."

Cassie snapped her gaze to his. "Is this a quiz of some sort?"

"The *getting to know you* quiz, and it worked. We know each other better now than we did a minute ago."

"You were a troublemaker in school, weren't you?"

"How can you tell?" His grin broadened. "I've been causing trouble pretty much my entire life. But not in a mean-spirited way. Speaking of which, I have a plan."

Cassie crossed her arms. "I'm almost afraid to ask, but go ahead."

"I understand we're going out to eat tonight." Leaning forward, Mitch rested his arms on his thighs, his brow furrowed. "Afterwards, let's take a walk outside, just the two of us. Then I'll tell you." He glanced over at her. "Are you game?"

"Is this some kind of legitimate plan or a joke?"

In the light of the late afternoon sun, the green hue of his eyes deepened. "I might joke on the surface, but I never play around with anyone's emotions, no matter what you might have heard."

"I haven't heard anything."

"Good. Your answers to my questions also proved we're compatible. That's actually an important part of the plan."

"Compatible. . .for what, exactly? I haven't said yes."

Mitch took another long drink of water, draining the contents of his glass. With a satisfied sigh, he stood up and stretched. "We can talk about it tonight. I'm going to take your hint and head upstairs for a shower. I do some of my best thinking in the shower. Sorry if that's too much information."

She finished her water. "At least warn me if this plan of yours is likely to get me in trouble."

Mitch walked beside her, carrying both of their glasses. "You shouldn't be in trouble, but I think our well-intentioned but misguided family members and friends are in for an eye-opening surprise this weekend."

"When you put it like that, I'm not sure whether to be frightened or full of anticipation." Although she found Mitch's unpredictability intriguing, Cassie wasn't sure she liked it, especially in a man she barely knew.

"So, are you with me?"

She heaved a sigh. "I'll agree to listen to the plan. Then I'll decide whether I'll go along with it or not."

"Stick with me, Cassie. I won't steer you wrong."

"I hope you're right."

It sure won't be boring.

Chapter 9

Friday Evening

MITCH STRUGGLED TO keep his mind on the subject at hand on the way to the restaurant. Cassie wasn't in the same vehicle, but he'd caught a glimpse of her climbing into Rebekah's car. As elegant and regal as she'd looked in her green medieval costume, she looked even prettier in her jeans and a light blue cotton top. With only minimal makeup and simple clothing, she attracted him more than any woman had in a long time.

Her skin was clear and healthy, and everything about her screamed of natural beauty. Her hair was still in the fancy braid minus the flowers, and he tried to picture in his mind what it might look like hanging loose around her shoulders. Ten to one that gorgeous color didn't come from a bottle. Slender with gentle, appealing curves, she was one of the most unaffected, feminine women he'd ever met while being funny and sexy with a rich laugh that completely enchanted him.

He wasn't the only guy who appreciated Cassie as the hostess led them through the restaurant and seated them at the table. Hard to miss the male attention directed her way. Why should that make him uncomfortable? For whatever reason, it did. Plenty.

One old geezer at the bar directed lecherous glances her way. Ditto the guy about his own age. In his expensive clothes and hair slicked back with enough hair gel for the entire Corleone family, the man was a player waiting to make his move. Mitch stared down the sleazy younger one, hoping he'd get the message. If either one of these wise guys so much as tried to talk with Cassie, he'd intervene.

Apart from the women in his family, he'd never felt so protective of a woman. Not that he believed for one second that Cassie couldn't take care of herself. Still, holding her own in a flirtatious exchange with him was a whole different ballgame than fending off unwanted attention from men.

After what he had planned for the weekend, Cassie would either love him or hate him. That thought wasn't welcome and unsettled him. It was true what he'd told her. He'd never been the type of person to toy with anyone's feelings or emotions although he could tease with the best of them. She'd need to agree with his plan one hundred percent or he wouldn't carry it out.

Maybe he should scrap the idea altogether instead of hatching some cockeyed plan borne from some ill-founded sense of. . .he didn't know what to call it. Revenge wasn't his motivation. The TeamWork crew meant well. He knew that. Still, a little lesson to show Amy, in particular, how her meddling could backfire might be a good thing. Put all the Cassie and Mitch innuendo and less-than-subtle suggestions to rest once and for all. Ignoring the misgivings in his mind, he pushed them aside.

With Cassie seated on his right, Mitch listened as she discussed a children's book with Chloe Grant. When they'd arrived at the restaurant, Joe Lewis practically fought Chloe for the right to sit next to her. They clamored for her attention whenever she wasn't talking with one of the other adults. Chloe told him she learned at least ten new words every day. What a cute kid with blonde curls and big green eyes. She certainly was as bright and articulate as any little girl he'd ever met and she couldn't be any more than six? Seven?

Trying not to be obvious, Mitch kept one eye on Cassie as they ate their meal. Gentle and patient, she was terrific with the kids. What a great teacher she'd make. A wonderful mother. He could almost hear his own mother whispering in his ear, encouraging him to get to know this woman better.

Marc Thompson sat across the table and engaged him in a rousing discussion of the fluctuating stock market. He was an impressive guy—intelligent, savvy and he knew his way around investments and the stock market. Advertising could be a risky business, but after listening to Marc, Mitch could understand why his Boston sports advertising agency thrived and held its own against the New York giants. He'd whistled under his breath when Natalie named a few of Marc's high-profile clients. Beautiful wife and child, home in the suburbs. . .the man definitely had it all.

Mitch noticed that Marc interrupted their discussion and paid close attention whenever Natalie or Gracie needed anything. From what he'd heard from Amy, Marc almost lost his family not long after he'd married Natalie. She'd fallen on the basement stairs in their home and lost all memory of him. Mitch couldn't imagine how tough that situation must have been, especially being a newlywed. From what he'd heard, Marc's dogged determination to keep his family together—with help from Sam, Lexa and their faithful TeamWork crew and a personal mini-mission to Montana—saved the day.

Early on during their fateful trip to Houston, Amy had given him a quick refresher course—starting with Lexa, the feisty volunteer who'd clashed with Sam at her first TeamWork camp in San Antonio in 1997. Their relationship endured a one-year separation when Sam went off on a year-long mission to the jungles of deepest Africa. They married the same day Sam returned to Texas and reunited in front of the Alamo, of all places. Fitting, but it made him chuckle.

Sam had kicked Josh Grant out of that same work camp, but not before Josh and Winnie had. . .coupled. That night resulted in Chloe's birth, unbeknownst to Josh until his daughter was a few years old. Quite a story that one, but their union seemed solid and now they'd added Luke to the family, and he'd been named after Josh and Rebekah's late father. The Grant family gene for green eyes must be incredibly strong since both Winnie and Josh's children had them.

Josh's twin sister, Rebekah, had slipped and fallen into a freezing creek on the Montana mission and Marc saved her from drowning. Amy told him Kevin had been in love with Rebekah for years but didn't make his feelings known for a long time. The way Mitch saw it, Kevin was unbelievably patient in waiting for Rebekah to kick the British guy she'd been dating back across the pond. They'd married in mid-December of 2002, and Amy and Landon embarked on their nutty road trip to love the next morning.

Cassie had been with the group since shortly before the Montana mission and Marta and Gayle joined not long after. He didn't know as much about them, as if their stories were waiting to be written, in a way. Mitch smiled as he glanced around the table. What a diverse and admirable group. If one of them had a need, they were there for each other. How many people could say the same?

Kevin interrupted his reverie and they talked for a few minutes. A humble and rather shy, quiet man, he owned and operated the Houston location of his family's Louisiana-based lumber store. Both he and Rebekah worked with the youth at their church. Another man who had it all. No kids yet, but they'd probably be making an announcement soon.

Sitting at the dinner table, surrounded by these godly people with all their blessings, Mitch felt oddly out of place. Sure, he'd grown up with great, Christian parents, but the pieces of his life hadn't fallen into place yet. More like there were pieces still missing. He was definitely a work in progress. The Almighty must consider him a challenge.

Sensing Sam's gaze on him, Mitch saluted their host. None of them were perfect, a fact he appreciated. They'd all stumbled at one time or another—even the mighty Sam. Just as *he'd* done, more often than he'd like to remember. The key was picking yourself back up, dusting off and getting on with it. And where was he in this personal journey of life? Well, he'd picked himself up and was in the process of dusting off. Then he'd get on with it. Whatever *it* was. That's what he was hoping to figure out, but it'd taken him almost thirty-two years to get this far.

That tired old cliché about everything being big in Texas? An understatement. Handing his plate to the server, Mitch released a small groan. He'd never consumed such a huge slab of beef in one sitting. The events of the day apparently hadn't dampened his appetite. Good thing he didn't indulge like this very often. A hard, fast run around Sam and Lexa's neighborhood tonight—a few times around—would be a good idea. Make that in the morning. The effects of the day were slowly starting to take their toll. Marc had loaned him a red polo and a pair of jeans, but the waist felt a little tight after his gluttonous feast.

Rolling his shoulders, Mitch felt Cassie's blue-eyed gaze on him. "You any good at massages?" He gave her a wink and rubbed the back of his neck. Even in the dim lighting, he caught the slow flush creeping into her cheeks.

As he departed the restaurant a short time later, Amy took him by the arm and steered him aside. "Cassie's not used to men like you," she whispered, leaning close. "You're making her uncomfortable."

"I beg your pardon. Men like me? What does that mean? I barely got two words in with her during dinner. Cassie's a kid magnet."

"I mean it, Mitch. I don't know if you're acting like this to get back at me or what, but stop it."

Opening his mouth to refute Amy's words, he closed it again. A stab of regret coursed through him. "I'll try to be better, but Cassie's a big girl and more than capable of protecting herself against the likes of big old bad me."

"I know what it is. You think if you're rude and obnoxious, she won't have any interest in you."

"Be quiet," he snipped. "I've already asked the lovely Cassie to take a walk with me when we get back to the house, and she readily agreed. I didn't bribe or offer to pay her either."

She gave him a startled look. "Oh? Have a good time."

"You are so transparent," he said, laughing as they walked outside together. "Don't think I didn't see the looks directed our way and all the twittering going on around the table."

"We never twitter."

"Oh, yes, you do. Like magpies."

Amy tugged her purse over one shoulder. "You probably don't even know what a magpie is."

"Sure, I do. It's. . .some type of bird. You look tired, Amy. You and Landon all right? I know it's tough for him to lose Madelyn."

"He'll be fine, and thank goodness the plane was heavily insured. You know my husband." She sniffled and offered him a weak smile. "Of course, he says what happened is all the more reason to buy a bigger plane."

"For your growing family, I hope?"

She blew out a sigh. "TeamWork is expanding by leaps and bounds, and I'm not talking about our immediate group. With a bigger plane, Landon will be able to transport more passengers and cargo."

"I guess that's another blessing to come out of Madelyn's demise, sad as it is," Mitch said. "Tell Landon to thoroughly inspect the landing gear before he buys another plane. Something tells me part of your trust fund is kicking in for this major purchase."

"In my estimation, it's worth it." She frowned. "Why? You don't think so?"

"Of course I do. You don't need my permission and it goes without saying Grandpa would approve. It's a very admirable investment." He'd always appreciated how Amy had fallen in love with Landon *before* discovering he'd been a major investor in TeamWork.

"What about you? Tam's Place and the fund for 9/11 widows and orphans have both been very worthy investments." They both waved as Landon headed with Josh and his kids to their minivan.

Mitch swallowed hard and gazed into the distance. "Yes, but I want to do more." He'd been pondering his options, wondering how best to put more of his trust fund to use. Through the years, the fund had been well-managed and it had grown considerably from their grandfather's initial generous gift. He made a good living and didn't need the money for personal needs.

"Pray about it, and He'll help you figure it out," Amy said. "Don't worry about Landon and me. We'll add to our family when the time is right. You, on the other hand, need to concentrate on marrying and settling down. Then we'll talk."

"And there we go." He glanced at his watch. "I wondered how long it would take you to mention matrimony and *moi* in the same sentence. No fair blaming my marital status for your disobedience of God's command to be fruitful and multiply." Interesting, though, how his sister hadn't added the *find the right girl* sentiment like she normally did.

Amy ducked her head, but not before Mitch glimpsed her smile. "We're headed to Winnie and Josh's for the night. You're right about one thing. I'm exhausted down to my bones. I'll see you in the morning." When Winnie pulled her yellow VW Beetle to the front entrance, Amy shot him a look over one shoulder as she opened the car door. "Make sure you give us magpies plenty to twitter about this weekend, okay?"

"I'll try my best. Sleep well." He closed the door after she climbed inside. Unwittingly, his sister had walked straight into his plan.

This will be fun.

Chapter 10

𝒞ASSIE APPRECIATED HOW Mitch kept his steps slow to match hers as they walked together around Sam and Lexa's neighborhood. Pulling her sweater closer about her shoulders, she snuggled into it and crossed her arms over her chest.

"Hang on a second." Mitch removed his suit coat and draped it around her.

For a moment, she was rendered speechless. "Thank you. I appreciate your chivalry, but as you can see, I have my sweater."

"I know that, but you also shivered. Where I come from, shivering equates with being chilled."

"Well, let me know if you want it back." Something about Mitch's expression told her he wouldn't ask for the jacket back even if he was freezing with icicles hanging from his ears.

"Cassie, I hope you'll accept my apology. Amy told me I've been acting like a jerk. She didn't use that exact word, but it's what she meant."

"I'd never call you a jerk, Mitch. You're. . .interesting."

His smile emerged as his gaze locked with hers. "Thanks. I'll take it. If I step over the line, say the word."

"Will do. You don't look like what I envisioned. A Wall Street broker, I mean. Ever had a beard?" What a dumb thing to say. The warmth invaded her cheeks all over again. Blushing seemed to be a given around Mitch. Good thing it was dark.

"No. You?" He shuffled his feet and kicked a pebble off the sidewalk.

She laughed. "Can't say that I have, no." Mitch had a wonderful way about him that helped her feel more at ease. Not to mention he was a lot more approachable than she'd expected. What she didn't expect was his teasing persona. Tagg used to tease her in the same way, and she'd missed that give-and-take relationship. Rebekah and Josh had a great rapport, and it seemed Amy and Mitch did, as well. How wonderful it must be to know someone always had your back.

Mitch rubbed one hand over his jaw and eyed her. "It's been a really long day, and I have some decent scruff now. Want to feel it?"

"That's okay. I'll take your word for it." He wore scruff well. "Before I met you—the first time, at Amy and Landon's wedding—I thought you might. . .well, I thought you might be stuffy. As in full of yourself." She giggled when he quirked a brow. "I knew you had to be smart, though. That was a given."

"Admit it. You pictured a boring guy with a high forehead and wrinkled clothes who talked incessantly about the stock market. Stuffy *and* scruffy. How am I doing so far?"

"Your forehead's not that high and from what I've seen, you seem inclined to talk about a lot of things but not the stock market. Thank you for that."

"Are you saying what I do for a living is boring?"

"No, I'm saying I don't know anything about it." How to converse intelligently about it was the challenge, but if she dared voice that thought, he'd probably give her another little lecture.

"Ah, right. You hate money. You're entitled to your opinion, but that doesn't stop me from wanting to talk about catering. I like food as much as the next guy. Who doesn't?"

"I don't hate money, Mitch. I just don't like how the lack of it, or too much of it, can make people do stupid things and let it rule their lives."

Mitch stopped walking. "Are you speaking from personal experience?"

He asked hard-hitting questions that made her think. Beneath the surface was a very caring man, and one she liked very much. Lowering her gaze, Cassie resumed her steps. "Yes, but from the perspective of not having any money. We were poor, and it caused problems. Let's say jail time was involved. And no, I wasn't the one sitting in a jail cell pondering my next crime." How could she tell Mitch her daddy was locked up most of her childhood? Drunk and disorderly, burglary and theft charges constituted his unsavory, lengthy police record. "No Felonies Thorenson" had become his unfortunate nickname—and, conversely—his source of false pride.

To her surprise, Mitch didn't appear shocked.

"I'm sorry to hear it, but rich people commit plenty of crimes, too. I'm sure I don't need to tell you how many stockbrokers have been tossed into prison for illegal trading activity and unethical business practices. When it comes right down to it, one sin isn't any bigger than the other. If it helps, I understand what you're saying."

Shoving his hands into the pockets of the jeans, Mitch glanced down at his feet. "I have to ask. What's your impression of me now? The fact that I'm wearing leather dress shoes with jeans doesn't count, in case that makes me a geek or a nerd."

She'd led herself right into that one. "You're fine. Nice. Funny. Unpredictable." Tall. Incredibly handsome in a nice, unaffected way. He wore the combination of casual and business attire well.

"Don't forget interesting. Come on, Cassie, that's all you've got?" After she started walking again, he jogged to catch up with her. "Give a guy a break. I survived a crash landing today. Doesn't that score me a few points on your empathy and sympathy scale?"

"I'll think about it." What did he want her to say? Her attention was diverted when she spied an older couple—neighbors of Sam and Lexa—further down the sidewalk, strolling toward them. Doris and Walt. She'd met them when they hired Doyle-Clarke Catering for Walt's retirement dinner the year before. Great people, but this could get awkward fast. Doris asked her about her dating prospects every time she saw her. Never missed an opportunity. Of course, she hadn't seen them in a few months, and tonight—the first time she'd been alone with an eligible, single man in forever—here they were. Doing an abrupt about face and marching in the opposite direction would be rude, and she suspected Mitch might enjoy it if Doris dropped her usual hints.

Sure enough, as soon as they came within range, Doris waved and called to her. "Oh, Cassandra, honey! How lovely to see you." She grabbed her husband's arm. "Look who it is, Walt."

"Who do we have here?" Mitch said under his breath.

"Doris and Walt Bicklebing. Be good and no teasing. They're lovely people but I never know what she'll say next."

"Bicklebing? Seriously? I'll enjoy this."

Doris gave them an appraising glance as they came closer. "Why don't you introduce us to your young man?"

"This is Mitch Jacobsen," Cassie said. "He's the brother of one of our TeamWork volunteers and visiting from New York."

"Well, how wonderful. Isn't that nice?" Mrs. Bicklebing stared at Mitch for a few seconds. "Why do you look so familiar to me?" Tearing her gaze away, Doris glanced up at the night sky. "In any case, would you look at that beautiful moon? It's the perfect night for a romantic walk. You never know what the weather will be like at this time of year, but this weekend is supposed to be unseasonably warm. So, how long are you visiting Houston, Mr. Jacobs?"

"It's Jacobsen, and only until early next week."

"You be careful." Doris's gaze darted between the two of them. "This young lady is incredibly special. Pretty as a picture and irresistible as cotton candy." She wagged her finger. "I'm warning you now, young man. If you spend more than a few hours with her, it'll be mighty hard for you to leave her when you go back home."

"Doris, don't embarrass the man. Sorry. She doesn't know when to quit." Walt darted an apologetic glance Mitch's way.

"No need to be sorry," Mitch said. "I understand exactly what you mean, Mrs. Bicklebat."

Cassie bit her lower lip not to laugh. She doubted Mitch's slip of the tongue was an accident.

Walt and Doris both laughed. "Bicklebing," Walt said after Mitch started to apologize. "Don't worry. We've been called Dingbat, Binglebat, you name it. Heard it all."

Mitch moved closer and draped his arm loosely around Cassie's shoulders. "As a matter of fact, I'm trying my best to make the lovely Cassandra fall in love with me as we speak. Considering it's Valentine's Day weekend, after all. Love is in the air."

"Oh, well then, we won't keep you," Doris said. "Far be it from me to stand in the way of young love. And, may I say, you two make an absolutely stunning couple. You enjoy your walk. . .talk. . .or whatever else you do tonight. Together."

Cassie wanted to groan.

Walt winked at Mitch. "Don't do anything I'd do."

Waving to them, Doris grabbed Walt by the arm. "Wait a minute, honey. You have that wrong," Doris said. "It's don't do anything I *wouldn't*—"

"No, I got it right." Walt's voice was firm.

"Happy Valentine's Day tomorrow!" Cassie called to them as the older couple started down the sidewalk again.

As soon as they were a few more paces down the street, out of earshot, Mitch dropped his arm. "Sorry. I couldn't resist."

"That statement about trying to make me fall in love with you was laying it on a bit thick. I hope you're not making fun of me. Look, Mitch, I'm not—"

"Shh," Mitch said, putting one finger over her lips. "I'd never make fun of you, Cassie. I'm tired and loopy and coasting on leftover fumes."

Cassie took hold of his arm and picked up their pace. "Then we'd better get you back to Sam and Lexa's quick before you drop from exhaustion." They walked together for a few minutes, murmuring greetings to a young couple pushing their baby in a stroller and a man jogging with his dog.

"This is nice, isn't it?" Mitch said as they walked with her hand tucked around his arm. "Reminds me of strolling the promenade or whatever they used to do in years past. Being friendly with the neighbors. Has a small town feel to it, you know?"

"Don't you ever take walks in New York?"

"Not really. New Yorkers are always too busy running here and there, me included. It's a lot colder back home than here at this time of year, but I should get out and make an effort. I've lived in the townhouse our grandfather left us since Amy married Landon and moved into his place, but I don't really know my neighbors. That's a pretty sad thing to admit."

"I don't think that's exclusive to New York," she said. "Other than people from church and the TeamWork crew, I don't really know my neighbors."

"Where do you live?"

"I rent a condo fifteen minutes from here. It's small, but it suits my needs. I'd like to get a dog, but I'm not home enough to keep one company. It wouldn't be fair to a poor pooch."

"I have a dog. I spend as much time with him as I can, especially on the weekends."

"Really? The city dweller has a dog? Shocking."

He smiled. "His name is Sam and he's a mutt—part sheepdog and part take your pick. Nobody knows. He's long-haired, big and lumpy but completely lovable."

"Sam, huh?"

"As in Samuel Langhorne Clemens."

"Wasn't that Mark Twain's real name?"

"See, I knew you were a girl after my heart, Cassie. Please tell me you're not adverse to a serious Mark Twain addiction."

"For you, no. For me? I can resist. I've read some of his books, but mainly those I was forced to for school. Until they banned some of them."

Mitch chuckled. "I choose to believe he was misunderstood. Falling off a log and stinking drunk, I think he was one of our finest American humorists. Sure, he could be profane, but he makes me laugh and lightens the burdens of life. Everyone needs a Twain in his or her life."

"I agree," Cassie said. "Walt and Doris have been married over sixty years. I heard him say once that one of the secrets to their long, happy marriage was being able to make each other laugh. They met in grade school and started going together when they were teenagers. Doris told me Walt gave her a promise ring in fourth grade during recess. Got down on one knee on the playground right in the middle of a dodge ball game. I find that incredibly sweet, don't you?"

"A little dangerous maybe, but sure. You know what's really sweet? Your sense of wonder. Ditto the phrase going together." Mitch's lips lifted. "Did you ever go together with a boy when you were in fourth grade?"

"Of course. I had boyfriends from the time I was in kindergarten."

"I don't doubt it for a minute."

"You?"

He chuckled. "Nah. I was a late bloomer. Ugly kid. Freckles, pimples, gangly and awkward."

"Don't know if I believe you. But, even if you were, something tells me you made up for lost time."

"You could say that."

Cassie didn't want to hear any more about Mitch's love life, but she'd led herself right into that one. Seemed easy enough to do where he was concerned. "I was hoping to hear about this big plan of yours before the night's over," she said. "I thought that was the purpose of this walk. If you're too tired, that's okay."

The silence between them grew long as they walked, but it wasn't uncomfortable. She stole a glimpse at his profile. With tiny lines etched around his eyes and on the sides of his mouth, the man was clearly exhausted. She probably should have declined the offer and let him go home and crawl into bed.

Finally, Mitch spoke. "Let's forget I ever mentioned a plan. It's not important anymore. In some ways, I think what happened earlier today is finally seeping into my subconscious. Changing my viewpoint on certain things." His tone was suddenly more subdued and serious.

"What do you mean?"

"The whole mortality thing, I guess. We can't know what's going to happen. None of us do. Only God knows when we're going to draw our final breath, say our final words, kiss our loved ones for the last time. I've always known it, but when you face the possibility of dying, it alters your perception."

Cassie chewed her lower lip. How well she knew.

"I guess what I'm trying to say is that it reinforced the whole idea of living for the moment, making each day count. We shouldn't waste our time or efforts trying to live up to the expectations of others. Am I making any kind of sense?"

"Yes, but it's not like we can live at warp-speed every minute. Sometimes it's in the quiet moments that I really feel the presence of God guiding and leading me. That's every bit as important as living in the moment. If you're always so busy going from here to there, you miss out on a lot of the blessings in the seemingly little things of life."

"Ah, an optimist," he said. "You're very wise."

"Aren't you? An optimist, I mean?"

"I used to be. Then something happened to change the way I view. . .everything." Raising his face to the sky, Mitch breathed out a sigh as they walked. "The evil within men can sometimes be unfathomable. It's a lesson most often learned the hard way."

Cassie waited until Mitch lowered his gaze to hers again. His expressive eyes held such a depth of pain that she ached for him. She could only guess he referred to the loss of his friend on 9/11, but she wouldn't ask. Not now, not tonight. Mitch would tell her if and when he wanted.

"I'll say one thing. Doris was right about the moon. It's incredible." He stopped walking and pointed to it. "I love how we can see the rays from the moon—moonbeams—like the rays from the sun."

Following his gaze, Cassie nodded. "I never really thought about it that way. It's beautiful."

"Doesn't it blow your mind how powerful God is to have made everything in the universe? I mean, think about it. He made the stars, sun and moon, mountains, oceans and valleys. I finally came to the understanding of how God is so much greater than the evil in men. He can't stop the evil, but He's always there to help pick up the pieces of our lives. We can overcome the feelings of inadequacy in not being able to stop the evil, but the key is allowing Him to work in us and not fight against Him."

"Is that what you did, Mitch? Fight back?"

His eyes were bright and he nodded slowly. "Yes, at first. Because of what happened, I stepped away from my faith. The problem is, I'd lost my hope and trust in God's sovereignty. I was filled with rage, and then anger, and then this overwhelming sense of grief. I lost sleep, fumbled through the motions on the job, stopped going to church and acted stupid in ways I'll forever regret. I felt like I was a miniscule speck of nothing, and I didn't think He cared."

Cassie found it difficult to believe how open he'd been with her about something so deeply personal. "I'm sorry you had to go through that, Mitch. But the way I look at it? We might be miniscule in the eyes of other men and the world, but in God's eyes, you have to know you stand tall." Wanting to connect with him, she took his hand in hers. "I hope you've found your center again."

He didn't answer for a long moment. "I did, but I'm a work in progress."

She smiled, tears in her eyes. "We all are. I guess we should head back to the house now. I'd still like to hear about the plan." She nudged his shoulder. "If nothing else, I'd like to know if my suspicions were correct."

"You asked for it. Careful." Moving his arm around her waist, he steered her around a large pebble on the sidewalk.

She drew in a quick breath. "Thanks. Knowing me, I would have found that pebble and taken a tumble. Even without your armor, you're quite the gallant knight."

He released her. "My armor has a ton of chinks in it, I'm afraid, both inside and out."

Why was it that everything Mitch said seemed weighted with subtext? Beneath the teasing, this man was a deep thinker. That could only be a good thing, in some respects. "You don't need armor to be a hero, Mitch."

"And you're definitely misguided," he said, the familiar smile teasing the corners of his mouth. "As far as the plan, I was thinking we could have some fun. Payback for Amy and the others who seem to be pushing us together."

"That's what I figured you were going to say." Why then, did her spirits sink? "For the sake of clarity, how were you going to propose we execute this scheme? I'm sure the fact we're on this walk—alone—is feeding into their speculation."

"You're right. It's more a scheme than a plan. And you, pretty lady, do not seem like a schemer. See, stick around me and I'll lead you down the road to ruin. Wait. That didn't come out right." He raked one hand through his hair and laughed. "In spite of the fact that I totally contradicted what I said earlier today, I trust you know what I meant, right? I'm afraid the circuit between my brain and my mouth must already be shut down for the night."

"You won't lead me down the road to ruin, Mitch. I'm perfectly capable of doing that all on my own. Let's stick with what you said earlier about not steering me wrong. Sounds better." When Cassie moved ahead of him, she heard his quiet laughter. Within seconds, he was beside her again.

"You're not suggesting we still carry out the plan, are you?" Unless she was mistaken, Mitch's tone made it sound as though he wouldn't be adverse to it.

"Why don't we see what happens?"

"Hey, I'm pretty charming when I'm operating at full throttle. Unlike tonight."

"I'm sure you are." They reached her blue Saab parked in Sam and Lexa's driveway. "Well, this is me." Clicking the button on the key fob, she reached for the car handle.

Mitch took hold of it, his warm hand over hers for the briefest of moments, and swung the door open. "I hear we're having a picnic tomorrow at noon."

"You heard right. Thanks for the reminder. I need to make Sam's peach pie." She heaved a sigh. "Just so you know, I never let anyone push me into something I don't want."

He tilted his head and stepped closer. "Somehow I don't think you're talking about baking a pie. I agree wholeheartedly. We're both free-thinking, independent people."

Cassie gave him a small smile, daring to lift her gaze to his. She couldn't move even though everything in her prompted her to get into the car. The scent of his aftershave filled her senses. Oh, it was better than nice. "Capable of making our own decision about who to like. . ."

"Or care about." His gaze, a soft, gentle caress, brushed over her. His face was only inches away. Overtaken by a momentary impulse, Cassie resisted the urge to rest her hand on his jaw and feel its warmth, that manly stubble.

"Nothing can happen between us," she whispered. "No matter what the others want." Shivers ran through her.

"Agreed."

Why was he looking at her like that? His eyes were nothing short of mesmerizing, especially in the reflected light of the moonbeams he'd talked about a few minutes ago. "Besides, you're going back to New York very soon."

"You live here and don't like what I do for a living. And maybe me."

"I didn't say that." If anything, the exact opposite was true. Cassie lowered her gaze as her pulse hammered. "I don't like being predictable, but you're nothing like what I expected."

"And you, Cassie, are everything I've hoped for but didn't expect to find."

She'd have to puzzle over that one later, if she could even remember it. Subtext was flying all over the place. She should wish him good night, pay him little attention and find excuses to avoid him the rest of the weekend. But no, somehow that would be impossible. Mitch was the kind of man who *commanded* attention. Whether she liked it or not, he'd captured her thoughts.

"I'd best go now," she said, climbing into the car. "Good night."

"Good night. I'll see you in the morning."

"I won't look forward to it."

"Neither will I." With that, Mitch closed the door.

As she pulled away a minute later, Cassie peeked in the rearview mirror. Mitch hadn't moved and watched from the driveway. Probably thinking how he couldn't wait to *not* see her again.

Chapter 11

Saturday, February 14, 2004

A THUNDERSTORM BLEW in the next morning with dangerously high winds and heavy rain. Waiting until there was a lull, Cassie ran from her car to the front porch but still managed to get a little wet. Meeting her at the door, Winnie took the salad and freshly baked pie and ushered her inside.

The scent of roses filled the air. "Did someone open a floral shop in here?"

Winnie pointed to a huge pink bouquet on a side table. "Marc went a little overboard, but I'm sure Natalie's not complaining. I'll go grab a towel for your hair. Be right back."

"Cassie!" Joe flew at her with open arms, wrapping himself around her.

"Hi, kiddo." She planted a kiss on the top of his head and ruffled her hand through his dark hair. "Want to read a story with me a little later?"

"Uh huh." Joe had the cutest smile ever that captured her heart every time.

"You're certainly the Pied Piper around here." Marc walked down the front stairs hand-in-hand with Gracie and Natalie followed close behind.

"I probably have more fun than they do. Hi, Gracie." The darling little girl—almost three but going on thirty according to Natalie—strongly resembled her mother with dark hair and classic features. According to some in the TeamWork crew, Gracie had also inherited her father's strong will. Hiding behind Marc, the child peeked out from behind him and stuck out her tongue at Cassie before running from the room.

"Grace Davis Thompson, you stop that right now!" Natalie gave her an apologetic smile. "Sorry. We're working on manners. It's all Marc's fault. He spoils her rotten."

"Get some good photos yesterday, did you, Marc?" Cassie said as Winnie came back down the stairs and handed her a white bath towel.

"You know it." Marc smiled. "Gaining leverage on King Sam never hurts. If you'll excuse me, ladies, I'd better go see what trouble Gracie's getting into now. She's been terrorizing Joe and Chloe's been running interference."

After telling the other ladies she'd help them with the lunch preparations shortly, Cassie darted into the half-bath to dry her hair as best she could. Afterwards, she headed to the laundry area off the kitchen, towel in hand. Pushing the swinging door, she stopped short when she spied Amy and Landon. Arms around one another, they were engaged in a tight lip lock. No one else was around, surprisingly enough.

Unable to move, Cassie stood transfixed, rooted to the spot. Wanting to give them privacy and not have them find her gawking, she backed through the swinging door and bumped into something firm and strong. Some*one*. Startled, she gasped and whirled around.

Mitch anchored his hands on her arms before releasing her a few seconds later. "Whoa. Steady. They're still in there going at it, aren't they?" In nice jeans and a heather green polo that enhanced the color of his eyes, he looked absolutely incredible. His hair was also damp, and she liked how it curled on the ends. She needed to stay strong. That task was already proving more difficult than she'd ever imagined. *He's leaving in a few days.*

"Cassie?" When he crossed his arms over his chest, it enhanced muscles she hadn't noticed yesterday. "Everything okay? What's behind door number one?"

She snapped to attention. "If you're talking about your sister and her husband, yes, they're in there enjoying one another's company. I'm not about to interrupt."

"That's very admirable of you and it's definitely a job for a big brother." Mitch barged into the kitchen. "Okay, you two. Time to break up your shameless display of public affection."

"Go away," Landon mumbled. Amy waved a dismissive hand and they increased their efforts.

Cassie ducked around them and into the laundry area. Coming back out a minute later, she averted her gaze and whispered to Mitch. "Are they like this often?" She gestured for him to follow her and led the way out of the kitchen.

"All the time," he said as they stood outside the door. "The stories I could tell. I'm just glad they're married. It's a beautiful thing to behold, though, isn't it? They have absolutely no shame, stuck to each other like that."

"After seeing them in action, I can see why they're nicknamed the Kissing Bandits. Technically, they're still newlyweds, so maybe we should go a little easy on them."

"I know." Mitch glanced at his watch. "Would you look at that? It's not even noon yet and they're already engaging in their wanton behavior." His gaze lingered on her.

"What?" she asked, bringing a hand to her cheek. "Do I have something on my face?"

"Not at all. I was admiring your hair. I really like it that way."

Cassie fingered one of her long curls. "Like what? Damp?"

"Natural and down around your shoulders. The color's so rich. It's gorgeous and reminds me of a Raphael painting. Almost ethereal. Feminine."

She released the curl. "Thanks." His sophistication was showing whether Mitch wanted it to or not, and she seriously doubted any of the single guys from church would know anything about Raphael much less compare her to the subject of one of his paintings. "It gets a little unmanageable sometimes. Aren't the women in Raphael's paintings severe looking with pointy noses and forbidding expressions? I doubt they'd win any awards for beauty. Or congeniality."

He grinned. "Ah, but you missed my point. In their day, they were considered beautiful. Suffice it to say it's a compliment. You're anything but severe and forbidding. Be glad I didn't say you have a Rubenesque quality."

"Fat?" She tried not to laugh but didn't succeed.

"Pleasingly plump. Which you are definitely *not*. Like I said, you're just right." Mitch cleared his throat and had the grace to flush. "Forget I said anything. Moving on. I heard the rain on the roof last night not long after I came back in the house. I hope you made it home safely before the deluge began."

"I did. Barely. I guess our picnic today will be indoors." She gestured to the kitchen with a grin. "That is, if we can get Landon and Amy out of the kitchen long enough to get everything ready. Tell you what. I'll give the Kissing Bandits five minutes. If they're not out of the kitchen by then, I'm kicking them out."

Mitch laughed quietly. "Decisive. My kind of woman."

~

Marta scooted close to Cassie as they waited in line for the food a short time later. "So, you and Mitch seem to be hitting it off well."

Cassie shrugged. "He's nice and fun, but please don't mail the wedding invites yet."

Marta laughed as they worked their way around the assortment of salads, sandwiches and chips lined up on the kitchen counters and then moved to the island in the middle for their drinks. Cassie acknowledged Sam's salute as he sliced a piece of her peach pie. The man did love his peaches.

"Come on, Cass," Marta whispered as Cassie poured lemonade for both of them. "The two of you didn't know anyone else was in the room earlier. I could have run circles around you singing some silly song at the top of my lungs and you wouldn't have noticed."

"I'd like to see that. Maybe you should try it sometime and we'll find out." Clamping an apple between her jaws, Cassie headed into the family room. As they ate, she read a story to Chloe, Joe and Gracie. Across the room, Mitch sat with Kevin and Josh. Cassie sensed his gaze on her a few times. She was every bit as guilty, stealing glimpses every other minute.

"Do you like Mr. Mitch?"

Because it was Chloe asking the question, she couldn't play it off and give her a non-answer. This child held her heart, as did Joe. Like they all did. And how obvious must she be for a little girl to pick up on her fascination with Amy's brother?

"Yes, Chloe, I do."

Chloe tilted her head. "Like my mommy and daddy like each other?"

"Different kind of like, sweetie."

"Maybe he's your prince."

Goodness, even the smallest TeamWork members were playing matchmaker now? Still, she didn't have the heart to tell Chloe that not every woman wanted a prince to make her happy. Or needed a man to rescue her. Why squelch a little girl's dreams?

Finding Mitch's attention settled squarely on her again, she wasn't quite sure what she believed anymore.

"We'll see, sweetie."

~

"I'm afraid I killed this poor guy." Cassie released a mock sigh and leaned back in her chair, shaking her head. "He didn't stand a chance." After playing Operation with Mitch the last forty minutes, she'd heard the annoying buzzer one too many times. "You're a lot better at this game than me. You have a very steady hand."

"Thanks. I'm afraid you're right, though. He's a goner for sure." Something in Mitch's tone sounded odd, but he gave her a smile as he closed the game box. "What's next on the agenda?"

"I think I'll go check on the kids who aren't napping and make sure they aren't getting in trouble."

"Mind if I come along?"

"If you dare." She felt the eyes of the others following them as they departed. They were scattered in the various rooms playing Monopoly, Battleship and Scrabble. "They won't ever give up, will they?"

"Would you really expect them to?" Mitch said. "Everything we do together feeds into their fanciful imaginations."

"I tried to join two of the other games but got flimsy excuses why I couldn't. They're horrible liars."

"And again, the plan doesn't sound like such a bad idea."

She heard the amusement in Mitch's voice as he trailed behind her into the family room at the back of the house. Finding it empty, Cassie moved her hands to her hips. "Well, this is interesting. I know they're not all napping upstairs. Wonder where they could be?"

"I think I might know." The rain had finally stopped. Mitch pointed out the window. "I see a yellow playhouse in the backyard. I don't remember seeing it out there yesterday."

Cassie smiled. "Kevin brought it over earlier this morning for Leah and Hannah. Today's their actual birthday and Sam and Lexa commissioned it from Kevin. Awesome, isn't it?"

Mitch smiled. "The TeamWork crew is definitely enterprising. Seems like anything they touch turns to gold."

"They work for everything they have." She ducked her head and smiled. "I'll say one thing, though—they all drive really nice cars."

"That doesn't bother you? The money thing? Nice cars generally cost a lot of money."

She felt like sticking her tongue out at him like Gracie had done earlier to her. That would be mature. "No, it doesn't bother me. A car is a necessary evil, as my grandpa used to say."

"I don't even own a car." He sounded quite proud of that fact.

"I'm sure you don't need one in the city. Plus, it's got to be expensive to store or park."

"Exactly," Mitch said. "A friend in Boston paid seventy-five thousand dollars for a parking spot. That's crazy. Mid-town Manhattan's even higher. Not worth the hassle. The public rail system is terrific and takes me anywhere I need to go. Tell you one thing: I don't plan on flying again in my lifetime after what happened yesterday."

Cassie arched a brow. "I can understand why you might be a little skittish about getting on a plane, but I can't imagine you'll never fly again, Mitch. How do you plan on getting back to New York?"

"I've already reserved a rental car. A road trip sounds like fun. I have vacation time I never take, so I figure why not? I'll take the scenic route. Wanna come?"

She averted her gaze. "That's pretty much what Amy and Landon did." Why, oh why, did she bring *that* up?

"Right, and it worked for them. Fell in love in record time. Are you saying you don't want to fall in love with me? I'm very competitive with Amy. We could try to beat their record."

"I don't think so." Did he believe falling in love was a game or a laughing matter? Not that she expected to experience an earth-shattering, life-changing moment where she knew the guy was *the one* at first sight or even within hours or days after meeting him, but that was ridiculous. "When are you leaving?"

"That eager to get rid of me, huh?" His grin made her pulse sputter. "I'll be out of your life on Tuesday morning. Bright and early. Amy might come on the road with me, but Landon booked a flight back on Monday afternoon."

"Want to go outside for a few minutes?" For one thing, she needed the fresh air.

"Sure." He opened the door and waved his hand. "Lead the way."

As they approached the cottage, Cassie heard Sam's voice coming from inside.

"Dada." That sweet little voice belonged to Leah, the more vocal of the twins although at this point it was mostly babbling. Moving over to the window, Cassie peeked inside.

"Once upon a time, there were two sisters," Sam said. Stretched out on the finished floor of the cottage, he balanced a baby girl on each knee. "They looked a whole lot alike—one with blonde hair named Hannah and one with dark hair named Leah—and they lived in a majestic castle under tall, towering trees in a kingdom called Houston."

Cassie's heart caught in her throat at the tender scene. She only had one or two memories of sweet shared moments like this with her father. But she clung to those memories when it seemed she was all alone in the world.

"Sam's the coolest dad ever." Mitch kept his voice quiet as he followed Cassie to the opposite end of the massive backyard. "Speaking of tall and towering."

"Kevin made sure the playhouse was big enough to accommodate him." As she leaned back against the trunk of a sugarberry tree, Cassie heard Sam's rich tenor. The happy giggles of the twins swelled her heart. *Wait a minute.* Another voice—a sweet, feminine one—joined in singing Sam's song.

"Is that Lexa?" Mitch asked.

"I do believe it is. She's so tiny, she was probably tucked in a corner of the cottage."

"They're a great couple. Great family." Mitch sounded almost wistful.

"Yes, they're the best. Tell me about your dad, Mitch. What was he like?"

He stared out over the yard, his gaze narrowed. "Strong in his faith. Honorable. Loyal. Trustworthy. He also expected too much of people and, in that regard, they always let him down. It's like that song by the Carpenters. *I know I ask perfection of a quite imperfect world and fool enough to think that's what I'll find.*"

How true. "When we expect the same of others that we expect of ourselves, that's when we're destined to be disappointed."

Mitch lowered his gaze to hers. "I'm sorry you've been disappointed, Cassie."

She shrugged and gave him a small smile. "It's part of life, so I've learned to adapt and go on the best I can." Drawing in a deep breath, Cassie slowly released it. "Don't you love how the earth smells after the rain? It's like a fresh renewal all over again."

"That's a great perspective. I don't enjoy the outdoors as much since I'm usually surrounded by the concrete jungle. Sometimes in the middle of the day, I'll go for a walk in the park. I take off my shoes and socks and sift my toes through the grass."

She slanted a grin his way. "You do *not* do that."

"Sure, I do. I don't have photos to prove it, but it's where I go if I need to escape and blow off steam. That's why they have parks in cities, you know. For harried executives to ditch their shoes, walk around and count their blessings. Keeps me sane."

"I imagine your job is very stressful," Cassie said. "Are your clients demanding?"

Mitch rested his hands on a low-hanging branch of the tree as he considered her question. "Probably no more than one of your fussy clients who wants a specific menu for a catering job. Or complains about a spice she hates and doesn't want in any of the food. We might have different occupations, but in theory, you and I both deal with the whims of people. Keeping them happy is job one. By the way, Lexa sang your praises as she drove the three of us stragglers to a mall this morning. She told me you're the solid backbone of Doyle-Clarke Catering and how she and Winnie couldn't do it without you."

Lexa and Winnie always made her feel valued and appreciated, but it was good to hear, especially from an objective viewpoint. "I don't know about that, but I enjoy it."

Mitch surveyed her. "What do you like most about the job?"

"The administrative part, I suppose. Brings out my bossy gene, and I'm an absolutely horrible cook. The worst. Terrible. Really bad."

"Not sure I believe that. The peach pie you made for Sam tasted great."

"Fooled you. I stayed up late baking a second one after I fell asleep and burned the first one."

"So, you're not a great baker or whatever. It's not poor baking skills but more a lack of setting an alarm. Lexa did say that—hands down—you're their best server. You swoop, dip, juggle, balance, schmooze and charm clients like no one else." Releasing the branch, he held up one arm as if balancing a serving tray and bowed low before her with a flourish. "Something else we have in common."

She laughed. "The schmooze factor?"

"You know it." Mitch nudged her shoulder. "Scoot over and share the real estate." He leaned against the tree beside her, close enough to smell his terrific aftershave—nice, but not overpowering. "Rumor has it you also run the catering office like a general. In the best of ways. If you don't mind my saying, I find that a little hard to believe."

"Why do you say that?" She liked being this close to him but felt heated in a way that had nothing to do with the rising humidity.

"You seem too. . .sweet."

She stiffened. "Watch your language. Maybe I don't want to be called sweet."

He shot her a curious glance. "Didn't mean to offend. Last time I checked, sweet was a good thing. On the flip side, what would you want to be called? Stinky sourpuss? Old battle-axe?"

She laughed. "No, thanks. How about sophisticated? No, forget that one. I could never pull that off."

Mitch rolled his eyes. "There you go again. We've already had this discussion. Get over it."

Not to be deterred, Cassie kept going. "Take Marta, for instance. Now, *she's* the epitome of sophistication. You and Marta would make a great couple. She's incredibly pretty with those blonde curls and gorgeous violet eyes. You don't find that combination every day. Don't you think she's pretty?"

Mitch grunted. "I'd be blind if I didn't notice she's pretty, but she's too—"

"Too. . .what?"

"I don't know, but nope. Marta's not the one for me. Plus, Amy's mentioned a guy named Eliot a few times and how she thinks something might be going on between the two of them."

"She's right. Those two play cat and mouse all the time. Eliot has a habit of disappearing for months-on-end sometimes. None of us really know what he does for a living, but I'm sure Sam does. One of these days, maybe Marta and Eliot will realize they could have something really great together."

She snapped her fingers. "How about Gayle? Her last name is Ferrari. Need I say more?" Mitch's startled expression made her laugh. "No relation to the Italian motor company. At least none that I know of, but with this crew? Anything's possible."

"Please don't tell me you believe I'm that shallow." Crossing his arms, Mitch leaned close, staring her down. "Why are you trying to pawn me off on one of the other TeamWork girls? Give me one good, valid reason I shouldn't be attracted to the woman standing here beside me right now."

"Because that's what they"—Cassie lifted her shoulder and nodded in the direction of the house—"want. We can't give in." She avoided looking at those distracting muscles that made themselves known every time he crossed his arms.

Mitch blew out a breath. "I know I was tired last night, but didn't we already talk about this? We have minds of our own, so I vote we go with it and see what happens. Have some fun this weekend and get to know one another." Shifting his position to face her, he leaned his hip against the tree. "I thought that's what we'd agreed to do. Am I wrong?"

"No, you're not wrong. I'm. . .confused, I guess."

"That makes two of us. I like you, Cassie. A lot. Marta and Gayle are great in their own way, but I don't think you realize how fantastic *you* are. Am I being clueless here in believing you like me, too, in spite of my numerous faults and flaws?" He tipped her chin, waiting until she looked up at him. "Am I?"

She held his gaze. "No, Mitch."

He dropped his hand. "So, tell me what's happening later on tonight before I forget about everything except how pretty you are and how much I'd like to kiss you."

Not used to a man saying such things—especially a man she barely knew—Cassie swallowed and tried to focus on answering his question. "Not sure. Dinner and then more of the same, I guess. I heard rumors about going out for some Texas line dancing. That's always a favorite, and it's fun."

He glanced at his watch. "We probably have a few hours to kill before then. "Want to get out of here? We can tell them we'll grab dinner on our own."

"Depends. Do you have ADHD, by any chance?"

She liked his laugh—deep, hearty and masculine.

"Why? Because I like to keep moving? If I don't have something to occupy my attention, I might as well march upstairs and fall asleep. And I didn't come to Houston to sleep, at least not during waking hours. If you'd rather not—"

"We could go critique the paintings at one of the art museums."

His grin surfaced. "Now you're talking, but that really *would* put me to sleep. Not that I don't appreciate an ugly woman every now and then."

That made her giggle. "As I recall, you said they were beautiful."

Mitch scratched his head and gave her a skeptical look. "I did, but in *their* day and age. Doesn't change the fact they're framed and on a wall. As in inanimate and flat. Lifeless." He raised his hands. "Suffice it to say, it's not what I prefer to do on Valentine's Day."

She quirked a brow. "What does Valentine's Day have to do with anything other than being February the fourteenth? And it's Saturday?"

His mesmerizing gaze brushed over her. "I want to spend time with a three-dimensional woman. If I'm not going to kiss anyone, I'd still like to have some fun. Staring at a painting and making pretentious comments about its texture and composition doesn't sound like my idea of fun. Does it to you?"

"Frankly, Mitch, you make anything entertaining." Why did he have to bring up kissing? Probably to plant the idea in *her* head. To her chagrin, it worked.

"How about another walk around the neighborhood? We might run into the Dinglebats."

"Bicklebing." Cassie shook her head. "Are you talking sightseeing, touristy kinds of things?"

"Not really. Something different and—"

"Fun. Right," she said. "Here's an idea. Ever been to a county fair?"

A slow grin lit Mitch's face. "Probably not since I was about ten, and never in February. You're talking fun house, bendy mirrors, bearded lady, funnel cakes and cheesy rides, right?"

"As much as I hate to admit it, the answer is probably yes to all those things. They've had a local fair on the weekend closest to Valentine's Day for a few years now. I saw it advertised on a billboard the other day. It's about five miles outside the city. I think the rain's cleared out now for the rest of the weekend."

"Then count me in. You're deceptively fun. It's a very appealing quality."

She laughed. "What's that supposed to mean?"

"Beneath this aura of cool, ethereal beauty lies the heart of a kid." He tugged on one of her long curls. "Come on, kid. What do you say, let's go have some fun?"

She started to remind him that she was, in fact, not a kid. Something in his eyes silenced her. He knew it as well as she did.

Cassie pushed away from the tree, her cheeks warm. "You're on."

Chapter 12

CASSIE WALKED BESIDE Mitch toward the ticket booths at the county fair. "What do you want to do first? Do you prefer the stay-on-the-ground-rides that spin or the ones that toss you all around in the air?"

"Tell you what, I'll get our tickets and then we'll get something to drink and negotiate." He'd changed from his jeans into a pair of khaki shorts, tennis shoes and a light yellow T-shirt. She couldn't decide which look she liked best, but the man obviously worked out.

"Sounds good. Thanks." Shielding her eyes with one hand, she squinted in the blinding mid-afternoon sun. "I've got some sunscreen in the car. You're not used to this Texas sun. Even in February, it can be pretty strong."

"See? That's sweet, like it or not. You're thinking of my needs."

"I was talking about me," Cassie said with a smirk, "but yes, pasty New York boys need protection if they don't want to get a bad sunburn."

He laughed. "Would you rather I have one of those fake, spray-on tans? That doesn't equate with manliness in my opinion."

"You're silly."

"And you're practical and incredibly pretty."

"Stop it," she snipped. "To be clear, this isn't a date. We're two people trying to kill time and have some fun."

"Whatever you say. I'll walk you back to the car."

"No, don't bother. It'll only take me a few minutes. I'll run back and get the sunscreen while you wait in the line for our tickets." Without giving him a chance to protest, Cassie sprinted back toward the parking lot. Opening the passenger door, she leaned inside and quickly sorted through a few brochures and manuals in the glove compartment. Hadn't she put a new bottle in here a month ago? She jumped when two hands encircled her waist from behind. Stiffening, Cassie whirled around, fully expecting Mitch although she might have to smack his face. "What are you—"

Not Mitch. Her eyes widened as she met a hard, steely gray gaze.

"Don't do anything stupid." He pushed her back around, against the side of the car. The man's voice was low and rough and the stubble on his jaw pricked her skin as he leaned close from behind. He tightened his hold on her and moved one hand across her lower abdomen in an invasive manner.

"Get away from me!" Jabbing both elbows into him as hard as she could, Cassie tried to scoot around him, but she was no match for his beefy arms.

Spinning her around again, he pinned her against the car with his body. "Shut up and take it like a woman, and I won't hurt you."

Cassie's mind was jumbled as she tried to recall something—anything— from the self-defense class she'd taken last year. *Don't let him see your fear.* Cassie spat in his face and tried to wriggle free. Scanning her surroundings, she couldn't believe the parking lot was deserted. Not one other person was in sight. How was that possible?

Cursing under his breath, the man clamped a big, dirty hand over her mouth. Biting down hard on the fleshy part of his hand, Cassie turned her head and screamed although her voice came out raspy and not as loud as she'd hoped. Kneeing him in the groin as he cried out in pain, she wrenched her arms free and started to run toward the entrance. From the heavy breathing coming from behind her, she could tell he was close on her heels. Although he was big, he moved unbelievably fast.

Only a few hundred more yards and she'd be in a safer area, visible to those near the ticket booth. She spied people waiting near the entrance and increased her pace. *Mitch, where are you?* Catching up to her, the man crushed into her from behind, wrapping his arm around her waist in a viselike grip. The choice name he called her under his breath repulsed her, making her cringe.

"Don't do that again," he rasped in her ear. "You're coming with me nice and easy now. I've got a knife in my left hand." Something cold and hard pushed into the small of her back. "If you don't cooperate, I'll use it." He ran one finger along her neck and a jagged fingernail scratched her skin. "Time to play nice. I wouldn't want to have to cut any of that lovely skin of yours. That'd be a real shame."

Cassie swallowed her fear and fought the tears stinging her eyes. *Lord, please give me Your words and Your strength.*

"Cassie!"

Mitch.

Her heart jumped when she saw him running toward her with a police officer two paces behind him. Surprising the man, she pushed against his arms and broke free of his hold. Her attacker screamed that vile name again and, after giving her a threatening glare, he took off in the opposite direction.

Both men ran after him and Mitch reached him first. Tackling him to the ground, he delivered one swift, hard blow to his nose. Raising his fist, shaking it in the air, Mitch rolled off the guy and then jumped to his feet. Taking over, the officer straddled the man and pulled out handcuffs while reciting the Miranda rights.

After talking with the officer, Mitch ran back over to her. Out of breath, he planted both hands on her shoulders. "Are you okay?"

"I think so." Cassie nodded, and her lower lip trembled. She would not—could not—allow the tears to fall.

Releasing her, Mitch stepped closer, his eyes searching hers. His jaw was set in a hard, firm line. "He didn't do anything to you, did he? Hurt you physically in any way?"

"No, but it was definitely on his mind." She shuddered. "Mitch, he had a knife."

"You're shaking."

"Am I?" She rubbed her hands up and down her arms.

"Come here." His voice sounded gruff, edged with compassion.

She didn't hesitate as he gathered her close, wrapping his strong arms around her. "Maybe I'm in shock. I've never had anything like that happen to me before." She wiped her hand across her eyes. "Thank the Lord."

"I knew I should have walked you back to the car. Forgive my stupidity. These kinds of fairs aren't exactly known for having the most reputable, upstanding citizens around."

"At least I was able to fight him off at first. I was the one being stupid and not paying attention. He came up behind me when I was at the car. I managed to get away, but he caught up with me when I started running back this way." To her chagrin, a few tears rolled down her cheeks. She sniffled and tried to keep them at bay.

"Aw, Cassie. It's okay to cry. You're safe now, and you handled it great. I saw the guy's hand, and you got him pretty good. Smart thinking." Holding her close, he stroked her hair as she rested her head on his solid chest. Being held by Mitch was wonderful, but it stirred feelings inside her. Feelings she wasn't sure she could trust. For now, it was what she needed.

"How's *your* hand?" she asked, her voice muffled by the soft fabric of his T-shirt.

"I haven't hit anyone like that since Landon, but I'll survive. Think I broke his nose."

Surprised by that revelation, she raised her head. "You hit Landon?"

"Decked him good in a coffee shop, as a matter of fact. It was after I found out what happened on that road trip through Louisiana and Texas with Amy. Long story, but after I slugged him, we sat and exchanged a civilized dialogue. He explained everything and it was obvious he was in love with her. He's an upstanding guy, and it wasn't like he purposely set out to deceive or hurt her."

"Landon's your sister's hero. And now, chinks in your armor or not— you're mine. Thank you."

"Welcome, but I only finished the job. You held him at bay on your own, impressively so. I heard a scream coming from this direction. The police officer was jawing around with one of the workers by the ticket booths, but he came right away when I called to him."

Easing out of his arms, Cassie brushed her fingers beneath her eyes and released a shuddering breath. "Sam and Josh insisted we take a self-defense class last year. I never honestly thought I'd need to put those lessons into practice. It goes to show you never know, do you?"

"I'll be sure and thank them later," Mitch said.

The officer called to them, one hand anchored on her attacker's shoulder. Cassie was relieved the man wasn't looking her way. He seemed more preoccupied with the blood coming from his nose. "We need to file a report if you two could come to the security office. It's to the left of the main entrance."

"We'll be right there," Mitch said.

When he looked at her, Cassie glimpsed tenderness in Mitch's eyes. Not like with Tagg or her father. Not like with Sam. Those men had hugged her, held her and comforted her, but this was different. She liked the strong, steady sound of his heartbeat. The way he'd held her. She couldn't deny she admired the firmness of his chest, the strength in his arms. Liked how he'd come running when he'd heard her scream.

Starting to relax, Cassie gave him a small smile. "Life is never dull with you around, that's for sure."

"I'd settle for a little less excitement, believe me. Do you want to head back to the house after we file the report?"

"Why? Do you?"

"You want to stay after what happened?"

"Sure. We're hardy types, you and me. Why let a little drama slow us down?"

He looked uncertain. "I agree, but it's your call. Whatever you want."

"I'll be fine," she said, shaking off the last of her apprehensions. "Let's go file that report and pray the guy's already been hauled off to jail. I hate the thought of him sitting there glaring at me. Or cussing me out again. That was bad enough."

"I'll check and make sure he's not in the office before you go in. You shouldn't be subjected to that, especially since the officer was right there to positively ID him."

"Oh, wait a minute," Cassie said as they started to walk back toward the fairgrounds. "My car door's still wide open."

Mitch turned in the opposite direction, pulling her around with him. "Let's go back together. We'd better hurry or that officer's going to think we skipped out on him." He squeezed her hand. "I'm definitely keeping you close the rest of the day."

Fine by me.

Chapter 13

*M*ITCH SAT BESIDE Cassie as they devoured pork loin sandwiches, the only occupants of a picnic table in a partially shaded area, shielded from the sun by a striped awning. After riding a few rides, they were both flushed with the heat. He'd been more thirsty than hungry, but as Mitch took another bite, he found he was ravenous.

They'd spent the better part of the first half-hour at the fair filing the police report in a cramped, makeshift security office set up in a trailer. The police officer hadn't been particularly agreeable, chomping on a wad of tobacco and revealing a remarkable lack of sympathy as he'd filled out the report by hand. The thought that Cassie could have been raped or worse made Mitch shudder. By God's grace, she'd escaped unharmed and her attacker had been hauled away to jail a few minutes before they arrived at the trailer. Another of God's mercies. She would have hated to face that scumbag with only a few feet separating them. In some ways, that experience would have been every bit as traumatic.

As much as Mitch disliked violence, the guy had deserved his wrath. He'd wanted to do a lot more than slug him in the nose. Men who hurt women or children were the lowest type of pond scum and deserved no leniency. *Except God's grace.* Yeah, he knew it, but it'd probably take him a while longer to see it God's way.

Cassie had been terrific as she'd answered the officer's questions. She was articulate, precise and relayed the events without caving into emotion. This woman's spirit and apparent inner strength amazed him. When Mitch offered his hand to her for comfort, he'd been pleased when she'd accepted without hesitation. Maybe it wasn't fair, but he couldn't help but compare her—positively—to some of the women he'd dated. Not by a long stretch of the imagination would any one of them ever suggest going to a county fair, and especially not on Valentine's Day.

"Why is it, even in the blazing heat, this sandwich tastes soooo good? You're a bad influence on me. I didn't think I'd be hungry again so soon after that picnic lunch earlier today." Cassie took another bite. Thankfully, her appetite didn't seem diminished by what happened. He'd noticed at dinner the night before that she seemed to eat whatever she wanted, another marked difference between her and most other women. While they were always on some strange fad diet, Cassie seemed the type not to worry about such silliness.

"I love your spirit," he said between bites. "You're so real and unaffected. Effervescent." Those weren't the only words to describe Cassie. Ever since he'd seen her earlier that morning, he'd been drawn to her. She should be off-limits, but he couldn't shrug off his physical attraction to her. She wore mid-thigh denim shorts and a sleeveless, white cotton top with athletic shoes. While modest, she stimulated every ounce of male testosterone in him. Mitch wished he could turn it off, and he'd said a few quick prayers under his breath. She'd pulled her hair back into a ponytail, and it highlighted her long neck, the graceful slope of her jawline and her slender shoulders. Cassie was a completely feminine, gorgeous girl who had no clue of the pure *power* she could hold over a man. That in itself was incredibly appealing. Doris Bickle-whatever was right. Even though he hated cotton candy, Cassie was irresistible.

I don't deserve her sweetness, her innocence. After Brad's death, during his time of rebellion from anything to do with God, he'd made foolish choices and succumbed to worldly desires. He'd done things he wasn't proud of, things that would shame his parents and the way they'd raised him. Things he'd regret until the day he died, but the temptation had been great and he'd been at the lowest point in his life.

He had no excuses, but if nothing else, he'd learned from his mistakes. Enough to know how he wanted to live his life. Enough to know the kind of girl he hoped he'd eventually find. Like the one sitting with him now. It wouldn't be fair to Cassie to start something between them. He'd been lousy at relationships with women who lived in close proximity, so how could he believe he could start—much less maintain—any kind of relationship with a woman halfway across the country? Problem was, the more time he spent with Cassie, the more he wanted to know her better.

Lord, if this is wrong, I trust You to clue me in somehow.

"What's next?" After finishing her sandwich, Cassie downed the last of her diet soda. Grabbing the plastic sandwich wrap and the empty chip bag, she climbed off the bench and tossed them in a nearby trash can.

He drained his iced tea and followed suit. "Great right hook you've got there. Ever play pickup basketball with a guy?"

"With Tagg when I was little. I had better hand-eye coordination and I never let him forget it."

Mitch smiled. "I'm sure you didn't. How about going on the Ferris wheel next? You okay with heights?"

"Not a problem for me. How about you?"

"I might need you to hold my hand."

"Afraid of heights are you?"

"I'm not afraid to fall, if that's what you mean."

What an ill-advised statement. *Great, Jacobsen. Watch it.* He admired how Cassie didn't flinch and held his gaze steady. One minute he was thinking how he didn't deserve her and the next he wanted to kiss her. Oh yeah, he definitely wanted to kiss her. See if her lips were as soft as they looked. Maybe this trip to the fair wasn't the best idea. And it felt like a date because he *wanted* it to be a date. He hadn't had such a great time with a girl in a long time. As much as he hated what happened to her in the parking lot, she didn't seem inordinately traumatized and he'd selfishly liked that he'd been able to defend her honor. Liked holding her, protecting her.

"Somehow I don't think you're talking about heights."

He'd leave that comment alone. Equally uncanny was how she seemed to read him. Amy was right about Cassie's intuitiveness. They strolled down the midway, making random observations. "Looks like they'll be loading again soon," he said as they approached the towering Ferris wheel, taking their place in line behind a teenage couple. Unashamed and oblivious to everyone around them, they couldn't keep their hands off one another. Rubbing his hand over his jaw, Mitch slanted a glance at Cassie to gauge her reaction. She appeared amused but also embarrassed.

"I can't believe they carry on like that for the world to see," she whispered, turning toward him and releasing a small groan. "Wow. I can't believe how old I sound. Give me a hair net, support hose and sensible shoes already."

Mitch leaned close to her ear. "Maybe I should plant a big wet smacker on you for the whole world to see. Then maybe you won't feel so old."

She giggled, most likely from his breath tickling her ear. He liked her giggle, and it sounded anything but childlike.

"Too late. It's time to get on the ride now. Don't dawdle, old man." Cassie tossed him a teasing look over one shoulder. If he didn't know better, he'd think she was flirting. Yes, she was definitely flirting.

A few seconds later, he plopped down in the seat beside her, rocking it. Mitch focused on keeping a respectable distance between them instead of dwelling on that fantastic *come here to me* perfume she was wearing. He'd noticed it when he'd held her close. Maybe it was her shampoo. Floral but light and undeniably feminine.

"When I was a kid, I used to go to the fair and ride all day long until my older brother finally hauled me home."

"Tell me about him. Does he live in Alabama?" The ride started and the breeze, warm though it was, cooled him down a bit.

She averted her gaze. With both hands on the bar in front of them, she leaned forward and peered over the edge to the ground below. "He died when he was seventeen. I was twelve. Boating accident."

The sadness that washed over her lovely features made him want to snatch back the question. Amy could have warned him Cassie had a brother who'd died. Was it possible she didn't know? He thought the TeamWork crew knew everything about each other.

"I'm sorry, Cassie. I had no idea. What was his name?"

"Taggart, but no one called him that. From the time he was a toddler, he was known as Tagg. I don't tell many people about him," she said. "Probably because it still hurts, even after all these years. The hardest part for me to accept is that I won't see him again on this earth. I won't get to meet the woman he'd marry. I won't have the opportunity to read stories with his babies. Won't be able to go to him when I have a problem with a guy and need his advice."

Family dynamics could be weird. How well he knew, but Cassie didn't seem to suffer from the *living in the shadow of her older brother* syndrome. Unlike Celeste who'd once told him how hard it was to live up to the expectations he'd set by being so good at everything in school. If nothing else, his failure in the medical field squelched that notion.

"Losing my brother in such a senseless tragedy was horrible, but it made it easier knowing that he'd trusted Christ when he was ten." A small smile lifted the corners of her mouth. "He had a cleft in his chin that he hated, but my grandma told him it was a symbol of distinction. Girls loved him and guys wanted to be his friend. He was popular, athletic and a good student, but he had a mischievous streak. I followed him everywhere, so my nickname became Tagg-a-long. I know Mama begged him to take me places, but I never heard Tagg complain. Not once."

Talking about Tagg didn't seem to make Cassie sad, but he needed to lighten the mood. No more heavy talk for the afternoon. "I hope you haven't had many of those guy problems you mentioned."

"Nothing I can't handle."

Mitch stretched his arm along the seat behind her. He touched the ends of her hair, playing with it. "You like a man with a streak of mischief, do you?"

She shot him a grin. "It's never boring. You remind me of Tagg in some ways."

"Just so you know, I'm nowhere near perfect. And guys don't like being told they remind a girl of her brother." Especially one who'd died and she'd obviously adored.

"You remind me of him in all the best ways, silly. Besides, perfect people are boring."

"Do you have any other brothers or sisters?" he asked.

"No. It was only the two of us. My mom wanted more kids, but after me, she couldn't have any more." She cleared her throat. "Sorry. It's not as Peyton Place as it might sound. My mom might have been drunk sometimes, and my daddy in jail, but they provided the necessities. We knew in their own way they loved us. Grandma Thor was always there for us. She lived three doors down, and she was waiting for us in the driveway every Sunday morning—rain or shine—to take us to church. Mama usually managed to go, too, although it seemed like such a contradiction. I was saved in that church when I was eight."

"I'm glad you had your grandmother to watch over you, Cassie." After hearing all that, Mitch wasn't about to ask any more questions or he'd risk spoiling the rest of the day. Not that he didn't want to know more about her, but they were at a fair. Time for fun. He'd steer clear of family-related questions. That should do the trick.

"You and Amy have a younger sister, right?"

"Right. That would be Celeste. The quick rundown is that she's engaged and works in a marketing firm in Philly. I've always been closer to Amy, both in age—we're eighteen months apart—and in every other way. Celeste always seemed to go more for the whole debutante thing."

"I thought your dad was a pastor. Was it a huge church?"

He shifted and straightened in the seat, regretting his mention of the word debutante. Most pastors' daughters weren't introduced into high society—especially in Philadelphia, land of such well-known debutantes such as the actress-turned-Queen of Monaco, Grace Kelly. Might as well tell Cassie the truth. No reason to hide it, and subconsciously or not, he'd broached the subject.

"Dad was a pastor, but my grandfather on my mom's side was a well-known actor," he said. "Suffice it to say he provided well for our family after his death."

"Really? Well, that's quite exciting." Cassie shifted to face him on the seat, knees touching. "Not that he died, of course." Her cheeks flushed. "What was his name?"

"He made a few popular films in Hollywood but missed the live stage. After twenty years in California, he returned to New York and spent the rest of his career performing on Broadway. He died a long time ago, so I doubt you've ever heard of him."

"Name, please?" Brows arched, she waited.

"Eric Carlisle."

She squealed, causing the young couple in front of them to take a break in the action and stare at them. "Seriously? Of course, I've heard of Eric Carlisle. That's awesome!"

Mitch laughed, enjoying her enthusiasm. "Have to say, I didn't expect such a positive reaction from anyone younger than sixty." They'd reached the highest point of the Ferris wheel's rotation. "Careful. Don't get too excited and rock us too much."

"My grandma talked about Eric Carlisle all the time. She watched. . .oh, what was it? *Destination Venice.* That was one of his films, right?"

"Wow. I guess you really *are* legit and not just trying to flatter me."

"Your grandfather was very handsome. Virile. Strong. Oh, and he had the most fabulous speaking and singing voice."

"Virile?" He chuckled. "Haven't heard that word actually spoken in. . .well, ever."

"My Grandma Thor said it once and I always remembered it." She swatted his arm when he gave her a look. "What? Christian women can't say virile? Grandma would say, 'I'm a Christian, but I ain't dead.' I've probably watched *Destination Venice* ten times." Sitting back in the seat, she shook her head. "Imagine that. You're Eric Carlisle's grandson. That explains why Doris Bicklebing said you looked so familiar."

"Grandma Thor sounds pretty cool, too."

"She was totally cool. I couldn't pronounce my last name until I was about three, so Thor was easier. And it stuck. She passed away three years ago, but she'd be so excited to know I've met you. And that I know you well enough to be sitting next to you on a Ferris wheel."

Leaning close, Cassie placed her hand on his jaw, moving his face right and then left.

"Like what you see?" Mitch said through clenched jaws.

"You really do look a lot like him."

"You think so? I'm not sure if he had the freckles. And, sorry to say, I can't hold a tune."

She smiled. "If he had freckles, the makeup artists probably covered them with makeup. I'll withhold judgment on your singing for Sunday morning if you go to the church service with me. Us," she added.

"And the virile thing?"

That made her laugh. "I'll reserve comment."

"Fine. I'll pretend my ego isn't bruised." Being silly, he raised his arm and flexed like he'd done on the plane with Amy. "Exhibit A."

"Like I said, you're my hero. I think that qualifies. But if forced, I'll deny I ever admitted it."

The smells—greasy foods and the cotton candy from the booth next to the Ferris wheel—invaded his senses. Good thing his stomach wasn't queasy. A quick glance at Cassie confirmed she took it all in stride and wasn't bothered. He couldn't imagine any of the women he knew wanting to ride a Ferris wheel at a county fair. They'd be more concerned about getting dirty or infected by something on the seat.

Enough with the comparisons. In every way, Cassie could outrun, outlast, and outshine any of them. Like a beautiful ray of sunshine bursting through the dark rain clouds of the past few years. Now he was growing poetic?

As soon as the ride ended, Cassie hopped down from the seat and led the way to a shooting gallery. "You any good at this? What do you say to a little friendly competition?"

Mitch laughed. "Bring it on, Annie Oakley."

He emerged victorious, but Cassie was a worthy opponent. The gamekeeper pointed to the prizes, mostly cheap overstuffed animals in garish, glow-in-the-dark colors. "Take your pick, buddy."

"I'll let the lady choose." Cassie thanked him and selected a purple bear with pink stars around its eyes.

For the next hour, they talked quietly as they waited in lines and then rode several rides. They were chased away from one kiddie ride. "Get out of here. You're too old!" the teenager manning the ride yelled, shaking his hand at them. After that, what else could they do but ride the tamer-than-a-turtle carousel? Mitch took photos of Cassie sitting atop a white horse. He handed her the phone and she snapped pictures of him riding a black stallion. Before the ride ended, he captured more spontaneous photos. Mitch had the feeling he'd be looking at those a lot when he went home.

On the bumper cars, Cassie relentlessly tore around the place with that purple bear sitting beside her. She'd named him Eddie. With his lifeless eyes and stitched-on grin, Eddie was beginning to get on his nerves.

"At least you don't drive like that in real life," he teased as they climbed out of the bumper cars. "That maniacal gleam in your eyes was scary. And don't get me started on Eddie. That bear's a little freaky."

She laughed and hugged her bear. "Don't insult Eddie. Come on. You know why he's special, don't you?"

"I can't begin to imagine. If you're hugging him like that, you could at least name him Mitch. Or Mitchell. Or Jacob or Ainsworth." He lifted his shoulders. "Some other variation of your benefactor."

"Benefactor? You're jealous." She planted a big smack on Eddie. "Ainsworth?"

"Family name on my dad's side a few generations back."

"Well, as Grandma Thor would say, it's distinctive. Aristocratic even."

"You're silly." Gorgeous and incredible, but silly. He'd needed a day like this—a day to be free and act like a kid again. More than he'd known. He couldn't imagine sharing it with anyone but Cassie. "Want to get something to drink and then head back to Sam and Lexa's?"

"Sounds like a plan." She fell into place beside him as they walked to a concession stand then found an empty bench and collapsed onto it. After taking a sip of her pink lemonade, Cassie pressed the sweaty paper cup against her cheek.

Mitch eyed her from behind the rim of his cup as he took a long drink of his Gatorade. "Thank you for today. I haven't allowed myself a day like this in years."

She frowned. "You don't do fun things on the weekends?"

Taking another drink, he gathered his thoughts. "I play pick-up basketball with kids and work on projects for TeamWork whenever I can. I mean fun things like coming to a county fair, for instance. Something that makes me feel like a kid again. It's been a long time. Too long."

"I imagine you miss your friend even more on the weekends, don't you? That's when I tend to think more of Tagg."

That question gave him pause. "You know about Brad?"

Her cheeks filled with color. "Only a little. Winnie mentioned it yesterday before you arrived. I'm sorry you lost a friend in such a senseless act of terrorism, Mitch." She lifted her gaze to his. "I didn't say anything during our walk last night because I didn't feel it was my place."

"You know what it's like, though, don't you?" After hearing about Tagg, he figured that Cassie—as much as anyone else—understood the deep-seated grief associated with such a sudden, tragic loss.

"Yes, but the difference is that we didn't lose Tagg because of the evil in men. Not that it makes it any easier. It cut deep, all the same. But God's grace gets me through it, step by step and day by day. I hope you've found it to be that way, too."

Ah, Cassie. So much he could say, but he wouldn't. Not now. He could only nod and reach for her hand again. She hesitated only a minute before giving it to him and smiled when he laced his fingers through hers. "Think you'll be up to line dancing later, if that's what the rest of the crew decides to do?"

"I'm kind of tired, but I can run home and grab a quick shower. Then I should be good to go."

"Papaw! Somebody, help us. Please!" The anguished cries sounded like they came from a child.

Cassie put a hand on his arm, squeezing it. "Can you tell where that's coming from?"

"Come with me." Tossing his cup in a trash can, Mitch darted off the bench and dashed to the middle of the fairway. He turned in a circle, scanning the immediate area. When the calls for help were repeated, a nearby food vendor pointed toward the Ferris wheel. That's all the direction he needed.

The instinctive need to help in a medical emergency took over, as it always did. No matter what happened in that Boston hospital during his residency, Mitch couldn't walk away when someone needed help. If he could offer it, he'd be right there on the front lines.

Lord, here we go. Again.

Chapter 14

CASSIE CHASED BEHIND Mitch as he canvassed the fairgrounds and reached the area near the Ferris wheel in less than a minute. Her eyes widened. An older gentleman was lying prone on the ground with a young girl who looked to be no older than seven or eight huddled next to him, her head on his stomach, sobbing uncontrollably. "Papaw!" she screamed.

"Cassie, I need your help." Mitch's voice was firm and authoritative.

"Sure. Anything."

"If you have a phone, call 9-1-1 or else ask one of the gawkers to call. It doesn't look like there's anyone else with them. See if you can get the little girl away from the man. Take her aside and try to calm her down as best you can. She won't want to leave him, but I need to get in there and work on him until the police officer or the EMTs can get here and take over."

Pushing his way through the ever-widening crowd, Mitch ran to the man, falling to his knees on the ground beside him. Cassie called to a woman standing nearby to phone for emergency service since she wanted to go to the child. Reaching the scene seconds after Mitch, she gasped.

What she'd thought might be a heart attack was something else entirely. The man's right arm was bleeding profusely, a puddle of deep red blood on the ground beneath him. The blood came from a jagged, deep gash, his arm nearly severed midway between the shoulder and elbow. From what she could tell, his arm was still partially attached by the bone, but the muscles and tendons were exposed. A wave of nausea swept over her. *You can do this.*

Mitch had already started an assessment of the man's condition, checking his pulse and vital signs. She prayed the man wouldn't go into shock. She didn't know much about emergency medical treatment, but Mitch certainly did.

Taking a deep breath, Cassie offered her hand to the little girl. "I'm Cassie. My friend's going to take care of your grandpa until the EMTs can get here."

Swinging blindly, the girl punched her on the upper arm. Then she pulled away, her eyes wide and fearful before she collapsed against her, her shoulders rocking with her sobs. "His arm almost got cut off!"

"Shh. Everything's going to be okay, sweetie, but I need you to come with me now." Cassie once again offered her hand. "We need to step back and let my friend help your Papaw." Leading the child to one side of the crowd, Cassie kept one arm around her, staying close while still in view of her grandfather. What could have happened? Now wasn't the time to ask questions. Those would come later, but for now, she needed to keep her as calm as possible.

A worker handed a cardboard box to Mitch. He positioned it beneath Donald's right arm, elevating it. In one swift movement, Mitch tugged his

T-shirt over his head and ripped it down the middle. Placing the fabric near the gaping wound, he began to apply direct pressure.

"You were very brave to call for help. Can you tell me your grandfather's name?"

"Donald Corman."

"Do you have anyone else here at the fair with you? Somebody else in your family?"

With her face pressed against Cassie's stomach, the girl moved her head back and forth.

"What's your name?"

"Mercy."

Cassie ran her hand over the top of the girl's head, smoothing her dark curls. "Mercy's your name?" Maybe if she kept her talking, it would help calm her. "I don't think I've heard that name before. Is it short for something else?"

"Mercedes." Although her voice was muffled, it was clear. She turned her head to watch what was happening even as she still clung to Cassie.

The man groaned, moving his head from side to side. Glancing about the crowd, Mitch's gaze found Cassie as he continued to apply pressure to Donald's wound. After she gave him a nod, Mitch leaned close and spoke to him. She imagined he wanted reassurance Mercy was nearby and that someone was with her. A police officer arrived, this one younger than the one on duty earlier. Crouching beside them, he talked quietly with Mitch.

In another few minutes, the sounds of an approaching siren could be heard. Cassie breathed a prayer of thanks as two EMTs ran to where Mitch still worked to apply pressure to Donald's arm. After talking in low tones with Mitch for less than a minute, they transferred the wounded man to a stretcher.

Rising to his feet, shirtless and covered with Donald's blood, Mitch gestured for her to follow them. A young guy standing nearby stripped off his own T-shirt and tossed it to Mitch. Catching it, Mitch called out his thanks.

"Let me talk with the EMTs for a minute," Mitch told her as they reached the ambulance. They'd loaded Donald into the back and the doors stood open.

"Come with me, Cassie. Please. You promised." Mercy held on tight to Cassie's hand as if she'd never let go.

"Of course, sweetie. As long as they say it's okay." Judging by the size of the ambulance, there wasn't a lot of room. She shot a look at Mitch, hoping he'd understand her underlying message and mouthed *she has no one else here with her.*

Mercy tugged on Cassie's hand.

After talking in low tones with the EMTs, Mitch held out his hand to her. "It's all set, but you need to ride in front, Cassie." He gave her the name of the hospital and said it was a few minutes down the highway. "I have the cross streets and the basic directions, so here's hoping I find—"

"You should stay with Donald," she said. "I'll come in my car." She crouched down beside Mercy. "Honey, I promise I'm coming to the hospital. I'll be in my car right behind you. This is my friend, Mitch, and he'll stay with you for now, okay? You'll be fine and they're going to take good care of your grandpa."

Mercy sniffled. Releasing Cassie's hand, she nodded but said nothing.

"Time's short. We need to go." Putting his hands around Mercy's waist, Mitch lifted her up into the back and climbed in behind her. "We'll see you there." His face blanched. "Promise me you'll go find that on-duty officer. He should walk you back to the car." Mitch's tone was firm, leaving no room for argument.

She nodded. "I will. See you soon."

He closed the doors and the ambulance pulled away seconds later, sirens blaring.

She stared at her purple bear, forgotten on the ground. "Come on, Eddie," she said, scooping him in her arms. "Time to go to the hospital."

Chapter 15

*W*ALKING INTO THE emergency waiting room, Cassie spied Mitch sitting with Mercy in one corner. Although it couldn't be helped, she hated that his clothing was splattered with Donald's blood. The T-shirt the young guy had tossed at him was about two sizes too small and strained across his chest. In spite of the drama and emotion in the situation, the corners of Cassie's mouth twitched when she saw the T-shirt featured a heavy metal rock group from the 70s.

She sensed Mitch's eyes on her when she asked one of the nurses at the station if they had scrubs he could wear, offering to pay for them. "My friend is with the patient's granddaughter, and with all the blood on his clothes, I hate for her to see the constant reminder."

The young nurse behind the counter gave her an understanding smile. "When the other nurse comes back—she's checking a patient's meds and should be back any minute—I'll go get some clean scrubs and bring them to you. You don't need to pay us for them. We're happy to help."

"Thanks so much." When she turned away, Cassie saw that Mitch held Mercy's hand and both their heads were bowed. Tears stung her eyes at the tender scene and she quietly took the chair on the other side of the little girl. As she'd done most of the way to the hospital, Cassie prayed—that the surgeons would be able to save Donald's arm and for Mercy and other family members who would be affected by what had happened.

When she finished her prayer, Cassie opened her eyes to find Mitch's gaze resting on her. They both looked up as a nurse approached and handed him a package of new, aqua-colored scrubs. After thanking the woman, Mitch rose to his feet and stretched. He looked weary but managed a small smile. "This was your doing, I imagine? Thank you." Excusing himself, he disappeared into the nearby restroom.

Cassie squeezed Mercy's hand, thankful she seemed much calmer. Hopefully, she understood her grandfather would be fine in spite of the pain he'd suffered. "Do you want me to call your mom or dad? Maybe your grandmother?"

"Mr. Mitch already called my grandma," the girl said. "And he talked to the police."

"The police?" Cassie sighed. Of course, another second incident report would need to be filed. What a day. Maybe they should lay low the rest of the weekend.

Mitch emerged a few minutes later. Dressed in the scrubs, he seemed at ease and comfortable in them. Based on his immediate reaction to the medical emergency at the fair, Cassie suspected he'd had some kind of medical training.

His manner had been too practiced. Another part of the mystery of this man. More and more, she was learning there was a whole lot more to Mitch than his teasing persona and surface casualness.

One of the nurses handed Mitch a plastic bag for his soiled clothes. When he walked toward where Cassie sat with Mercy, his familiar smile helped to ease the tension. "What do you think, ladies? Is it my color?"

Mitch would look good in anything, in any color. She suppressed her sigh.

"You look like you're wearing your jammies, Mr. Mitch." Giggling, Mercy eyed him up and down.

Digging his wallet out of the bag with his clothes, Mitch gave the little girl money for the vending machine. Then he dropped into the chair beside her and told Cassie in whispered tones that Mercy's grandmother should arrive momentarily. He also confirmed he'd spoken to the police.

"It was very sweet to see you praying with Mercy."

Mitch's smile worked itself further into her affections. "In so many ways, I love how kids show us how simple it is to pray. Adults tend to make everything complicated. It's like we're afraid we'll fail. We stumble over what to say, or how to say it, and we stew over whether we're even saying it right. But God doesn't care about that. I hope I never lose that childlike faith and implicit trust."

"I hope neither one of us does," Cassie said. "Do you know how the accident happened?"

"One of the workers was cutting up wooden crates with an axe. Donald was walking behind him. From what I can tell, he was talking with Mercy about going on the Ferris wheel. He didn't see the guy, and the guy obviously didn't see him, and. . ."

"I've heard enough." Cassie shivered. "How horrible." Another senseless, freak accident.

"The worker ran off when he realized what happened. Probably scared out of his mind. He's nowhere to be found."

"I hope he's okay," Cassie said. "We probably should pray for him, too. It wasn't his fault, and I can't even imagine how he feels right now. I'm thankful you were there and knew what to do. You're an intriguing man, Mitch Jacobsen. Famous grandfather *and* medical skills. Who knew?"

Mercy ran over to Mitch and thrust a candy bar in his hands. "I got this for you."

Mitch smiled. "Thanks, but you were supposed to get something for you, not me. That means you've got to help me eat it."

"Okay." Mercy settled back in her chair. Her feet didn't touch the ground and she tucked them beneath her, boosting her up in the chair. When Mitch offered Cassie a bite of the candy bar, she shook her head and listened as he asked Mercy where she went to school and what subjects she liked.

A plump, middle-aged woman suddenly burst through the doors of the ER, out of breath. She let out a sigh of relief when she spied Mercy.

"Mamaw!" Scrambling down the chair, Mercy opened her arms for her grandmother's embrace.

"Ah, honey, I'm so glad you're okay." The woman gathered Mercy in her arms and held her tight. "I'm sure Papaw's going to be fine." Releasing her, she nodded to them. With her hand outstretched, she approached Mitch. "I'm Barbara Corman. I believe we spoke on the phone. Forgive me for being a bit confused, but are you also my husband's doctor?"

"No, ma'am. Mitch Jacobsen. This is my friend, Cassie Thorenson."

"He's the one who saved Papaw," Mercy said. "He got blood all over him and the nurse brought him some doctor clothes to wear."

A few tears slipped down Barbara's face and she threw her arms around Mitch and kissed his cheek. "Your quick thinking saved my Donald's life." Pulling back, she pumped his hand. "I can't thank you enough for what you did for him. And Mercy. You're a good man. Donald was lucky you were there."

"I'm thankful God planted me there when Donald needed me. Glad I could help."

Barbara stepped back and wiped her wet cheeks with the back of her hand. "I'd better check in with the nurses. From what I gathered on the phone, they're prepping Donald for surgery and they need my permission. I need to go and sign some forms."

"We should probably take our leave, but I hope you'll call us later and let us know how he's doing," Mitch said. He pulled out his wallet and removed a business card, handing it to Barbara. "My cell phone number is on the card. If I don't answer, please leave a message."

After looking at the card in her hand, Barbara's brown eyes rounded and she looked up at Mitch. "You work in New York? On Wall Street?" She shook her head and ran her hand over her forehead, her brow furrowed. "Forgive me, but this is a bit much. I'm starting to think you're an angel and, like you said, God Himself planted you at that fair today." She shrugged and put her arm around Mercy's shoulders. "Stranger things have happened." Barbara smiled at them through watery eyes. "I hope to give you a good report later today."

"We'll look forward to it," Mitch said, handing Mercy the uneaten portion of the candy bar. "Here you go, young lady. You were very brave today. The best. Help your grandma and take good care of your Papaw, okay?"

"I will." She gave him a smile filled with unabashed adoration. Easy to see why.

"Bye, Mercy." Cassie pulled her into another hug. "I have something I want to give you. Let me run out to the car and I'll be right back." Within two minutes, she handed over the purple bear. "This is Eddie, and if it's okay with your grandmother, I'd like to give him to you."

The little girl's eyes lit and she reached for Eddie. "He's so cute! Purple's my favorite color."

"Thank you for giving the bear to Mercy," Mitch said, moving one arm around her waist and steering her back outside. "What do you say we head back to the Lewis homestead? I think we've had enough excitement for one day. I'm wondering how I can get inside and up to my room without Amy or one of the others seeing me in this getup." Leaning his head back against the seat, he closed his eyes.

Pulling up in front of Sam and Lexa's house a short time later, Cassie stole a glance at Mitch and silenced the engine. He'd fallen asleep, and she hated to wake him. Who *was* this man? He worked on Wall Street but somehow seemed completely comfortable in the hospital scrubs. Once again, he'd been a hero. Twice in the same afternoon. How many more layers would she discover about Mitch before the weekend was over?

Brushing a lock of dark hair away from his forehead, Cassie trailed the back of her hand down his cheek. He stirred but didn't open his eyes. Turning his head, he leaned into her hand.

Something about seeing Mitch so vulnerable like this, so peaceful in his slumber, touched her deep inside, in a place never reached before in quite the same way. Something indefinable.

Something I like very much.

Chapter 16

After Cassie dropped Mitch off in front of Sam and Lexa's house, telling him she'd be back in a little over an hour, he'd been surprised to find the front door unlocked. The door leading into the kitchen was standing wide open as he'd entered the front hall. Amy and some of the others were sitting and talking on the back patio. He headed straight for the stairs, hoping to get up to his guest bedroom unnoticed. The bright color of the scrubs didn't exactly help. Three stairs up, he heard Amy call to him to wait. He hesitated and turned back around.

Amy's jaw gaped as she eyed him up and down. "Well, this is something I never expected to see. Is everything okay?"

"Yes," he said, his voice hoarse as he rubbed one hand over his eyes and then moved his hands to his hips. "Cassie took me to a county fair and there was. . .an incident. Two incidents, actually."

"Sounds eventful. Cassie's all right?"

"She's fine." He appreciated his sister's concern for their well-being. Besides their Mom, Amy had been his greatest source of encouragement and support when his future as a doctor tanked. Likewise when he'd lost Brad. She'd navigated the chaos to reach his side and stayed with him for days, praying with him and forcing food into him.

"Come out back with us and have some iced tea," she said. "Unless you're not up to it."

He debated it for a moment since he didn't particularly feel like chatting, but figured he might as well tell them so they could pray for Donald. He had the feeling Cassie might not tell them about her traumatic experience, and he needed to be sure and thank Sam and Josh for insisting the ladies take that self-defense class. "For a few minutes," he said, "and then I need a shower."

"Did you eat? We fended for ourselves with the leftovers from earlier, but I can fix you a sandwich."

"That'd be great. Thanks." Amy knew his preferences and that in itself was a comfort. Climbing back down to the landing, he followed her to the back of the house. Winnie, Rebekah and Natalie had taken the kids to the park before the adults headed out for the evening. For the next few minutes, Mitch told the rest of the group what happened. The release felt good, and in the course of the story, he also gave them the short, sad saga of what happened in Boston during his residency.

"God put you there today, for both Cassie and Donald," Lexa said.

"He's also using your medical training to help others in unexpected ways and places," Sam said. "Don't ever discount the value of that, Mitch."

After finishing his sandwich, he excused himself and climbed the stairs. If he didn't want to spend more time with Cassie, he'd pass on the evening's festivities. The idea of going to a noisy, packed restaurant didn't appeal to him. The promise of holding Cassie close and dancing with her was the greatest lure in going. From what he knew, Texas line dancing didn't mean a lot of slow dancing, but he'd sit out most of it and seize whatever opportunity presented itself.

The thought of Cassie made him smile. Amy was right about her. They were good together. No, better than good. They were great together.

~

Cassie tried to focus on anything other than how handsome Mitch looked. How tall. How broad his shoulders. He'd always been attractive, and maybe the events of the day turned her head, but tonight? The man was gorgeous. His eyes reflected the deep green of his shirt. His dark hair was styled, but it looked soft and touchable. She shook her head. Well, this was ridiculous, mooning over the man. He was the same guy as yesterday, and the same as he'd be tomorrow.

Mitch pulled on a lightweight jacket and waved to the others as they all paraded out of the house and started loading into the various vehicles. "Ready to go? I know it's been a long day for us already. If you're too tired—"

"Raring to go. Are *you* too tired?" Maybe that was his underlying message but he didn't want to state it flat-out.

"I wouldn't miss the opportunity to spend more time with you, Cassie."

Thanking the two teenage babysitters from the church they'd hired for the evening, Cassie grabbed her small purse and a lightweight sweater, draping it over her arm.

"Bye, Cassie. Bye, Mr. Mitch! Have fun." Chloe gave them a bright smile. Luke was in a playpen while Gracie and Joe sparred over something. Less than a year apart in age, the interactions between those two were fascinating to observe.

"We will. You, too," Cassie said. "Be good for Miss Kimberly and Miss Traci tonight."

Mitch gave Joe a high-five in the air when the little boy glanced over at them during a momentary lull in his debate with Gracie. "You're in charge tonight, big guy." Joe broke out into a wide grin. Goodness, that child looked more like his daddy every day, right down to the smile lines and piercing blue eyes.

"Looks like you've got a new friend," Cassie said as Mitch closed the front door behind them. He'd played a couple of games with the kids after their indoor picnic earlier in the day and made new friends for life. "Why does it feel like you've been here for a week instead of only a day?"

Mitch gave her a grin as they walked toward her car. "When you put it that way, I'm not sure that's a good thing. It's true we've packed a whole lot into a short time." His phone rang. Pulling it out, he stared at the display. "I'd better take this call. It's probably Barbara Corman."

Listening to his comments, Cassie gathered the news was positive. *Thank you, Lord.*

"The surgeon was able to save Donald's arm." Mitch pocketed his phone. "Praise God."

"Mitch, I have to ask you something." She prayed it wouldn't upset him, but she'd been wondering about it all afternoon. "Were you once in the medical field?"

"Yes," he said, narrowing his eyes and staring into the distance at the sun beginning its descent on the horizon. "A long time ago."

"In my opinion, the skill and confidence you demonstrated when you rushed to Donald's aid today can only come from someone who's been trained. Well trained." She waited until he looked at her. "Is that why you punched that guy in the nose and not his stomach? To keep him down but not do internal damage? Because that's what I imagine a doctor would do. . .in a case like that."

Mitch dropped his gaze from hers. "You're right. I'll tell you about it some other time but not tonight if you don't mind."

"Of course." Cassie clicked the key fob. "Would you like to drive? For the practice?"

In the middle of tapping a rhythm on the top of the car, Mitch stopped. "Don't tease me. I hope you're serious because I'd love it. Not for the practice either. It's rather emasculating to have the woman do all the driving."

"Well, far be it from me to detract from your manhood," she said. "As long as you drive more defensively than you did in that bumper car. That was a pitiful display."

"Hey, I let you slam into me, woman. Wanted to empower you."

"Male chauvinist."

"Ka-ching! Another chink was added to the old armor." One thing she admired about Mitch was how quickly he seemed to recover his sense of humor, even if it was only a mask.

She tossed him the keys. "All yours. Don't put any chinks in my car, please."

"Let me guess. Your car is named Eddie?"

"Nope. I'm not that unimaginative and boring. This, my friend"—she patted the hood of the Saab—"is Edwina."

"Cars aren't named Edwina. I thought women gave their cars a masculine name."

"I don't care," she said, wrinkling her nose. "Call me a maverick."

"Then you should call the car Maverick. What is it with you and variations of the name Edward, anyway?"

"That was my grandpa's name. Call me sentimental, I guess."

"Ah, I see. Nothing wrong with being sentimental."

Mitch closed the car door and started the engine. "Like the purr of a cat. I love that sound, especially sitting behind the wheel. Make sure you're strapped in tight."

"Wait," she said, putting her hand on his arm. "You do have a valid driver's license, right?"

"Yes, but I'm not showing it to you unless forced. It seriously looks like a mug shot."

"Now you have to show it to me. Let's see it. Dig it out already."

Laughing, he reached into the back pocket of his jeans and tugged out his wallet. He flipped through a few photos and handed it over. "There. Are you happy now?"

"I can't see it very well."

"Maybe you should get out your granny glasses."

"Be quiet. I guess all the excitement earlier today has made you punchy."

"Speak for yourself. You're the one who mentioned the hair net and support hose."

Even though it wasn't dusk yet, she needed the inside light to study the photo. "Not bad, but I have to say, you look like a. . .devilish rogue more than a knight in shining armor."

"Told you. And you asked for it. Let's see yours. Hand it over, please."

"No."

"Why? Embarrassed by your facial hair?"

Laughing, Cassie pulled out her wallet and handed over her driver's license. "Hope you're still my friend."

He twisted his lips and brought it closer. "Not bad. You couldn't have a bad hair day if you tried. It's one of your best features. Don't ever cut it."

"I was actually thinking of cutting it for Locks of Love. I've done it before."

"As long as you'd grow it back. Right away."

She sat back in the seat. "As if you have any say in the matter. The truth is revealed. You only like me for my locks." Crossing her arms, she huffed. "Hush and drive."

He patted the dashboard. "Come on, Maverick. Let's show this girl what you can really do."

"Mitch—"

"I'm teasing, Cassie. I promise to take very good care of"—he grunted—"Edwina."

"Hey, he who has no car has no reason to tease."

"Okay, that's a low blow. I've owned a few cars in my lifetime, and I had a Jeep when I moved to New York. In any case, I'll get you back for that one."

"I'm so scared."

Mitch pulled away from the curb. "I hope you're going to navigate. We don't want to get lost. With our track record, anything could happen."

True enough. "For starters, turn left at the end of the street."

~

As he drove, Cassie settled into the passenger seat. She told him it was about a twenty minute drive and left him alone with his thoughts except to give him occasional directions. He couldn't remember when, if ever, he'd been alone with a woman in a car without feeling compelled to keep the conversation moving. He'd love to know what she was thinking, but he was likewise content with the quiet.

His thoughts wandered back to the talk on the patio. Sam had highlighted something he'd never considered. All his medical training hadn't been wasted. Sure, he might not have the M.D. behind his name. Neither did he have the long hours and loss of sleep doctors experienced as a way of life. He used to wonder how he'd balance life as a hospital physician with having a wife and family. From what he'd seen, it was difficult to balance the heavy demands, especially being a physician in a bustling, urban hospital. Although it could be done, something usually suffered as a result. Unfortunately, it was often the family.

After Brad died, he'd turned sour on the whole concept of marriage. As a result, he'd dated a lot because he genuinely enjoyed female companionship. And again, Amy was totally right. He'd dated aimlessly, choosing women he knew weren't right for him long-term. He liked the softness of a woman, the way a woman could make him feel more like a man. Most of the women he dated didn't share his faith if they had any beliefs at all. He'd turned away from his beliefs, and in essence, turned his back on God. Like Peter, he'd denied the presence and importance of Christ in his life. Denied Him. Maybe he didn't verbalize the words, but in his heart? Yes, he had. Not speaking up for his faith was perhaps his greatest sin, and it grieved him. His apathy made it too easy to invent flimsy reasons to excuse his reckless behavior. *Wrong, wrong, wrong.*

Time to face facts.

I want what these people have. In the short time he'd been with the TeamWork crew, he'd seen how great it could be to have a wife and family. Especially after his dad died, he'd known he wanted what his mom and dad shared all those years. He wanted someone to come home to at the end of a long day. When he made a bad trade or lost a client, who would he turn to for comfort and reassurance that he wasn't a complete screw-up? He didn't want to go through life alone. At Amy and Landon's wedding, as he'd listened to their vows, it was like some internal light switch got flipped on to illuminate his shortcomings.

"Turn right at the next light," Cassie said, interrupting his thoughts. "The restaurant's two blocks down on the right."

Within five minutes, he'd parked the car and they walked inside. The hostess greeted them and he spied Rebekah and Kevin waving to them from a large table near the dance floor. As they chatted with the others, Mitch was glad none of them brought up the earlier events in the day. More than that, he was grateful that Cassie didn't seem unduly traumatized by what happened to her. Beneath the aura of small-town charm was a woman strong in character. If Cassie wanted to talk about it, she'd say something. Otherwise, he was content to relax and enjoy the evening.

Sipping his Coke, Mitch watched Cassie without bothering to disguise his fascination with her. She was a natural on the dance floor. A live band set up in one corner of the restaurant played until they took a break and a DJ spun country western tunes, none of which were familiar, but they were catchy.

Marc and Natalie weren't as adept with the line dances, but they danced beside Sam and Lexa, briefly trading partners for the livelier dances. Amy and Landon held their own—Landon *was* originally from Texas—but Kevin? Another surprise. Who could have guessed the shy, quiet man could dance like that? Kevin and Rebekah danced near Josh and Winnie and they also traded partners every now and then. Mitch watched Kevin twirl his wife beneath his arm before bringing her smoothly back into the circle of his arms. *Way to go, Kevin.*

At the first hint of a slow dance, he'd make a beeline for Cassie. A couple of guys cut in and danced with Marta and Gayle, but Cassie politely declined when asked. That pleased him, although he had no claim on her, no right to deny her the opportunity to meet other guys. After all, he was going back to New York in a little over two days. That thought disgruntled him, irrational as it was.

Chomping on a tortilla chip, Mitch caught the inside of his cheek. Hard. "Ow," he said under his breath, carefully finishing the bite. He leaned back, throwing his arm on the back of the chair vacated by Cassie, trying to appear nonchalant. Tapping his foot in rhythm to the music, his back stiffened when a tall cowboy approached her. Slightly long, dark hair, muscular and not bad looking. Mitch grunted under his breath and straightened in the chair. The guy didn't have a hint of a receding hairline and not an ounce of fat on that lean frame.

"Stone!" Cassie threw her arms around the cowboy and gave him a warm reception. "It's so great to see you."

Stone? Seriously? If he was honest with himself, the name *was* fitting. The guy looked solid as a. . .well, a rock. A very big, immovable rock. Grabbing another chip, Mitch stuffed it in his mouth. He tried to train his attention elsewhere, but it didn't work, and he moved his gaze back to where Cassie talked with the man. If that guy grabbed her and headed to the dance floor, he'd cut in. Make a fool of himself, if needed. Whatever it took.

In too snug jeans, a short-sleeved red shirt—unbuttoned one too many buttons—and a black Stetson, Stone what's-his-name epitomized the stereotype of a cowboy from the cover of one of those romance books he'd seen women sneak into their grocery carts. And did every single man in Texas own a Stetson? What was it about those hats that women loved so much, anyway? Did the hat make the man? No, it was probably more the combination of outdoors, brawny man and the Stetson. Women fawned all over guys like that.

Leaning to the left to get a better view, Mitch clenched his jaws. Well-worn cowboy boots made from some kind of an animal. Probably rattlesnake or alligator. He wouldn't doubt this Stone guy killed the animal with his bare hands. Might even be one of those champion bull riders women went nuts over, judging by the obnoxious silver buckle.

"Having a good time?" Kevin slid into the chair beside him.

Mitch moved his arm. "Yep. The TeamWork crew sure knows how to have a good time." He nodded in Cassie's direction. "So, who's the cowboy in the red shirt?" As casual as he tried to be, he couldn't fool anyone. He'd always been regrettably obvious with his feelings.

Kevin chuckled under his breath. "Stone? He's a friend of Cassie's from a few years ago."

"I take it you've met him before?"

"You can be straight with me, Mitch. I've been there. When Rebekah dated Adam, I'm sure I had the same look on my face that you do now."

"The British guy?"

"The same." Kevin was a handsome guy, and Rebekah was tall, blonde and leggy—the girl-next-door version of a supermodel. Rebekah could have had her pick of men, but from what Mitch could tell, she was unaffected by her God-given beauty and adored her husband. Who wouldn't? Kevin was a walking pillar of faith, loyalty and strength of character. Their personalities meshed well.

Crossing his arms, Mitch rested them on the table. "I hear you waited a while—as in a few years—to stake your claim for Rebekah. Can I ask why?"

As Kevin considered his answer, Mitch darted another glance to where Cassie talked with Stone across the room. What could they have to talk about for this long?

"I wanted Rebekah to make the conscious decision that she wanted to be with me," Kevin finally said. "It wasn't a contest between Adam and me. We'd dated and she knew the way I felt about her. The only way to explain it is that God gave me a peace that Adam would eventually mess up the relationship. And that she'd figure out what she wanted."

"The waiting must have been tough." Kevin's smile confirmed his words. "You've got a lot more patience than I would have. It's not my long suit and I'd have barged right in there. Tell me something. Is this friend of Cassie's a casual acquaintance or did they date?"

"Not sure. You should ask her. The main thing is, even if she did date Stone in the past, she doesn't now."

"Right." Good point. Mitch finished his Coke. "I'd better get over there in case there's a slow dance soon. Aren't we about due?"

Kevin nudged his arm. "Go get your woman, city boy."

"Thanks, man. I think I'll do that." That's all the impetus he needed. Rising to his feet, Mitch squared his shoulders. He hadn't a clue what to say to a guy like this and felt a little less worthy as a man the closer he came to all that rugged masculinity. If he knew how to swagger, he might try it, but he'd probably end up looking stupid and feeling even more inadequate.

Bottom line? No way, no how was this Stone guy going to hone in on a slow dance with Cassie.

Time to stake his claim.

Chapter 17

$\mathcal{C}$ASSIE'S HEART SKIPPED a few beats as Mitch approached where she talked with Stone. The man was completely adorable wearing that *who is this guy?* expression. Why would a man as confident as Mitch be intimidated by the man standing beside her? Stone might be impressive physically, but he was a total goof. She'd met him shortly after her arrival in Houston. They'd gone out a few times, shared one awkward kiss totally lacking in chemistry and been friends ever since.

Something about the pasted-on expression on Mitch's face struck her as comical. Could it be he didn't know what to say for once in his life? She'd let him speak first.

"Mitch Jacobsen," he said, offering his hand to Stone. Was it her imagination or did his voice suddenly sound deeper?

"Stone Bicklebing." He pumped Mitch's hand a few times before releasing it.

Cassie bit her lip not to laugh as Mitch darted a glance at her. "Don't tell me you're related to my old friends Doris and Walt?"

"They're my aunt and uncle. How long have you known them?"

"Cassie introduced us when I first got to town."

"And when was that?"

Mitch grunted. "Yesterday, as a matter of fact."

"I see."

"Great people," Mitch said. "We talked about the moon, among other things."

"Okay then," Stone said as he cast a curious glance in her direction.

"Your aunt told me I'd be a fool to leave Cassie behind when I leave Houston."

Stone crossed his arms. "And how long have you known Cassie?"

Mitch's face grew pale, visible even in the dim lighting inside the restaurant. "Long enough."

This was going nowhere fast. Not Mitch's best moment, to be sure. The band returned and began tuning their instruments for the next set. She turned to Stone. "It's been great to see you again."

"You, too, Cass. Take care." He leaned close and whispered. "This guy really likes you. Do yourself a favor and put him out of his misery." Telling Mitch it was nice to meet him, Stone departed.

"Well, that was strange." Mitch tugged on the lapels of his jacket. "Is Bicklebat a big name in Texas or is the world really that small?"

"Come dance with me." Cassie pulled him by the hand and led him onto the dance floor. That's where Mitch took over. Resting one hand lightly on her waist, he took her other hand in his as they started a fast waltz.

"I have to say, you're surprisingly good at this."

"I've learned a few of the social graces in New York."

"Social graces?"

"How to waltz the old-fashioned way, for one. I'm using the same technique now, but it's set at a faster tempo. The key is in knowing how to properly hold a woman." He twirled Cassie around the floor, moving them expertly among the other dancers. Sam and Lexa smiled as they passed them, as did Winnie and Josh. She couldn't miss a few broad winks here and there. Ah, the TeamWork matchmakers must be having a field day. Not that she even cared anymore.

Cassie relaxed and enjoyed being held in his arms. She didn't like it when a dance partner wouldn't—or couldn't—lead. Or had two left feet. Not that they could help it, but she was glad Mitch had no problems in that arena.

"By the way, you're incredibly cute when you're jealous." She'd put her hand on his chest, a reminder of how firm and muscular it was. Lord forgive her, but she couldn't get the image of shirtless Mitch leaning over Donald out of her mind. In more ways than one. Maybe it was the combination of his selfless, heroic actions and his strong physique? Rebekah told her how seeing Kevin shirtless on one of the TeamWork mission projects made her see him in a completely different light. Call it vain, call it inappropriate, but she couldn't help it. God made her this way, right?

Mitch grunted. "Don't know what you're talking about."

She hadn't voiced that thought, had she? No, she'd said something about him being jealous. "What? They don't teach you how to talk to a rugged cowboy in those social grace classes?"

"I'm sure they have those classes, yes, but you won't catch me in one of them." He tugged her closer, moving his hand around her waist with firm control. The movement seemed natural and comfortable. Possessive almost, but she wasn't about to complain.

"Which class *did* you enroll in?" She could only blame it on the night and the headiness of being held in Mitch's arms. Must bring out her flirting gene.

"How to charm a girl the old-fashioned way." With that, Mitch proceeded to whirl and twirl her with the best of them.

She loved every minute.

~

Two Hours Later

"Oh, no." Shifting to face Mitch, Cassie slid right into him. As in flat up *against* him. She burst out laughing. She'd moved way beyond the point of embarrassment.

Laughing with her, Mitch struggled to sit up. His feet slipped out from under him and he landed flat on his back. "Now, this is fun."

"Shh." She stifled her giggles and moved a finger over her lips. "Listen. Do you hear that?"

He stopped. "Um, no. What am I supposed—?"

"Listen closely. That hissing sound."

"You've got to be kidding me." He turned incredulous eyes on her. "We broke the castle?"

"Unless my ears deceive me, yes, we've managed to puncture the castle." She tugged on the back pocket of his jeans.

"Excuse me?" Mitch angled his body away from hers, laughing. "Sweetheart, you need to buy me dinner first before you—"

"Oops. Sorry." She raised her hands. "Didn't mean to invade your privacy, but do you have a knife in your back pocket?"

"Well, yes, but it's not like the blade is out, if that's what you're thinking." He slid his hand into the pocket. "The bottle cap thingee has apparently broken loose."

"Great. What are we going to do?"

"I say we find the humor in it all. It's not like we can find the source of the leak tonight and fix it with duct tape or something. Chances are, the leak is directly beneath me."

"That's a great idea! I know where Sam keeps the duct tape." When Cassie started to scramble to her feet, she slid and landed beside him again. "We're never going to get out of here, are we?"

"It has to be deflated, anyway and I'll tell Sam and he can let the rental company know. I'll pay them well to find and patch the puncture. I'm sure this isn't the first time it's happened."

After a few tries, they finally managed to climb out of the castle. Mitch stepped outside first and took hold of her hand to assist her, giving it a tug. "On solid ground again."

"Thanks," she said, smoothing her hands down her clothes. "On Christ the solid rock I stand. . . Do you know that one?" She quietly sang a few bars of the hymn.

"My faith is built on nothing else," he said. "Your thought process fascinates me. I'd sing it with you, but you don't want to hear my voice if you plan on sleeping tonight."

She laughed. "That good, huh?"

"That nightmarishly bad, yes, but your voice is beautiful. Alto?"

"Second soprano. I'd better scoot on home. It's past my bedtime."

He bowed. "In that case, the gallant knight will walk the fair maiden to her horse."

"I had fun tonight," she told him as they slowly rounded the side of the house. Neither one of them seemed to be in a hurry to end the evening.

"You were right, you know."

She glanced up at him as they reached her car. "What do you mean?"

"I was jealous of Stone. I didn't want to take the chance he'd whisk you onto the dance floor first. . .and have you bask in all his. . .virility." He scratched his head. "That's a word, right?"

"It is, and there's no reason for you to be jealous."

"I know that now."

"I've seen your bare chest. You have nothing to worry about in the virility department." *I can't believe I said that.*

Mitch's gorgeous, heart-stopping smile spread across his face. Needing a distraction, Cassie opened her purse and retrieved her keys. That took all of three seconds. The man was uncanny in seeing so much, and she avoided his gaze. "Well, I guess this is good night. I'll see you in the morning."

Mitch stepped in front of the car door, blocking her way. Shoving his hands in the pockets of his jeans, he rocked back on his heels. "I think you can figure out what I want to do right now."

"This isn't a date," she said, trying to sound firm. "We're two friends who had a good time. A really good time. With their friends. And danced together. It was nice."

"It was better than nice and you know it, date or not. Don't forget I fed you when you were hungry." True enough, he'd bought her a cheeseburger and fries. He'd amused her by dipping the fries in mayonnaise, and teased her because she'd asked for extra pickles and eaten every one of them.

"Doesn't count since you helped me eat my burger. Wait, are you playing the entitlement card?"

"Not at all. I'm not entitled to anything, but what I'd like—"

"Please stop talking for once in your life." Tugging on his jacket with both hands, Cassie yanked Mitch close.

His eyes crinkled at the corners and his mouth creased into that addictive smile. She was growing accustomed to this man. He lowered his head and hesitated, waiting. "Yes? Did you want something?"

"You can be incredibly infuriating."

"Are you complaining?" He rested his hands lightly on her shoulders. "You and I understand one another a lot better than you're willing to admit, Cassie."

"Don't know about that, but I don't. . .kiss. . .men I don't know," she said, helpless to resist him. Mitch had her tongue-tied ten ways to crazy and then some.

He laughed. "Neither do I. After today, we know each other quite well. As a matter of fact, I'm already falling—"

She put a finger over his lips, silencing him. "If it'll make you stop talking, go ahead and kiss me already." The only thing she'd protest was if he *didn't* kiss her.

"With pleasure," he murmured as he brushed his lips over hers before settling into a short but memorable kiss. Oh yes, there was a definite spark between them. More like a minor explosion, but who was counting?

"That's pretty much what I had in mind." Slowly brushing his fingers down the length of her arms with a feather-soft touch, Mitch stepped back with a grin that made her all kinds of silly. "You'd better go if you don't want more where that came from."

Cassie cleared her throat. "Didn't mean a thing. I definitely won't be thinking about you the rest of the evening."

"Then we're even since I definitely won't be looking for you tomorrow. You can come find me."

"Arrogant man." She clutched her keys against her chest and fought the strong urge to grin.

"Pushy woman." He stepped closer, his eyes searching her face, making her heart pound.

"Say good night, Mitch." Somewhere in the background, she heard the sound of metal hitting the pavement.

"You dropped your keys."

"Don't care." She couldn't tear her gaze from his if she tried.

He chuckled and skimmed his thumb over her cheek. "Happy Valentine's Day, Cassie."

"I thought you weren't planning on kissing anyone on Valentine's Day. Guess you're not a man of your word."

"Correction. I'm not kissing just anyone. I'm kissing a very incredible *some*one. We've shared a lot today. Try and keep me away." Slipping his arms around her, he tightened his hold as if he'd never let her go.

"Insufferable," she whispered.

"Beautiful." Mitch lowered his lips to hers once more.

Oh, she was in trouble all right. The best kind of trouble.

Chapter 18

CASSIE FIDGETED. . .AND then fidgeted some more. What was she, ten? Finally, she sat on her hands. She'd lost count of how many solos she'd performed since her arrival in Houston eight years ago. The thought of singing with Mitch in the congregation made her antsy. Why, she had no idea because he made her feel at ease under normal circumstances. To be fair, standing and singing in front of more than seven hundred people would make most people a little queasy. And doing such a thing didn't exactly qualify as an everyday occurrence.

Mitch nudged her arm. "Everything okay over there?"

She swallowed. "Think so."

"Anything I should know?"

"You'll find out soon enough."

"Sounds ominous."

"Let's hope not," she mumbled. Lowering her head, she prayed and remained on the pew when he rose to his feet for a hymn. He started to drop back down on the pew, but she waved her hand. *Don't worry about me*, she mouthed. Trying to calm her nerves, she tapped her foot, thankful it was a rousing hymn, and glanced down the long row of her friends. Kevin had taken the week off from his youth and music ministry so he could attend, and he shared a hymnal with Rebekah. Natalie, Marc, Gayle and Marta were on the row behind them. Sam caught her eye and gave her an encouraging smile. Cassie nodded, taking a deep breath. How happy Papa Bear must be to have so many of his TeamWork crew worshipping together.

On Cassie's right, Amy put her arm around her and squeezed her shoulder. "Lexa told me you're singing this morning," she whispered. "You'll do great."

Cassie leaned her head on Amy's shoulder for a brief moment. "Thanks."

Mitch shot them both a curious glance.

When the pastor began the prayer for the offering, she hopped up from the pew and tried to scoot past Mitch. Kind of hard to do when his masculinity—when *he*—filled all the available space. She tugged on his arm and motioned to the aisle. With a concerned expression, he stepped aside to allow her to pass. Closing her eyes and whispering a prayer under her breath, Cassie walked to the front where the worship leader handed her the microphone.

The pianist struck the first chord of the song they'd practiced before Sunday school. *Lord, use me as Your instrument. May my song touch someone's heart today.*

"I'd like to dedicate this song to all the men and women who've served our country, some of whom paid the ultimate sacrifice. Someone else paid the ultimate sacrifice for you and for me, and His name is Jesus." She took a deep breath as she listened to the opening prelude, avoiding looking at Mitch. Slowly, quietly, infusing the lyrics with feeling, Cassie closed her eyes and began to sing. A few bars into the song—as always—the Holy Spirit began to take over, easing her nerves and soothing her.

A friend had written the tune, and she'd penned the lyrics about a young soldier who'd gone off to fight in the war—a song full of poignancy and heartfelt sentiments about family, love, and binding ties. The type of song to wrap itself around your heart, hold on tight and never let go in all the best ways. While she hadn't enjoyed the benefits of professional voice training, she sang from the deepest part of her soul. As she began the chorus, Cassie dared to glance at Mitch. He nodded his head in time with the song, and she could tell Sam was tapping his foot.

Barely registering the reaction of the congregation as she finished, she made her way back to the pew and dropped into the space beside Mitch.

"That was incredible," he whispered. "I was right last night. You've got a great voice."

Cassie enjoyed having Mitch sit beside her, but without trying, he was distracting. Overwhelmingly so, especially wearing that fabulous aftershave. Her knees felt weak, her insides were turning into mush. Everything in her reacted to this man she barely knew yet also knew better than most men in her life. *Silly girl. What a disrespectful thought while sitting in church.* At least the bulletin listed the scripture verses for the morning message so she wouldn't come across like a complete idiot if Mitch wanted to discuss something about it later in the day.

Walking out of the church after the service, they shook hands with the pastor and exchanged pleasantries with other members. Sam was busy introducing the visiting TeamWork volunteers, and he motioned for Mitch, Amy and Landon to join them.

"You really like him, don't you?"

Cassie turned to face Rebekah, unable to stop her smile.

"Yes, although I have no idea why I'm spending so much time with him since he's going back to New York soon. He's also made a vow never to fly again."

"After what happened, I can understand why he'd feel that way," Rebekah said. "Give him time, sweetie. I'm sure he'll change his tune. Wait and see. If not, there's other ways to travel between New York and Houston. Lots of people hate to fly."

"Let me guess. You two must be talking about Mitch." Marta joined them, draping her arms around their shoulders. "The man's gorgeous, he's got a solid career and he's obviously not hurting financially. He's the total package." She winked at Cassie. "Glad to see you're hitting it off so well with him, Cass."

Marta always spoke her mind. Seeing Winnie nearby, Cassie excused herself. "Here. Let me help you," she said, easing the diaper bag from her friend's shoulder.

"Thanks. I'm like a walking nursery these days. I heard you helped Chloe take Gracie to her Sunday school class this morning. I appreciate it. I can't imagine how Lexa does it with two kids the same age, but she *is* the most organized person on the planet." Winnie smiled when Cassie pretended the bag weighted her down. "I promise I don't have a bowling ball in there. Josh usually carries it for me, but he's in a meeting."

"Let me walk you to your van. Chloe, is that a new dress?"

"Uh huh." She twirled in a circle, modeling it for her. "Mommy made it for me."

"She did? Why, your mommy did a fantastic job. You look very pretty." Winnie had found yet another creative outlet. Next to Lexa, Winnie had more energy than any woman she'd ever met. Sometimes she wondered if her two bosses ever slept.

Chloe tugged on the hem of her dress. "Mr. Mitch told me he likes you. He thinks you're beautiful and likes your hair."

Feeling her cheeks grow warm, Cassie waved as the little girl climbed inside the minivan.

Opening his palm, Luke offered her a handful of mushy, sticky cereal as Winnie strapped him into his car seat.

"Chloe, how'd your brother get cereal? He's too young for that." Pulling out a baby wipe from the diaper bag, Winnie cleaned his hand.

"I'm not a tattletale, but her name starts with G and ends in E. And she lives in Massa. . .however you say it."

Cassie hid her smile and ruffled Luke's blonde hair. It had grown long enough to curl on the ends now. What a doll. Both Chloe and her little brother would break a few hearts one day.

"Chloe's right about Mitch, you know," Winnie said, closing the door of the van. "Mitch is quite infatuated with you. If I'm not mistaken, the feeling is mutual."

"We've become friends, if that's what you mean." Cassie turned her head and scanned the parking lot.

"Oh, I think it's more than that. Be careful, sweetie."

Cassie snapped her gaze back to Winnie. "I will." She bit her tongue not to say more. Of all the TeamWork ladies, Winnie understood the lure and temptation of a powerful man. "So will Mitch." Mitch was a different man than Josh Grant had been years ago—handsome but reckless.

A glimmer of something flittered through Winnie's blue eyes. Cassie suspected she wanted to say more. "If you ever need to talk, I hope you know you can come to me," she said. "Or Lexa. You've always been our friend, first and foremost."

Cassie swallowed and gave her a quick hug. "Thanks, Winnie. That means a lot." She appreciated Winnie's sentiments more than the other woman could know. Until moving to Houston, she'd never felt valued—truly accepted, understood and appreciated—by anyone other than a few select family members. Both Lexa and Winnie had given her so much more than a paycheck—they'd helped instill self-confidence and self-worth in a lost, hurting little girl from Alabama.

"Your song really impacted Charlie Robertson." Winnie leaned against the passenger door. "He was sitting down the pew from us. While you were singing, he kept wiping his eyes. Soaked that hankie clean through. I think he served in the Persian Gulf, and the lyrics seemed to touch him in a special way. I'm sure he's not the only one. Did you write the lyrics?"

"She nodded. "Yes, and Danica in the praise team wrote the music."

"You make a good team. Have you thought any more about recording your songs?"

"You ask me that every time I sing a solo."

"And you put me off every time."

"I'm afraid recording them for the world's consumption would rob me of some of the joy," Cassie said with a shrug. "I can't expect you to understand."

"Oh, I do," Winnie said. "But, approaching it from another angle, it would also give others a lot of joy."

"As long as you're not trying to kick me out of the catering business. I know I can't cook a lick, but—"

Josh strolled toward them and gave Cassie a quick hug. "You don't need to cook when you can sing like you do. Terrific song and you wowed them, as always. Are you and Mitch coming to Myerson's for lunch?" He ushered his wife into the van and closed the door.

"Wouldn't miss it."

~

Mitch laughed at Marc and Josh's teasing but he couldn't stop his thoughts—and his eyes—from straying to Cassie. Sitting across the table from her was more distracting than having her seated right beside him. Her auburn hair was wavy and loose, flowing down her back. The pretty light blue dress and matching sweater she wore highlighted the color of her eyes. *Rein it in, Jacobsen.* Maybe he shouldn't have kissed her last night, but he'd been powerless to resist her. He loved teasing her, sparring with her. . .matter of fact, there wasn't anything he didn't love or admire about her.

The group sat around a long, rectangular table and traded stories and reminisced while they ate lunch. In moments of quiet, as he listened to the others, he replayed her song, and especially the catchy chorus, in his head. After the service, he'd pulled Kevin aside and asked him to mail him a CD of the morning service, hoping it would include Cassie's solo. When Winnie told him Cassie wrote the lyrics, he'd made her blush with his shower of compliments. Maybe he'd gone a little overboard, but she deserved every one of them.

"What do you say we find a park, camp out under a tree, read some poetry and feed each other grapes?" he said as they walked out of the restaurant together.

"A nap sounds good after that big meal." She patted her stomach. "I can't believe it's so warm this weekend, but I'm glad. Saves some layers. You never know with Texas weather. There's a nice park not too far from here. Want to try that?"

"Sure. Want to walk or drive?"

"Let's walk," she said, tucking her hand beneath his arm. "I have a blanket in my car. Let me grab it and take it along so we don't stain our Sunday best."

Mitch couldn't stop his grin. How adorable was this woman? Sunday best indeed.

As they walked, he told her about Barbara's latest call he'd taken before the church service. "Donald's expected to be released in a day or two and he's already started physical therapy. If he keeps up with it, he has a good chance of recovering full mobility in his arm."

"Before you leave, I want to get her phone number so I can keep in touch." Cassie slanted him a wry grin. "I also want to check on how Mercy and your good friend Eddie are getting along."

He nodded but didn't respond. All sixteen hundred miles of that long trip, he'd be thinking of Cassie, replaying the events of the long weekend in his mind. Earlier that morning, Sam had given him a road atlas and he'd mapped out his trip. He'd be going through Tuscaloosa, Alabama. From what he knew, Cassie grew up there. A germ of an idea planted itself in his brain when he'd noted that fact, but he didn't want to bring it up with Cassie yet.

"What have we here?" Mitch said as they approached the park. A small crowd numbering at least a hundred men and women gathered across the expansive grounds. Most of the men wore black and the women were dressed in white or pastel shades. Some were dressed in formal wear—tuxes and long gowns—and a few wore casual outfits. A number of the women carried bouquets and the buzz of excited activity filled the park.

Leaning close, he whispered in her ear. "Do you think we've stumbled upon a mass wedding ceremony?"

Cassie visibly shivered from his nearness, and that pleased him more than it should. "Either that or it's a really big photo shoot." Cassie smiled at a young girl who barely looked old enough to drive much less get married. What was the legal age in Texas, anyway? A quick glance around the park revealed couples of every age. Stepping aside, Cassie engaged her in a short conversation. "You're right," she told him a minute later. "It's a Valentine's Day weekend of mass wedding ceremonies—two yesterday and two today. Bilingual, different faiths, and apparently something for everyone."

"And which kind is this?"

"English speaking and ecumenical."

"Then I believe we've found our next adventure."

Cassie's expression was comical and adorably cute when she scrunched her nose. Her blue eyes widened and she stared at him. "I'm *not* crashing a wedding, Mitch. Mass weddings, that is."

"Come on. It'll be fun. It's not really crashing since there are lots of bystanders and we're outdoors. For public consumption, if you will."

"I'm not sure about this." She resisted when he tried to take her hand.

"Look," he said, keeping his voice low, "it's not like we're getting married because I'm pretty certain you'd need a marriage license and be registered. Have a reservation or something."

"I suppose." She chewed on her lower lip.

He arched a brow. "Time's a wasting. It's not every day you stumble on something like this. We can observe the ceremony, shake some hands, congratulate a few happy couples and then be on our merry way. Haven't you ever been curious about these things?"

"Can't say I've ever thought about it," she said. "Do you really believe God is pleased by"—she waved her hand around the gathered group—"this? En masse?" Lowering her voice, she stepped closer to him. "Somehow it seems. . .wrong. Too casual."

"For you and me, maybe, but for some people, it makes sense. It probably doesn't cost much, it's quick and it's in the beautiful outdoors. Didn't Sam and Lexa elope?"

That made her frown. "Yes, if you want to get technical about it. But—"

"We can't judge their hearts, Cassie."

A look of alarm passed over her face. Grabbing his arm, she pulled him aside at the same time as a large man plowed into his shoulder. Caught off-guard, Mitch stumbled and nearly fell. Recovering his balance, he stared at the guy and rubbed his shoulder. Considering he was built like a linebacker, he figured his shoulder might be sore in the morning.

"Whoa, buddy! What's the hurry?"

His face was beet red and he clenched his fists like he was prepping to take a swing at him. Instead, he threw something on the ground at Mitch's feet and spat on it. "I'm never asking another broad to marry me. I can't believe Denise did this. Thought she was different. I'll be single the rest of my life, and these women can—"

Mitch held up his hand, interrupting him. "No need to finish that sentence. I'm sorry if—Denise, is it?—stood you up, but maybe she had a legitimate emergency. Have you tried to call her?"

"Yeah," the man snarled. "Her emergency was meeting some guy at a bar last week. Now she's *doing some thinking* and says she's not ready to commit and settle down. Some messenger dude showed up with her engagement ring." He shook his head and tugged at what little bit of hair he had at the back of his head. "She didn't have the common decency to do her dirty work herself."

"Well, then, maybe it's best you found out now," Cassie said.

Mitch didn't like the way the guy raked his dark eyes up and down Cassie as if seeing her for the first time. Maybe Denise had the right idea. At the moment, any female would probably garner his anger. And his leering stare. Cassie, however, appeared more irritated than intimidated.

Stepping closer to Cassie, Mitch wrapped his hand around hers. "Whatever," the man said. "You women are all alike. No good, none of you."

"That's not fair," Mitch said. "You can't believe that. That's the heat of the moment talking. Listen, we'll pray for you to find—"

"Lay off, man. Prayer won't help me none. If that's all you've got, I don't want your kind of help. Take the stupid rings. They're yours. Do whatever you want with them." With one last glance at Cassie, he stormed off in the opposite direction.

"What's your name?" Mitch called after him, but he raised his hand in the air and kept walking. "Sorry for what he said to you, Cassie. I feel for the guy, but I hope he doesn't go off and do something stupid."

"I didn't take it personally. You tried, but he wasn't in a rational frame of mind to listen. Sad, though, that he doesn't want our kind of help when it's what he needs most. What was that he threw on the ground?" Leaning down, she reached for something at his feet. "Mitch, this is a diamond ring!"

Taking it from her, Mitch rotated it between his fingers. The sunlight reflected the facets of the stone. "No matter how mad he is, I can't believe he'd toss something this valuable on the ground. Hang on. I'll see if I can catch him. Wait here. I won't go far. Promise."

"Go," she said. "I'll be fine. Standing in a park surrounded by people about to be joined in holy matrimony seems safe enough."

~

Within five minutes, Mitch returned. "He had too much of a head start and jumped in a cab at the edge of the park. Running after a guy and hollering 'Hey, angry jilted groom!' didn't seem appropriate." He glanced at his watch. "I figure the ceremony should be starting soon if it's on the hour."

"Guess what else I found?" She held up the matching wedding band. "We have a few minutes, so maybe we could turn the rings over to the people in charge of the ceremony. Or take them to the police. In case he decides he wants them back later." Shielding her eyes with one hand, Cassie nodded toward the left side of the crowd. "There's an officer standing over there."

"Great idea. Let's go ask."

"My advice is to keep them," the officer said after they explained the situation. "Anybody else would hawk them for whatever money they could get, anyway. Let me see that ring." Mitch handed the engagement ring to him but didn't show him the matching wedding band. "Nah, it's not worth anything. Cheap cubic zirconia."

"Denise wasn't even worth a real diamond?" Cassie said as they thanked the officer and walked away. "That's plain wrong and I say angry jilted groom doesn't deserve her. He's a cheapskate."

"I agree, but I still think we should stay."

She stopped in her tracks, giving him her best *you're crazy* look. "Why? I don't take marriage lightly, Mitch. It's sacred and ordained by God."

"Agreed. Totally."

"Then why are we here?" Something unsettled her, but she hadn't figured out what or why.

"To see what it's like. Call it a cultural or educational experience to broaden our horizons. Humor me. It'll be fun." He offered his hand. "Are you with me?"

In spite of her lingering misgivings, Cassie put her hand in his as they walked to the edge of the crowd. Close enough to hear the ceremony yet not be mistaken for participants. *How do I let him talk me into these things?* The man couldn't be boring if he tried.

"According to our neighbor on the left, over five hundred couples will be enjoying marital bliss as a result of these ceremonies," Mitch whispered a minute later.

"We can only hope," Cassie said. "Did you know that marital is commonly misspelled as martial?"

He chuckled. "No. How can you possibly know that?"

"I have a friend who's a paralegal and she works with marital trusts. Unfortunately, a lot of that marital bliss turns sour and the couples end up in horrible battles. It's a tragedy, really." Wow, speaking of sour. Even though it was true, she could use an attitude adjustment.

Mitch was silent as they waited for the ceremony to begin. She wondered what made him quiet since he rarely lacked for something to say.

Cassie took a deep breath, determined to break the silence. "I probably shouldn't have said that. It's just that, when I marry, it'll be for life."

"What brought that on?" The warmth of his breath tickled her ear.

So, he wasn't irritated with her, but now she felt foolish. "I'm only saying."

"Seems to me like you're waiting for my response."

"Don't flatter yourself, Mr. Jacobsen."

He chuckled. "Me, too. For life. Just saying, *Miss* Thorenson."

Oh, the man could be insufferable. Wonderfully so. When she crossed her arms over her chest, he must have assumed she was cold since he put his arm around her and nestled her close. She had neither the heart nor the inclination to shrug him away.

A minister, wearing a long black robe that flowed in the gentle breeze, welcomed everyone. In his hands, he held a Bible. Opening it, he began to read a passage of scripture from 1 Corinthians, Chapter 13, famously known as the love chapter.

"Love is patient," Mitch whispered, echoing the words of the minister.

"Love is kind and is not jealous." Cassie kept her tone low and stared straight ahead.

"Does not brag and is not arrogant." Taking her hand, Mitch stroked his thumb over hers.

"Does not act unbecomingly." Standing beside Mitch, the words assumed an entirely new meaning.

As the minister finished, Mitch's expression was solemn as he turned to face her. He wasn't teasing now. Something stirred in her belly and she couldn't move. Couldn't tell him they needed to leave. This was wrong and yet somehow it seemed incredibly right.

The minister spoke again. "Grooms, repeat after me."

Mitch's lips moved, but no sound came from his mouth as the minister continued with the vows. "In the presence of God, our family and friends, I offer you my solemn vow to be your faithful husband in sickness and in health, in good times and bad, and in joy as well as in sorrow. I promise to love you unconditionally, to support you in your goals, to honor and respect you, to laugh with you and cry with you, and to cherish you for as long as we both shall live."

The warm breeze blew over Cassie's eyelids like a soft caress when she closed her eyes.

"I do."

What?

Startled, she opened her eyes, staring at Mitch. "You can't say that. You *shouldn't* say that."

"Too late. I just did." His hold on her hands increased. "Don't worry. You don't have to say it."

"You don't need to worry about that." This was nuts. Why did *he* say it? What did this mean? It certainly wasn't legal, thank goodness. They had no marriage license. They weren't even a couple. They shouldn't be standing here. In essence, weren't they mocking the other couples, mocking God? Hanging her head, shame flowed over her. Cassie stewed, her inner thoughts waging war as she half-listened while the women repeated their vows.

"You're safe," Mitch said, leaning close and whispering. "He didn't use the word obey."

She couldn't even respond although that particular word had never been a problem for her. She'd willingly say it if she were actually getting married. If she loved a man and wanted to walk through life with him. Not that Mitch couldn't possibly ever *be* that man. Still, this was completely crazy.

"This is wrong, Mitch. We're making a mockery of marriage, what they're doing here"—she waved her hand—"everything."

"I disagree. We're not mocking marriage. We're celebrating and affirming it."

He sounded so confident and acted as though he wasn't about to relinquish her hand and allow her to run away. Mitch could be very persuasive, but not in a controlling, manipulative way. She could leave if she really wanted and he'd respect her wishes.

"If you want to leave, then lead the way." She liked that he was giving her the out, but the problem was, she wasn't sure what she wanted anymore. In some ways, how was this any different than playing dress-up as a little girl? Rebekah had mentioned that very thing when they were dressed in their finery for the birthday party. They'd played roles to make the day special for the children and had a lot of fun in the process. Pretend. It wasn't real. *And yet it was. Like it is now.* The couples standing nearby considered it real and binding. This whole scenario was absurdly fascinating.

They'd reached the ring exchange part of the ceremony.

Cassie started to pull her hands from his, but the obvious affection in Mitch's eyes stopped her. She hesitated, unsure what to do. He quirked a brow with a *what do you want me to do now?* expression and pulled out the ring—the fake ring, she reminded herself—and held it up with a look of expectancy.

"Fine," she said with a sigh. "Put it on my finger." It wasn't a wedding band, after all. Only a diamond wannabe. Perhaps the biggest surprise was that it fit. Perfectly. No sliding around her finger. Like it was sized specifically for her. How could that be? Fake or not, the round stone certainly looked real to her untrained eye. She'd never worn a ring on that finger before—never worn a ring on any finger—and she couldn't resist as she twisted and turned it, admiring it from all angles.

"This isn't real, remember?" She could hear the smile in his voice.

"I know that," she said, sounding more flippant than she intended. "I'm sorry that I don't have a fake ring for you."

"Doesn't matter." Their hands still laced together, Mitch turned to face the front. "Here it comes."

"What God has joined together, let no man put asunder. I now pronounce you husbands and wives. You may now share your first kiss as a married couple. Congratulations, one and all."

"Don't even think about it," Cassie said, pushing against his chest, laughing more from nerves than anything else.

"It's all I *can* think about since last night." Mitch's voice was husky. He tilted his head and gave her his best smile.

"Fine." They'd already gone through the rest of this charade. Why not?

I'm crazy for indulging this whim. Leaning on her tiptoes, Cassie kissed him, but she pulled away a few seconds later. No sense in lingering and prolonging it. *Wait a second.* When she met his eyes again, she knew he wanted more. Her breathing grew shallow. She wanted more, every bit as much as Mitch did. *Step back. Do something.* Why couldn't she move?

Without a word, Mitch slowly drew her to him again. He moved his arms around her waist and wrapped her in his warmth. So close she felt his strong heartbeat.

"Mitch. . ." She sighed as he lowered his lips to hers and cupped her jaw with one gentle hand. This kiss was sweet and achingly tender. No kiss had ever moved her. . .until now. But *this* kiss? She felt it everywhere.

Quite simply, it was perfect.

"Thank you." Mitch leaned his forehead on hers. "If you were faking the emotion just now, I don't want to know."

"I wasn't," she whispered. "You're the one with the acting gene in the family."

"This isn't acting, Cassie." To prove his point, he kissed her again.

Chapter 19

CASSIE REACHED INTO the bag of food beside her. "Want another leg?"

"Are you trying to fatten me up?"

She laughed, surveying the remains of their feast after they'd grabbed dinner at a fast food restaurant within a few blocks of the park. "I sure am. After all, isn't it a fake wife's job to keep her fake husband fat and happy?"

Taking the piece of grilled chicken, Mitch winked. "I don't like the word fake. Let's say pretend, if you don't mind. And, based on that theory, it's my duty to keep you barefoot—"

"You are unbelievable! Fake—*pretend*—or not, you're a total chauvinist." Shaking her head, she took a bite of her biscuit dripping with honey.

"Nah. I'm just insufferable." They shared a grin. "I've witnessed your fondness for pickles. Isn't that what pregnant women crave?"

"I wouldn't know," she said, reaching for a napkin. They ate in silence for a couple of minutes, sitting under a tree in the same park. This was nice. "For the record, I love ice cream, too, but that's neither here nor there. There's a great little ice cream shop not far from Sam and Lexa's house. It's called Richardson's." The owner, Bea Richardson, was one of TeamWork's biggest cheerleaders. She should also have a degree in Matchmaking 101. "If you're good, I might take you there tomorrow. What else is on your schedule?"

Mitch finished off the chicken leg and tossed it in the bag. "Sam and Josh are taking me downtown to the TeamWork office. They want to tell me more about upcoming projects. I think they recognize a potential recruit in me. For the Houston branch of TeamWork, that is. Imagine that."

That surprised her, but in a good way. "That'll be fun for you. Beck works in the office, too." She handed him a napkin to wipe his mouth and hands. "She used to teach and sets up the schoolroom operations for the TeamWork missions all over the world."

"Wanna come with me?"

She smiled. "I should probably show up at my job. We have a huge catering event on Thursday and lots to do to get ready for it. Not that your offer isn't tempting."

"How about I talk to Lexa and see if I can get the afternoon off for you? I can play the whole *it's my last day here in Houston* card on her. I can be pretty persuasive."

"Yes, I know. Let's play it by ear, shall we?" Mitch knew as well as she did they'd spend some quality time together tomorrow. No way would he start the drive back to New York without saying good-bye.

Mitch's cell phone rang. Retrieving it, he flipped it open. "Hey, Amy." Nodding his head a few times, he was obviously trying to get a word in edgewise between her questions.

"Yes," Mitch repeated more than a few times. "If you'd ever let me speak, I'll tell you. Cassie and I are having a great time together. She's an absolutely incredible girl. You were exactly right about her." He gave her a wink. "Maybe I should trust your instincts, after all." He listened for a moment more. "Well, I've got to go. Thanks, but we're having dinner now, as a matter of fact. Tell Sam and Lexa not to wait up. Something tells me we're going to be out very late tonight. Catch you later." With that, he snapped his phone closed.

She frowned. "Was that last comment necessary? Now, they're going to think the worst of me if we're out really late. On top of everything else, are you purposely trying to sully my reputation?"

"Haven't you ever done anything really spontaneous and fun in your life? Besides, teasing my sister is fun. One of the joys of my life."

Cassie's cell phone rang. She mouthed *Winnie* to Mitch. "Hi, Winnie. Yes. We're having a great time. Yes, he's wonderful. Everything Amy said about him and then some. What's that?" she asked, giggling in surprise when Mitch kissed her on the cheek. "I'm sorry, what did you say?" She waved him away when he made silly faces, trying to distract her even more. "I don't know. Don't worry. Sure thing. I'll open the Doyle-Clarke Catering office in the morning like I always do."

She closed her phone a few seconds later after signing off with Winnie. "Wow, I am such a creature of habit."

"Well, having a job *is* important," he said, chuckling. "I was talking more about doing things out of the normal routine."

She laughed. "I've been doing that ever since a certain Wall Street broker arrived in town."

"Time for a confession. You love it."

"I'll admit to no such thing." Cassie wiped her hands and tossed the last of her biscuit—the hard edge she didn't like—in the trash bag. Standing, she stretched. "We'd better be getting back now, I suppose."

"We don't really have to go back yet. Do we?"

Something in Mitch's tone made her look at him. "I'm almost afraid to ask what you have in mind."

Leaning back against the broad base of the tree, he crossed his arms behind his head. That grin of his was irresistible. "You tell me. We've got a blanket, God's beautiful world all around us, and each other. What more could we possibly need?"

The *each other* part of his statement gave her pause. Winnie's warning came to mind. "Okay, but only for a few minutes and then we should head back to the house. Sam's planning on devotions tonight at ten." Perhaps keeping that in mind would keep her thoughts on the right track.

"Sounds good," he said. "Come over here and tell me more about yourself. Time to get better acquainted."

They talked. And talked some more, unable to get enough of each other's stories. Mitch told her how they'd lived on a tight budget when he was little since his dad's pastoral salary didn't cover anything more than the necessities. His mom taught school part-time. "Mom and Dad taught us the value of a dollar," he said. "They wouldn't allow Grandpa Carlisle to give us anything more than twenty dollars for birthdays and fifty at Christmas. I think they knew he slipped us extra money here and there, but they never said anything."

Cassie loved hearing his memories. She relaxed and rested her head on his chest. When he moved his arms around her and nestled her closer, she felt protected and safe. "What about your grandparents on your dad's side?" she asked, loving the way she could feel the steady beating of his heart.

"They lived in Pittsburgh and the three of us kids spent a couple of weeks with them every summer until we were teenagers. They're both still living and in the same nursing home. It's sad to see them there. Granda—my grandfather— is still sharp as a knife but Gran has suffered from Alzheimer's for years and doesn't remember him. I can't imagine not recognizing, not knowing, the person you've loved for over fifty years."

She squeezed his hand. "I'm sure that's difficult. Maybe somehow—deep down—she knows."

Mitch kissed the top of her head and leaned his cheek against her hair. "I love your optimism. Knowing how fragile life is makes me appreciate the relationships in my life more."

Did he consider whatever this was between them a relationship of some kind? Well, considering they'd participated in a mock wedding—sort of—that question was debatable. Cassie pushed the thoughts from her mind, determined to enjoy the evening with him. The harsh realities would stare them in the face again soon enough.

"What about your Grandma Carlisle?"

"She died from breast cancer when she was in her early 50s. Grandpa never remarried, and I think he poured a lot of his leftover pain into his work. His acting on the stage was brilliant, even better than his films, in my opinion. That raw emotion was almost tangible, and it lent an air of authenticity to his performance that most actors never achieve."

"Did you see him perform often?"

"Whenever he was in a new play, he'd always send us tickets for the front row. Grandpa was a strong Christian and something of an enigma to his peers because of it. I never heard him say a swear word—onstage or off—and the characters he portrayed never acted immorally without clearly showing the consequences. He stood by his personal convictions and understood the importance of a man's word. Integrity and honesty meant everything. Like my dad, he was a hero to me. I hope I can do them both proud and eventually become half the man they hoped I'd be."

Mitch's chest rose and fell with his sigh. Shifting her position, Cassie faced him. "You're becoming the man God wants you to be, Mitch, and I know your dad and grandfather would be very proud of you."

"Thanks." She glimpsed the gratitude in his expression, felt it in his smile.

"Your turn. Tell me about your parents." Mitch intertwined their fingers.

Cassie turned her head, unable to look him in the eye, hoping he wouldn't think less of her once she told him the truth. "My mom tried hard to be a good mother, but she became too dependent on a bottle for comfort when Daddy wasn't around. She had a deep faith when I was a little girl. She'd dress me up like a doll, ironically enough"—she caught Mitch's smile—"and march me off to Sunday school every week, rain or shine. With Grandma Thor. We walked to church most of the time since whatever car we had at the time usually wasn't reliable. Then, when Tagg died, Mama shut down, closed inside herself." Her eyes misted when Mitch took her hand, stroking his thumb over hers. "She died five years ago. Acute alcohol poisoning. I tried so many times to help her, but she pushed me away. Pushed everyone away."

"What about your dad?" She'd removed her hand from his, but he took it again and idly traced the lines on her palm with the tip of his finger.

"He managed to get himself thrown in jail a lot for various and assorted misdemeanor crimes. Petty stuff, really, but crimes all the same. Daddy became known as 'No Felonies Thorenson.' It was his claim to fame and he took some warped sense of pride in the nickname."

"I'm sorry, Cassie. That must have been tough."

"Tagg was my greatest supporter. He always believed in me and made it bearable."

"And Grandma Thor, too, right?"

"She was, yes. Looking on the bright side, we didn't always have food on the table, and we didn't have new clothes very often, but we weren't physically or verbally abused." She shrugged. "It could have been a lot worse, and Tagg and I did the best we could with what we had. For a long time, we didn't know we were that different from anyone else. Tagg won over everyone and made it okay, even acceptable, to be poor, as weird as that might sound."

Mitch pushed aside a long strand of her hair that had fallen across her cheek and gently tucked it behind her ear. "Did you feel like you were living in Tagg's shadow?"

"A little, but I never minded. Why? Did Amy hate living in the shadow of her handsome, intelligent older brother?"

His smile made her weak all over again. She was a goner. "Celeste more than Amy. You think I'm handsome?"

She swatted him. "Of course not. I only marry ugly boys. Makes it easier since I don't have to fight off all the other girls."

Mitch caught her hand and his smile sobered. What was on his mind now? She'd learned Mitch could change the topic in a heartbeat. "Something wrong?"

"No, but I'm hoping you'll tell me more about Tagg."

She swallowed hard. "Okay."

"I don't want to make you sad, but I want to know you better. I think a lot of your history, a lot of who you are today, has to do with your brother."

Again, Mitch had zeroed in that part of her she'd tried to keep hidden for so many years. Obliging him, Cassie scooted close again. "He was in a boat with some friends on the lake closest to our house. I sat on the dock, watching them. One of the girls started hollering for help and waving her arms. She wasn't wearing a lifejacket. Tagg jumped in to save her. Turns out, she was trying to get his attention, and it worked."

She hung her head and, as much as she wanted to stop them, a few tears escaped. "I felt left out and decided to try the same ploy. I wasn't wearing a lifejacket either, but"—she took a gulping breath—"I really *couldn't* swim, but I sort of knew how to tread water. I called to my big brother to come save me, and sure enough, he dove in the water again."

Cassie choked down a small sob. Since the time of the accident, she'd never told anyone the details, afraid to relive that horrible scene. "Another boater saw me calling for help in the water and sped in my direction. Tagg didn't see the boat, and. . ." She sniffled and paused to catch her breath. "The boater jumped in and got me out of the water, but it was too late for Tagg."

"Oh, Cassie," Mitch said, stroking her hair as she cried. "I can't even imagine what that must have been like for you."

"I *killed* him, Mitch. If I hadn't acted so selfishly by trying to get his attention, Tagg would still be here." Her sobs came out in anguished waves and she was helpless to stop them.

"You can't know that. It was a tragic accident." Mitch's calm, gentle voice was a soothing balm for her weary soul.

"I always felt like Mama and Daddy blamed me. After Tagg died, she more or less spent most of her time curled up with her bottle and Daddy went off on his little crime sprees. Sometimes I think he wanted to be thrown in jail so he wouldn't have to come home and face her and. . .me." The last word rushed out on a sob.

Cassie pulled back and wiped her hands beneath her eyes. "Oh, look at your shirt. I'm so sorry." She put one hand on the spot near his shoulder where she'd soaked it clean through with her tears.

"I don't care about that. What I care about is you," he said. "Have you carried this around inside you for all these years?" His eyes held compassion in their depths.

"It's my deepest shame. I haven't shared it with anyone else because I'm afraid they'd call me a. . .a murderer or something."

"You were a kid trying to get her big brother's attention. Speaking as a big brother, in identical circumstances, I would have done the same thing as Tagg. And, as horrible as it was, it was a blessing he didn't linger and suffer. That would have been harder on everyone, especially you."

She sniffled some more. "Tagg died a hero and the governor came to his funeral. He broke a lot of hearts when he died."

Mitch tipped her chin. "None more so than his little sister's."

Her eyes filled with tears again and when he opened his arms, she willingly fell into them. "I'm here for you, Cassie," he said. "Whatever you need."

"Thank you," she murmured, closing her eyes. "I'm really glad you're here."

Mitch was what she needed. She just hadn't known it until now.

Chapter 20

CASSIE RUBBED HER eyes and yawned. *Where am I?*

She was lying on her right side beneath the blanket—now coated with heavy morning frost—and her sweater was bunched beneath her head as a makeshift pillow.

I'm not alone.

Almost afraid to look, she turned her head and bumped noses with Mitch. Also on his right side, he was asleep with his arm draped around her. Holding her. He'd been. . .*spooning* her!

This can't be happening!

Giving his arm a gentle nudge, Cassie tossed the blanket aside. A glance at her dress confirmed it was a wrinkled mess. Her shoes sat on the edge of the blanket, and the crumpled bag containing the remains of their picnic was still parked beneath the tree. "Mitch," she said, a sharp edge in her voice as she shook his shoulder. "Mitch. Wake up!"

"What's wrong?" Opening his eyes and yawning loudly, he blinked hard a few times. Propping himself up, he rested his weight on his elbows. "Where are we?" He grimaced and winced, rubbing his shoulder. "I figured I'd feel the effects of being bowled over by that linebacker yesterday."

She smoothed both palms over her hair. "I'm sure sleeping on the ground didn't help." With a frustrated sigh, she gestured at their surroundings. "I can't believe we slept here all night! You'd think a cop might have come along to wake us up and send us home."

"Considering we've seen three cops since yesterday, you'd think so." Sitting up, Mitch rubbed one hand over his face before slapping both stubbled cheeks. "Well, this is quite a situation. At least no serial killer decided to stop by."

"This is not amusing." Cassie jumped to her feet and grabbed her shoes. Hopping on one foot, she pulled the strap of her sandal over her right heel before tugging on the left shoe. "I'll never be able to live this down."

"Forgive me if this is a dumb question, but why does anyone have to know?" From his tone, it was obvious Mitch thought she was overreacting.

Cassie rested her hands on her hips. "Are you serious? Sam knows things like this. I swear the man's got some kind of radar. I mean, sure, he's loving and a great leader, but he can be tough. And Amy!" She started pacing. "This can't be good."

"Don't worry about Amy. I can handle her."

"Yes, but. . .oh, I hate this because she's your sister. She'll probably think I'm some wanton woman out to snag her brother."

Mitch laughed, but he stopped when she shot him a warning glance. "Cassie, you're like the last woman on the planet who would try to lure me into—"

"Did you say lure? Like into my lair or"—she gasped—"my. . .my bed?"

He chuckled low in his throat, incensing her even more. "No one's going to think that. I happen to think you're the sexiest woman I've ever met, but you're even more so because you don't purposely flaunt it. Besides that, you don't have an insincere or dishonest bone in your body."

He thinks I'm sexy? Well, that was a first, but she didn't have time to dwell on it. She wasn't sure whether to be mad or how to react.

Mitch yawned again and glanced at his watch. "Seven o'clock. Still early. Here's the plan: you'll drop me off in front of the house and I'll sneak inside. No one will be any the wiser. Although Sam probably locks his front door at night." He shrugged. "Not a big deal. If it is, I'll see if the side door's unlocked."

"Sam will be up. The man rises at the crack of dawn, raring to go. He'll be in the kitchen, reading the paper and drinking his morning coffee. The person I really *don't* want to see for once in my life."

"Relax," he said, yawning again. "They'll probably assume I'm upstairs in their guest bedroom and you're home snuggled in your own bed."

"And if they see you come in the door?"

His frown revealed his growing frustration. "Then I'll tell them the truth."

Cassie considered that for a moment. "You're right. Sam may actually be a lot more understanding than Amy, and she and Landon are staying with Winnie and Josh. Have you checked your phone lately?"

He took his phone out of his pocket. "No, considering I've been asleep. I turned it off after Amy called. I never turned it on again for the simple fact I didn't want us to be interrupted."

She sighed. "I turned off my phone for the ceremony since I didn't want the phone going off during something so important. Then I think I turned it off again after Winnie called."

"Then maybe subconsciously you didn't want to be interrupted either. Three calls from Amy," he said, checking the phone. "How about you?"

Was Mitch correct in his assumption? She'd told him more about her family than she'd confided in her closest friends, Rebekah included. Although Mitch had shared some things with her, she'd been the one doing most of the talking. He'd listened to her, dried her tears, and consoled her. What a saint to put up with such a needy, emotional wreck.

Her purse had been tucked halfway beneath her during the night. Grabbing it, Cassie tugged out her phone and quickly perused the list of calls. "One from Beck, one from Winnie, and one from Amy. Oh wait. Another one from Beck." A wave of fear coursed through her. "We're going to have some explaining to do. They're probably gathering at Sam and Lexa's right now."

"If anything, they're probably worried for our safety," he said. "And for that, I'm sorry. Look, Sam and Lexa trust you, and I hope they know me well enough to trust me. If they're up when we get back to the house, maybe Lexa can run interference if Sam starts an interrogation. We're adults and it's not like we're prone to wanton behavior."

"Speak for yourself." She didn't like the amusement in his voice, but her barb was uncalled for and unkind. Judgmental. Would she never learn? "Sorry," she mumbled.

"Not a problem." Eyeing her with a raised brow, Mitch reached for his leather shoes and started to put them on. "Great. They're wet from the frost and now I can't get them on. The leather must have shrunk." He grunted and peeled off his socks.

"I guess we'd better face the music, take it like adults"—Cassie raised both hands in the air—"and every other cliché we can think of to describe this situation. I've never been in a. . .a compromising position like this before. No off-color comments about that one, please."

"Wouldn't think of it," Mitch said. "You know what? Don't listen to the voice mail messages. They'll only agitate you more. Let's not even call them since it's so early and we'll be back at the house soon enough. For now, you need to try and relax. You're all worked up, and that's not doing anyone any good." Mitch scrambled to his feet and walked to stand in front of her. "I vote we tell them the truth. We slept together and time got away from us."

She groaned. "Not funny, Mitch. Spare me the crass jokes, please."

"I'm not trying to be crass and I'll take the full brunt of the blame if our actions are questioned. I'm not trying to be distasteful or disrespectful, but technically? Yeah, we *did* sleep together, but it was completely innocent. An honest mistake. Could happen to anyone."

"Yes, for a couple of lunatics! Which is exactly what they'll think. See what being around you for two days has done to me? Two days, Mitch! I can't even fathom being around you longer than that."

"That's not the impression I got last night. If it's more palatable to you, I could rephrase and say we fell asleep together. Still means the same thing." Mitch swept the blanket off the ground. Walking a few feet away, he shook it out and then began to fold it.

Cassie blindly watched his actions while her mind whirled with plausible explanations for their overnight absence. How could he be so calm and act as if nothing happened? Shrug it off like her reputation wasn't hanging on the line?

The stubble on Mitch's handsome face was way too appealing, a fact which irritated her. Ditto the lazy grin. He had the folded blanket under his arm and ran his hand quickly over his hair. "At the risk of incurring more of your wrath, I really enjoyed last night."

"That's beside the point. Don't even go there." Yes, she'd enjoyed it, too, but she wasn't about to give him the satisfaction. Fuming, Cassie grabbed her purse and car keys.

When she reached for the blanket, Mitch put his hand on her arm. "I've got it. Let's go."

She stopped a minute later as they approached the edge of the park. "Oh, good grief. We left the car in the restaurant parking lot. We'd better pray it's still there."

"I'd offer to run ahead," he said, "but I'm not about to leave you alone here at this hour of the morning."

"Thanks. Let's pray as we walk." Her frown was deep. "But let's hurry."

~

Mitch stole a few glances at Cassie as she drove them back to the house. Maybe he should have insisted on driving. She was awfully quiet, and that worried him. Tiny lines had surfaced around her mouth and eyes. His cool, ethereal friend had turned into a tight, twisted bundle of knots. And he was to blame. The one saving grace was that her Saab hadn't been towed from the restaurant.

He didn't feel sorry they'd fallen asleep together in the park, but he did regret that he'd subjected her to a potentially dangerous situation. More than that, he hated that *she* felt remorseful for what happened. Cassie seemed inordinately bothered by what Sam and the others would think of her, as if they'd assume the worst. Granted, he didn't know them as well as she did, but he felt sure they'd understand. If he worried about what others thought of him, he'd have hung up his saddle a long time ago.

A few large raindrops splattered on the window. "Great," she said, slapping one hand on the steering wheel. "Now it rains. If it'd done that last night, we wouldn't be in this predicament."

"Don't go blaming God." Mitch shook his head. As soon as the words were out of his mouth, he knew they were misguided.

"I'm not! And stop patronizing me." Taking a deep breath, she visibly appeared to calm down and then repeated, "I am *not* blaming God, Mitch. Yes, He allows things to happen."

"Right. I think we need to try and figure out why He allowed it to happen and talk about where we go from here."

"Where we go from here?" She glared at him for a couple of seconds before returning her attention to the road. He hated to incense her even more, but she was beyond gorgeous with fire spitting from those sapphire eyes. Full of passion. If she wasn't already so agitated, he'd kiss her. Unfortunately, kissing him was the last thing she'd want to do given their current situation.

"For what it's worth, I really am sorry, Cassie. I didn't mean to sound flippant earlier, and I hope you know I never intended to put you in the situation of having to explain yourself to your friends."

"I know. You were wonderful last night, listening to me. I'd never felt so. . .safe and protected." She released a long sigh of frustration and shook her head.

"Careful there. Better keep your eyes on the road."

She shot him a sharp glance. "Have you, um, been in a situation like that before?"

He hadn't expected that question, and true to her nature, she'd couched it in the politest of terms. Still, was a moving vehicle the best place for this conversation? "I haven't been the best example of morality since Brad died, if that's what you're asking. Not that it's an excuse, but I lost my way for a while after 9/11 and drowned my guilt and anger in living a worldly lifestyle. I let my family down, and I betrayed myself in a lot of ways. I freely admit I've done things I regret, but that all stopped after Amy and Landon's wedding. I rededicated my life to Christ, and I've tried my best to live like a Christian."

"Is this a confession? If that's the case, you don't need to feel compelled to tell me." She waved her hand as if dismissing the matter. "Doesn't matter to me."

The muscles in his jaw twitched. "Then why'd you ask? I think it does matter."

"I'm sure a man like you hasn't been holed up in your Manhattan townhouse like a. . .a monk."

"Not sure I like your implication." He fought the rising sense of defensiveness mixed with regret. Who'd she been talking to, anyway? Still, if that wasn't jealousy in her tone, he'd never heard it before. "I've been weak in the past, Cassie, so I know how easy it is to succumb to temptation. I don't claim to be a saint. Matter of fact, I'm a first class sinner. In spite of my upbringing in the church, in spite of being a Christian since I was six, I've fallen." He winced at his own words. They sliced through him, and he wished like anything he could change his past.

"I'm careful not to purposely put myself in a situation to be tempted now. But yes, I've still dated." A lot, but saying that now wouldn't be in his best interest. "A string of casual relationships isn't what I want. I tried it, but all that does is leave me empty inside. Most of all, dating someone who doesn't share my faith is wrong. God expects my best, and I've failed Him. He wants more for me, and I should expect more of myself."

Maybe it was better that Cassie find out about his past now. If she couldn't forgive him for his indiscretions, then that would effectively end any possibility of a relationship between them. A relationship that seemed destined to flounder eventually when they were more than a thousand miles apart. That thought pierced him like an arrow.

"If you're asking me to return the favor, I have nothing to say."

"That's fine. I don't expect you to tell me anything. I hope you can find it in your heart to forgive me for. . ." How to finish that sentence?

"Mitch, there's nothing to forgive because it's not *my* place to give it. That's between you and the Lord."

"I still wanted you to know."

Her shoulders visibly drooped. "I know it's more difficult for a man. You're a high-powered executive. I imagine working on Wall Street with all those professional women must be extremely. . .attractive."

"No, Cassie." He turned in the seat to face her. "You know what's attractive?"

She pulled up to a stoplight and turned her head to look at him. Much better, especially with what he wanted to say. "What's incredible is the sweetness I see in your face, the purity of your spirit, the undiluted innocence in your eyes. You have what most women will never have. You have Christ in your life. He's part of you, as sure as you're living and breathing." He placed his hand over his heart. "I'd lost sight of how incredibly *beautiful* that can be."

A tear rolled down her cheek. In one swift movement, he brushed it from her face with his thumb. When a second tear fell, he did the same. Mitch waited for her to speak, unsure whether Cassie wept because of sadness or overwhelming emotion. The only sound was the steady rain hitting the roof of the car.

"What I meant about not returning the favor was because there's nothing *to* tell." She'd said it so quietly that he almost didn't hear the words. But he did. He wanted to reach for her hand, but felt it best to restrain himself since she was behind the wheel. The stoplight turned green and she pulled through the intersection.

"Cassie, pull over to the curb."

"We're almost at the house and it's getting later by the minute."

"This is something we need to do. Please."

She breathed out a deep sigh. "Hold on." A minute later, she'd pulled beside the curb on a residential street. Turning off the engine, she stared at the rain streaming down the front window. "What did you want to say?"

Twisting his body in the bucket seat, feeling cramped in the confines of the car, he faced her. "It'd be nice if you'd look at me."

"The truth is, I'm embarrassed." Her gaze finally met his. "I've never done anything like that in my life."

"I want to see you again after I go back to New York."

Her expression was guarded, making it impossible to try and read her emotions. Surely he hadn't misread the way she'd responded to him. Not that he expected her to fall in his arms and pledge undying love, but some sign of affection might be nice right about now.

"Cassie, I need you in my life."

He could see her swallow and she twisted her hands in her lap. "How can you say that? What can I possibly offer you that you can't find in every other woman in New York? You're accomplished, sophisticated, highly educated. . .everything I'm not."

"Oh no, you don't." Mitch grabbed her hands, not allowing her to withdraw. "Don't make this out to be some rich boy, poor girl scenario."

She wrenched her hands away from his, her expression anguished. "I've had boyfriends, but I've never—"

"You don't have to tell me."

"Yes, I do. Be quiet. You had your turn and now it's my turn." Her eyes flashed.

He fell silent and braced himself to hear a story of the boy back home, the childhood or high school sweetheart who'd broken her heart and sent her running away to the big city. An image of Stone Bicklebing popped unbidden into his mind, making him want to groan. Anyone but that guy.

"I've kissed guys before, but you're the first guy I've ever wanted to kiss. And not stop, if you must know." She frowned and slumped back in her seat. "Don't let it swell your head. At least you didn't run screaming. I wasn't even sure I was doing it right."

Sweet Cassie. He reached for her and cradled her face between his hands, feeling silly as he leaned across the console. "You're a rare woman, Cassie. A treasure. I'm honored." Humbled beyond reason, Mitch kept the kiss light and sweet. When Cassie bit her lower lip, it yanked hard on his heartstrings. This woman was getting to him, settling in his heart. *I'm going to miss her like crazy.* That truth hit him like a punch to the stomach.

"We work together on every level," he said, releasing her. "On the way to Houston, Amy ran down the long list of my faults and told me why I haven't been able to commit to a woman. Turns out, she was spot-on. I've kept company with women who were completely wrong for me. I knew it, but I've never thought about the reasons why. Amy finally forced me to see the truth."

When Cassie looked at him, her sweetness stole his breath. If he perished today, he'd die content for having known this woman. Extreme yes, but it was the truth. "I'm afraid to risk giving away my heart because I'm afraid of losing it all." He raked his fingers through his hair, disheveling it even more. "I'm tired of being afraid, Cassie. Look, I pretty much laid myself bare a minute ago. Remember how I said I wish I could step through that door to change my past?" His voice broke. "How I wish I could."

"Shh," she whispered. "I understand." Her blue eyes were moist as they roamed over his face. She smoothed his hair away from his forehead, her fingers lingering. "Beneath this bravado you put out there for the world lies a very tender, compassionate soul. Let's take this one step at a time." Settling in her seat again, Cassie started the engine. "And now, it's time to go home."

Mitch kept his voice calm and as soothing as he could. "If they even ask where we've been, we'll explain it and then we'll all have a good laugh."

"I hope you're right." He could tell Cassie didn't believe it for a second. Problem was, neither did he.

Amy was going to kill him.

Chapter 21

No SOONER HAD Cassie turned the corner of Sam and Lexa's street than her spirits sank. "We've been found out. Ladybug's here."

"Who or what is Ladybug?"

"That's what Winnie calls her car. The yellow VW in the driveway."

"I thought that was Buttercup."

"No, that's her nickname for Chloe, although Chloe's growing out of it."

"Thanks for setting me straight. Lots of nicknames with this group. My mind is spinning."

She appreciated Mitch's attempt to lighten the mood, but her stomach was turning somersaults. Call it intuition, a hunch or whatever, but. . . At least the rain had stopped and the sun was beginning to make its appearance in-between the low-hanging, dark clouds.

As they approached the house, the front door swung open and Amy stepped out onto the walkway, her expression not especially warm and welcoming. Landon stood right behind her, but he looked a little more amenable.

"Nice to see you two finally decided to come back."

Cassie squeezed past her and into the house, but no way could Amy miss her bedraggled appearance. Perhaps she should have swung by her house and changed first, but the thought hadn't even entered her muddled brain in her haste to get here and hopefully avoid a scene. Too late for that, apparently. Raking her gaze over Mitch with his wrinkled dress pants and shirt, Amy shook her head. "Aren't you a sight?"

"Hey, Amy." Tossing his suit coat over his shoulder, it flopped in Amy's face as Mitch passed by her and into the house.

"Something happen to your shoes?" she asked, staring at his feet and then at the shoes he carried.

"I'm afraid they shrunk. Got shrunk. Shrank. You're the journalist. You tell me the proper word."

"Doesn't matter. What does matter is how this happened. Spill it."

"I tossed them in the dryer. What do you think?" Mitch was already getting testy, and this couldn't bode well for them. "I'm famished. Think Sam and Lexa would mind if I raid their kitchen for some breakfast?"

"Not until you tell me where you've been all night."

Amy's voice had risen and Landon put a quick hand on her arm. "Amy, honey. . ."

Leaning close, she lowered her voice. "I don't know what you do when you're in New York, but this is unacceptable behavior, especially when you're a guest in Sam Lewis's home and keeping company with one of his TeamWork girls."

Mitch darted a quick glance at Landon. "What exactly is unacceptable behavior? And keeping company? Really, Amy, this isn't 1950. You're making broad and spectacularly unfair assumptions because Cassie and I decided to stay out all night? I'm sorry to tell you this, but we're both adults, and frankly, it's no one else's business but ours."

Cassie could only look back and forth between them. Maybe if she kept quiet, Amy would leave her out of it. She could only pray they could make their explanations and clear up this misunderstanding before everyone else in the house got involved.

"That answer is ambiguous and only feeds into those assumptions, Mitchell. From your rumpled clothes to your cocky attitude, you're doing nothing to discourage me from thinking the worst." She crossed her arms. "I guess I shouldn't really be surprised by your behavior, but"—she moved her gaze to Cassie, making her want to sink into the floor—"I would have expected better from you, Cass."

Cassie bit her tongue, but she was peeved now. "What exactly are you implying?" She darted a nervous glance at Mitch and could tell he was equally irritated.

Landon grunted. "I believe Winnie calls it macking."

Mitch threw him a grateful glance. "Oh, there was plenty of macking. Among other things." He winked at Cassie. "How's that for an amphibious answer?"

Landon burst out laughing. "Man, it's a good thing you work with numbers. You wouldn't make a living if you were a writer."

Wide-eyed, Cassie could only stare at Mitch and she closed her mouth. What was he saying? Teasing was one thing, but this situation was plummeting from bad to worse incredibly fast. Sure, Amy might have provoked him, but did he have to imply things that hadn't happened? Not to mention they hadn't even kissed last night. Before that, yes, there had been some. . .macking earlier in the day. So, it wasn't a flat-out lie. Surely Mitch wouldn't purposely tell an untruth.

Amy's eyes grew wide. Clamping one hand over her mouth, she turned without another word and hurried up the stairs.

"Is she pregnant or is it possible I actually shut her up?" Mitch said to Landon.

"I wouldn't count on either one," Landon said. "She didn't get much sleep last night. You must not have checked your cell phone. She called you a few times."

"Why?" Mitch moved his hands to his hips. "Contrary to what Amy believes, she's not my keeper. Eighteen months notwithstanding, I'm still and forever her elder sibling."

"Cut it out, Mitch," Landon said. "Time to stop acting like you're an overgrown adolescent. Own up to whatever you did—or didn't do—with Cassie and then we can move on. As it is, I've got to get packed and head to the airport early this afternoon. After this little episode, you might hope Amy decides not to go with you on the road."

Cassie had never seen Landon lose his cool, but he looked close to it now. Since Mitch had decked him once, she wondered if Landon might be considering repaying the favor.

"I'll be happy to do that," Mitch said, "but first I'd like to know why it's anyone else's business but mine and Cassie's. We're consenting adults and what we do, when we do it, where we do it, and how we do it is our private business."

"Is that so?" Landon spread his feet apart and crossed his arms.

The door from the kitchen opened and Winnie stepped into the living room. Glancing at the stairs, Cassie saw Amy coming back down again with Marc and Natalie right behind her. Wonderful. Where were the kids? Why not bring them into the TeamWork lynch mob? And where were Sam and Lexa? Hard to believe they wouldn't come tearing down the stairs at any moment.

"Okay, everyone. We don't need an audience." Cassie raised her hands, wishing she had a white flag to wave. "Don't I get to speak? Seriously, nothing happened. . ."

Moving forward, Winnie gasped and pointed to her left hand.

Oh, good heavens. *The ring!* How could she have forgotten to remove it? Mitch's lips twisted, but it was difficult to tell whether he wanted to laugh or groan.

"How can you say nothing happened when you're wearing an engagement ring?" Winnie's blue eyes raised to hers, questioning, unbelieving.

"Relax. It's fake." Mitch waved his hand.

Amy gawked at Mitch and moved beside her, staring at the ring. "It looks real enough, but that's beside the point. Before I blow another gasket, you'd better explain why you'd give Cassie a ring in the first place, much less a fake one. And then act so callously dismissive. I'm not sure which is more disrespectful." When Amy lifted her hand to inspect the ring, Cassie wriggled free and clasped her hands behind her back.

Mitch balked. "What's that supposed to mean? Whatever happened to the trust factor? Don't make snap judgments, Amy. That never leads to anything good, and you know it."

Amy's eyes sparked. "I agree, but how can you say nothing happened when Cassie has a sparkly stone winking at me from her ring finger that wasn't there yesterday? Considering the fact Cassie's not dating anyone else, and knowing how you can be a fast worker when you put your mind to it, I put two-and-two together and guess what I came up with? M-i-t-c-h. This one has your stamp all over it. Question is, are you playing some kind of joke or are you serious?"

"Yes, Mitch," Winnie said. "What are your intentions toward our Cassie?"

Cassie loved the reference to *our* even as she bristled. She wasn't too fond of Mitch for being so lackadaisical about the ring on her finger, fake or not. What on earth was happening here?

When Winnie asked to see the ring again, Cassie pulled her hand back out to show her but shot a *Help me!* glance at Mitch. The man could think quicker on his feet than anyone she knew. He'd gotten her into this mess with his whole crazy scheme, so he could good and well get them out of it. Besides, she rather liked the idea of watching him squirm. Just a little. He'd get Amy back for her teasing and matchmaking. Then they could laugh it off and get on with their lives. No harm done, right? Then why was her stomach rolling like she was in a tiny boat on a choppy ocean? Without a paddle?

"I don't know why I thought you might actually be happy that Cassie and I hit it off so well," Mitch said, his voice tight. "You've been pushing me into her arms for over a year."

"Thanks for that," Cassie mumbled. When she glanced at Landon, the expression on his face was one of bemusement. This entire situation was absurd.

"Come on, Natalie," Marc said, turning to leave. "This is obviously a private discussion. Someone please give us the go-ahead when the fireworks are over and it's safe to go in the kitchen."

"Might as well stay, Marc." Mitch laughed, but it lacked humor. "Ever since I arrived in Houston, you've all been guilty at one time or another of giving Cassie and me winks, sly grins, innuendo and everything else but physically pushing us into each other's arms. You want to know the biggest irony of all? I'd formulated a plan to get you back, more or less." His gaze zeroed in on Amy. "To teach you a lesson that you can't always get your way or—to the other extreme—what you get might not be anything like what you'd intended. Well, surprise! I decided against any plan, but then something happened between us, anyway. So, you tell me, who's the joke on now?"

Amy's gaze softened as she looked into her eyes. "Cassie, I apologize for my brother if he acted inappropriately in any way last night. I have to ask, though—and I'm not judging—but did you spend the night with him?"

"I can't believe this! Give me some credit for propriety." Mitch's tone was incredulous.

"We did spend the night together," Cassie sputtered, "but not in the. . .biblical sense." Oh great. That hadn't come out right at all and would only fuel the fire. She raised her hands to her cheeks, knowing they had to be positively flaming. "After the ceremony, we—"

"*What* ceremony?" Amy slapped a hand on her forehead. "Please tell me this isn't happening."

Marc paused on the stairs with Natalie beside him. From the looks on their faces, they weren't going anywhere.

"Mitch, a little help here, please?" Cassie stared him down.

"An English-speaking ecumenical mass marriage ceremony." Mitch grinned in smug satisfaction.

"You didn't!" Cassie wasn't sure which of the women said it.

"We did *not* get married!" Cassie raised her voice and clenched her fists. Now everyone would think the worst since her co-hort in crime sure wasn't doing anything to stop it. In fact, he was encouraging it. What happened to the sensitive, compassionate man who'd comforted her last night? The romantic man she'd enjoyed getting to know the past few days? Apparently, he'd gone missing.

Winnie pushed forward to stand beside Cassie, slipping an arm around her shoulders and squeezing. "Cassie's important and special to all of us. We can't allow you to disregard her feelings like this and take your smooth New York manners back to the big city along with our friend's good reputation and virtue."

"I'd never do that, Winnie." Mitch lowered his voice, but the set of his jaw hardened. "Cassie and I need to make plans. She's an incredible woman and I care for her. I definitely want to see her again after this weekend." Stopping, Mitch stared at Winnie, open-mouthed. "Wait a second. Did you say her virtue?"

"Yes, I believe I did." Winnie gave him a defiant stare.

Mitch's jaw gaped. "Anyone else in this room have a comment about that, too?"

Amy put one hand on his arm. "Mitch, you know how much I love you—how much we all love you—but if you did something reckless, I hope you intend to make this right. Think of Cassie, after all."

"Make what right, exactly? Now isn't the time to turn puritanical on me, little sister. That has got to be one of the most ironic things you've ever said considering you barely knew Landon before you were kissing him from Baton Rouge to Texas and points in-between, not to mention spending the night with him."

"Let's leave me out of this, shall we?" Amy said. "Completely different situation. We didn't have a choice in the matter."

"Well, to be fair, he *is* right," Winnie said.

Cassie felt the urge to say something. She couldn't stand idly by and let Mitch take the brunt of Amy's anger. She cleared her throat and squared her shoulders. "I was a party to what happened yesterday, too, you know. Not that anything happened."

Inhaling a deep breath, she was determined to get it out and not stop until she was done. "If you must know, we fell asleep. Together. As in next to each other. Fully clothed. All night. And that's all. End of discussion." She hoped the indignation in her tone would convey her disappointment in their assumptions.

"Thank you, Cassie." Mitch shot her a grateful glance. "Now maybe the sanctimonious finger pointing can stop"—he glared at Amy—"since some in this room seem to automatically assume the worst about me."

Amy raised her hands. "You have to admit it looks bad, sneaking back into the house this early in the morning. You didn't answer your phones last night, and none of us knew where you were." She stopped and drew in a breath. "My point being, there are consequences for your actions."

"We know that." Both she and Mitch said it in unison. At least they were in sync about something. A positive sign. If ever a morning could be erased off the slate of time and repeated, this would be the one.

The kitchen door swung open. "Someone care to explain what's going on?"

Sam.

Mitch's face drained of color as he slowly turned around. Cassie almost wished she was prone to fainting so she could escape this madness although Sam's calm authority and presence gave her a sense of relief. He might give them a stern lecture, and they'd deserve it, but he'd be fair and truthful. And Lexa would encourage and support her, as she always did. If anyone understood being young and impetuous, it was Lexa.

Putting his keys in the bowl on the hall table, Sam removed his suit jacket and tossed it over the nearest armchair. "I think we'd better take this into my study. All of you, come with me."

Rebekah, Kevin, Lexa and Josh filed in behind Sam from the kitchen, also dressed in business attire. Cassie collapsed against her as Rebekah wrapped her arm around her shoulders. "Are you okay? What's going on?"

"Long story," Cassie mumbled, leaning her head on Rebekah's shoulder.

Mitch gently pulled her aside with a pleading look in his eyes. "When this is over, we need to talk privately."

"I think you've done enough talking for now. But. . .you're right." Cassie moved ahead of him into Sam's spacious study, plopping down on the floor in front of the loveseat where Kevin and Rebekah were seated. The day had only begun and she felt like she'd already hiked a mountain. Somehow she knew she wouldn't be skipping down the other side of that mountain.

"Have a seat wherever you can find one," Sam told them. "I'll bring in more chairs if we need them."

"I'd better go check on the kids," Lexa said. "I'll be back in a few minutes."

"They're fine," Natalie told her. "Chloe and Joe are up reading together. Gracie, the twins and Luke are still sleeping." Lexa nodded and took a chair closest to Sam's desk.

"Cassie, you sit here beside Rebekah." Kevin helped her up and then perched on the arm of the loveseat next to his wife. Thanking Kevin, Cassie noted Mitch sat on the floor with his back resting against the sofa where Marc and Natalie sat huddled close together on one end, Josh and Winnie on the other. Amy took the chair near the loveseat while Landon sat on the floor at her feet.

Cassie cleared her throat. "I'd better call Marta or Gayle and ask one of them to open the office."

Winnie shook her head. "The answering service will pick up any calls and we don't have any scheduled appointments. It'll be fine until we can get there a little later this morning."

"This is more important right now." Lexa's voice was quiet but firm. "Seems this group has some things we need to discuss. Clear the air."

Sam locked his hands together on top of his desk and looked around the room at all of them in turn. "The first thing we need to do is pray. Let's ask the Lord to search our hearts, and to guard our minds and tongues as we air our grievances"—he focused on Amy and then Mitch—"or whatever we feel the need to say. I'd encourage you to be open in sharing, but let's try to do it in a non-confrontational way in the spirit of truth and uplifting one another."

Amen, Cassie thought even before Sam began his prayer.

Chapter 22

*H*OW COULD MITCH have allowed his temper to take over? What started out as a completely innocent situation had snowballed out of control because of his thoughtless words and careless actions. *Lord, forgive me. What an idiot I've been.*

Seeing Cassie's deep frown, he wanted to cross the room and sit beside her, but she might not take kindly to that gesture. Sam's prayer appeared to have a calming effect on her. He could only hope she wouldn't push him out of her life altogether.

"Is this an intervention of some kind?" Josh said, his voice teasing as he squeezed his shoulder. "Morning, partner. Missed you and Cassie last night. What time did you get in? Dawn?"

"Josh, stop," Winnie said.

Sam nodded to Mitch. "Why don't you start by telling me what instigated such a lively discussion this morning?"

"Cassie and I decided to take a walk in the park yesterday afternoon and we happened upon a Valentine's Day weekend mass wedding ceremony. A guy who'd been jilted by his fiancée ran into me and almost knocked me over. He was upset and threw an engagement ring and wedding band on the ground, saying he didn't want them and we could have them. I ran after him to try and reason with him, but he got away from me and jumped in a cab. We showed the ring to a cop but he could tell the ring's not a real diamond." He took a deep breath. "I guess I got caught up in the moment and we play-acted part of the ceremony, but only for fun."

"Marriage is not a laughing matter, Mitch." Amy's voice was calm but firm.

"I agree."

"So do I." Cassie nodded.

"I take full responsibility for what happened," Mitch said. We didn't get a marriage license, didn't have our names on any roster. It wasn't legal in any sense of the word."

"Are you absolutely sure about that?" Landon asked.

"Yes." No need to tell them he'd said the words "I do" out loud or wished in his heart that the ceremony had somehow been real. Still didn't make it official. No way could saying those two little words make the ceremony valid between the two of them—with or without a marriage license. It meant absolutely nothing in legal terms, but he didn't like the niggling doubt Landon's question planted in his mind. "I put the engagement ring on Cassie's finger but not the wedding band."

Cassie lifted her chin and looked over at him. "I didn't say the vows out loud or in my heart."

Mitch lowered his gaze to the floor, stung by her words. What could he realistically expect? He'd take what he could get and be grateful Cassie didn't seem to hate his guts. A lot of women would have a short fuse and kick him to the curb. Then again, in all the best ways, Cassie wasn't anything like any other woman. It was true what he'd told her. She was a treasure.

"Cassie would never act so rashly of her own volition," Rebekah said. Kevin put his hand on her shoulder and she reached for him.

"So, you didn't get married but Cassie's wearing a diamond. To each his own, but what's the big deal here? Did something else happen?" Marc was in boss mode and he checked his watch. "We've got a plane to catch back to Boston in a few hours. Let's get all the cards out on the table, shall we? Sorry to be blunt, Mitch, but did you two get a hotel room or spend the night together? Not that it hasn't been done before by some in this room." That last comment was mumbled under his breath but still loud enough to hear.

Winnie gasped and Mitch angled his body so he could better see the occupants of the sofa.

"Uncalled for, Thompson." Josh's voice sounded tight and irritated. "Say what you might about me, but have the guts to say it to my face in private. And don't bring my wife into it."

"Sorry. Only stating a truth as I know it," Marc muttered.

"What happened between them is no one's business but their own," Kevin said.

"Thank you for the voice of reason." Mitch slapped his hand on his thigh. When Cassie gave him a look, he shrugged and gave her a sheepish grin.

"Marc, you've got my loyalty forever for pulling my sister out of that creek in Montana," Josh said, "but it doesn't give you the inherent right to say hurtful things." He glanced around the room. "Might as well set the record straight since we're among friends and this seems to be the time for confessions. Everyone in this room knows my less-than-stellar past. I've confessed my transgressions and sins to the Lord and He's forgiven me. I've also tried my level best to make it right, as much as humanly possible, with those I've wronged. Even so, I get the impression some of you believe I took advantage of Sheila in the San Antonio work camp. That stops now. You have my word that nothing happened."

"I have to say, I'm relieved to hear you say that," Rebekah said.

Josh shot his sister a look. "Wow. Really, Beck? You, too?"

"You know I'll defend you to the ends of the earth, Josh, but there was always the tiniest doubt in my mind. You gave Sheila the money from the safe, though, right?"

"Yes. I felt sorry for her when she came to me with the story of Howard. She needed money to get away from him and I borrowed the money with the full intention of telling Sam the next day. But in his infinite wisdom, Sam tossed me out of the work camp before I had the opportunity. I know I should have mailed the money back to him when I got home, but I was too embarrassed and, frankly, too lost in sin. When I came to Houston to ask Sam's forgiveness, I gave him a check to cover the debt with a greatly inflated interest rate."

"As I told Josh, Sheila repaid that debt a long time ago." Sam smiled. "But I accepted the check as a TeamWork donation."

"Not to get off-track, but how are Sheila and Angelina now? And Howard?" Natalie asked.

"We see Sheila and Angelina a few times a year," Lexa said. "Sheila's a social worker and helps place foster children. Angelina's a teenager, very pretty, and a good student. She's come into her own and isn't nearly as shy and she's been a big help and emotional support for her mama."

Sam's voice was low when he spoke again. "As far as I know, Howard never laid another hand on Sheila. He spent a lot of time behind bars, but he was shot and killed a few years ago in a botched robbery attempt." Regret hung heavy in his words. "Sheila never divorced him and he tried to be a good father to Angelina, but he battled strong addictions and couldn't seem to keep himself out of trouble."

Hearing that, Mitch shot a look at Cassie and her eyes met his. From what he knew, her father didn't battle addictions. No, that was her mother's problem. Cassie looked so small and vulnerable, and he was thankful the attention had shifted from them to the others in the group. Maybe this was a good thing, clearing the air of long-held assumptions. Hopefully, that would be the end of it as far as he and Cassie were concerned although he figured Amy would have a few more choice words.

Mitch heard tears from Natalie. She had her head on Marc's shoulder. "We'd like to ask you all to pray about something with us, if you would," she said.

"Of course," Rebekah said, echoed by the other ladies and a few of the men.

"We've been trying to have another baby for over a year. I'll admit, sometimes it's hard to be around the rest of you when you're such Fertile Myrtles or whatever." She wiped beneath her eyes as a tear slipped down her cheek. "I can't believe we've made it through an entire weekend together without someone making the announcement they're pregnant."

"Maybe the Lord wants you to focus on the one you have for now."

Mitch raised a brow at that comment from Cassie, of all people.

"Maybe you shouldn't call her Princess all the time. That only feeds into the whole entitlement idea. Besides, not everyone has the privilege of growing up in a wealthy Connecticut town or being able to attend Wellesley," Winnie said with a pointed look at Natalie.

"As opposed to *your* daughter who talks about princesses all the time?" Natalie shot back. "Winnie, you didn't even tell Josh he had a daughter for four years. He had a right to know he was a father."

"I can't believe you said that," Winnie shot back. "I had my reasons. It was all very…complicated."

Marc rubbed one hand over his face. "Winnie, it's obvious Chloe inherited your tendency to hen-peck and mother everyone. Not that it's not a good thing. You keep us in line, and we love you for it. But can we please leave our children out of this? Look, don't you think we know Gracie's spoiled? We're working on it. Maybe it's my fault. I work hard at my agency to provide a nice life for my family, and I do a pretty decent job of it."

"No one's questioning your work ethic. It's above reproach," Josh snapped. "But maybe if you spent a little less time in the office and more time at home, Gracie would have a younger brother or sister by now."

"For once I'm going to have the good sense to restrain myself." Marc snarled out that comment.

Natalie laced her fingers through Marc's. "I think when we relax and try not to think about it, we might actually be able to get pregnant again." She patted her husband's arm. "Stop picking on Josh. He's a good man and God's grace allowed him to make a beautiful family together with Chloe and Winnie." Tears welled in her eyes again as she glanced at Winnie. "And now Luke. You're so blessed."

"We need to let our girls have their tea parties, play with dolls and indulge in the idea of being a princess while they're young," Lexa said, most likely trying to keep the peace and stem more outbursts. "As long as we keep it all in perspective of being a princess in the eyes of the Lord. Real life will come fast enough. Natalie, honey, I'm sure the Lord will bless you and Marc with more children. Medically speaking, there's no reason you can't, right?"

"Right." That emphatic word came from Marc.

Mitch ducked his head between his propped legs to hide his grin. Marc sure wanted everyone to know he was the man.

"Maybe we should all be praying instead for Kevin and Rebekah to have their first baby," Marc said. "Hopefully, it won't take him as long to be a father as it did for him to speak up—"

"Enough." Natalie said, silencing her husband with that single word.

"Nothing to be ashamed of, Kev," Josh said to his brother-in-law.

Kevin grunted and shifted his position. "I have no reason to be ashamed of anything."

"For the record, Beck, you nearly lost Kevin because you were so wrapped up in that twit of a Brit," Natalie said.

Mitch felt like he was at a tennis match watching the volleys go back and forth over the net. Natalie was really on a roll now. She and Marc seemed the most quick-tempered of the group. On the other hand, those two must have some serious fun making up after a fight.

"Why you even paid Adam any mind in the first place is beyond me," Natalie continued. "You're fortunate Kevin was so sweet and loyal to wait for you while you were busy playing *eenie meenie miney moe, which man shall I choose?*" Her voice had taken on a high-pitched, sing-song quality. "Oh, I don't know. Maybe I'll go look at my beautiful gazebo for a while, and *then* I'll choose."

Amy stifled a giggle at the gazebo remark while the other women glared at her. "Sorry, but I find it funny."

"Natalie, pipe down and leave Beck alone." At Marc's comment, Natalie crossed her arms and pouted.

Rebekah cleared her throat. "Trust me, I know how horribly indecisive I was about Kevin. I'll admit the idea of the life Adam offered sounded appealing at first—dining with royalty, summer mansions, Christmas in London. It's like the whole princess thing, the idea of the perfect fairy tale. Kevin wasn't slow in speaking up for my heart. He was smart," she said, reaching for his hand, "and loving, and incredibly patient. It took me a little longer to grow up, but he knew I'd reach that point eventually. Remember, I was a schoolteacher at the time. Working around kids all day can alter your reality a bit. When my daddy died," she said, shooting a glance at Josh across the room, "that was my wakeup call. I finally understood my prince had been here all along."

"And the newlywed has spoken," Landon said, clapping. "Where's my tiny violin?"

"Have you all been drinking?" Winnie's eyes were wide, unbelieving. "Landon, need I remind you that you and Amy are the newlyweds in this bunch? Don't even get me started."

Winnie's last comment was directed more at Amy. Surprising, since Mitch knew how tight these two women were. This was getting better by the minute. From a psychological standpoint, Freud would salivate over an in-depth character analysis based on all the accusations flying around the room. It'd be a fascinating case study of the interpersonal dynamics of a group of close friends, some of whom saw one another infrequently, some every day, and with varied temperaments and thresholds of frustration.

Lexa glanced at Sam, her brow furrowed. Would she ask him to step in and stop the madness? These people apparently had some deep-seated grievances with one another they'd needed to air. Best to get long-held hurts out of the way now and then try to clean up the mess. Mitch didn't envy Sam, but if anyone could get this crew whipped back into shape, Sam would be the man who could handle it.

Amy waved to get their attention. "To make up for laughing about the gazebo comment, I'll make a confession. In case any of you in this room believes we're above reproach in our past behavior."

"I don't think you need to worry about that," Mitch said, sitting up straighter. The expression on Landon's face was priceless. He didn't look happy with Amy's revelation, but he remained silent.

Amy took a quick breath. "Landon and I spent a night together on the road between Baton Rouge and Houston."

"And this is shocking how?" Marc asked. "We're Christians, people. We're not perfect."

Kevin chuckled under his breath. "Maybe that should be a new TeamWork slogan."

At least his comment served to lighten the tensions running rampant. Being an advertising guru, Marc would be the one to put it in concise terms. And he was right. Their behavior this morning was indicative of how imperfect they all were.

"Our rental car broke down and we were stuck in a fleabag motel. In the same motel room."

"Look, nothing happened that shouldn't have," Landon said. "I know I had to answer for some things on that road trip. Things I'm not particularly proud of," he said, staring at Mitch, "but I assure you, it wasn't some elaborate plan I'd cooked up to lure Amy into the den of iniquity for my sinful desires."

At the word *lure*, Cassie finally met Mitch's gaze. Was that a tiny hint of a grin? She was sitting too far away, but he dared not make a move. The natives were restless and he didn't need to draw any more attention to either one of them.

"I can't wait for you two to have kids already," Josh said to Landon. "Maybe that'll slow you down a little. The Lord knows nothing else seems to do it. Mr. *Meet and Marry Me in Lightning Speed*. Your courtship of my favorite journalist lasted all of what, six months?"

"The span of time is irrelevant." Indignation was clear in Landon's tone. "Amy, we should go before the tensions in this room get any more contentious."

"Why? To go *nap*?" Marc said. "The sparks between you two at any given moment are palpable. Spare us, please."

Josh chuckled. "We all know nap is a code word for something else, Warnick."

"Josh!" Winnie's cheeks flushed.

"Oh, this is rich." Marc laughed but stopped after Natalie swatted his knee.

Mitch couldn't stay silent any longer and knew he needed to say something. "You know what? I take full responsibility for starting this brouhaha or whatever, but I have to say, all the bullying and catty comments in this room surprise me."

"Think of the children," Cassie said in a tearful voice. "I should go get Chloe and bring her in here. I can only hope I'm like her when I finally grow up some day."

Several of the women sniffled. Natalie reached for Winnie's hand across the laps of their husbands. Marc and Josh spoke in low tones and Marc slapped Josh's shoulder and chuckled. Well, that was good to see.

"Enough." Planting his hands on his desk, Sam rose to his imposing height. "No one leaves this room," he said, darting a glance at Landon and Amy.

Mitch wondered how long Sam would let them go at each other before he finally intervened. Walking around to the front of the desk, he leaned back against it. With his arms crossed, his face was a study in consternation.

Mitch waited, as he knew they all did, for their leader to speak.

Chapter 23

$\mathcal{S}$AM'S PIERCING BLUE stare encompassed every TeamWork volunteer in his study, one by one. Cassie scooted a little further back into the cushions of the loveseat. She noted how Kevin massaged Rebekah's fingers, the same as he'd done for her ever since her fall into that frozen creek in Montana.

"If anyone else in this room has a grievance, complaint, accusation or problem with another person in this room and feels the need to air it in public, feel free to speak up now." Sam's voice was calm but as firm as she'd ever heard it. "Any takers?"

The word *no* reverberated around the room.

When Sam's eyes met hers, Cassie lowered her gaze, embarrassed and ashamed. She and Mitch had started this horrible mess. In days ahead, she could only hope they'd all be able to laugh about it. They'd remained civilized although it highlighted the sensibilities in their tight-knit group. No one right, no one wrong. If nothing else, no one could accuse this group of being perfect. Far from it. Didn't mean they didn't love each other fiercely. They were family. Why was it the deepest hurts usually came from those you love most in the world?

Because they're the ones you allow access to your heart. That gives them the power to hurt you the most.

Sam reached for his Bible and his eyeglasses. Positioning the glasses, he flipped through his Bible. "Listen to these verses from the fourth chapter of Ephesians, starting with verse 25: '*Therefore, laying aside falsehood, speak truth each one of you with his neighbor, for we are members of one another. Be angry, and yet do not sin; do not let the sun go down on your anger, and do not give the devil an opportunity. He who steals must steal no longer; but rather he must labor, performing with his own hands what is good, so that he will have something to share with one who has need. Let no unwholesome word proceed from your mouth, but only such a word as is good for edification according to the need of the moment, so that it will give grace to those who hear.*'"

Closing the Bible, Sam laid it on the desk and paused to gather his thoughts.

"We're all sinners capable of hurting one another, as we've proven here this morning. Each one of us is human in all our glorious imperfections. I like to believe the hurt is temporary but the good remains. Because of our shared faith, we're also capable of supporting, praying for, encouraging and loving one another. What I want you to understand is that God had a divine plan in bringing this particular group of people together. Believe in the *blessing* of that bond. As a matter of fact, Lexa, Josh, Beck and I just returned from a breakfast meeting. We're in the beginning stages of planning an upcoming mission. There's a Native American congregation planning to build a church near

Albuquerque and they've asked TeamWork for help." Sam's blue-eyed gaze swept the room. "We're going to give them assistance, and I'd suggest this group could definitely use another hands-on mission."

When Sam glanced at Lexa, she nodded with a lovely smile. "Each one of you in this room has something uniquely special to bring to TeamWork. God doesn't care where you're from, whether you're poor or privileged, orphaned or come from a large family, how much education you've attained or how many professional accolades you've received."

With a curled fist, Sam tapped it over his chest. "God is concerned about the condition of your heart, my friends. Some of you probably wondered why I let you carry on with your petty criticisms and insults as long as I did. You needed to get it out, that much was clear. If you didn't, you'd continue to harbor these feelings." When he smiled, the lines on either side of his mouth deepened. "I have to say, it was very enlightening."

Cassie shifted her position and heard a few low chuckles from the others.

Sam's gaze rested on Marc and Natalie. "Marc, you've been blessed with intelligence and ingenuity. You command respect and loyalty. Natalie has a heart for reaching young souls for Christ with unequaled passion. Natalie, you're a loving mother and bring out the best in Marc, the tender side that makes him an even better leader and father to Gracie."

Marc kissed Natalie's temple and whispered something in her ear as Sam moved his focus to Josh and Winnie. "Josh, you've been refined by the fire and risen from the ashes. As you once said, you found your redemption in a little girl named Chloe. God makes no mistakes. Winnie is your perfect helpmate and mother to your children. She's also the best business partner Lexa could ever have. As my TeamWork general counsel, you're a great asset to our organization and I've seen glimpses of true greatness in your character."

Winnie snuggled close and put her head on Josh's shoulder.

Sam focused on Rebekah and Kevin. "Beck, you've been one of my best encouragers for years. Your support of Josh in his darkest hour, and your tireless efforts on behalf of the schoolroom projects for TeamWork are an invaluable addition. Kevin, you've always been a stalwart defender of the faith, but you're even stronger with your wife by your side. I have no doubt your children will one day be a loving testament of the love you share."

Finally, his gaze rested on Amy and Landon. "Amy, one of your greatest strengths is your fearless spirit. You do nothing halfway and everything with fierce passion. Landon, Amy is your equal and soul mate. Your dedication to TeamWork Missions—including the use of your plane and piloting skills—has enriched the ministry immeasurably."

Sam's eyes softened as he turned to her. "Little One, your unbridled enthusiasm has been a huge blessing from the first day you came into our lives and told Lexa you wanted to be a part of TeamWork. You've gone above and beyond for Doyle-Clarke Catering and in helping with all our kids. Your willing spirit is beyond compare. Mark my words, the Lord's got something very special in mind for your future ministry."

Mitch cleared his throat, prompting Sam to turn toward him. "Mitch, I know you've helped Amy and Landon with Tam's Place and other TeamWork projects in New York. From what I've heard, you work well with kids and teenagers as well as the other volunteers. The incident at the fair shows how God is using your training in ways you might never have imagined. As with Cassie, I have no doubt He'll continue to use you mightily for His purposes and glory."

Lexa stood and moved beside Sam, slipping her hand in his. "I'd suggest each of you search your hearts and ask forgiveness from the others you might have offended or wounded by your words here this morning. No one leaves this house—not leaving this *room*—until you're straight with each other. I want some prayers being lifted. Now, let's get started."

For such a petite woman, Lexa loomed tall and commanded tremendous respect. The pride and admiration on her husband's face was a love story all its own.

Mrs. TeamWork had spoken.

~

Glancing out the kitchen window, Mitch saw Cassie sitting on the back deck. The kids played in and around the cottage, giggling and chasing each other. He smiled when he spied Gracie and Chloe whispering together. He leaned closer to the window. Now they were hugging.

Lexa came over to stand beside him. "Here," she said, handing him a lightweight jacket. "Cassie might be a little chilly. The heat wave's over now and we're getting back to our usual temperatures for this time of year."

"Thanks. Lexa, I'm really sorry about what happened this morning. I take full responsibility for keeping Cassie out all night. She was embarrassed and hated to think she'd disappoint you and Sam."

"She didn't disappoint us, and neither did you, Mitch. Cassie's become part of our family. I think what happened was the trigger to air some issues and things that needed to be said. In some ways, we should thank you for bringing them to the forefront. This group is special in how our different personalities mesh well together overall. Sure, we have quibbles with each other. It's inevitable, I suppose, but the important thing to remember is—whenever one of has a need—we're there for each other. Those kinds of deep, abiding friendships are rare and you don't find them every day. Some people never find it."

"For a minute there, I thought Marc and Josh were going to start throwing punches."

"With those two, they respect one another, but they don't know each other as well. Add Landon into the mix and you've got some strong testosterone." Her lips twisted. "They'll work out their differences. When I left Sam's study, they all seemed to be fine."

He looked out the window again. Cassie had taken a cushion from one of the deck chairs and put it on the ground beneath one of the trees. Chloe, Gracie and Joe were playing around her and his spirits lifted to see Cassie laughing and smiling. "I used to be Amy's hero. Does every woman need a hero, Lexa?"

"It doesn't have to be in the physical sense. But in her heart? Speaking for myself, I'd say yes." The depth of grace and wisdom in Lexa's aquamarine eyes gave him renewed hope. "You want to know what makes a man a hero? A hero is the little boy who picks a flower and presents it to his mama. The teenage boy whose single mom had a ring stolen, so he saves up enough money to buy her a new one. The college student who calls his mother to let her know he got back to school safely after the holiday break."

Lexa moved beside him at the window. "Sam told me once that he'd never skip unless he had a daughter someday. That would be the only thing that would ever make him want to do such a thing. Then, a few months ago, I was doing the dishes and looked out the kitchen window. Guess what I saw in the backyard?"

Mitch grinned. "A skipping Sam?"

"Yes. He was holding Leah in one arm and Hannah in the other. In another year, I'm sure he'll be teaching them to skip on their own speed."

Mitch's smile faded. "I'd love to be Cassie's hero, but I stand for everything she's never wanted."

Lexa's smile was gentle. "That might be so, but you can offer her everything she *needs*."

Mitch leaned forward and kissed her cheek. "Cassie's blessed to have you and Sam. *All* of you. I know Cassie's supposed to be at work right now, but I hope you'll excuse her long enough for us to talk."

"No worries. Winnie's headed over there now and I told Cassie to come whenever she's ready." Lexa patted his arm. "I know this is more important. Go on out there and take your time."

"Any advice?" Funny how he'd never needed advice before on how to talk to a woman. What should he say? What *could* he say? He wasn't used to being twisted in knots. He needed to start packing his bags and study the map some more but didn't want to do any of it. Spending more time with Cassie was uppermost in his mind.

"Be yourself and speak honestly. That's a big part of being the hero of a woman's heart."

With a nod to Lexa, Mitch stepped outside with Cassie's jacket. Behind him, he heard Lexa call to the children to come inside. Bless that woman. Joe,

Chloe and Gracie came running and they called out greetings as they flew past him. He heard the door close and the sounds of their voices grew faint.

Cassie didn't look up at him as he crossed the yard. "Hi," he said, dropping down beside her a minute later.

"Hi." Her voice was quiet, subdued.

"Would you believe I'm at a loss for words?" Mitch draped the jacket around her shoulders and then smoothed his palms over the knees of his jeans.

"I'm not sure what either one of us can say right now."

Mitch swallowed hard. "Amy's flying back with Landon. Right after the big brouhaha, she told me she'd decided not to go on the road trip with me."

Cassie looked at him, her surprise apparent. "Did she say why?"

"Only that she needs to be back in her office before next week and it'll take the rest of this week to drive. She also thinks I need some time alone to think things through and being on the road might give me that time. I suppose she's right."

"Things?"

He breathed out a breath. "I know I've joked about it, but I never expected to like you as much as I do. You're an incredible woman, the type of woman I've wanted and needed in my life all along. Now that I've found you, I don't know what to do. You're based here in Houston and don't like New York. I'm in New York with no plans or desire to move to Texas. And, frankly, I don't think I'd do well with a long-distance relationship."

"Well, then, why are we even talking about it?" When Cassie started to rise to her feet, he reached out a hand to stop her. After a few seconds, she sat down beside him again.

"I don't want to lose you, Cassie."

"You won't lose me," she said, her voice quiet. "We can remain friends. We have the bond of TeamWork and—in spite of a rousing brouhaha every now and then—we love each other. Sam mentioned the mission they're starting to plan for next year. So, if neither one of us is attached, maybe we can get reacquainted then." Her tone was flat and lacked enthusiasm.

"As in longer than a year from now?" Mitch shook his head. "You can't be serious. Sorry, but that doesn't wash. I need to see you before then."

"I hate to point out the obvious, but you don't want to fly."

"I can drive or I can take the train, bicycle, skateboard, hot air balloon, pogo stick. How about you? Are you willing to come to New York?"

Her cheeks flushed. "I've never been much of anywhere."

"Then how can you say you don't like New York?"

Cassie ran a hand through her long hair, tousling it, and the action momentarily distracted him. "I never actually said that. You misinterpreted my statement to Amy after you first arrived. I'm sure New York is a fascinating city, but it's so. . .big. Huge, actually."

"That's kind of ironic, considering what they say about Texas." He didn't want to remind her that she'd been attacked here on her home turf, so to speak. "Crime and crazy people are everywhere, but you can't let that stop you. We have to step out in faith every day, right? I guess the main thing here is whether you want to see me again, Cassie. If you do, then we can try and figure out how we can make this relationship work between us."

Mitch waited, and when she didn't answer right away, his pulse skidded to a grinding halt.

Shifting toward him, Cassie drew up her knees and clasped her hands around them. "Don't you get it?"

His brows rose. "I guess I don't. Men can be clueless. Can you give me a hint?"

"Mitch, I like you so much it scares me. But, I have to wonder, is it just because you're new and exciting? I've never met a man like you. You're different in so many ways, but it's a *good* different."

"Not exactly what a guy wants to hear, but if you say the word sophisticated, I might have to kiss you to make you quiet."

"Tempting," she said, her humor resurfacing and making him smile.

"What are you saying? We should give it some time?" He didn't like that any better. That was a non-answer if ever he'd heard one. "How much time?"

"I don't know any more than you do. I don't see how anything lasting can develop when there's so much distance between us. Geographically, I mean. Like sixteen hundred miles or something."

"Trust me, I know. Don't remind me." His jaw was set hard, his voice strained. *Fight for her. Fight for the right to pursue a relationship with her.* "What I'm asking is that you give me a chance, Cassie. Give us a fighting chance at making a go of this relationship. We started something between us this weekend, and I'm not about to end it before we have the chance to see how truly great we can be together long term. That would be the greatest mistake of all."

Her expression was one of curiosity. "Why?"

Although Cassie sat inches away, Mitch felt her deep sigh. "You're the best thing that's ever happened to me. I don't want to lose my chance with you because of my own stupidity." His voice caught on that last part. He couldn't help it, but neither could he worry about appearing like the fool. While he waited for her response, his heart raced like it hadn't since he'd taken that leap down from Landon's plane.

"It's not like I mock-marry guys all the time, you know, and I don't currently have any better offer on the table." Her coy grin belied her words. Ah, yes, he'd found his solid footing again.

"Come here." His voice had turned husky. Hauling her into his arms, Mitch kissed her. "You are so lovely," he whispered, pouring his affection for her into the kiss without deepening it like he wanted. It was too soon, and he didn't want to risk losing her before he had the opportunity to earn her love.

How easy it would be to fully immerse himself in this woman's softness. After brushing another gentle kiss across her lips, he smiled. "Is that enough to convince you?"

She widened her eyes. "I think so, yes."

Mitch dropped a light kiss on the tip of her nose. "You are addictive. I hope you'll be prepared for the onslaught of emails, telephone calls, text messages—"

"Okay to the first two, but I don't text. Don't like it."

"No texts. I can live with that." Pulling her up by the hand, they leaned against the tree, side by side. The breeze ruffled through the trees and it looked like a storm might be brewing off to the south.

"I know guys like to be logical," she said. "You want to know the path between Point A and Point B."

"And women use maps and ask for directions. Your point?"

"I think we need to see what happens—"

"Naturally, you mean?" He winked, enjoying her blush. "Then be prepared for a thorough wooing, Miss Thorenson."

"I can live with that."

Chapter 24

$\mathscr{C}$ASSIE COUNTED IT a miracle she could concentrate on her work when she finally made it to the catering office. Lining up workers for several upcoming events and confirming food orders kept her busy and her mind occupied. She knew Mitch had gone with Kevin to take Amy and Landon to the airport, and then they planned to swing by the TeamWork office to meet Sam and Josh who'd transported Marc, Natalie and Gracie to the airport.

Lexa breezed into the office later in the afternoon and told her there'd been some serious fence mending at the house, especially between Josh and Marc. What a relief. Cassie followed Lexa into her office, taking a report to her.

"Don't let the guys fool you, Cassie."

"What do you mean?"

Lexa motioned for her to have a seat in one of the armchairs facing her desk. "Marc and Sam developed a special kinship in Montana. Before that, Josh and Sam had been close friends for years until the San Antonio work camp. Now, Josh is working alongside Sam and they have a restored relationship. Better than ever. Let's just say Marc and Josh are rather wary of one another."

"Are you saying there's a rivalry of some kind between Marc and Josh. . ." Cassie wasn't sure how to phrase the question.

"Yes, that's exactly what I'm saying. It's not much different than two little girls fighting over the right to be best friends with a third girl." Lexa smiled. "Our big strong men would deny it, but I think there's jealousy there and the desire to be the winner in some kind of crazy contest for Sam's loyalty. As far as Natalie, her personality changed a bit since she suffered from the amnesia. It's difficult to explain. She's still the same and yet she's a little more hot-tempered, as evidenced by this morning's events."

"Could be Marc's influence," Cassie said.

"Agreed." Lexa moved aside some papers on her desk and checked her calendar. "Marc's always had a strong personality. Most men in his position of authority and control do, but he learned the valuable lesson in Montana that—in order to win back Natalie—he had to surrender all."

"At the throne of grace."

"Exactly." Lexa smoothed a hand over her brow. "What a morning, huh? But it was good in a lot of ways. I believe we'll all be stronger for having gone through it."

"Papa Bear okay?"

Lexa's eyes softened. "He was shaken up, but it served to reinforce our humanity and the sovereignty of the Lord's leading in our lives."

"You and Sam make a great team, Lexa. Thanks for all you do."

Lexa's eyes were moist. "Thank you, sweet girl. You and Mitch okay?"

"I think we will be, although I have no idea what the future will bring."

"None of us do, but that's where faith and trust come into play. Mitch is a good man, and it's plain to see how much he cares about you."

Cassie lowered her gaze. "I don't have much experience when it comes to men, and I'm not sure I can trust these feelings."

"Remember, I was pretty much standing where you are now when Sam picked me up for my first work camp. I didn't know what to think of this tall, inquisitive cowboy who exasperated and yet attracted me at the same time. Trust me, God will work out the details."

Lexa blew out a breath. "And now I need to put together the monthly expenditure spreadsheet and hope two plus two equals four."

~

Mitch waited outside the house when Cassie pulled the car to the curb. She tossed him the keys as she hurried around the car to the passenger side. His smile was thanks enough. Oh, the man looked gorgeous in a red sweater, jeans and dark jacket. Must be part of the new wardrobe he'd bought at the mall. She navigated and he drove them to a favorite local pizza place where they shared a large pepperoni and sausage pizza. He made a crack about not eating garlic, and she promptly stuffed a pepperoni in his mouth to make him quiet.

As they ate, Mitch told her more about his work, stressing how he helped people secure their financial future. In a way, what Mitch did for a living sounded similar to Sam and Lexa's financial planning careers before Sam had joined TeamWork full-time. She found it incredibly endearing how Mitch wanted her to understand his job. As if he somehow wanted her approval.

"You don't have to prove anything to me," she told him, glimpsing relief in his expression. "If you're happy in your job, that's the most important thing." He grew quiet and sadness flitted over his features, making Cassie wonder if he missed his medical career. From all indications, that had been his first love, his great, deep passion.

"How about ice cream for dessert?" she suggested as they finished the pizza.

"The place you were telling me about? Sounds like a plan," he said.

"Well, now, who do we have here?" Cassie hid her smile at Bea Richardson's question as the bell on the front door sounded of the small ice cream shop. The owner surveyed Mitch with approving eyes from behind the counter. "Welcome to Richardson's."

"Bea, this is Mitch Jacobsen. Mitch is Amy Warnick's brother and he lives in New York." Cassie knew Bea didn't know Amy as well, but she'd met all of Sam's volunteer crew at some point. She was an honorary member of TeamWork with a plaque on the wall to prove it. She doted on Lexa and Sam, Winnie and Josh and all their kids, treating them like her own family.

"Any friend of Cassie's is a friend of mine. Tell me what kind of ice cream you like, Mitch. I made a fresh batch of cookie dough ice cream tonight, if that interests you."

Mitch turned to her. "Since we already shared a pizza, would you care to share a banana split with me?"

"Extra hot fudge and two cherries and you've got yourself a deal."

Sitting next to one another at one of the round tables, they acted silly, spooning bites of the dessert and then feeding one another. They kept their conversation light. Cassie didn't want to think about saying good night to him. Good night meant good-bye for now, something she didn't want to say.

"Mitch is head over heels for you," Bea whispered after Cassie grabbed extra napkins at the counter. "How long have you known him?"

Cassie hesitated. "Not long although I first met him at Amy and Landon's wedding."

"It's a pity he lives so far away. My late husband and I kept up a long distance romance for a while." Bea's eyes misted with her long ago memories. "I met him when my parents sent me to visit my grandparents in California when I was seventeen. Bob was two years older and stole my heart in two days' time. He was tall, handsome and funny and I'd never met anyone like him before. I didn't want to leave him at the end of my two-week visit. I cried and clung to him like a blame fool, but I didn't care. The minute I met him, I knew he was the man God planned for me. We fit." She smiled. "Turns out, Bob thought the same thing about me. Good thing, too."

"How did it all work out so you could be together?"

"We wrote letters back and forth for a year. My Bob couldn't write a postcard to save his life, but he wrote novels to me. Mushy stuff even though he wasn't a real emotional man." Bea's cheeks flushed with color.

Cassie darted a glance at Mitch. Giving her a smile, he gestured to the banana split.

"I won't keep you from Mitch, honey, but long story short—Bob worked in his daddy's ice cream shop and saved up enough money for a down payment on a house. He came to Texas a little over a year after we'd first met. Then he proposed and we married two months later. He decided he liked Houston and didn't want to take me away from my family, so we saved up to buy this shop. Took us a few years, but Bob loved the people contact and getting to know his customers. When the kids came along, we put them all to work learning the trade. Been here in this location going on forty years now."

"That's such a great story, Bea." She'd known Bea for years but never knew that part of her story. Bob had been gone for over a decade, and Bea had poured her considerable energies into the continuing success of the popular shop. The Lord had blessed her with several children and grandchildren, all living nearby, some of whom also worked in the shop.

Bea patted her hand and gave her an empathetic smile. "If it's meant to be, God will help make it happen. Keep your eyes on Him, child. He'll show you the path."

~

Mitch smiled when Cassie pulled him by the hand after they returned to the house.

"Where are you taking me now? A walk around the park?"

"No, but it's time you met another member of the TeamWork family."

Walking to the back of the Lewis home, Cassie led him to a one-car garage. "This is the place where Sam and Lexa send feuding couples to talk." She shot him a look. "Not that we're feuding."

When she started to lift the garage door, he rushed forward to help her. "Let me do that." As soon as she turned on the light and he caught a glimpse of the car inside, he laughed. "This has to be the famous bomb. Wow. I had no idea it was still around."

"This is it, all right." Cassie ushered him inside, leaving the garage door open. Walking to the passenger door, she opened it and waved her hand. "Have a seat, please."

"Am I in trouble?"

"Not at all."

"You did say feuding. I was hoping it was more like a place. . ." He ran a hand through his hair and gave her a sheepish grin. "Never mind."

"It's cold out tonight, and this is the most private place around."

"Then let me close the garage door to keep the heat inside."

"Good idea." She scooted around to the driver's side while he closed the door and then joined her in the car.

"So, this is the bomb." Mitch smoothed his hand over the black leather seat.

"Sam had it restored and they take it out on the open road every now and then. For old time's sake, I guess. He drove this car for years and it played quite a role in his relationship with Lexa in that San Antonio work camp."

Cassie twisted to face him. In doing so, the bottom of the long, flowery top she wore under her jacket got trapped beneath her leg. Her face scrunched into a frown, and she was adorable in her discomfiture as she wiggled to free it. As she tugged on it, she somehow managed to whack her chin with her hand.

Mitch couldn't stop his chuckle. "Are you okay? Need some help over there?"

"I'm fine," she said with a quiet grunt. "The clown show's over. Time to be serious now." She composed her features. "I was, um, hoping you'd tell me more about your medical career. I'd really like to know if you don't mind telling

145

me. I think it'd help me understand you better." She lowered her gaze and twisted her hands in her lap. "We've shared a lot, but there's still a lot to learn."

Mitch wasn't sure he wanted to talk about it, but he'd more or less promised he would. If he clammed up now, he'd be doing her a disservice. Hurting both of them in the long run and any possible relationship between them. He wanted her to know everything about him, and this was a big part of his history and the man he'd become, for better or worse. "Okay, you asked for it." He blew out a breath. "I went to Harvard undergrad, economics major and pre-med."

Cassie didn't blink. "That actually makes perfect sense."

"The sad truth, Cassie, is that I almost killed a patient in the second year of my residency."

"I think the key word in that sentence is *almost*." When she reached for his hand, Mitch laced their fingers together. If she'd resisted, shied away from him, he wasn't sure how he'd have handled it. Not well, most likely. Cassie seemed to believe in him, and that meant the world. "Will you tell me about it?"

"I ordered a drug to be administered to a patient without first checking to see if he was allergic to other medications. He went into shock and we almost lost him. He survived, but he sued the hospital and that was the sad and quick end of my illustrious medical career."

"Wouldn't the nurse have checked the chart?"

"It was one of those unfortunate situations where the mistake started with me and then it snowballed. The nurse on duty was new and young. I was the one responsible and the blame rested solely on my shoulders." He leaned his head back on the seat and closed his eyes. "I have no excuses except that I was tired and worn out. Med school had been grueling and I was lucky to grab a couple of hours of sleep between classes and rotations. That particular night of my residency, I'd been up for about thirty-six hours straight."

"Doctors are human and make mistakes," Cassie said. "I've heard how high the cost of medical malpractice insurance is, and there's a reason for it. I'm thankful the patient didn't die, but did the powers that be at the hospital ask you to leave?"

Opening his eyes, Mitch refocused his gaze on her. "I didn't give them the opportunity. I resigned before they could ask me to leave. That would have been the ultimate humiliation. Because of what happened, I was a liability. I'd failed them, but more than that, I'd failed myself." And like that, the heaviness he'd carried with him for years—an invisible anchor that weighted him with guilt and anger—eased. Not completely lifted, but it wasn't quite so bad because she'd listened and cared enough to know.

"You're the only one other than my family that knows the details of what happened." He squeezed her hand. "Thanks for caring."

"Mitch, maybe it's not my place, but I have to speak up. The other day at the fair, you didn't hesitate when we heard Mercy's screams. You ran straight to

Donald's side. You knew exactly what to do, and you saved his arm as a result. Talking about what happened in your past, I can hear the regret in your voice. But there's a passion there that I don't hear when you talk about your job as a stockbroker."

Somehow Cassie had managed to cut through his psyche, peeled away the layers to discover the hidden truth. Although it cut deep, Cassie was right. "I'm good at it. And I help—"

"I heard the spiel during dinner. Yes, you help people—and I know you must be very good at it—but where's your heart in all this?" She sat back on the seat, still holding his hand.

"What about you?" He kept his voice low. Not that he wanted to avoid further discussion, but he wasn't sure how to answer her question. "Why are you in the catering business? I know you're good at it, and you love Lexa and Winnie. Those are givens."

"Without a college degree, there's not a lot I can do."

"Have you thought about going to college?"

She nodded. "I'm considering taking some evening classes."

He leaned his elbow on the back of the seat. "What would you like to do? If you could do anything in the world you wanted, what would it be?"

"Teach." She didn't even hesitate.

Mitch's smile resurfaced. Her answer didn't surprise him at all. "You're great with kids. You have a gentleness, a kindness about you. Children respond to that. I've seen how great you are with the TeamWork kids. You'd be an awesome teacher." His phone buzzed in his pocket. "Who's calling me at this time of the night?"

"You'd better check," she said. "It might be your mom."

Glancing at his phone, Mitch nodded. "You're right, in a manner of speaking. It's my self-appointed mom. What's up, Amy? Isn't it about time for your nap with Landon?"

Beside him, Cassie laughed quietly.

"Very funny, Mitchell," Amy said. "Although you didn't ask, we made it back home fine. Thanks for your concern. Welcome to Manhattan. It's snowing and it took us three hours to get back from LaGuardia. I wanted to tell you I'll be praying for your safety on the road. I'd also like to speak with Cassie now, if you don't mind."

"What makes you think I'm with her? It's getting kind of late."

"I heard her laughing."

"Wow. Your hearing is exceptional for an old married lady."

"Funny. Please hand her the phone."

"Yes, boss. Oh, and by the way, she introduced me to Sam and Lexa's bomb. It's really quite cool." He offered the phone to Cassie. "Amy would like to speak with you."

Me? she mouthed. "Hi, Amy." Cassie nodded a few times before saying, "I'll keep that in mind." She darted a glance his way. "Thanks for the advice. I'll talk to you again soon. Good night." Closing his phone, Cassie handed it back. "She said to tell you she'd see you on Saturday if not before."

Mitch knew there had to be more to it than that, but he wouldn't push for details. "I hate to say it, but I guess I'd better be getting inside." Never in his life had he dreaded saying good-bye to a woman as much as he did now. With everything in him, he wanted to stay longer in Houston, get to know Cassie better. Spend time with her. Be silly with her. Kiss her. Find out her idiosyncrasies, her quirks, her joys, her sorrows, where she was ticklish, her hobbies, what she liked to read. . .everything about her.

"Mitch?"

"Huh? Sorry," he said, shaking his head as he climbed out of the car. When he started to lift the garage door, it wouldn't budge. He tugged harder, but that door wasn't going anywhere. "Great. We're locked in. Not that I'd mind being stuck in a garage with you. I'm sure we could find something to do."

With a grin, Cassie pushed the button on the side wall and the garage door slowly lifted.

"I guess this is it," she said a few minutes later. Giving him a shy smile, she tugged on the bottom of her jacket.

He could ask her to sit with him on the sofa. No, that might be too tempting. They could go in the kitchen and share a glass of milk. Milk was wholesome. Anything to keep his thoughts distracted from how much he wanted to hold her and not say good-bye.

"Cassie." The name rolled like a caress from his tongue. When she walked into his arms, he leaned his head against hers. "It's not an exaggeration to say I'm going to think of you the entire way back to New York. I'm going through Tuscaloosa, as a matter of fact."

"You are?" She raised her head, her blue eyes bright.

He nodded. "I had this crazy idea to ask you to go with me, but logistically, it didn't work. But I guarantee, if you were with me, it'd be an eventful trip."

She laughed softly in the quiet of the house. "Like you said before, we've had enough excitement."

"What's your opinion on the whole love at first sight thing?"

"Where you and I are concerned? Nope, I don't believe in it. Impossible." Cassie patted his chest and chewed her bottom lip. "What are your thoughts about it?"

Mitch shrugged and covered her hands with his. "I figure you'll find another guy in a week's time and forget all about me. Some guy named Stone, or Heath or—

"Be quiet and kiss the girl who won't think about you while you're driving back to New York."

"Gladly since I'll dismiss her from my mind as soon as I leave this house tonight." He brushed his thumb over her hand and nuzzled her cheek.

"You're not leaving. I am." She giggled when he dropped light kisses near her ear.

"Can't wait until you leave." Hungry for her, Mitch stifled her next comment by covering her mouth with his. He deepened the kiss when he sensed she wouldn't be resistant, wouldn't push him away. She met his kiss with an eagerness that thrilled him.

"Why, my little Alabama flower. You amaze me," he said at length, resting his forehead on hers. "Let me walk you to your car. It's pretty cold out there. Don't get any ideas about warming yourself up by kissing me or anything."

"Wouldn't think of it," Cassie murmured, tugging on the collar of his jacket.

After one last kiss outside by her car, she climbed inside and Mitch reluctantly closed the door. An overwhelming sadness engulfed him and he missed Cassie as soon as she drove away into the cold, lonely dark night.

Chapter 25

The Next Morning

*I*N SLEEP SHORTS and wearing a T-shirt and his glasses, Sam sat at the kitchen counter reading the newspaper when Mitch sleepily wandered into the kitchen. Although it was insanely early, he appreciated the other man's presence. Taking a seat across from Sam, Mitch downed a cup of strong black coffee and gnawed on a bagel smothered with cream cheese. He wasn't really hungry, hadn't really gotten much sleep, but—this morning, in particular—he needed something in his stomach and the caffeine.

"Wanna talk about it?"

"Nope. Appreciate the offer, though." Mitch yanked off a piece of the bagel and stuffed it in his mouth. That should keep his jaws busy.

"If it helps, I know how you feel."

"Uh, huh. Thanks." Mitch chewed some more. His somber mood must be written all over his face and he'd closed the cabinet door with a little too much force when he'd pulled out a mug.

Removing his glasses, Sam picked up a peach from a bowl on the counter. "What's it like Sam?"

"What's that? The peach?" Sam took a hearty bite with a small smile.

"Love. Marriage. The whole thing."

"Have you ever experienced love before?"

Mitch nodded but avoided his direct gaze. "I've told girls I loved them before. Foolishly."

Sam eyed him as he took another bite of his peach. Man, it was juicy. Sam grabbed a napkin and wiped his chin. "You know," he said with a wry grin, "this peach could be a good object lesson if I wanted it to be."

"Go for it." Mitch took another bite of his bagel.

"Love can be pretty messy sometimes, for one." He winked. "Juicy and delicious, too."

"You're creative, Sam. And corny. I'll give you that much."

When the other man laughed, his deep smile lines surfaced. "It's still early and I'm just getting started. I have something I'd like to give you. Call it a parting gift."

Mitch watched with interest as Sam walked over to the small desk in the corner of the kitchen and pulled a hardbound book from the bottom drawer. Coming back to the counter, he pulled up his stool again and sat down. "Here," he said, pushing it across the table. "For you."

Seven Rules of Marriage: A Husband's Guide to Loving Your Spouse. Opening the front cover, Mitch noted Sam's signature scrawl and the 2003 publication date.

LCJW Publishing, the first release from Landon's newly formed publishing company. Landon and Sam had both worked hard to promote it, and the book had sold well and become a commercial success. Now Sam had a second book in release, and it seemed to be doing just as well as the first, if not better.

"Nice try, Sam."

"Take the book with you on the road. Your assignment is to read a chapter every night. Guaranteed, by the time a week's up, you'll know the secret to a satisfying relationship. Applies every bit to unmarried men. Most of it, anyway. Trust me. You'll learn some things."

Mitch nodded. "Thank you. Sam, I want to personally apologize to you for what happened here yesterday morning. I never meant to hurt Cassie in any way or cause trouble."

Sam's smile was kind. "I appreciate your words. You're a good man and it's clear you've developed feelings for Cassie. In spite of it all, we couldn't be more pleased. Not that you need our approval. A lot's happened in a short time this weekend. A crash landing's bound to shake you up, but I'm sure it's made you realize how blessed you are. How fleeting life can be, how fragile. Then you meet a sweet, smart and beautiful girl who's not at all what you expected. A girl you were prepared to resist for various reasons. A girl from a completely different background and yet you discovered you have a lot in common." Sam took another bite of his peach, chewing slowly. "How am I doing so far?"

"I'm thinking you're either God's mouthpiece or pretty good at reading my mind." Mitch chuckled under his breath. "Please. Keep going."

"You've reached a point in your life where you're seeking God's purpose for your life, both professionally and personally."

Mitch whistled under his breath. "Am I that obvious to everyone?"

Sam tilted his head. "What do you mean?"

"Cassie told me she believes I should pursue something in the medical field again. Even though my medical career tanked, she thinks I should. . .consider other options."

"How do you feel about that?"

"You sound like a shrink."

Sam's laugh was hearty. "Lexa would get a kick out of that."

"I'm too old to change course, Sam. When I was able to help Donald at the fair, it reawakened something inside me. Reenergized me like nothing has in a long time in terms of my career."

"Early thirties isn't too late to change." Sam finished his peach and tossed the pit in the nearby trash can. "That's the age I was when I went on a year-long mission. When I came back, I knew mission work in some capacity was what I wanted to do full-time. The position had opened up with TeamWork, so I left my financial planning business behind and haven't looked back. But that training and experience helped me in ways I never expected. As I said before, Mitch, the Lord's using your abilities and talents in a different way now. Just be open to the opportunities that might present themselves. Never forget your well-being is in the hands of Someone infinitely more capable. Take the time to stop and listen, and be willing to step out in faith—that's the key as I see it."

Mitch nodded. "Sounds right to me. I'll keep that in mind."

"It's exciting to see how the Lord works things out above and beyond what we can ever imagine." Sam's smile was kind. "I've seen Him work in the lives of my TeamWork crew over and over again. Not that we haven't had our challenges, but God never promised it'd be easy. I'm here if you need me, brother. Feel free to call anytime."

"I appreciate that, Sam. It means a lot."

Lexa came down the steps with the twins and Joe as Mitch was saying his final good-bye. They all held hands and prayed for his trip and then Lexa gave him a quick, warm hug. "I'll be praying."

Man, he needed that hug. Since their short exchange the day before, he'd felt a special bond with Lexa. "Thank you. For everything." He kissed the cheeks of the twins and then high-fived Joe. "Take care of your little sisters, partner." What a great family. A stab of something—envy?—pierced him as he turned to leave.

"Our door's always open." Lexa said, walking him to the door. "I hope we'll see you again soon."

"I hope so, too, Lexa. Thanks."

With a salute to Sam, Mitch picked up his bags and headed to the rental car parked in the driveway. Ready to leave Houston. . .and a pretty big chunk of his heart behind.

Chapter 26

Mid-March 2004

M̂y ADORABLE MISS Thorenson,

I'm sitting here in my Wall Street office, unable to concentrate on stock quotes today. You are completely capturing my thoughts. Signed, Donald Trump

With a goofy smile plastered on his face, Mitch sat back in his office chair. Waiting. He glanced at the clock on the wall. Houston was an hour behind, but Cassie should be back from her lunch break. Sure enough, within a couple of minutes, she replied.

My Dashing Mr. Jacobsen,

I'm sitting here in my Houston catering office, unable to concentrate on quiche tarts today. You have completely captured my appetite. Signed, Martha Stewart

Mitch laughed. Their email flirting could go on all day, and he'd love nothing better. Forcing himself to concentrate on his work, he stopped after another two hours to send another email.

My Dearest Juliet,

I missed an important phone call from a client because I was buying something for you. It's all your fault. Answer the door when someone comes calling in the next half-hour. Signed, Mitchell a/k/a Romeo

Concentrating on a report, he kept the email inbox open. He'd sent her a dozen, multicolored roses—two dozen would probably be too much—along with a card commemorating the one month anniversary of their "nuptials." Had he gone too far? Maybe, but he'd wanted to send her flowers and what woman didn't love flowers? Within the hour, he heard the sound signaling he'd received a new email.

My Dearest Romeo,

Your messenger arrived and now the office is so fragrant my clients will be distracted. It's all your fault. Answer your phone when someone calls you tonight at 10 p.m. Don't be late. Signed, Cassie a/k/a Juliet

Shortly before the appointed time, Mitch settled at his kitchen table with his phone resting beside him. Promptly at 10:00 p.m., the phone rang as if on perfect cue.

"Hi, Mitch."

"Hello, Moonbeam." He'd adopted the nickname, and she'd embraced it. "How was your day?"

"Unproductive. Yours?"

He laughed heartily. "Same. Some woman kept flirting with me via email. It was very distracting. She somehow seems to think I find her irresistible."

"And do you?"

"Completely. I'm a fool over her."

"A fool, eh?"

"Totally. I love flirting with her. She's extremely witty."

"No, I didn't know. I assume she's only responding in kind to the intelligence and natural charisma of the fool."

"I imagine she's wearing something incredible tonight."

"Oh, my, the fool's getting a little too personal, isn't he?"

"That's why he's a fool."

"I hate to disappoint you, but I'm only wearing jammies and my hair's in a ponytail. You?"

He envisioned the appealing image in his mind. "Plaid flannel sleep pants and a red T-shirt. No ponytail tonight, though. Where are you?"

"On my living room sofa. You?"

"At my kitchen table."

"Are you eating this late?"

"I'm snacking, yes. Cereal, actually. You caught me in the act, I'm afraid. I'm cheating."

"Really, now, that's a very foolish thing to do, isn't it? I hope it doesn't happen often."

"I love your sense of humor, Cassie. I wish you were sitting here with me right now. Do you think you could fly up here late next week? Stay from Thursday night through Monday or Tuesday?" He heard her sharp intake of breath. "Cassie? Something wrong? Too soon?" It wasn't like he hadn't brought up the idea frequently.

"No," she said. "I'm cat sitting for a neighbor and the little bugger tried to take a bite out of my finger."

"The cat sounds lovely. Did it draw blood?"

"A tiny bit." He could hear the sound of water running.

"Wish I could kiss it and make it all better." He made loud lip-smacking sounds into the phone. "What's the cat's name? Dracula? Prince of Darkness?"

"Socks."

"Like the smelly things like I just peeled off my feet? What about them? How your mind does wander, woman."

"That's the cat's name, silly. Speak for yourself. Maybe it's a good thing I know about your foot odor problem now."

"We all have flaws, sweetheart. Name one of yours."

Cassie sniffed. "I have none. I'm perfect."

"Well, arrogance has to count for something," he said. "If this is going to work between us, we need to do something about your self-importance complex."

"My, my. You're assuming an awful lot, aren't you? Tell me more about this woman who's been emailing you. She sounds like a pest. How long have you known her?" So, she was fishing, was she?

"Not long enough. Forever. A few weeks. Always."

"Feeling amphibious tonight are you?"

"Hey, I never claimed to be a word person. That's Amy's responsibility in this family. Speaking of amphibious, I have to ask you something."

"What's that?"

"Please tell me you learned how to swim." Random thought, but ever since she'd told him about Tagg's death and how she couldn't swim, he hadn't been able to forget it.

He didn't expect the silence on the other end of the phone. "Cassie? It's a simple question."

"Um, no, if you must know."

"That's not good. Everyone should know how to swim. Amy and I had lessons when we were like three or something."

"Well, we couldn't afford lessons and after Tagg's death, I had even less of a desire to ever go into the water again in my lifetime."

"I can understand that, but we need to do something about this. I'm serious."

"Are you ordering me to take swimming lessons, Mitch?"

"I guess I am. Or come here and I'll personally take care of it. That would be fun." An image of Cassie in a swimsuit popped into his head. Man, he really shouldn't go there. "If you'll recall, I asked you about coming to New York a minute ago, but then Dracula bit you. If you're not bleeding profusely, or needing immediate medical attention, I'd sincerely appreciate an answer."

"I can't afford it, Mitch, and I don't want you paying for anything."

His lighthearted mood took a nosedive. Stubborn woman. They'd shared this same conversation a few times. Why wouldn't she allow him to pay for a plane ticket? With one finger, he absently followed the wood grain of the table. He closed his eyes and leaned back in the chair. "Cassie, we're at an impasse here. How are we ever going to find out if this relationship will work between us if you're not willing to accept anything from me?"

Based on the silence on the other end of the line, she was trying to figure out how to respond. Mitch counted to ten under his breath.

"That's not true. I accepted the flowers you sent today."

"I didn't know your favorite color rose, so I sent—"

"One of every color in the rainbow. Thank you. They're gorgeous."

"Tell me your favorite flower, or at least your favorite color rose."

"It doesn't matter. I like them all."

"Talk about ambiguous." Above all else, he didn't want to push her too fast. Cassie was different from the other women he'd dated in that regard, too. He'd never had to do a lot of pursuing in the past, never participated in the chase or the games. While Cassie had been responsive to him, she was also skittish and inexperienced when it came to dating. Not being in the same city—not even the same state or region of the country—threw a huge monkey wrench into the equation. Going in, he knew trying to maintain a romantic relationship long distance could be frustrating and tentative at best. But he needed to try and give it his best effort. Cassie was more than worth it.

He could hear her sigh. "I've never received flowers from anyone in my entire life. I'm not picky. It's the thought and the giver that's most important."

"Fair enough. Promise me you'll think about coming for a visit. Soon."

"Promise, Mitch."

~

After putting his empty cereal bowl in the sink and running water over it, Mitch went into the bedroom. Flopping on the bed, he dialed Amy's home number. "Hey, bro," he said when Landon answered. "My sister around?"

"She's right here," Landon said. "Hang on a second. Everything okay?"

"On second thought, maybe you're the one who can help me on this one."

"Something tells me it's a woman. Cassie, I hope?"

"Of course. Listen, I'm trying to get her to come for a visit but she's being stubborn and won't accept a plane ticket from me. Short of breaking my vow and getting on a plane, I'm not sure how this is going to work between us. We talked and she's at least promised to think about it. That's a big step in the right direction."

"You know, I picked up the new plane last week. Maybe it's time to forget that *no flying ever again* vow."

Mitch sat up cross-legged on the bed. He heard Amy in the background and waited impatiently for Landon to come back on the line. "Hello? Anyone there?"

"Sorry about that. Amy wants to talk to you."

"Let me work on Cassie," Amy said a second later. "I'll enlist Lexa and Winnie, if needed. Beck, too. You know they'll do what they can to talk you up, big brother."

The tension in Mitch eased with the knowledge the other ladies had confidence in him. "Amy, I miss Cassie more than I thought possible. It's killing me that she's so far away. And so incredibly stubborn and resistant to taking anything from me. You know what I mean," he added lest she misinterpret his words.

"Mitch, first of all—not that it makes you feel any better—it's only been a month since we were in Houston. Secondly, have you ever stopped to think maybe Cassie's not resisting you so much as the idea of physically getting on a plane?"

"What are you talking about?"

"Think about it. Do you know if Cassie's ever been on a plane?"

No, he hadn't even thought of that one. "Come to think of it, she made a comment about not going anywhere but on the highway between Tuscaloosa and Houston."

"So, in her own way, maybe Cassie's skittish about flying, too. I don't know that for a fact, but it's one possible reason. Then there's the pride factor. She might be hesitant to accept something of value from *any* man, so don't take it personally. I'll say one thing about her, though."

Lost in thought, Mitch tugged a string off the bottom of his sleep pants. Amy had made several good points he hadn't considered. To his shame, he'd been selfish and put his own feelings of self-pity above Cassie's needs. Definitely not the best way to begin a relationship. Not to mention he'd already broken one of the cardinal rules mentioned in Sam's terrific book. "What's that?"

"Cassie might not have had any of the same advantages growing up that we did, but that girl's got more class in her little finger than a lot of the people I deal with on a daily basis working at the magazine."

That made him smile. "Speaking of which, when are you going to quit working for that seedy-sounding rag and go to work for your husband? I hear he's big into acquisitions these days."

She laughed. "We're negotiating. Maybe I'll stop working at *Habits* at the same time as I fulfill your wish for a niece or nephew."

"Is this an announcement?" Mitch was only half-joking. He couldn't wait to spoil Amy and Landon's kids.

"Not yet. Listen, get some decent rest and keep talking to Cassie. Keep those lines of communication open. That's the most important thing at this point."

After brushing his teeth, Mitch climbed into his bed. He picked up the spy novel he'd started reading the night before but tossed it aside two paragraphs into the chapter. With Cassie uppermost in his mind, no way could he concentrate on serious espionage drama.

Grabbing his phone, on a whim, he dialed Cassie's home phone number, hoping he could entice her to sing to him over the phone. She'd done that for him a few times—even humoring him with special requests—and he'd love to hear her voice tonight. Was that the act of a desperate man? Probably, but he didn't care.

Cassie didn't answer, and he decided to leave a short voice mail message. Clearing his throat before the beep, Mitch prepared to sing. He had to be nuts about the woman to even attempt to sing for her. *Beep.*

"You are my sunshine, my only sunshine," he began, closing his eyes and feeling every bit the fool.

~

Three Weeks Later

A New York exchange flashed across Cassie's office phone. Was Mitch calling from his office to sing to her again? His heartfelt, out-of-tune songs had to be the sweetest, most romantic thing a guy could ever do for a girl. Bless his heart, he tried, and he'd started doing it more frequently, even taking her requests. That first message he'd left with his rendition of "You Are My Sunshine" would remain on her home phone answering machine for a very long time. He'd embellished it and added lyrics about moonbeams before his voice had soared gloriously flat. How she loved it. The first morning after he'd left the message, she'd listened to it three times as she'd eaten breakfast and dressed for work.

She startled when the phone rang again. "Doyle-Clarke Catering. This is Cassie."

"Hi, Cassie. It's Amy."

"Hi, Amy. How are you?" Before she'd met Mitch, Cassie usually only talked with Amy when she called to speak with Winnie. Not this time. She was downright chatty. Chances were high the reason for Amy's call involved Mitch.

She listened as Amy told her about Landon's purchase of his new plane. Pulling open her desk drawer as she listened, Cassie's gaze fell on a stack of postcards nestled inside. Twelve in all from Lake Charles, New Orleans, Tuscaloosa, Huntsville, Knoxville, to points in Virginia, Washington, D.C., Philadelphia and New York. Fun, colorful cards that traced Mitch's drive from Houston to Manhattan.

She smiled at the thought of Mitch picking up the cards during his trip. On each of them, he'd written something about her that he liked, things he'd miss or things he hoped to learn. Once she knew he'd arrived back home safely, Cassie shared the postcards with Bea Richardson. For whatever reason, she hadn't shared them with anyone else. She considered them little treasures she hugged to herself, and of all people, she'd known Bea would understand.

"Sorry to go into all that," Amy said, drawing Cassie's attention back to the conversation. Why was Amy telling her so much about Landon's new plane? Must be because Landon intended to use it for TeamWork missions and relief efforts. Always a good thing.

"The real reason I called is to see if you might be interested in going on a test run in the plane?"

Cassie almost choked. "What do you mean? When?"

She listened with wide eyes as Amy told her Landon could fly into Houston the following week and take her back with him to New York. "He could pick you up on Thursday and fly you here, but you'll need to fly back to Houston commercial. Sorry about that."

"Amy, it's a very generous offer, but I can't agree to Landon taking me on his plane. The cost of fuel is sky high and—"

"Landon's flying down to Houston on TeamWork *and* publishing business, so he's coming anyway. I'd come along for the ride, but I have important meetings for *Habits* next Thursday afternoon that I can't miss. I can probably take the day off Friday, if you'd like. Honey, if you're worried about what happened with Madelyn, there's no need."

"No, it's not that." Cassie swallowed hard. "I suppose I could consider it. But I insist on paying my own airfare for the return flight."

"If it helps, Mitch's birthday is next Friday. He'd love me forever if I could convince you to come for a visit. Since he came back from that Valentine's Day trip, he's been a miserable grump. He misses you, Cassie. Think about it, pray about it, and let me know as soon as you decide."

Mitch had been miserable? Amy must be exaggerating, but the fact Amy had called made it sound as though she approved of a relationship between them. Why did it have to be complicated? Cassie ran her finger over the glossy postcard of Tuscaloosa, wondering if Mitch had gone anywhere near where she used to live. She doubted it. Her old stomping grounds looked nothing like the photo on the card. He'd never asked for an address or specifics about her family home, and for that she was grateful.

The thought of seeing Mitch again sounded more appealing by the minute. Could she really do this? She'd never stepped foot on an airplane before. Mitch could have died in one. Rebekah was probably right in that he'd eventually change his mind about flying again, but it would be on his own timetable.

Her eyes fell on the calendar on her desk. She smiled when she read the verse for the day. How timely, and perfect for what her heart needed.

For God has not given us a spirit of timidity, but of power and love and discipline. 2 Timothy 1:7.

Chapter 27

Thursday, April 22, 2004 ~ Midtown Manhattan

$\mathcal{T}$HE CLOSER THE taxi brought her to the address for the townhouse, the more Cassie felt like a little girl on Christmas morning. Knowing Mitch was so close made her pulse race. She couldn't wait to throw her arms around him and kiss him. Show him how much she'd missed him. How much she wanted to be with him again, even if only for a few short days.

"That's it! Number 3405." Cassie pointed out the window at the red-brick, two-story structure, barely able to contain her excitement. Reaching for her purse, she pulled out more money than she needed, determined to give the man a great tip just for bringing her here. Stepping out of the cab, she waited on the sidewalk.

Last minute misgivings stirred inside her. Ever since Amy called with the idea to surprise Mitch for his birthday, she'd anticipated this moment. Imagined Mitch's surprised smile and teasing comment on discovering her on his doorstep. But. . .what if he wasn't so thrilled? *Silly girl, the man calls you every night and emails you every day.*

The driver came around to her side of the cab and closed the door.

"Thank you so much." She started to hand him the money but he waved it aside.

"You're welcome. Any friend of Miss Amy and Mr. Mitch is a friend of mine."

That stopped her and Cassie glanced into his kind eyes. What driver in his right mind wouldn't accept payment?

His laugh was genuine, from-the-gut. "Ask Miss Amy about Luis Delgado sometime. I've known Mr. Warnick for a few years now and been driving him all over the city. I got to know Miss Amy when she lived here and she helped my daughter, Angelina, get an internship at one of them fancy magazines. That Mitch is a real good man, but I don't see him as much. He works himself too hard, but he's been through a lot the last few years, losing his friend on 9/11 and all."

Cassie stared at him for a long moment. This man was no random acquaintance. Her eyes widened. "Landon arranged for you to pick me up at the airport, didn't he? I mean," she stammered, "it wasn't random. . ." Wow. How naïve of her to think otherwise. Landon had arranged for an airport employee to escort her from the plane, telling her he had reports to complete and didn't want her to wait. Then her taxi driver had been outside the airport and moved forward as soon as he'd spotted her.

This explains a lot. And how glad she was.

"They told me to look for the beautiful girl with long auburn hair and a smile that'll make me glad I'm alive and living in the city."

She smiled. "They really said that?"

"Sure enough they did. They also told me your coming today is a big surprise for Mr. Mitch." He gave her a wink. "He's a mighty blessed young man."

"Thank you, Mr. Delgado. You can call me Cassie." He'd pointed out a few famous landmarks as he'd driven her into the city, giving her little history lessons here and there. Based on the humor she'd glimpsed in his eyes in the rearview mirror, he enjoyed her enthusiasm.

His grin was broad, ear-to-ear. "And you can call me Louie. Pleased to make your acquaintance, Miss Cassie. I've heard a lot about you from Mr. Mitch."

"You have?"

"The guy can't stop talking about you. You've brought the smile back to his face."

Cassie nodded, pleased by his words. "I think we're going to be good friends, you and me."

"I'd like that. Miss Amy told me to bring your suitcase on over to their place. You okay with that plan?"

"Yes, that's fine," she said. "It's nice to know people are looking out for me."

"I'm going to pull the cab around to the other side of the street and wait until Mr. Mitch answers the door or else comes home. Wouldn't be right for me to leave you here all alone, sitting on the man's doorstep." He glanced at the sky. "Besides that, I think a storm's brewing."

"I'm not sure if he's even home, but Landon gave me a key if Mitch isn't home." She'd feel weird going inside the townhouse without him being there, but she'd do it, if needed.

Unexpected tears stung Cassie's eyes as Louie pulled out a card from his coat pocket and handed it to her. "Then I'll see you again on Monday morning. We need to get to the airport by noon for you to catch your flight since I understand you're flying commercial back to Houston. If your plans change or if you need to go anywhere while you're here, you call on Louie. I'll take good care of you." He tipped his cap. "Enjoy your stay here in New York, Miss Cassie."

"I'll do that. Thank you again." On impulse, she leaned forward and kissed his cheek. "Since you won't accept a tip."

He laughed again, deep and hearty. "A kiss from a lovely lady, especially a southern one, is better than a tip any day. I'll see you in a few days." With a wink and a wave, he climbed back into his taxi.

Climbing the stairs to the front door of the townhouse, Cassie took a deep breath and knocked on the door.

~

Finally finished with his meeting, Mitch swung around the corner leading to his office. "Jen, do you have any messages for me?"

"Hey, Mitch." He'd never minded his assistant calling him by his first name before, but today she'd infused it with a little too much breathiness. He paused beside her desk long enough for his messages. Flipping through the slips of paper, he mentally prioritized them.

"You have a few voice mails, too." She gave him a coy smile which he ignored. Jen wasn't much younger than he was, dark-haired and attractive but she wore too much makeup. She'd never been married to his knowledge, and— if the office gossip was true—hoped to snag a broker as a husband. Her hemlines had crept higher and her necklines had plunged lower in the past month alone, along with her increasingly blatant invitations to join her after hours for a drink. Being friendly was one thing, but if Jen stepped over the line—even came too close to the line—he wouldn't hesitate to request another assistant.

"Thanks. I'll check them." He started into his office.

"Oh, I almost forgot. A girl named Cathy Sorenson called a few minutes ago. I didn't write it down because she said she'd call you back."

He turned back from the doorway. "Cassie Thorenson?" His pulse thrummed. Best news he'd heard all day.

Jen snapped her fingers. "That's the one! Her accent's so cute. Sweet and refreshing in a downhome, cut-offs and barefoot-down-by-the-river kind of way. Wholesome, you know?"

Mitch nodded, lost in thought. "I'll be in my office. No interruptions, please."

"Sure thing, boss." He closed his door, away from her prying eyes and big ears. As it was, her off-base description of Cassie got his heart pumping. Little did Jen know her words only made him think about Cassie even more. Not that it took much. He'd love to see her in cut-offs and barefoot—all that gorgeous auburn hair tumbling around her shoulders, her long legs lightly tanned. The image was way too appealing and distracting. He could think about Cassie all day, but he needed to concentrate on his work.

Dropping into his chair, Mitch closed his eyes and massaged his temples. He'd battled a headache ever since he'd arrived that morning. A few good trades hadn't eased the tension as he'd hoped. Could be the stress of the last few months catching up with him, but it was more than that. Easing back into the plush leather, he rested his elbows on the arms of his executive chair.

I don't belong here.

Stocks, trading, money, investments. . .all of it. Cassie was right. Having too much money made people do stupid things. Not having enough money made them do stupid things. The sad fact was, money was a necessary part of life. Sure, he helped clients make wise investments for their retirement and long-term security for their families. What he did for a living wasn't wrong in and of itself. Sam and Lexa had worked as financial consultants before they'd married and he'd joined TeamWork full-time. Mitch liked Sam's analogy of investing one's funds wisely as a means to having earthly security whereas accepting Christ was the only way to achieving eternal security.

Bottom line? Overall, he was happy in what he did, but he wasn't *content*. Cassie hadn't said it, but she might as well have: he'd settled. He couldn't have the career he wanted because of his own foolish mistake, but he'd walked away when perhaps he should have pursued his options. All his medical training shouldn't be washed down the drain. But what was he qualified to do?

Loosening his tie and trying to clear his thoughts, Mitch pushed in the voice mail code to retrieve his messages. He listened and jotted a couple of notes, chuckling as he listened to a personal message from a friend. When he heard the other man mention Alabama, that's all it took. He wanted to call Cassie. She'd been on his mind constantly. Call it a pity party, but he'd hoped she'd come visit for his birthday. He hadn't even told her it was tomorrow. Why he hadn't, he didn't know. Maybe because he wanted her to come visit without that knowledge.

He dialed her cell phone number.

She picked up on the third ring. "If this is a solicitor, I don't need anything you're selling."

"Too bad. I'm running a special on whispered sweet nothings." He loved how they didn't even need to greet each other but jumped headfirst into a conversation. The kind of familiarity he'd only previously shared with Amy and Brad.

"Hmm. I can tell you're a good salesperson. Keep talking. How much?"

"If you happen to be from Alabama, for today only, it's a free introductory offer."

"But if this offer comes from New York, I've already taken advantage of it."

"It's non-transferable, but I'm willing to extend the offer. Your complete and total satisfaction is guaranteed."

"Do you offer a warranty? Or a return policy?"

"You can't even know how much I want to kiss you right now."

Her laughter made him smile. "I must be your ideal customer."

"Oh, you're my ideal, all right."

She groaned. "I guess I led myself right into that one, huh?"

"I'd say so. I need to see you, Cassie."

She hesitated for a few seconds before she spoke again. "Are you okay?"

"Not sure. Starting to ponder some half-crazy things."

"Care to share them with me?"

"Let me ruminate on them a little more. I'm actually returning your call, in a manner of speaking. My assistant said you'd called."

"I wanted to tell you I had dinner with Barbara and Donald Corman last week. They settled their lawsuit against the operators of the fair and will be getting a nice lump sum. They're going to put most of it in a trust for Mercy's college education."

"That sounds great. Wise use of the funds."

"I thought you'd want to know that, but there's more."

"What's that?" Leaning back in his chair, Mitch kicked off his shoes and crossed his feet on top of the desk. "They're naming Eddie the Freaky Bear as the trustee?" He stared out the window, not focusing on the high rise office buildings but on the rain streaming down the window while steady pellets of hail beat a staccato tap dance against the glass.

"I think you have a problem with Eddie. Maybe you should seek professional help."

"I will if they have a twelve-step program. Cassie, you make it incredibly easy to get off-topic."

"Sorry," she said. "Anyway, Sam was talking to a new guy at church on Sunday. His name's Billy. He's young, in his early twenties and he's been coming regularly the last month or so. Long story short, this guy was working at the county fair the day we were there. Turns out he's the employee who wielded the axe that injured Donald."

"Wow. That's unbelievable." Mitch rubbed his hand over his face. "Did you tell Donald and Barbara?"

"No, but that's the other strange thing. File this one under the *only in God's world* category. During our dinner, I mentioned something about the church. Barbara said Mercy's been trying to get them to come to church. So, guess who walked into church on Sunday morning?"

"You're kidding." Mitch loved the enthusiasm in Cassie's voice. Loved how God worked.

"Nope. I sang a duet with my songwriting friend, and the song was about forgiveness. Common theme, but I knew that was the song we should sing. When I looked at Barbara while I was singing, tears were streaming down her cheeks. Then Sam and Lexa invited them to lunch and. . .you can probably imagine how it turned out. Donald and Billy aren't going to be best buddies, but there's an understanding between them. More than anything else, Donald could see how sorry Billy was for what happened. I think the meeting between them will go a long way toward bringing emotional healing for both of them."

Mitch nodded then realized Cassie couldn't see him. "You've got to love how God orchestrates these things like a symphony. I'd better get moving. Keep singing, Cassie."

"I will. Talk to you again soon."

After disconnecting the call, Mitch blew out a deep sigh. If she wouldn't get on a plane to see him soon, he'd have to suck it up and board a plane. It was either that or he'd be rolling down the highway again.

Chapter 28

INSIDE THE TOWNHOUSE, Cassie's heart skipped a beat as she heard a key being inserted and then turned in the front door lock. Then she heard Mitch's wonderful laugh. He was talking with someone, maybe on his phone. The door opened a crack.

"Aren't you going to check your mail?" Definitely a female voice. Young. Sounded pretty, too. Cassie wouldn't be able to explain it if asked, but as a general rule, an unattractive woman didn't sound like *that*. Her voice was low, teasing, and downright sultry.

"Okay, I'll check to humor you. I might have a birthday card from my insurance agent."

The woman laughed and her next comment was muffled. Mitch must know this woman well to have such a good camaraderie with her.

"Thanks for the surprise visit. A night out will be good for me. I've needed this."

Cassie wished she hadn't heard that comment. *Have I made a huge mistake?* When she'd talked with him earlier on the phone, she had to resist the urge to blurt out that she was standing inside his townhouse. She'd enjoyed it, believing it would only add to his surprise. Now, she was second-guessing herself. What *was* she doing? Goodness, standing in the front hall of the man's home like she belonged there. She felt like she'd done something wrong, as though she'd broken into Mitch's private residence and had no right to be there. Even though Amy had arranged it and Landon had given her a spare key, their plan to surprise Mitch suddenly didn't seem like such a great idea. What to do?

She darted a frantic glance around the living room of the elegant home. Should she clasp her hands together and greet Mitch and his female guest as they came through the door? No, that wouldn't do. At best, she'd surprise him and at worst, he'd throw her out on his front doorstep. Spying a door she assumed led to the kitchen, Cassie made a mad dash toward it. Just in time. Within seconds, she heard them coming into the townhouse.

How did she get herself into these situations? She took a deep breath, trying to calm down. Digging her cell phone out of her purse on the kitchen table, Cassie punched in Amy's cell phone number. She could hear their animated voices on the other side of the door. Did the woman laugh at everything Mitch said? Please. She started to pace, but the floors were made from hardwood and her sandals made a clacking sound. Clack clack. They had to go. Holding the phone against her shoulder, Cassie leaned her hip against the table and tugged off one shoe and then the other.

Mitch's dog—Sam Longhorn Lemons or whatever Mark Twain's real name was—padded over to her. He was a terrible watchdog, thank goodness, or

166

this could get dicey real quick. As soon as she'd let herself in the townhouse earlier in the afternoon, the dog had greeted her with a wagging tail. He'd bowled her over on the living room floor and covered her with sloppy wet kisses. She'd had a few pets in her life, and this dog was a complete love bug.

"Not now," she told him, keeping her voice low when he used his paw to push his ceramic food dish across the floor. When he moved closer and nudged her leg with his furry head, she sighed. "I don't know where your food is, you big, old shaggy love bug. Your master's home now. Go see Mitch!" She pointed to the door as if the dog could understand. Surely he heard Mitch's voice. Then again, maybe he was half-deaf.

"Come on, Amy. Pick up, pick up, pick up." Cassie's heart pounded so hard, she hoped she wasn't in danger of dropping from a heart attack right on-the-spot. Wouldn't that be something? Mitch would come into the kitchen with this other woman and find an Alabama hick sprawled on the fancy hardwood floor. What an embarrassment.

The dog was still in the kitchen, too, seemingly more interested in being fed than slobbering all over his master. Sitting beside his empty bowl, he gave her a forlorn look. "Right. Like you're neglected. Is that all males can think of?" Cassie started to chew on a fingernail, something she hadn't done in years. Not wanting to mess up the nails she'd taken great care to manicure and paint a pale pink, she dropped her hand to her side.

"So, how's the romantic reunion going?" Amy said a few seconds later.

"Mitch got home a few minutes ago, but he's with a woman." Nothing like spitting it out without so much as a friendly greeting. *Calm down.* She trusted Mitch and needed to give him the benefit of the doubt. She hadn't expected to see him with another woman. Why, he might be hugging and kissing her right now. The mere thought of it made her want to throw up. This was a scenario she hadn't imagined in the many times she'd envisioned their reunion. Swallowing hard, Cassie took a deep breath and moved one hand over her stomach.

"What?" Amy sounded as incredulous as *she* felt. "I'm sure there's a perfectly logical explanation."

"Maybe there is, but now I don't know what to do. Jumping out and yelling *Surprise!* somehow doesn't seem appropriate."

"Mitch often goes out with work colleagues after hours. Maybe he stopped by to change his clothes."

"With a woman in tow?" Cassie lowered her voice. Was that a habit with him? She didn't like it, but it wasn't as though she had any claims on the man. Or did she? This was so weird.

"Okay, I can see why you'd be a little upset, Cass, but let's withhold judgment until we have the facts. What does she look like?"

"Why does *that* matter?" She practically hissed the question, but it wasn't wise to alienate Amy.

"Humor me. Open the kitchen door a crack and see if they're still in view. Then tell me what she looks like."

"All right, but it'd better not creak." Tiptoeing to the door, Cassie tentatively pushed it open.

"So, when are you going to tell her?"

Mitch removed his tie and unbuttoned his shirt a couple of buttons. *You'd better not remove anything else, mister.* She could hear Amy talking on the phone and covered it with her hand, smothering the sound. Being caught in the act of spying would be the ultimate humiliation. This wasn't good any way she looked at it. She wanted to know who they were talking about. Was *she* the topic of their conversation? Maybe it was egotistical to think that way. She certainly hadn't flown all the way to New York to find him with another woman. Oh, what a fine mess.

"I'm hoping the next time I see her," Mitch said. "It's not exactly one of those things I want to blurt out in a random moment, you know? And I'd prefer a face-to-face meeting."

Stretching out on the sofa, Sultry kicked off her ridiculously high pumps and flexed both feet. She appeared to be of medium height, slender with her mid-length dark hair cut in a chic style. "I'm sure you'll figure it out. You've never had a problem with women before."

Cassie's cheeks warmed and she stifled a groan. This is what she got for trying to surprise him. And eavesdropping. Neither one led to anything good. Why couldn't the floor open up and swallow her? All she wanted to do was march into the living room, put that woman's shoes back on her feet, wish her a good life and push—send—her out the front door.

Mitch moved toward the kitchen door. "Want something to drink?"

Oh, oh. Cassie moved away from the door. Although large, the kitchen was pretty much like Texas—wide and full of open spaces. Where could she hide? This was stupid. She should go out there and announce her presence. Wouldn't that be a kick in the pants?

If this was a huge mistake to come to New York, she might as well find out now.

~

"Hang on a sec." Mitch reached for his phone and checked the display. "Better take it. Hey, Amy. What's up?"

"Who's the woman, Mitch?"

"What are you talking about?" How could she know?

"The woman with you in the townhouse now."

He glanced around the living room and strolled into the front hall. "I repeat, what are you talking about now? Did you have cameras installed in here to spy on me?" Talk about invasion of privacy.

"No, of course not. Answer the question, please."

"If you must know, Celeste is in town on business and stopped by the office to wish me an early happy birthday. We're going to dinner."

Silence ensued on the other end of the line for a few seconds. "Good to know, I have to say. Why didn't Celeste call me?"

"Because we're in cahoots to shut you out of our little sibling reunion, that's why. She's been in town all of a half-hour. Give me a break. I suppose I can convince her to include you in our private celebration. We're headed over to Café Eduardo for dinner in about an hour. You know, the scene of your most famous conquest."

She laughed. "Stop calling it that. Makes it sound illicit. What time's the reservation?"

"Eight o'clock. Under my name. It's fashionably late, but it was the only reservation I could get at the last minute. Hope to see you there. Bring your husband along. He's always good for a few laughs, plus he's got some serious clout with Eduardo and his staff."

"Landon's still working, but I'll call and tell him to meet us there. Don't hang up."

"Why not? Are we going to discuss the weather? I'm glad the rain finally stopped."

"Stop being so flippant and go into the kitchen."

"My kitchen? Why?"

"Yes. Do it, please. Now."

"Actually, I was about to get Celeste some water. Wait. How *did* you know she's here in the townhouse?" This was getting pretty weird.

"Go into the kitchen and you'll know."

"Tell me why you're being a crazy woman."

"Just go into the kitchen, Mitch. *Now!*"

"Okay, you win," he said, laughing as he pushed open the door and headed straight to the cabinet to get a glass for Celeste's water. Something caught the corner of his eye. Something bright and sitting on his kitchen table, all demure and sweet in a pretty dress and. . .looking absolutely incredible with his dog on the floor at her feet.

"Cassie?" His heart jumped. "Amy, I'll talk to you in an hour. Or two. Whenever."

"I heard," Amy said, laughing. "I think you slobbered through the phone."

"Be quiet. I'll deal with you later."

"Café Eduardo. An hour. And happy birthday, Mitch."

"Best gift you've ever given me, sis. Thanks forever." He tossed his cell phone on the table and planted his hands on the table, sandwiching Cassie between his propped arms. "You are a sight for these weary eyes." His gaze roamed a leisurely path over her lovely features, drinking her in like a thirsty man at the well. "Welcome to New York, Moonbeam. Hands down, this is the best surprise of my life."

"Spying on you from behind your kitchen door is very draining. I need to be revived."

"Gladly." He lowered his lips to hers, hoping his kiss conveyed how much he'd missed her. This kiss was the best ever, even better than the ones they'd shared in Houston. Delicious. Tantalizing. From all their phone conversations, Skype sessions and emails, this girl from Alabama was settled in his heart. He'd always teased Landon about falling so hard and fast for Amy. But ever since being with Cassie in Houston and spending such quality time with her, he'd lived the reality.

Mitch heard a throat clearing behind him a minute later. "Aren't you going to introduce us?"

Cassie flushed deep red and struggled to get down from the table. After helping her down from her perch, Mitch put his arm around her and they faced Celeste together. He hoped she wouldn't make this awkward. "Celeste, may I introduce Cassie Thorenson. Cassie, this is my youngest sister."

"Nice to meet you." Celeste was as cool and professional as ever. She didn't hug Cassie, didn't offer her hand, but neither did she look her up and down like she was appraising her worth. He'd seen her do that very thing with a number of women before, so he had to thank the Lord for small favors.

"Mitch has told me quite a bit about you." Celeste gave him a wry grin.

"Oh?" Cassie's voice sounded nervous and he reached for her hand.

"Totally good. No need to worry," Celeste said. "I thought my brother had come in here to get me some ice water. I came to check on him."

"Let me get it for you." Amazed, Mitch watched as Cassie made herself at home in his kitchen. If he allowed his imagination to run away with him, he'd envision her wearing his shirt, getting ready to fix breakfast for them. *Whoa, rein it in.* Where had that thought come from? She'd only just arrived and already his imagination had run amuck. If he didn't know better, he'd think he was delusional. Now who was the crazy one? Besides, that scenario would only happen if she ever agreed to marry him for real.

"Watch it, brother," Celeste whispered, leaning close. "Your thoughts are showing."

"Be quiet." Openly admiring Cassie was one thing, but he needed to be careful not to cross the line into disrespect. Women had no clue what a fine line it was for a man sometimes. Cassie was the sexiest woman he'd ever known because *she* didn't know it. That fact in and of itself was a huge turn on that women didn't seem to understand. Yeah, he'd be asking the Lord's forgiveness later tonight. *Help me keep my thoughts pure, Lord.*

Cassie opened a couple of cabinets. "Third one to the left of the refrigerator," he said, walking toward her.

"I've got it." Grabbing a glass, she asked Celeste if she wanted crushed or cubed ice.

"Crushed. You're a doll. Thanks," Celeste said a minute later as she took the glass from Cassie. When she raised her pinky finger, Mitch wanted to swat her. Both of his sisters did the same thing—Amy from unconscious habit, but with Celeste, it was downright affected. Pure snobbishness all the way down to her designer suit. Amy always shopped off-the-rack, but Celeste had to have the latest creation from the best designers. No wonder her fiancé had cut her loose. The guy probably figured out he couldn't afford the stress, both monetarily and emotionally.

"Mitch, would you like some water, too?" Cassie smiled. "You look a little parched."

"Can you give us a minute alone?" Mitch said to his sister.

Celeste's hazel-eyed stare moved between him and Cassie before she mumbled, "Certainly. You know where to find me when you're. . .done."

He shot her his best *that's uncalled for* look. She must have missed the course in tact at her Ivy League college. "We'll be sure and do that. If you need to freshen up before we meet Amy and Landon at Café Eduardo, you might want to do it now."

Celeste hightailed it out of the kitchen, making him chuckle. That's all it took—one subtle suggestion that something about her appearance might be amiss. Heaven forbid.

"Where were we?" Mitch walked back to where Cassie crouched beside the table, stroking his dog. "You've made a lifelong friend, haven't you, Sammie?"

"Sammie," she said, kissing the dog's head and ruffling his ears. "I like that nickname."

He liked how Cassie had bonded so quickly with his dog. He hadn't taken kindly to a few of the women he'd brought home, and Sammie liked most everyone. Perhaps he should have paid better attention to that obvious clue. "I only use his full name when he's in trouble."

"Oh, I doubt you ever get into trouble, Sammie." Giving him another quick kiss, Cassie rose to her feet. "We'd better feed him. He was pretty insistent before you came into the kitchen."

Mitch walked over to the pantry, opened the long door and pulled out a plastic container. "I keep his food in here. For reference in case it ever comes in handy." The food dish wasn't in its usual corner beside the water dish. "Sammie? What'd you do with your dish?"

"I think I know." With a smile, Cassie ducked under the table and emerged a few seconds later, holding the dish in the air like a prize. "Got it! Come on, sweet boy." She filled the food dish and returned the container to the pantry while Mitch grabbed the water dish.

As he carefully lowered the water dish to the floor, he caught Cassie's frown. "I don't think Celeste likes me."

"Well, I don't think she likes me very much, either, and I'm fairly certain Amy's on-the-fence on that one, too." He shrugged. "At least Celeste gets along fine with Mom."

"She must like you and Amy or she wouldn't come to visit."

"The thing is, I don't think Celeste likes herself very much right now. You were right about one thing, though. I'm absolutely parched, but for *you*." Pulling her into his arms, Mitch gave her a gentle, light kiss. "How long can you stay?"

"Until Monday morning."

"Plans can be changed," he murmured, unable to stay away from her. "Let's negotiate."

"Your negotiating methods are underhanded. Come on. We'd better get out there or Celeste will definitely think the worst of me." Cassie tugged on her shoes and then, taking him by the hand, led him back into the living room.

"No need to worry. She's still primping."

Cassie glanced down at her pretty dress and sweater. "Do I look okay? Maybe I should go over to Amy and Landon's and change into something a little more fancy?"

"You're perfect as you are and I'm not letting you out of my sight."

"Fine by me." When her lovely smile emerged, it made everything right in his world.

Chapter 29

CASSIE HAD NEVER seen so many utensils on a dinner table. She knew the difference between the dinner fork and the salad fork, of course, and she recognized the soup spoon. The sideways fork at the top of her place setting was the one that stumped her. And why did Celeste stick out her pinky every time she took a drink? Was something wrong with her finger so she couldn't bend it?

Mitch, Amy and Landon drew her into the conversation as much as possible. "Tell me about your fiancé, Celeste," Cassie said after their salads had been delivered and Mitch asked the blessing. Why were they all looking at her like she'd asked if they'd forgotten their deodorant? She stopped chewing in the middle of her first bite. She'd thought the question would gain her some favor with Mitch's youngest sister, but her apparent blunder managed the opposite.

"I'm not sure I have one of those anymore." Celeste sniffed and took another drink of her water with lime.

"I'm sorry. I didn't know." Cassie's spirits plummeted lower when she noted the absence of a sparkling diamond on her ring finger. Mitch couldn't have mentioned the broken engagement during one of their many phone conversations?

"It's okay." Celeste waved her hand. "Ashton and I are currently on a break. It could go either way, but right now, it's not looking hopeful."

Cassie prayed under her breath that Mitch's sister wouldn't burst into tears, but somehow she didn't seem the type. "Guess you can't take me anywhere," she whispered to Mitch, grateful when Amy engaged Celeste in a conversation about something work-related.

"I should have told you," Mitch whispered in her ear. "Sorry. The breakup happened a couple of weeks ago, so it's still raw." Beneath the table, Mitch reached for her hand, giving it a little squeeze.

After the salads were cleared and replaced by their entrées, Cassie focused on her chicken breast and fresh steamed vegetables. Speaking of raw, the carrots were so crunchy she thought she'd send one flying across the table when she bit into it. At least the rest of the meal was uneventful.

"Amy, would you mind if I camp out at your place tonight?" Celeste asked as they prepared to leave the restaurant together. "It's late, and I'm too tired to drive. I still need to be up and out early tomorrow, though, since I have an event tomorrow night."

"Our home is your home," Landon said, helping Amy with her lightweight wrap he'd claimed at the coat check. "You're welcome to stay for however long you need." Cassie caught the grateful glance Amy gave him.

"Thank you." Celeste's gaze moved to her. "I assume you're staying with Amy and Landon, too?"

Cassie couldn't miss the implication that perhaps she might be staying with Mitch instead.

"Yes, she's staying with the Warnick side of the family. Good night, Celeste," Mitch said, moving forward to give his sister a quick peck on the cheek. "Thanks for the birthday surprise. As always, it's great to see you."

"You, too. I'll watch over your Alabama rose tonight."

Mitch wisely refrained from making a comment and she tried not to be offended by the rather condescending manner in which the line was delivered. Celeste certainly knew how to push buttons, both in Mitch and Amy. Families. Did they realize how thankful they should be to even *have* each other? Although she knew they did, it made Cassie miss Tagg all over again. That sharp little pinch shot through her again. Would she ever get over that feeling of loss? More importantly, would she ever *want* to stop missing him?

I never want to forget him.

She missed Tagg more than Mama. Maybe that was wrong, and she'd prayed about it quite often, but Tagg had always been there for her in ways her mother had never been able to fulfill. Same with Daddy.

"Let me say good night to Cassie and then I'll send her on the way with you," Mitch told the others as he led her to a private alcove. "Tell me why it's not even my birthday yet, and I feel as though it's already been the best of my life."

"Mr. Jacobsen, the things you say." Cassie lowered her gaze, unexpectedly shy.

He lifted her chin with his fingertips, forcing her to look at him. Such a handsome man. She could hardly believe she was in one of the most exciting cities in the world with Mitch. She'd seen the way other women watched him. The way he moved, the way he looked, his obvious respect for women and his deep, masculine voice.

"Cassie, don't stop me from saying it this time. Promise me."

She eased into a gentle smile. "How can I stop you if I don't know what you're going to say?"

Mitch brushed his fingers over her cheek, his touch the softest caress that sent shivers through her. "I'm in love with you. I was pretty much there when I left Houston. When you're with me, I'm more alive than I've been in years. The kind of alive that makes me wonder what I did all these years without you in my life. The kind of alive that makes me want to spend the rest of my years finding out more about you, discovering you and loving you."

She blinked hard and tried to stop her jaw from gaping. Such beautiful words, but they confused her. "Is that. . .are you *proposing* to me, Mitch?" Sure sounded like a proposal.

"Not officially, but put it this way: if we stumbled upon a mass marriage ceremony in Central Park tomorrow, I'd be seriously tempted. We could get on with our lives and then have another ceremony later on for our family and friends. And assorted pets." He smiled. "You've already won over Sammie. That's a huge plus in your favor."

"Maybe we should stay away from Central Park then."

"Are you turning me down?" A flicker of hurt passed over his features.

"No, I'm not." She kept her voice quiet, her tone soft. "I'm saying we should take things as they come and not rush things. But I miss you every day, Mitch. When I think of you, it makes me smile. You don't know how many times I've looked at those postcards you sent to me. You've kind of worked your way into my affections, you know. Is this what you meant when you told Celeste you wanted to tell me something face-to-face?"

He feigned shock and chuckled. "Eavesdropping on me in my own abode, were you?"

"Never," she murmured, lost in his touch when he cupped her face and lifted her lips to his. His skin was warm, his lips firm but gentle, and she loved the aftershave he wore. She met him willingly, without fear, without hesitation and hoped her kiss might convey what she might not be able to express with words.

"I'd better escort you out now or they're going to send a search party." A couple of minutes later, Mitch helped Cassie into Landon's white Range Rover, tucking her in the back beside Celeste.

"Sleep well tonight, Moonbeam, and have fun with Amy in the morning. Keep your phone on because I'll be calling."

"I will. Good night, Mitch." She leaned close and kissed his cheek, rough with the beginnings of a new growth of beard. "I'll see you tomorrow afternoon."

Cassie missed him as soon as Landon pulled away from the curb.

Chapter 30

"WELL, NOW, WASN'T that sweet?" Celeste crossed one long leg over the other and gave her a smile. "I'd say my big brother is smitten."

"As well he should be," Amy said from the front, her voice a hair above chastisement.

"Amy tells me you've known Mitch since they flew down to Houston for Valentine's Day. I, for one, couldn't be more thrilled that he's found someone real. Someone. . .down to earth. Simple and uncomplicated. Heaven knows," Celeste said, glancing out the window, "he's dated a string of women who could barely tell time or tie their shoelaces."

"Celeste!" Amy gasped, twisting in her seat to give her a pointed stare. "Please show a little sensitivity. What's wrong with you tonight?"

Landon glanced at her in the mirror. "Celeste, we're sorry about your parting ways with Ashton, but there's no need to badmouth anyone."

She released a sigh. "Okay, perhaps that was an exaggeration. But you know as well as I do that our brother hasn't always let his head rule his heart. Seriously, Cassie," Celeste said, shifting slightly towards her, "he's picked women that were completely wrong for him. No wonder he likes you so much. You're a breath of fresh air that's blown into his life at exactly the right time."

Cassie couldn't let that one go. "What do you mean, the right time?" Her stomach had suddenly turned sour. How thankful she was that Amy was the sister who lived in New York. She already suspected she wouldn't be sorry when Celeste left early tomorrow morning.

"I think he's finally reached the point where he's come to some kind of resolution about Brad's death. Tragic as it was, he allowed it to color his actions. He made some bad choices, including women who weren't what he needed. Too bad he hadn't met you before he did all those dumb things."

"No one can say how they'd react given the same circumstances," Amy said. Her voice was low but she spoke clearly and succinctly. Her tones were almost clipped and so unlike her. Cassie sensed Amy's barely contained anger, and that, too, was unlike her even-tempered friend. She prayed Celeste didn't push her to the limit. She saw Landon move his hand across the seat. If anyone could keep Amy calm, it would be her husband. These two shared a great relationship—passionate, mutually respectful, and loving.

"Right. Just like no one could imagine people would hate us so much they'd use our planes as weapons, fly them into our towers and destroy the innocence of an entire nation."

Cassie glanced over at Celeste. Her words, bitter as they were, also conveyed a great sadness.

"Celeste, did *you* lose someone you cared about in the Twin Towers?"

Celeste snapped her gaze back to her so fast it was a wonder she didn't seriously hurt her neck. "How could you even know that?"

What could she say that Celeste would accept and believe?

"Cassie's very intuitive," Amy said, lowering the visor and giving her a barely perceptible nod, reflected in the mirror. If it was meant to be an encouragement, it worked.

"I didn't know her well, but I lost a friend, yes. I used to work with her at my marketing firm in Philly. The worst part of it was that she had an appointment in the North Tower that morning. Didn't even work there."

"I'm sorry for the loss of your friend. As bad as you feel for your friend— and not to downplay the sadness—I imagine it was multiplied even more for Mitch."

"He turned against God Himself, Cassie. Did you know that?"

"He told me about it, but I don't know that I'd call it turning away from God." Cassie knew she had to defend Mitch, but to his own sister? She had no doubt Amy would have a word with Celeste later in private. "Yes, he lost his way for a while and acted out of pain and grief from the deep loss of Brad, but he never completely lost his faith because. . .well, that's not possible. Once you place your trust in Him, He's always there, living inside of us."

"Our dad was a pastor, so we know all that and don't need a refresher course." Celeste checked her watch and crossed her arms.

"Celeste. . ." A note of warning surfaced in Amy's voice.

"Mitch is a quitter," Celeste snapped. "He ran away from his medical career when he should have stuck it out. Doctors make mistakes all the time and they're either covered up or people are paid off to keep them quiet."

Lord, please help me. Give me Your words. "I might be simple and uncomplicated, but I appreciate Mitch for his strong character and honorable qualities. He has so *many*, Celeste. As far as his medical career, he almost lost a patient. I can't begin to imagine what that would be like, can you? Maybe God used that situation to show him he's not the right man for the job, so to speak. That he's not destined to be a doctor. But he has the right amount of compassion to help others in whatever he chooses to do. If that's as a stockbroker, then so be it. I think Mitch knows there's something better for his talents and abilities. He trusts the Lord to lead him, and I have no doubt He will."

"You haven't known our brother as long as we have," Celeste shot back. "Whether or not Mitch pays attention to the Lord's will or decides to do things his own way is the key. Next thing we know, he'll change his mind again and go off on some other career path."

"Nothing wrong with that," Landon said from the front, and Amy echoed her agreement.

Cassie settled back in her seat, content to remain silent for the remainder of the hopefully short trip. Sounded like Mitch wasn't the only one in the family to do things his—or her—own way.

~

Cassie sat on the bed, dressed in her sleep pants and a T-shirt, trying to read her Bible. Hard to do when her thoughts kept wandering to a handsome man in a townhouse not that far away. After hearing Celeste's harsh words, she felt protective of Mitch. Celeste's breakup with Ashton notwithstanding, it was no excuse for her bad behavior and critical comments. Bowing her head, Cassie began to pray.

She startled when a light knock sounded on the door not long into her prayer. "Come in." She glanced at the clock. Almost eleven. The door swung open and instead of Amy, as she'd expected, Celeste stood in the doorway. She'd changed from her business suit into jeans and a red Phillies T-shirt. That was a shock, but it made her more real, more approachable. Without her high heels, she seemed a few inches shorter and closer to her own height. Her face was devoid of the heavier makeup she'd worn earlier, revealing her pretty complexion and lovely features.

"I'd like you to come with me, if you're not too tired."

"Um, okay. Where are we going?"

Celeste frowned. "Trust me."

The woman had been condescending, arrogant and borderline rude, and now she asked her to trust her? *No judgments. Trust her.* Since Celeste was leaving early in the morning, maybe she'd come to make amends for her earlier behavior. And now Cassie needed to swallow her misgivings and treat her with Christian kindness.

"Let me change and I'll be right out."

"No, you're fine like that."

Some girls might go outside in their pajamas, but she wasn't about to do such a thing. "Celeste, these—"

"No one else will see you but me. What size are you? Four? Six?"

"Eight, actually. Why?"

"That'll do fine. Wait for me in the living room and I'll meet you there in five minutes." Celeste paused in the doorway. "You don't need your purse." With that, she did an about face and headed back down the hall.

"Are you serious?" Cassie muttered under her breath, swinging her legs over the edge of the bed. "Lord, help me with this one. Life is never dull around the Jacobsen family, that's for sure." Walking across the room to the dresser, she picked up her brush, scooped her hair into a long ponytail and then secured it with an elastic band. She caught a glimpse of her purse sitting by the bed. Where on earth was Celeste taking her that she wouldn't need her ID? If, God forbid, something happened, shouldn't she have it with her? After pulling out her driver's license—for peace of mind—and tucking it in the pocket of her sleep pants, Cassie closed the door behind her.

"Let's go," Celeste said, meeting her in the living room and heading to the front door. She swung it open and waited for her to pass into the corridor of the high rise residence.

"Now can you please tell me where we're going?" Cassie asked when Celeste clicked the doors of Landon's Range Rover. "And does Landon know you're taking his car?"

"Yes, he knows. Amy knows. They're fine with it. Happy about it, as a matter of fact."

Cassie settled back into the leather seat, wishing either one or both of the Warnicks were along for this little midnight joy ride. Apparently all three Jacobsen siblings had an unpredictable nature. At least Amy and Mitch demonstrated a good amount of humor and made everything more of an adventure. Maybe she should try and make conversation, but she was tired and wasn't up to it tonight.

"It's not far," Celeste said. Thankfully, less than three minutes later, she pulled into the parking garage of a hotel a few blocks away.

Climbing out of the Range Rover, Cassie glanced at their surroundings and resisted the urge to plant her hands on her hips. "Are you kidnapping me, Celeste? You have to admit, this is more than a little strange, hauling me away so late at night, not telling me where you're taking me and—"

"Here," Celeste said, tossing something at her she'd retrieved from the backseat. She closed the car door and clicked the lock on the key fob.

Cassie stared at the slinky blue fabric in her hands. A one-piece swimsuit with the tags still attached? She raised a skeptical brow. "We're going swimming? At this hour of the night?"

"Yes." The way she nodded, her face composed and serious, Celeste must not believe doing such a thing was in any way out of the ordinary.

"But I can't—" Cassie hesitated, not sure how much she should admit to the other woman.

"I know, and that's why we're here."

"Because you're trying to drown me?" No wonder Celeste hadn't wanted her to bring ID. It would take longer to identify an out-of-town Jane Doe.

Celeste cracked a smile. "Look, I know we got off on the wrong foot, but you mean a lot to Mitch and you've been friends with Amy a long time. And. . .I hope eventually we can be friends."

"So," Cassie said slowly, trying to formulate her next question.

"Mitch is worried about you because you can't swim." Celeste brushed a loose strand of dark hair behind one ear. "I keep a few swimsuits on hand at Amy's and figured no time like the present."

"You're going to teach me to swim? Tonight? I don't think there's a *Learn to Swim in an Hour* class, is there?" Cassie hadn't meant to sound so sarcastic and she bit her lower lip.

"No, but I can teach you a few basics that will help. Can you at least tread water?"

"I think so, but I haven't done it in a long time."

"It's easy," Celeste gestured for her to come alongside her as she started to walk through the garage. "Like riding a bike or whatever. Basic survival skills."

"Did Mitch ask you to do this?" Cassie followed as Celeste opened another glass door leading to a service elevator in the middle of the building.

"No. It's totally my idea, so you can blame me for this one."

Cassie remained silent on the ride to the top floor of the hotel. "Please tell me we're not breaking any rules or won't get arrested and hauled off to jail or something. I've already entered a Manhattan townhouse, probably illegally. For the record, I'm not proud of it."

Celeste laughed then, and it softened her features, making her even prettier. "Mitch isn't complaining. Bringing you here in the first place was Amy's brilliant idea for his birthday, and this is my gift to him. Rest easy. I know the manager of the hotel and I'm welcome to use the pool anytime I'm in town."

Headed out of the elevator, Celeste led the way to another glass door. *Pool Area. Swim At Your Own Risk.* No kidding.

"I called to let my manager friend know I was bringing you here," Celeste continued. "Hotel Security's been informed, and no one should bother us since the pool's closed to the guests as of eleven o'clock."

"I see." She didn't really, but Cassie was tired and her brain was muddled. And now she was supposed to have a swim lesson and be happy about it. At least it'd been a couple of hours since dinner. Wasn't that the rule—wait a couple of hours after eating so you don't cramp, thereby decreasing the chances of drowning? She shook her head. No reason to think of the "d" word.

"I was a champion swimmer in high school. Went to nationals and briefly entertained going for the Olympic trials, but I didn't. I also swam for Bryn Mawr."

"I'm impressed. Congratulations." Hopefully that came across as enthusiasm, not sarcasm.

Celeste stopped in front of the women's locker room. "We can change in here." She flipped on a light switch and fluorescent lights systematically illuminated the area.

An hour later—after a rigorous swim-by-numbers lesson in the indoor, heated pool—Cassie rested a moment, arms crossed at the edge of the pool. She panted a bit, not having worked out so strenuously at anything in a long time. Celeste offered her hand, and grabbing hold of it, Cassie lifted out of the pool.

"Thanks, Celeste. That was energizing. You're a good swim coach." She squeezed the water out of her ponytail and rotated her shoulders. She'd definitely *feel* this workout tomorrow.

"You're welcome. Remember the rules about what to do and not do and you should be fine if the occasion ever arises."

"You didn't have to do this."

Celeste gave her a small smile. "I'm not such a bad person, but I don't know when to quit sometimes, as you witnessed earlier."

"I don't think you're a bad person at all," Cassie said. A couple of hours ago, she might not have been able to make that statement with complete honesty. If nothing else, Celeste's caring gesture in bringing her here showed she genuinely cared about Mitch, and that's what mattered most.

"I'm glad you feel that way. Like I said, I hope we can be friends."

Cassie smiled. "I'd like that, too." She could rest easier knowing they'd formed some type of bond, however odd, on that hotel rooftop. And when he found out, Mitch could rest easy that she'd learned a few things about staying afloat in the water.

"Tell me about growing up with Mitch," Cassie said after she'd changed and they were headed back to Amy and Landon's residence. Leaning her head back on the seat, she listened and laughed once or twice at Celeste's retelling of pranks Mitch had played on her.

"Mitch was a great big brother. He always watched out for Amy and me and even slugged a guy once when he got too fresh with me."

"Really? My brother did that once for me, too, but I was only six at the time. Chase Rollins tried to kiss me on the playground." They shared a grin. When Celeste asked about her family, she gave her the basics.

"I'm sorry you lost your brother, Cassie. That helps you understand the kind of tragic, sudden loss Mitch suffered, though, doesn't it? Sometimes people can express sympathy and regret, but unless they've gone through the same thing—or almost the same thing—they can't truly understand at a ground zero level, so to speak. Maybe that's a bad analogy, and I don't say it to be cruel or disrespectful to those who died on 9/11, but it's true all the same."

When they parted ways, Cassie thanked her again. "Have a safe trip back to Philly."

"Will do. I'm glad we were able to spend some time together. You're good for my brother," Celeste said. "Our mom's going to love you."

Cassie didn't expect Celeste's approval to mean so much, but it did. And she hoped she was right in terms of their mother. The thought struck her as she climbed back into bed that Mitch would eventually ask to meet her father. What then? She only prayed Daddy wouldn't be sitting in jail at the time.

"Lord, I'm too tired to worry about that one tonight," she mumbled, closing her eyes as soon as her head hit the pillow. "Giving this one to You, my friend."

Chapter 31

ℭASSIE AND AMY poked in and out of a few shops on Friday morning in an elusive search for the perfect gift for Mitch's birthday. She'd waited until coming to New York to find something, believing it would be easier on his home turf. Not so. More like an impossible task. Everything was either too expensive, too trite, too silly. . .or not right for one reason or another. Not that she thought Mitch would be picky, but *she* couldn't be pleased. "Call me Goldilocks," she said under her breath as they left yet another store empty-handed. Never one to shy away from a challenge, she held out hope she'd find something before returning to the townhouse.

Maybe it was the thrill of being with Mitch or being in a new, exciting place, but New York wasn't nearly as scary as she'd expected. Amy warned her which areas to avoid if she ever ventured out of the townhouse on her own. "Call Louie if you ever want to go anywhere while Mitch is at work. He'll take good care of you."

Some of the shopkeepers eyed her as though she was a curiosity once they caught wind of her accent. Apparently, some native New Yorkers hadn't met anyone from Alabama up close and personal before, making her somewhat of an anomaly. As with most people, a smile and a kind word went a long way. Trying to understand some of *their* accents proved challenging. Same words, but she found it interesting how different they could sound depending on where someone was raised. That point was driven home when a woman with a British accent stopped them to ask how to find a place called Bonnie's.

"Oh, you must mean Barney's," Amy said. "It's over on Madison."

As Amy gave the woman directions, Cassie waited, content to observe the world go by—a mix of tourists and locals, business professionals, high society matrons, and families with children whose clothing cost more than her monthly condo rent payment. The skyscrapers were so tall they seemed to touch the sky. Limousines were lined up in front of some of the higher-end stores and uniformed chauffeurs congregated on the sidewalk. How the other half lives indeed. She'd never seen such opulence everywhere she turned. Then again, she was in one of the ritziest sections of Manhattan. She found the energy of the city invigorating. The pace of her life had been slow compared to the hustle bustle of the big city, but experiencing it firsthand, she could understand why Amy, Landon and Mitch liked living here.

"I'm sorry about Celeste," Amy said as they perused the offerings in an upscale men's clothing store. "She was worse than usual last night. I think she was tired, and as you witnessed, that's never a good thing. She puts on fancy airs because she's always had this misguided attitude that acting haughty and snooty will make people admire her. Sometimes it has the opposite effect and she comes across as being cold. What most people don't realize is that Celeste is rather shy. As a general rule, she tends to be quieter, believe it or not."

"She is? I mean, she does?" Cassie wished she hadn't blurted that one out although it was her gut reaction.

Amy smiled. "The idea to take you to the pool last night was all Celeste, for the record, a way of giving her approval of your relationship."

"We had a nice talk on the way back," Cassie said. "Sometimes those late night or early morning talks can be good. You know, when you're calm at the end of the day, and more introspective. I think we actually bonded a little." Her shoulders were a little sore, but no need to bring that up since getting to know Celeste was definitely worth aching muscles.

"I'm glad, and I know Celeste feels the same way. Oh, look. Landon would love that shirt over there." Amy led the way to a nearby counter and checked the tag. "Don't think so," she said, shaking her head. That statement made Cassie love her all the more. Amy didn't spend extravagant amounts even though she could. One peek at the price tag on a red silk tie was enough to make Cassie want to leave. People really paid that much for a necktie? She knew Mitch loved the color red, but no way could she justify the expense.

"Why don't we duck into the coffee shop around the corner and grab something to eat and drink?" Amy said as they exited the store.

"I like that suggestion. We could use a little break."

"This is the scene of the crime, so to speak," Amy told her as they settled at a back table after picking up their orders at the counter.

Cassie's eyes grew wide. "You mean this is the place where Mitch decked Landon?"

"Exactly." Amy's lips upturned. "He told you about that, huh? Guess you're the woman to ask if I want to know anything about my brother."

They sipped their coffee while exchanging more gift ideas for Mitch and sharing a piece of delicious cinnamon pecan coffeecake. "I already picked up a couple of small items for him, but bringing you here is going to be pretty hard to top." Amy's eyes met hers over the rim of her cup. "Please don't feel like you have to get him anything for the sake of giving him a wrapped gift, Cassie. Seriously, all you need to do is put a pretty bow on your head and that'll do the trick."

"Thanks, I think," Cassie said, laughing.

"Has Mitch made any plans to show you around the city? I know you're not here for long—this time—but Saturday is a good day to get around much easier since there's fewer people downtown."

"I'll let him decide, especially since he didn't know I was coming. Being together will be fun. I didn't come to see any sights but Mitch." She blushed when Amy laughed. "You know what I mean." A random idea popped into her mind. "Is there a library near here, by any chance?"

"There's one four blocks away. It's the one closest to the townhouse. Why?"

"I'm thinking we can go there and check the computer for a list of Mark Twain's books. I'll print out the list and then we can take it to one of those secondhand bookstores Mitch likes."

Something lit in Amy's expression. "I think I see where you're going with this, clever girl. Excellent idea. I got him a first edition of *Innocents Abroad* a few years ago in a bookstore in SoHo and he went nuts over it."

Cassie's smile downturned. "Forget it, then. I've saved up some money, but I'm sure a first edition will cost more than I can afford. Not that Mitch isn't worth it, but it doesn't sound like it's a very original idea."

"Nonsense. If it comes from you—first edition or not—he'll treasure it even more because you cared enough to indulge one of his passions. I'll pitch in to help, if you want. Trust me, nothing will thrill him more. That's why we should also check the suggested prices for first edition classics—so we'll have a ballpark idea of the cost. Most of the dealers are reputable and know Mitch. He's spent more than a few hours perusing the shelves in some of the local bookstores. Matter of fact, if we drop his name, we'll get first class service." Amy tucked her hand over her arm. "Come on. This will be fun."

"If you say so." She might as well see what they could find and hope the cost didn't give her a stroke.

Entering the front doors of the massive library a few minutes later, Amy pointed her in the direction of the computers. "This was my old stomping grounds when I lived in the townhouse."

Cassie glanced around in awe. From the black-and-white-tiled floors to the Tiffany-style hanging lamps, brass fixtures and dark wood furniture, the library was magnificent. It had to be at least a century old. "I love this place," she said, lowering her voice when she heard it echo. Turning in a slow circle, lifting her gaze to survey the atrium-styled structure, she breathed in deeply of the familiar smell of old books. Call her weird, but she'd always loved it.

"I could spend a lot of time here. One of my favorite places to escape into a whole new world was in our library back home," Cassie said, her voice wistful. "It was free entertainment and I spent hours there every week. But it was nothing like this."

Amy smiled. "No wonder you and Mitch get along so well. He's here almost every Saturday morning." She pointed to a nearby group of tables. "He parks himself over in that general area."

"I can see why," Cassie said. "Let's go check the computer."

Fifteen minutes later, they'd printed out a list of Twain's works as well as some basic information about pricing for vintage books. Amy made everything fun and Cassie had to stifle her laughter a couple of times.

"Hold on a second," Amy said as they walked back toward the entrance. "See that girl behind the reference desk? The one with the dark hair?"

Cassie followed Amy's gaze. "Do you know her?"

"Not really, but Mitch dated her last year. She has a mermaid name. Like that animated movie that came out a few years ago."

Why was Amy telling her about his ex-girlfriend? Cassie's eyes widened. "That's Arielle?"

Amy snapped her gaze back to her. "He actually told you about her?"

"Yes, he mentioned her because. . ." Maybe she shouldn't have said anything considering this was the woman Mitch suspected of "lifting"—his polite term for stealing—a prized sculpture belonging to Grandpa Carlisle from the townhouse. "Okay, don't tell your brother you heard it from me, but he believes Arielle. . . took something from him."

Amy crossed her arms. "Tell me straight, Cass. What 'thing' are we talking about here?"

Cassie's mind worked furiously as she formulated a plan. "So you've never met her, huh?"

"No, I never have. They didn't date very long." Amy eyed her closely. "You've got that look. Reminds me of Mitch. What are you thinking?"

Cassie stepped closer to her friend. "I'm going to tell you, but you can't make a scene or gasp or anything like that. Rein it in, Mrs. Warnick."

Amy's brows rose. "This must be big. Spill it."

Cassie inhaled a quick breath. "Mitch told me he believes Arielle took a sculpture from the townhouse that once belonged to your Grandpa Carlisle."

Amy's eyes grew wide, but she twisted her lips and nodded without saying a word.

"If my plan works, we'll save the first edition Twain idea for another time." Cassie gave her a shaky smile. Her nerves could get the best of her if she allowed them, but she wanted to do this for Mitch and his family. Suddenly, she *needed* to do this for him.

With new resolve, Cassie squared her shoulders and lifted her chin. "Come with me, Amy. We're going to get that sculpture back."

Chapter 32

𝒞ASSIE'S HEART POUNDED as she approached the reference desk and her palms felt damp. Her gaze fell on the nameplate in front of where Arielle worked. Yep, it was the mermaid klepto all right, although that wasn't a charitable thought. Whispering a quick prayer under her breath, hoping this wasn't a completely stupid idea, Cassie stepped up to the counter. *All for Mitch.*

She'd played the lead role in one of her high school productions. Sure, it was pretty much an all-girl play because none of the boys wanted to be caught in a "sissy play." Now seemed the time to call on the old acting skills, rusty as they were.

Arielle acknowledged her with a polite nod as she helped another patron. An older librarian moved over to her with a kindly smile. "How may I assist you today?"

"I'd like to speak with Miss"—Cassie glanced at Arielle's nameplate—"Carson."

"She might be busy for a while longer. May I be of some assistance?"

Well-meaning though she might be, the woman's helpful attitude was starting to irritate her. For once in her life, she didn't *want* someone to be so nice. Life could be so ironic sometimes. "No, thank you. This is a personal matter. I'll wait."

"Very well, then. I'm sure Arielle will be with you soon. Have a pleasant day." The woman quickly disappeared around the corner.

Cassie drummed her fingers across the counter, stopping when Arielle gave her a pointed look. Amy nudged her shoulder. "Let me know if you want me to do or say anything."

"Will do." Beneath veiled lids, she noticed how Arielle spoke in low tones with a man in a red knit stocking cap pulled low over his forehead even though it was fairly warm outside. He wore ripped jeans made to look old. The kind that cost a small fortune because they had some fancy designer's name embroidered on the backside. They hung low on his hips without any belt in sight and the top band of his underwear was clearly on display.

Multiple gold chains were draped around his neck and more dangled from both wrists. Since when did guys wear more jewelry than women? He didn't look like what she'd consider a typical library patron, but what did she know? She'd seen a number of guys dressed this way on the streets. One thing she *did* know? If she spied gold chains anywhere on Mitch's body, she might have to do a little "lifting" herself. Somehow, he didn't seem the type.

The guy handed Arielle an envelope. Was that. . .money? It sure looked like money peeking out from the top flap—not fully visible but enough to know it was there. Whatever they were discussing, it was clear it wasn't a book or rental fee.

Cassie grabbed a listing of library classes from the counter and pretended to study it—*Origami for your Mommy* sounded plenty interesting—while darting glances at the duo huddling together at the end of the counter. Her hands shook and she lowered them to the counter, needing an anchor.

"I'm sorry for your wait," Arielle said, coming over to her a couple of minutes later. "Can I help you find something?" Her blue eyes grew rounder when she spied Amy standing beside her. "You have to be Mitch Jacobsen's sister," she said, extending her hand across the counter. "You look too much like him not to be related."

"Amy Warnick." She shook the other woman's hand. "Nice to meet you. This is my friend, Cassie Thorenson."

"How is Mitch these days? I've missed him."

As Amy talked with Arielle, Cassie shifted from one foot to the other, thankful for the desk that separated them. Was it a good or bad thing that Arielle recognized the family resemblance? She hadn't thought of that angle. Not that she'd thought this plan through at all.

Lord, please let this work. What, oh what, did she think she was doing? Hoping she wasn't obvious, Cassie pinned her gaze on Amy and tilted her head slightly toward Arielle. *Keep her talking,* she mouthed.

"Cassie's visiting New York for the first time," Amy said. "I thought I'd show her our fabulous local library. I used to live in the family's townhouse before Mitch moved in, and like my brother, I spent a lot of time here."

Was Amy trying to imply she knew Arielle had also been in the townhouse? Cassie had to give her credit for being civil after hearing Mitch suspected the woman of stealing the valuable heirloom. That news would send some people flying across the counter to try and force a confession out of her. But what if Mitch was mistaken and Arielle *hadn't* taken it? From what he'd said, the librarian was the only suspect. Too late for misgivings now. She'd already set Operation Statue in place, so she needed to get on with it.

Unzipping her purse, Cassie reached into a small inside pocket. She'd kept the fake diamond engagement ring there ever since Mitch left Houston. Finding it, she pulled it out and slipped the ring on her finger.

"How nice," Arielle said to Amy, turning back to her. "Is there something specific I can help you ladies find today?"

"I was wondering if we can talk somewhere privately." Cassie made a point to put her left hand on top of the counter, and she tapped her fingers up and down.

"May I ask what this is about?" Sure enough, Arielle's gaze drifted to the ring.

"Cassie, I'll be right over here when you're ready to leave." Amy pointed to a grouping of chairs and strolled away. Cassie wanted to beg her not to go, but perhaps it was for the best. Might as well get straight to the heart of the matter.

"Something's gone missing from the townhouse, and I sus—I'm hoping you might know something about it."

Arielle visibly stiffened and her eyes narrowed. As much as she hated to admit it, the woman was very pretty with straight, long dark hair and classic features. The precise and perfect type with not a single hair out of place that always made her feel somewhat self-conscious by comparison. "I thought Amy said you were only visiting."

"I am. Mitch and I are. . .very close friends, but yes, I live. . .somewhere else."

"Somewhere southern, I'll bet." Coming from this woman's lips, it wasn't a compliment. "Are you a detective?"

Cassie swallowed. She couldn't lie but neither could she leave the library without trying to get the truth. "Let's just say I can put up a big stink if you don't answer my questions." She infused that statement with as much authority as she could muster. *Put up a stink? Really?*

"I'm not answering any questions unless you have some kind of official badge or warrant."

"I don't think you want to do that." Cassie touched the sleeve of the other woman's tailored white blouse as Arielle started to turn away.

"Look, I don't care who you are," Arielle seethed, leaning halfway across the desk. "Kindly remove your hand or I'll call security and have you forcibly removed from the premises. The alert button's right here, an inch away. I won't hesitate to push it."

When Arielle moved her hand, Cassie clutched her forearm. Time to run—gallop—with her idea and hope it worked. "I'm sure your supervisor would like to know why you accepted money from the library patron who was here at the desk just now. You know, I've always held such high respect for librarians, but I hardly believe this is proper and acceptable behavior. Do you?" She glanced up at the ceiling. "And would you look at that? A handy dandy surveillance camera right above the desk." She started to raise her hand as if to wave at the camera.

"Fine," Arielle said through clenched teeth. She lowered her voice. "Tell me what you want."

Cassie's gaze bore into the other woman and Arielle motioned for her to step to the end of the counter. That appeared to be the place where she conducted her personal business. "Where's the sculpture, Arielle?"

After a long moment, Arielle blew out a breath. "None of your business." At least she didn't deny any knowledge of its existence.

"On second thought, maybe I'll push that button," Cassie said. "Security would come running over here, right? I'm sure they'd love a good juicy story about one of their junior librarians."

"You're not as innocent as you look are you, Little Miss Mary Sunshine?"

"It's Cassie, for the record. If you tell me willingly, the police might go easier on you."

Arielle closed her eyes for a long moment before her lids fluttered open again. "I didn't do anything with it, if that's what you're thinking. It's safe in my apartment."

"Why'd you take it?"

She lifted her shoulders. "I don't know except that I like it. Maybe I wanted a souvenir. Call it a parting gift from Mitch." Her voice held barely disguised sarcasm. "He'll dump you, too. He's not the kind of man to commit to anything more long term than a fly-by-night relationship."

Cassie stiffened at that comment but kept her gaze steady. Arielle's words gave her hope that she could still hope to recover the sculpture.

"I'll sell it to you."

Cassie gasped but then closed her mouth. The nerve of the woman. She wanted to throttle her. "You can't sell something that doesn't belong to you. Listen to me because this is how it's going to happen. How far do you live from here?" Where she got the gumption to say all that, she had no idea, but this was getting a little fun now. Weird, but fun.

"It's a ten minute walk."

"Fine. I'll spring for cab fare. Time to take a little field trip."

"Who do you think you are? You can't waltz in my library with your hick country accent, threaten me and then order me around. The way I see it, Mitch owes me."

"He owes you nothing."

Arielle's gaze fell on the ring. "I'll trade you for the ring."

Worthless or not, she'd grown rather accustomed to the ring. She didn't need to consider it and valued it for the sentimental value alone. "This ring's not for sale or trade." Ever.

"Then no deal."

"Listen, you little literary shyster." Time to pour on the arsenal. "You're going to take a coffee break now. I'm going with you to your apartment and you're going to hand over the sculpture or Amy and I will have no qualms about going to the police and filing charges against you for theft. Maybe *grand* theft since I suspect that sculpture is worth a pretty decent sum of money." She didn't know that for a fact, but it seemed the right thing to say given the circumstances. Nonetheless, it was probably true. Cassie drummed her fingers on top of the counter again to irritate the other woman further.

"Why are you doing Mitch's dirty work?"

That question stopped her for a moment. *Of course.* Arielle was playing the old ploy of a woman dropping her handkerchief on the ground with the hope a handsome man would retrieve and return it. And come back for more. From what she knew of kleptomaniacs, they didn't take anything for monetary gain but because of a lack of something in their own lives. In this case, it could be a lack of affection from Mitch, but more than likely, from someone else in Arielle's past.

Cassie snapped to attention. "That sculpture is part of his heritage, his family, and it's very important to all of them."

Arielle's shoulders slumped. Could it be she'd finally gotten through and pierced her conscience? One could only hope.

"If I give you the sculpture, you won't press charges, right? I can't lose my job." The other woman appeared frightened and at least sounded repentant.

Cassie mustered a small smile. "I can't very well report something as stolen if I'm holding it in my hands, now can I?"

~

Cassie and Amy rode with Arielle in the elevator to her tenth floor apartment where she surrendered the Lew Lawrie sculpture. She handed it over to Amy and managed a small apology. As surprising as that was, it confirmed in Cassie's mind that Arielle wasn't a bad person. Not at all, but she was misguided and most likely hurting from more than Mitch's rejection.

Before leaving the apartment, Cassie told Arielle they'd pray for her but received a dirty look in response. "Yeah, well, good luck with that."

"Mitch didn't want to report you to the police, Arielle, but there's Someone else you should report to and ask forgiveness from," Amy said.

"Who's that?" From the round, questioning eyes to the clueless comment, Arielle obviously wasn't a woman of faith.

Cassie's heart softened, and she resolved to pray for her. "Arielle, God—Jesus—wants to have a personal relationship with you. He cares about you and He loves you, but you have to invite Him to be a part of your life. I asked Him into my heart when I was a little girl, but I didn't really know what it meant to live for Jesus until I moved to Houston. He blessed me with people to help me learn more about Him. I'll pray He'll do that for you, too. Godly people who'll always care about you and pray for you."

The other woman waved her hand. "Jesus gave up on me a long time ago and I'm going to ask you nicely to leave my apartment now. I have to get back to work before they fire me, anyway."

"Think about what we've said and know we'll be praying for you," Amy told her as they departed. "So will Mitch." She relayed the name of their church and the street before Arielle soundly slammed the door behind them.

"Here, you carry it. You earned the right," Amy said, giving her the sculpture as they hurried to the elevator.

Giddy with anticipation, Cassie could hardly wait to see Mitch's reaction. Even to her untrained eye, she could appreciate the master craftsmanship and artistry of the sculpture. But when it came right down to it, it was a nice statue of a naked man holding a book. Her cheeks flushed when she realized how she'd been holding him. Goodness. Sculpture or not, she needed to watch where she placed her hands.

Apparently noticing her awkwardness, Amy laughed. "Why do you think I wanted you to hold him? He's quite the man, isn't he?"

"Yes, he is. Look out world, Cassie's feeling empowered," she said as they exited the elevator and flagged down a taxi outside Arielle's apartment. She glanced over her shoulder a number of times as if she halfway expected Arielle to come running outside and snatch it from her hands.

Glancing out the window as the taxi passed the endless skyscrapers en route to the townhouse, Cassie's thoughts wandered to a long ago memory. She'd almost forgotten about it until the events of the last half-hour brought it to mind. "When I was in third grade, right after Christmas, Sally Reynolds grabbed my favorite doll I'd brought for show and tell. She threatened to drown her in a playground puddle."

Amy raised a brow. "What made you think of that?"

"Arielle reminds me of Sally in some ways. That girl was meaner than spit, but I'd seen the way she looked at my doll. Grandma Thor gave her to me for Christmas. Sally didn't want the doll so much as what it represented. What she lacked in her own life, I guess. I felt sorry for her, but Sally didn't want my pity."

"Let me guess," Amy said. "You gave Sally your doll."

Cassie nodded slowly. "I did, and I knew Grandma Thor would understand. Sally came from one of the best families in town. Goes to show it's true that money can't buy love or anything else. The last I heard, Sally's married for the third time with no children. Sad, isn't it?"

Amy reached for her hand, squeezing it. "The Lord was working inside you even then. Preparing your heart and working through you. Have I told you today how wonderful you are?"

Cassie smiled. "Thanks for sticking with me in that crazy scheme. The difference between Sally and Arielle, of course, is that there was no way I was going to allow Arielle to keep the sculpture. It's a lot different than a doll and represents so much to your family."

They shared a smile.

"I appreciate your taking the day off work to come with me," Cassie said. "That was quite the adventure, wasn't it?"

"It worked, and Mitch will be thrilled. On behalf of the Jacobsen family, thank you, Cassie." She gave her a quick hug.

"Welcome. You may call me Detective Jacobsen."

Amy's eyes grew wide. "Do you realize what you just said?"

Cassie half-laughed, half-coughed. *Oh, my.* Glancing down at her lap, she marveled at how the ring sparkled in the reflected sunlight streaming through the windows of the taxi. "Blame it on the ring. I should probably take it off." In her heart, she didn't want to remove it, but it was for the best. Slipping it from her finger, Cassie tucked it back into her purse.

"Do you think there's a reason you've kept it all this time?" Amy asked. When Cassie hesitated, not sure she was ready to answer the question, Amy gave her an understanding smile.

"What's Mitch's all-time favorite birthday meal?" Cassie said as the taxi driver dropped them off in front of the townhouse. She'd experimented with different recipes in the last two months, mostly easy, fail-proof recipes Rebekah and Winnie shared with her. With the exception of two burned casseroles, they'd turned out well. Maybe she shouldn't get too proud of herself, but making them had helped boost her self-confidence.

"Fix him plain old spaghetti and meatballs," Amy said. "No fancy stuff for Mitch. He's happy with anything, and he's a pretty basic guy when it comes to his food. Mom usually comes for his birthday and fixes it for him, but she's in Florida with some friends for a few weeks."

"Well, then, that's what I'm going to fix him for dinner tonight. You and Landon are welcome to come."

"Thanks, but you two deserve a romantic evening alone. I'll take you to Hanrahan's Market and we'll get everything you'll need. Let's run this prized commodity back inside where he belongs"—she nodded to the sculpture—"and then I'll take you there. It's only a short three-block walk."

Within minutes of entering the market, Cassie made new friends with the owner, Fred, his wife, Sandra, and their business partner, Akhil. Amy scooted around the small aisles of the store beside her, and together they selected the makings for a simple tossed salad. Amy told her Mitch loved a sliced hardboiled egg and sliced cucumber in his salad but wouldn't want bacon bits and definitely no radishes or what he called "wilted, gross, rabbit food."

Next they selected bottled Italian dressing, a box of linguini, a jar of spaghetti sauce—homemade sauce sounded too risky—frozen meatballs and a loaf of Italian bread.

"I'm so glad you're here," Cassie said. "This is fun."

"Now, for the *piece de la resistance*? Chocolate mousse. I have a recipe that's easy peasy and Mitch absolutely loves it. It only takes four ingredients. When you're ready to start on it later, call me and I'll walk you through it." Amy dropped a bar of Ghirardelli dark chocolate into her basket. "You use seven of the eight squares for the mousse and shave the last one as a garnish." She patted Cassie's arm. "Trust me. He'll love you forever."

Cassie blushed at that comment and followed Amy to the dairy section where she picked up a carton of heavy whipping cream. "We might as well get eggs, too, since I never know what Mitch has on hand or if they're expired." Flipping open the lid of a carton of large eggs, Amy nodded with satisfaction. "These look good. Next we need sugar. The extra-fine stuff." Within seconds, she'd added the sugar to Cassie's basket. "There now. That should do it."

"Mitch said he's going to try and get off early," Cassie said as they walked back inside the townhouse with the grocery bags. "Amy, you don't think he'll mind me being here when he gets home, do you? I don't want to come across as a stalker, but this will be the second night in a row where he comes home and—guess what?—Cassie from Alabama's standing in the man's kitchen."

"Are you kidding me? It's his dream come true."

"It is?"

"Believe in yourself, Cass. You're so good for Mitch, and I'm thankful my brother finally woke up to that fact."

"Thanks. To be honest, Mitch and I woke each other up. Um, that didn't come out right." Sometimes she needed to think things through before she opened her mouth.

Amy's smile relieved her worries. "All in God's timing. I'm excited to see what He's going to do in your lives."

They stacked the bags on the counter and started to remove the groceries. Cassie giggled when Sammie trotted over and nudged her leg. An insistent *pay attention to me* nudge. "How's my sweet Sammie today?" Crouching to his level, she ruffled his ears and gave him a kiss. "Amy, before you leave, could you help me find a tablecloth for the dining room table and maybe some candles?"

"Sure, as long as Mitch hasn't moved them." Two minutes later Amy returned to the kitchen with the items in hand. "Here you go. Do you need some wrapping paper for the sculpture?"

Cassie considered the question for a minute. "I'd like to wrap a little sarong around him to cover him up, but I don't think Mitch would appreciate it." Her grin escaped. "I'm sure I'll figure out something."

"I'm sure you will," Amy said. "You've proven yourself quite resourceful today."

Chapter 33

"HAPPY BIRTHDAY, MITCH." An unexpected shyness rolled through her and Cassie clasped her hands behind her back as he entered the townhouse. True to his word, he'd left the office early and it was a few minutes after five o'clock.

"Welcome home." She bit her tongue. Maybe she shouldn't act like a 1950s housewife waiting for her husband to come home. Wearing a pearl necklace and heels, no less.

"I could definitely get used to this," Mitch said. Pulling her into his arms, he gave her a sweet kiss. She liked how he kept the kisses light—except for the good-bye or good night kisses—as much for her sake as his. The man was so addictive that kissing him could easily become a habit that would be difficult enough to break when she left town. She pushed those thoughts out of her mind, determined to enjoy their time together.

"You're spoiling me. Amy called. Sounds like you had fun today." He shot her a wry grin. "Too bad Celeste couldn't stay."

"No comment." She wrinkled her nose.

He laughed. "You've learned to be politically correct since coming to the big city."

"I think Celeste and I came to an understanding of sorts. Did she or Amy tell you about our little midnight swimming lesson?"

"Celeste called me on her way out of town this morning. She sounded apologetic for whatever it was she said to you last night. She thinks you're a quick study and sweet as pie." His appreciative gaze swept over her. "She's right. You look incredible, Cassie."

Her cheeks warmed. She wasn't used to compliments from men, but coming from Mitch, she cherished them. Right after she'd returned to the townhouse with Amy, she'd called Louie to see if he could help her out for an hour. He'd dropped her off in front of a mid-priced department store and returned forty-five minutes later. She'd never really liked to shop because she'd never had much money to shop. But she always had an idea of what she wanted, and this time was no different. Her sage green and white skirt fell slightly below her knees, and she loved the silky, matching sage-colored blouse. On her feet, she wore beige wedge-heeled sandals since they boosted her height and made her legs appear longer.

"Oh, wait. I have something for you." Darting back out to the hall, Mitch hung his jacket on a hook and rolled his sleeves. When he picked up his briefcase and set it on the floor by the closet, she spied a gorgeous bouquet of a dozen roses in different colors, wrapped in cellophane and sitting on the floor.

With a wide grin, he bowed low and presented them to her. It was his birthday and yet he was giving *her* a gift?

"They're so beautiful. Thank you." Cassie buried her nose in the flowers, but they were damp and she was careful not to brush them against her blouse. She couldn't resist teasing him. "I see you're as indecisive as ever about which color to get."

"Ah, you could put that idea to rest if you'd pick a favorite color already. So, it's my contention you're the indecisive one." He brushed a finger across the bridge of her nose. "You had some water on your nose. I think there's a vase in the kitchen. Amy left it behind when she moved in with the hotshot publisher in case you're thinking I get flowers on a regular basis."

He sniffed the air as he entered the kitchen. "You cooked for me?" Walking across the room, he lifted the lid of the pan on the stove. "Linguini? Now I know why you told me not to make a dinner reservation."

"I'm trying my best to make your favorite birthday dinner. Amy told me your mom usually made spaghetti and meatballs for your special day. Kind of hard to burn pasta, but don't get too excited since it's only tomato sauce from a jar. And frozen meatballs—heated up, of course. You can reserve comment until after you've tasted it. We have a salad, too. Can't go wrong with salad, right?" The chocolate mousse was also chilling in the refrigerator. From what she'd sampled, it turned out fine. Maybe she wasn't a total failure at cooking, after all.

"Moonbeam, I could eat peanut butter out of a jar and it'd taste like the best thing I'd ever eaten if you're sharing it with me."

"Stop it already," she said, laughing. "Now you're going overboard. I've set the table in the dining room. Why don't you go have a seat and I'll be in with our meal in a few minutes."

He peeked around the corner. "Candles? And are those rose petals scattered on the tablecloth?"

She smiled. "On a whim at the market, I picked out a couple of roses. I thought sprinkling them on the tablecloth might be. . .romantic. You have to bear with me. It's been a long time since I've had a boyfriend, if you could even call it that." That thought stopped her. "Is that what you are, Mitch? My boyfriend?"

He'd pulled out a cut crystal vase from beneath the sink and filled it with water. At her question, he placed the vase carefully on the table. "I want to be your boyfriend, Cassie, if you'll allow me the honor." He paused, as if gathering his thoughts. "Based on what I said last night at the restaurant, I think my intentions should be clear. You have to know how special you are in my life."

"Like I said, bear with me. The last time I had a boyfriend, I was worried about whether or not he'd ask me to the Friday night dance. This is uncharted territory."

"Didn't you go out with Stone Bicklebong?"

She stared at him. "Bicklebing." Would he never get the name right? "And what on earth makes you think that?" Surely the man wasn't still jealous of Stone for some unfounded, ridiculous reason.

"Nothing. You two seemed pretty friendly at the restaurant that night."

"We went out a few times, yes, but if you must know, we decided we worked better as friends." Tears pricked her eyes. "For that matter, I *choose* to be here with you, Mitch. You were honest with me about your past. You know, it's not easy when I think about you. . ." She stopped and turned aside, determined not to cry in front of him. Why did she have to bring that up? Why did he? She'd never thought of herself as overly emotional, but this weekend seemed to be on overload.

A moment later, she felt Mitch's strong hands on her shoulders. He turned her around, but he didn't pull her into his arms like she expected. Instead, he dropped his hands to his sides, his expression earnest. "Cassie, do you remember how—when we were sitting in the car together on that crazy morning in Houston—I told you I wished I could change my past? Well, I, um. . ." He ducked his head and ran a hand through his hair. When he raised his head, moisture shone in his eyes. "You're an incredible woman of God, the type of woman I've always wanted to find. I'd give anything I own to be able to come to you without the sins of my past, but I can't. All I ask is that you accept me as I am, a broken but forgiven man. Can you find it in your heart to do that?"

All over again, she melted at how completely open and honest this man could be in expressing his emotions. "Mitch, you were forgiven a long time ago. But thank you for telling me."

He wrapped his arms around her and pulled her close, resting his head on her shoulder.

She smoothed her hands over his strong shoulders and hugged him tight. "You're straight with God, and that's most important. None of us are perfect. You've survived things in your life that most people can't even fathom and emerged stronger from having lived through them." Easing back, she made sure she had his eye contact. "If I pushed you away, if I kept searching for that so-called perfect man, I'd never find him. He doesn't exist. I've never met a man like you. You steal my breath away with your sensitivity and compassion. And you always make me laugh. Remember what Doris said—a man who can make you laugh is. . ."

"Afraid the sauce is going to burn." Mitch darted to the stove.

"Oh, no! Don't open the lid. It might splatter all over your shirt!" Rushing over to stand beside him, she swatted his hand aside and turned down the burner.

"Now you're manhandling me?"

"Excuse me for trying to save your shirt. I saw the monogram before you rolled your sleeves. Spaghetti sauce can stain and I won't be held responsible for killing anything by Brooks Brothers."

He laughed as she checked the oven temperature and slid the tray with the Italian bread inside. "Let me go put on some music and then I'll help you bring everything out to the table."

Cassie followed him to the doorway, watching as he pulled out a record album from a nearby cabinet.

"Miles Davis okay?"

"Sure." She'd heard the name but didn't know any more except that he was a jazz musician. He removed the album from its sleeve and positioned it on the vintage turntable. The whole time, she held her breath, wondering if he'd discover the Lew Lawrie sculpture sitting on the ledge of the bookcase. If he didn't see it by the time they finished their dinner, she'd do or say something to draw his attention to it.

This will be fun. She walked back into the kitchen with a big smile of anticipation.

"Cassie!"

Chapter 34

MITCH TURNED THE sculpture in his hands. Unbelievable. Did Cassie have something to do with its sudden reappearance?

She stood in the doorway to the kitchen, looking deceptively innocent and for all the world like she harbored a delicious secret. "Hmm?" Yes, she definitely knew something.

"How. . ." He turned it upside down. Lew Lawrie's original signature mark. "How. . .what. . .where?" Bringing it closer, Mitch studied it for nicks or damage. Still in mint condition, thank the Lord. "Is this—"

"Yes, it's the sculpture that belonged to your grandfather."

He looked up at her. "Cassie, this is incredible. Did you have something to do with getting it back?" Had she scoured pawn shops for his birthday gift? Not that he cared, but he couldn't envision her doing such a thing.

"A little, yes. Amy took me shopping this morning, and we stopped at the library. When we were leaving, she saw. . .Arielle Carson behind the reference desk."

He cringed. "So, Amy knows it's been missing?"

"She does now. Sorry, Mitch, but I had to seize the moment and she happened to be there."

"Perfectly understandable," he said quickly to reassure her, "but I might need you to protect me next time we see her."

"Won't that be on Sunday morning? In church?"

"Good point. Maybe that'll save me, in a manner of speaking. I'd mentioned to Amy that Arielle had taken some things, but I never explained how I knew that. Come to think of it, I'm surprised her journalistic instincts didn't kick in with that one. But I never told Amy she'd stolen something of value to our family."

"A priceless heirloom, you mean."

"Exactly, and trust me, I am forever indebted to you. This is an early Lawrie piece before his style evolved into Beaux-Arts Classicism and then Art Deco. Grandpa got to know him in his later years and Lew gifted him with this sculpture. It's insured, but I figured Arielle had probably pawned it."

"Why didn't you report it to the police?"

"Because I knew Arielle wasn't a bad person. She was pretty mad when I broke it off with her. I figured I'd eventually get it back. . .one way or another." He shrugged and placed the sculpture on the bookcase. "Did you happen to go by Rockefeller Center when you were out with Amy earlier today?"

She raised a brow. "No, but Louie—the greatest taxi driver in all of New York—took the scenic route on the way here yesterday, and he pointed it out to me. Tell me why you're asking and then I've got to get back in the kitchen if you don't want peanut butter for dinner."

"There's a big statue of Atlas in Rockefeller Center, opposite St. Patrick's Cathedral."

"You mean the big bronze guy holding something that looks like the world?"

"The same. That's probably Lee Lawrie's best known work."

Cassie's face blanched. "Oh no! Not again!"

He was almost afraid to follow her into the kitchen. If he did, he'd probably pull her into his arms and kiss the rest of the night away. Maybe he should stand firm, but he'd reward her later for recovering the Lawrie. He still couldn't get over it. What an inventive, amazing woman. He'd definitely need to hear that story later. It was bound to be a good one. Beneath her sweet exterior, Cassie could be pretty tough. Independent and stronger than even she realized. He loved those qualities about her.

A minute later, she pushed open the door, panting, her cheeks flushed. "I didn't burn it. This is a personal victory. For once in my life, I didn't burn the bread!"

Cassie might not have burned their bread, but inside, Mitch melted.

~

Feeling a bit nervous, Cassie couldn't eat much of her dinner. Knowing how much Mitch enjoyed it was gratifying. She wondered about the remainder of the evening, not sure what to expect. He'd dimmed the lights and they dined by candlelight, the smooth sounds of Miles Davis's trumpet serenading them.

Her thoughts went back to that first day he'd arrived in Houston and how awkward she'd felt sitting with him on the patio. Tonight she felt every bit as young and inexperienced. Was it appropriate for her to be in a man's townhouse? How silly was it that at age twenty-six she didn't know the boundaries? They'd shared so much in Houston, they'd flirted and had such fun with emails and phone calls, but now—sitting across from the man—she felt tongue-tied. She trusted Mitch, and she knew right from wrong, but she hoped they'd both be able to withstand and resist temptation.

Throughout the meal, Mitch complimented her so much she finally stuffed a piece of bread in his mouth to stifle him. "It's your birthday, not mine," she told him. "Not that I don't appreciate it."

"Tell me the story of how you got the Lew Lawrie sculpture back," he said, swirling linguini on his fork. He listened with great interest when she told him the story of confronting Arielle, then gave her a sweet kiss and told her how he loved her for what she'd done for his family. "Besides your being here, this is the best birthday gift you could have ever given me."

"I think it's wonderful how you appreciate and value your family's heritage," Cassie said. "From the classic furnishings, the vintage record player and albums, books and sculptures. . .so many things. Too many things today are flyaway."

"Right," he said. "There's not pride in workmanship like in years past. Take Kevin and that one-of-a-kind gazebo he built for Rebekah. Or that yellow cottage he designed and built for Hannah and Leah. You might think I'm crazy, but I love all the crackles, hisses and popping sounds in that Miles Davis album. It gives it unique character. Today's technology is so smooth. It's almost too perfect. But life's not smooth, it's not perfect."

"You sound like an old soul." Leaning her elbow on the table, Cassie rested her chin on her propped hand. "Tell me more."

Mitch's smile reached his eyes. "I know I completely understood Grandpa Carlisle's desire to return to the live theater. Hollywood was mostly gloss and glamour, but it wasn't real in the same way as the Broadway stage. He used to tell me that when he was on the stage, the character would take over. He'd fully inhabit the role and—for a couple of hours each night—it's like he became another person."

"I wish I could have known him," Cassie said. "Sometimes I think people play roles in real life. We all do, to some extent. We say what others want to hear. Do things the way we believe others expect. That's sad because it's not honest and keeps us from becoming the unique person we're meant to be." She shook her head and smiled. "Something like that."

The lines around Mitch's eyes crinkled when he smiled, making him even more impossibly attractive. In some ways, she found it difficult to believe he could be interested in her when he could have his pick of any woman he wanted.

"You're the most transparent woman I've ever met, and I mean that in the best possible way." He took her hand and skimmed his thumb over it, focusing his gaze on their joined hands. "There's not a dishonest bone in your body."

He'd mentioned that once before, but considering the timing now, she had to wonder if he thought of Arielle.

Cassie smiled as he finished the last spoonful of his chocolate mousse a few minutes later and licked his lips with satisfaction. "Hands down, this was the best birthday dinner of my life. Just don't tell my mom I said that, please." He reached for her hand again. "Thank you, Cassie."

She slowly withdrew her hand and rose from the table. "I'd better go wash up our dishes."

"I'll help you."

They laughed and teased as they worked side-by-side in the kitchen. Mitch stole light kisses on her neck, especially when she was vulnerable with her hands in the dishwater. From his favorite corner of the kitchen, Sammie watched their antics, his head resting on his crossed paws.

"Sammie want a treat? Watch this," Mitch said. Holding up the chew bone, he waved it at the dog. "Let's show Cassie what you can do. Come on, boy."

Sitting upright at attention, Sammie began to make noises unlike anything she'd ever heard. Kind of like a low howl combined with a humming sound. Cassie pulled the stopper from the sink and dried her hands. If she didn't know better, she'd think Mitch's lovable mutt was trying to sing. "Is he. . .exactly what *is* he doing?"

"Singing, of course. Sammie doesn't take requests, but he's got 'Jingle Bells' down. I can't sing, as you know, but maybe if *you* start singing, then he'll jump right in." The expression on Mitch's face was too cute to ignore.

"Jingle bells, jingle bells, jingle all the way," Cassie began and Sammie started his accompaniment. She didn't get far into the song before she dissolved in laughter. "That's the weirdest but cutest thing I've ever seen."

After drying the last of the dishes she'd washed, Mitch tossed the towel on the counter and wrapped his arms around her from behind, rocking her back and forth. "I'm weird and you're awfully cute, so I think we make a very good team," he said. "What do you think?"

Turning around in his arms, she gave him a very special birthday kiss. "Does that answer your question?"

"Uh, yeah." He looked dazed and goofy. Cassie recognized that look on a man's face, but she'd never been the reason before. She liked being the reason for Mitch.

"I can finish putting the things away," she said. "I think you have some cards on the hall table you haven't opened yet." He'd brought them in when he'd arrived home earlier.

"Go on," she said, nodding toward the door. "I'll be out shortly."

"Okay." He gave her a light peck on the cheek. "Only because you insist and you're so beautiful."

When Cassie walked into the living room a few minutes later, Mitch sat on the sofa. His face had drained of color, and the look on his face was one of shock. "Mitch, is everything okay?"

"I'm not sure, to be honest."

"What do you mean?" Her pulse skipped with a beat of foreboding as he gestured to the envelope and unfolded piece of paper on his lap. It wasn't a card but looked more like plain white ruled paper. "Did you receive a letter for your birthday?"

"In a manner of speaking." His voice was tight and oddly quiet. "It's from Brad."

Chapter 35

Saturday Morning ~ April 24, 2004

"IT'S MORE MASSIVE than I could have imagined." Cassie's eyes filled with tears as she surveyed the site where the majestic Twin Towers once stood. Words could never explain the overwhelming sense of loss and grief. She was glad she'd been with Mitch right after he'd opened the letter from Brad. His widow, Felicity, had sent a note saying she'd found it in a box in the back of their bedroom closet.

Although Brad had written *Dear Mitch* at the top of the page, it wasn't so much a letter to him as it was Brad's personal musings of the good times they'd shared. From what Cassie heard her married friends say, a lot of guys thought it wasn't manly to show emotion much less shed actual tears. Mitch was as strong of a man as she'd ever met, but she'd held him as he'd cried, wrapping him in her arms and crying with him, their tears mingling together. Sharing that moment with him—as sad as it was—had been precious and one she'd never forget. He'd done the same for her when she'd told him about Tagg. Nothing could bring their loved ones back, but sharing their loss helped ease the heavy burdens in their hearts.

"God knew, Cassie." Mitch had rested his head on a pillow positioned on her lap and he'd stretched out on the sofa. "He knew I needed this closure, and the timing couldn't have been more perfect. In spite of his love of comic books—abbreviated literature, he called it—Brad was a great writer. I'm glad Felicity sent this to me." Even though Mitch had already read the letter twice, he'd listened as she'd read it to him a third time. When he closed his eyes, it was almost as though a wave of serenity washed over his features, bathing them in a peaceful calm.

Now, standing behind her at the site, Mitch wrapped her in his arms. He must need the connection and she needed it, too. The loss of humanity, the loss of dreams represented by the gaping pit, humbled Cassie in a way nothing else had ever done before.

Finally easing out of his embrace, Cassie dropped to her knees and lowered her head, clasping her hands together. Beside her, Mitch did the same. After a few minutes, he reached for her hand and they prayed together. Afterwards, they sat on the ground and talked more about his memories of Brad.

"He worked in the South Tower, the second one hit." Mitch's voice was thick with sadness. "He worked on one of the floors near where the plane tore through the building." He snapped his fingers. "Like that, hundreds of people are gone. *Do not be overcome by evil, but overcome evil with good.* Never again will I hear Brad's crazy, from-the-gut laugh. See that wild red hair of his. He used to tug on it when a trade was tanking and then it'd stick straight out from his head. The little boy in him collected comic books and he loved superhero movies. Devoured spicy Thai food like candy and played practical jokes on me almost every week." Mitch fell silent for a long moment and when he raised his head, a single tear rolled down his cheek.

"He'd probably say his last joke was on me. I find it ironic how he said in the letter, 'No matter where you go in life, don't forget me, buddy.' And now 'Never Forget' has become a catch phrase and a slogan for 9/11." He shook his head and heaved a huge sigh. "I can't begin to imagine the terror of those people trying to evacuate, not knowing what was happening. Wondering if they'd ever see their families again. Sending frantic messages, leaving reminders that might never be found."

Raising his knees, Mitch rested his elbows on them. "Here we are, a few years later, and yet they're still finding things to return to loved ones. A watch, a ring, or some other small memento. Beauty for ashes, right? I know Brad wouldn't want me to be sad for him, though." A hint of his grin emerged. "Well, maybe a little. He loved life, loved people. He also knew the Lord, but he wasn't a practicing Christian, I guess you could say. That's one of my biggest regrets because I wasn't much of a good influence on him the last few years. But I have no doubt he's in Heaven harassing someone. Brad would want me to remember the good times, take away what I learned, and then get on with the process of living." Leaning close, Mitch kissed her cheek. "That's what I'm trying to do."

"How's Felicity doing now?"

His eyes narrowed as Mitch surveyed the site. "She's engaged to a man named Stephen. Stockbroker at another firm. I only know him by reputation, but he seems like one of the good guys. I'm happy for her, and I know Brad would approve and be glad Felicity moved on. They wanted kids, and now she'll have that opportunity."

"Do you want children?" Cassie's heart raced. After all they'd shared, she didn't think it was too personal to ask. "Chloe and Joe are always asking me about you. They talk about how Mr. Mitch would do this or say that. You made quite an impression in a very short time."

"They're great, and I feel the same way about them. Without question, I want kids. Speaking of which, I have somewhere else to take you. Somewhere not so sad." Rising to his feet, he dusted off his jeans and she did the same.

"It was important to come, and I'm glad we did."

"Have you heard anything about the teenage girl in Texas that Amy befriended?" Mitch said as they sat together in the back of a taxi bound for Queens. "Her name is Tamara, but she goes by Tam."

"I think Winnie mentioned something about her once or twice, but I don't know much of the story."

"Amy met Tam during that infamous road trip with Landon from Louisiana to Houston after Beck and Kevin's wedding," he said. "They stopped in a restaurant somewhere in Texas and Tam was their waitress. Then some guys were hassling her outside the restaurant as they were leaving. Long story short, Amy gave her a business card and then got a call from Tam a couple of days before Christmas. She was pregnant and thinking of terminating her pregnancy."

Cassie drew in a quick breath. "I'm glad she called Amy. I know how active Amy's always been in the pro-life movement. That must have broken her heart. What happened?"

"Landon flew Amy back down to Texas in his plane. She spent that night and the next morning with Tam, counseling and talking with her about the Lord's plan for her life, telling her every single thing she could think of to try and convince her not to have the abortion."

Almost afraid to hear what was coming next, Cassie braced herself for the rest of the story.

The little smile lines around Mitch's eyes surfaced. How she'd grown to appreciate them. *Love* them. "Then Amy's favorite cowboy showed up with Winnie and Chloe."

"Winnie was a single mom for more than four years, and it goes without saying how adorable Chloe is." Cassie leaned her head on Mitch's shoulder.

"Amy accompanied Tam into the clinic," he said. "She told me she about lost it when they called Tam's name and she went behind those closed doors. But within a few minutes, she came back out again and told Amy she couldn't go through with it."

"Oh, thank the Lord." Cassie moved one hand over her abdomen. "So, everything turned out all right for Tam and her baby?"

"You're about to find out." The taxi stopped in front of a three-story, red brick home. "Here we are. Look," he said, pointing out the side window.

Cassie looked out the window where he indicated. In the front yard stood a large sign: Tam's Place.

Chapter 36

"COME ON. LET me show you around."

Mitch jumped across a newly poured concrete sidewalk and assisted her. Together, they bounded up the wide front steps, hand-in-hand. Opening the heavy wooden door, he ushered her inside. When he closed the door behind them, a bell jingled, reminding Cassie of the bell at Richardson's.

The older home smelled slightly musty, but glancing around the large front hall and adjoining rooms, Cassie admired the rich woods and neutral colors. The furniture and bright decorative accents made it warm and welcoming. Walking further into the home, Cassie spied a number of potted plants and paintings with pretty landscapes adorned the walls. A few young women were talking together in the living room and gave them curious glances. One of them waved to Mitch and he raised his hand and nodded.

"Mitch Jacobsen, as I live and breathe! What a sight for sore eyes you are. It's about time you came to see us." A robust woman with a beaming smile walked toward them, carrying an armload of towels. Lowering them onto a nearby chair, she opened her arms. Within seconds, she'd gathered Mitch in a huge bear hug. "Imagine finding you here in the house," she said, stepping back and turning to her. "Tell me. Who's this beautiful young lady you've brought to see us today? Is this why I haven't seen you for over a week?"

"Helena, this is Cassie Thorenson. Cassie, may I introduce you to Helena Goodall. We couldn't run Tam's Place without her. I'm sorry I haven't been by, but things got crazy at work."

"Any friend of Mitch is a friend of mine," Helena said. "He works too hard at that fancy Wall Street job, but this man's got a big heart. Together with Amy and Landon, they're our founders and major investors in Tam's Place. They roll up their sleeves and pitch in with whatever needs to be done. You tell me how many people as busy as they are would take the time."

Helena beamed and winked at Mitch. "And now they've brought in their friends from TeamWork. These good people know how to show God's mercy to those who need it, but then again, don't we all need that same mercy?" She leaned toward Cassie and put a hand to the side of her mouth as though telling her a secret. "I think they come to check up on me and Tam and make sure we're not getting into trouble."

"If you're trouble, then you're the best kind," Mitch said. "Cassie's a volunteer for TeamWork, too." He put his arm around her shoulders and tugged her close. "The Houston branch."

"Ah, then you must know Mr. Lewis and his wife, Lexa," Helena said. "They show up every now and then. Mercy, that tall cowboy gets this old heart fluttering." The good-natured older woman laughed when Mitch rolled his eyes. "You need to get yourself one of those Stetsons."

Mitch laughed. "I'll think about it."

Helena pointed to the door. "Our new front door's courtesy of Mr. Lewis's most recent book success. And Josh and Winnie Grant are big contributors for the meals and maternity clothes."

"I work for Lexa and Winnie's catering business," Cassie said.

"Do you now?" Helena's warm brown eyes twinkled. "You must be a mighty good cook then. Keep her around, Mitch."

That made her laugh, but Cassie mock-frowned when Mitch chuckled. "They keep me in the front office and away from the food, but I help serve and supervise at catering events."

"Tam around today?" Mitch asked.

"She had to take Henry to the doctor, but they'll be back any time."

"Nothing wrong I hope?" Mitch's brow creased with concern.

"Oh, no. It's his regular checkup. He'll be one in July," she told Cassie. "Cutest little baby boy you've ever seen. He livens up this place and the girls love him. I'm sure Tam will want to meet you, Cassie. Let me get one of the girls to run these towels upstairs and then I'll give you the nickel tour."

"Sure. Thanks," Cassie said. "What exactly is Tam's Place?" she whispered to Mitch, hoping her voice didn't carry as they waited in the hallway for Helena to return.

"At its core, it's a personal counseling service for pregnant and abused women. If they need a temporary place to stay, it's also a safe haven. Based on Christian principles but also run with other state and local agencies. Lots of upkeep since it's an older home and there are many rules and regulations. It seems there's always something that needs to be repaired, replaced, painted or tweaked. But we've got everything in order and been blessed to help a number of women who've come here for assistance of some kind."

Within a minute, Helena motioned for them to follow her. "Tam's Place started more than twenty years ago but under another name, and it offered most of the same services. Of course, we're more modernized now and keep up with the newest technology and programs." The women, some with Bibles on their laps, glanced up at them as they walked through the living room. Next Helena led them into the inviting, spacious kitchen where three ladies sat at the table, enjoying a light lunch. "Being Saturday, this is our busiest day," Helena said. "Lots going on, and we have our weekly Bible study and prayer time tonight. Our numbers are growing, and we had thirty here last week."

Helena leaned heavily on the wooden railing as she started up the main staircase leading to the upper level.

"Helena, we don't need to go upstairs," Mitch told her. "I know you had knee surgery, and that's a whole lot of steps for you to climb."

"Good enough." Helena's breathing sounded a bit labored.

"I'm going to talk with Landon about installing an automated chair lift," Mitch said.

"That's a very good idea," Helena said, stepping back down to the landing. "If they're needed, Cassie, we have six bedrooms on the second level. Then there's a large attic that we've converted into another large bedroom that can hold up to six more women."

"Do you have many overnight guests?"

"More in the winter than this time of year, but you never know. We want to have a warm bed and food available for any woman who needs them."

"What a wonderful ministry," Cassie said. "Does Tam live here in the house?"

"Yes, she's our live-in manager and I live here, too. I'm more or less their Dorm Mother," Helena said. "That girl's awfully young, but she's smart, organized, sassy and got a heart of gold. A born leader if ever I've seen one." She moved her gaze to Mitch. "That sister of yours is real smart and recognized a good soul when she met Tam. As soon as Tam told Amy she wanted to do something to help TeamWork, the idea was born. I happen to know for a fact Landon flies her down to see her family in Texas every now and then, too, so they can see Tam and her little boy."

The back door closed and they heard some of the women greeting Tam.

"Tam, we have a visitor," Helena called to her.

Within a few seconds, a darling little moppet with curly brown hair hanging nearly to his shoulders ran around the corner and straight into Mitch's legs. Laughing, Mitch fell onto the floor with the squealing child on top of him. "Cassie, this is Crazy Man, also known as Peter Thomas Goodall."

"My three-year-old grandson," Helena said.

Mitch struggled to sit up with Peter hanging onto his neck. "Cassie, save me, please!" He waved one hand in her direction.

"I'll save you, Mr. Mitch!" Cassie planted both feet on the floor and pretended to have an invisible tug of war. Peter finally released his hold and rolled off Mitch, tumbling to the floor.

"Peter," Mitch said, sounding official, "I'd like to introduce you to my very special friend. This is Miss Cassie."

Cassie bowed. "It's my honor to meet you, Sir Peter." The little boy giggled and ran to his grandmother, giving Helena a kiss. The older woman's face lit with pure joy.

"What's all the commotion out here?"

A young woman holding an infant boy rounded the corner, and her eyes lit when she spied Mitch. Tall and thin, she was pretty with several bright purple streaks in her otherwise dark hair. "Well, look who's here. About time you came back over here, Wall Street. We've missed you the last couple of weeks."

Cassie smiled at the nickname as Mitch gave the girl a quick hug.

"Hi, I'm Tam," she said, stepping forward and offering her hand to Cassie. "And this is my son, Henry James Coughlin." She smoothed her hand over his downy brown hair. The child rested his head on his mama's shoulder and gave Cassie a sleepy, blue-eyed stare.

"It's nice to meet you, Tam. I'm Cassie. Wall Street brought me. This is such a great place."

"Yeah, it is. Wall Street, Mr. Handsome and the Mrs. have been real good to me, Henry and all our guests."

"Enough with your nicknames." Helena waved her hand, laughing.

"Ah, give it up, Helena. It's fun and it's not hurting anyone." Tam turned back to her. "I'm guessing you're from Mississippi? Alabama?"

"Alabama."

"Then that's what I'll call you. You two want to stay for lunch? I can whip up some soup and sandwiches in no time. We can chat."

Mitch glanced at Cassie for confirmation and she nodded. "We'd love to," he said. "Thanks."

Cassie worked with Tam to prepare the simple meal and then sat beside Mitch at the large, oblong table in the kitchen. Henry had been taken upstairs for his nap and Peter sat in a booster seat at the end of the table. As they ate, the ladies told Cassie more about the different services they offered.

"You're so young to have this much responsibility," Cassie said to Tam as she dried the dishes after their lunch. "You seem more than capable of handling it, though. Looks to me like you've found your niche."

Cutting up potatoes for the evening meal, Tam darted a quick glance at Mitch. Playing with building blocks, he sat on the floor with Peter. Like with the TeamWork kids in Houston, Mitch possessed an easy, comfortable manner and kids gravitated to him.

"You know, all it took was one person who cared enough to say she believed in me," Tam said. "Amy told me she could tell I was smart and encouraged me to make my child a part of *living* the dream instead of letting it hold me back from whatever I wanted to do in my life. That's why when she, Mitch and Landon took over this place and asked if I wanted to come and work here, I jumped at the chance. I was itching to get away from Texas and start fresh, you know?"

Cassie nodded. "I did the same thing when I left Alabama. I couldn't wait to get away, meet new people, and go places. I'd never been so scared. . .or more excited."

"Right." Tam scraped the cut potatoes into a bowl of water and set it aside before retrieving a bag of carrots from the refrigerator. "Not that I'll be here my entire life," Tam said next, pulling a roasting pan from a bottom cabinet. "But it's where the Lord's planted me, and I plan on blooming here until the next opportunity comes knocking. Then again, I could be here forever." She shrugged. "Who knows?" In that moment, Tam sounded younger, more vulnerable. "Now I've got someone else to think about, so it's not all about me anymore. You got any kids, Alabama?"

"No, but I hope to someday. Hand me a peeler and I'll work on the carrots."

Tam pulled one from a utensil drawer and handed it to her. "Here you go. Thanks."

They worked together in silence for a couple of minutes, smiling at the antics of Mitch and Peter. They'd moved to a small table set up in one corner, and Mitch's long legs were scrunched under the table as he colored with an oversized, fat crayon. Could the man be any cuter? She wondered all over again why he wasn't married.

Maybe God saved him for you.

That thought startled her. Then again, more and more, Cassie believed the Lord had saved *her* for Mitch. She'd never believed in destiny, fate or any of those New Age philosophies, but she definitely believed in God's providence.

Tam opened an upper cabinet and rotated a spice carousel. "I never asked them to name this place after me. Just so we're clear on that."

"We're clear," Cassie said as she added another peeled carrot in a bowl on the counter. "I'm sure Tam's Place has been a huge blessing for a lot of women."

"I hope so. Helena keeps me straight. She can be a real pain sometimes, but then, so can I. She helps me out a lot with Henry, and I've adopted her as my official mother since my mom died last year."

"I'm sorry, Tam. My mom died five years ago."

"I'm sorry for your loss, too, Alabama. That's tough. I pray every day the Lord will use me in some special way for the girls here. I know exactly how they feel because I've been there. A lot of them are young, pregnant and scared. They're not sure what they're going to do or how they'll support themselves much less take care of a baby. Pure and simple, we're here to give them hope."

Tam paused in her work. "I know that's what God wants me to do. He's blessed me with so much, and now it's my turn to share the wealth." She grinned. "Mitch said you're part of TeamWork, too, and that's what they're all about, right? Rebuilding lives?"

She nodded. "Yes, and I love being part of such a great organization. In a lot of ways, they're my family."

"You're blessed," Tam said. She angled her head toward Mitch. "Don't mind admitting to you that I've had a crush on Mitch since forever. That man's so fine. I mean, that red polo he's wearing can't keep up with all those bulging muscles." She laughed under her breath. "Whoever said brokers can't be hot has never met Wall Street."

Cassie ducked her head but couldn't hide her smile.

"You're special to him. I can tell. It's in his eyes." Crossing the room to the pantry, Tam pulled out a bag of onions. "Speaking of eyes." She laughed as she put the bag on the counter. "Never met an onion yet that didn't make me cry."

"Do you have anyone. . .special in your life?" Cassie asked, unsure if that was appropriate, especially since Tam was so young.

"I've got a guy back home in Asher, Texas. His name's Denton. He was so sweet when I was pregnant with Henry and stayed with me through the whole thing. He even changed Henry's diapers and gave him his bottle when I was too tired to take care of myself much less a baby. Denton's sweet on me, and I love him, but there's no heat, you know? There's a new girl in town, and I'm praying Denton might take up with her. She's nice and I think they'd be real good together. He deserves the best."

"The right guy will come along for you, too, when you least expect it, Tam. I'm adding you and Tam's Place to my prayer list. Do you have a business card?"

"Sure." Tam dug in her pocket and handed Cassie a card. "Is that how it happened for you and Mitch? The not looking for it but it dumped in your lap kind of thing?"

That question gave her pause for a moment, but it also made Cassie smile. "Yes and no. We were kind of pushed together by some well-meaning matchmakers, and neither one of us was really looking for a relationship. It's tough since I live in Texas." She lifted her shoulders. "We're taking it as we go and trying to figure it out."

"Well, I'll pray for you and Wall Street to make it. You owe it to yourself to give it a fighting chance."

Cassie and Mitch said their good-byes with hugs all around a short time later.

"Instead of taking a taxi, can we try the subway?" Cassie turned big eyes on him, laughing at his expression of shock.

"You sure about that?"

She nodded. "I'm feeling brave, I guess."

"Would you listen to you?" he teased. "And to think you didn't even like the big city. You're here all of a day and a half and now you're ready for the subway."

"Why not? I like trains."

"Well," he scoffed, "the subway's a train, but you might want to hold your nose and shield your eyes. And maybe cover your ears. You never know what you'll find on a New York subway. I'm thankful you'll be there to protect me."

Cassie laughed and curled her fingers around his arm. "Just another adventure. Let's go."

Chapter 37

"I LEARNED A lot about you today," Cassie said over dinner in Mitch's kitchen. "And survived a ride on the subway. All in all, I'd say that's not bad for a first trip to New York."

"And we still have all of tomorrow," he reminded her.

"Can't wait." They'd picked up Chinese food and she sighed as she attempted to use chopsticks, failing miserably. Of course, Mitch was very adept with his. "You are such a city boy," she said, dropping her chopsticks on the table. "It's impossible to actually get something in your mouth with these skinny wooden sticks. If I were forced to use these things all the time, I'd either starve to death or else become a pig and lap up everything with my mouth. I assure you, it would *not* be pretty."

Mitch's eyes sparkled from across the table. "Not to change the subject, but I'm glad you got to meet Helena and Tam. Peter poked me in the arm and said the word pretty."

"Oh? About the picture you were coloring together?"

"No," he said after chewing another bite. "You are so adorably clueless sometimes. He was talking about *you*, Alabama." Picking up some noodles and a piece of chicken between his chopsticks, Mitch leaned across the table and offered it to her. "Here, take this before you make me feel guilty that you're not eating."

"You *should* feel guilty about not allowing me to eat with a fork." She balked when he practically shoved the bite in her mouth. Laughing, Cassie captured a runaway noodle and then Mitch fed her a few more bites. The man was smart, after all, and he'd obviously figured out they'd be sitting at the table all night if he didn't help her.

"Now it's time for our fortunes." Rising to his feet, Mitch took his plate to the sink. He reached into the bag on the counter and pulled out two plastic-wrapped fortune cookies.

"You don't really believe those things, do you?" Cassie accepted the cookie he offered.

"No, but they can be fun. I'll go first." Unwrapping one, his eyes widened as he returned to his chair.

"Well?" Cassie prompted.

"Maybe I, uh, shouldn't read this one out loud." His cheeks flushed, a rare sight.

"What could that fortune possibly say that would put a blush in Mitch Jacobsen's cheeks?" Surprising him, she tugged it from his grasp. "*Your true love will grant you all the desires of your heart tonight.* Oh, my. I see what you mean."

"Told you." Mitch sat back with crossed arms, a smile teasing the corners of his mouth. "Your turn."

"Okay, here goes." She pushed her long hair behind one shoulder. Tearing open the wrapper, she pulled out the thin white strip of paper from between the jaws of the hard cookie. "*Your true love will climb many mountains for you and hold your hand through the valleys.*" Cassie considered the words. "That's a lovely sentiment, wouldn't you say?"

"I would, you know." When she glanced up at him, Mitch took both her hands in his. "I'd do anything for you, Cassie."

"Me, too," she murmured. "For you, I mean."

"Let's go sit on the couch for a while before I take you back to Amy's." Gathering their empty food cartons, he tossed them in the trash. After filling Sammie's food dish, they walked out to the living room together, arm-in-arm.

For a few minutes, they talked about nothing in particular. Cassie loved the closeness, the knowledge that she could say anything and he'd accept it, accept *her*. Not that they agreed on everything. They'd sparred about little things here and there, but she had the feeling if they both got going on opposite sides of the fence, it could get heated. Then they'd have fun making up again.

Before she knew what was happening, their comments became more infrequent, their gazes full of longing. She wasn't nervous, and she welcomed his kiss. Drawing her close, Mitch lowered his lips to hers. His kiss was light, teasing, and then became more firm. Sinking into the kiss, Cassie enjoyed the feel, the taste, of his mouth on hers. All-consuming. Dangerous. Exciting. Heated.

We need to be careful.

"You're such a natural at this." He kissed her again and murmured how beautiful she was. He moved his warm lips to her jaw, her cheek and then nibbled behind her ear. Oh, that was good. Maybe *too* good. She shivered, and not from being cold.

After one last kiss, Mitch eased away, putting distance between them. "As much as I hate to say it, I need to take you back now."

Flushed from his kisses, Cassie nodded, thankful yet more than a little dazed. "I know." She could kiss him all night, and he wanted to kiss her all night. But, no. Time to go. "Is it too far to walk?"

"Not at all," he said with a soft chuckle. "That's a great idea. It'll help clear the cobwebs from my head. Who knows? Maybe I'll finally meet some of my neighbors."

Wrapping Sammie's leash around his hand, Mitch asked her to lock the door behind them and then they headed down the front steps of the townhouse together.

Cassie laughed as Sammie pranced like a stallion. "Why, Sammie, you're a closet stud muffin."

"That's my guy." Mitch grinned and hooked his free arm through hers.

They walked slowly, making observations about everything and nothing. Stealing kisses, stargazing and admiring the moon. They didn't meet any of Mitch's neighbors, but they had fun and enjoyed the mild spring evening.

"Hey, are you up to sharing a foot-long hot dog?" He nodded toward a corner street vendor.

She laughed. "What? You don't think you shoved enough Chinese noodles and chicken down my throat?"

He cocked a brow. "Oh, trust me. You haven't lived until you've had a Corner Dog." Three minutes later, they sat side-by-side on a park bench. Pinching off a piece of the bun, Mitch tossed it to Sammie.

"I hope you have antacids handy," Cassie said. "You're right, though. This is really good. You can't beat a good hot dog every now and then. Don't tell me what's in it, just give me a dog. It's one of my mottos." She shot a look at Sammie sitting beside her. "Hot dog, Sammie. No offense."

"I like your mottos," Mitch said, licking his lips after giving her a quick kiss. "The mustard from your half tastes really good."

"Mitch, doesn't it seem like we've known each other for years instead of only a few months?" she said as they stood outside the building where Amy and Landon lived.

"I think my soul's known you my whole life."

What could a girl say to that? She beckoned him closer. "I love you, Mitch."

With Sammie tugging on the leash, Mitch chuckled under his breath and met her lips. "Fine by me. Love you, too, Cassie."

~

Sunday Morning ~ April 25, 2004

Cassie's beautiful voice garnered more than a few admiring glances from the members of the congregation. She reached for his hand after the offertory hymn and left it there for the remainder of the service. He loved having Cassie next to him, worshipping together, praying together. She didn't hush him and order him not to sing, so that was a positive sign.

I want this. Not only for today.

Mitch opened his Bible and Cassie leaned close as the pastor read from James 2:14-17. "*What use is it, my brethren, if someone says he has faith but he has no works? Can that faith save him? If a brother or sister is without clothing and in need of daily food, and one of you says to them, 'Go in peace, be warmed and be filled,' and yet you do not give them what is necessary for their body, what use is that? Even so faith, if it has no works, is dead, being by itself.*"

"That's the theme verse for Tam's Place," Mitch whispered. Although he tried, his focus wasn't on the pastor's message. He kept stealing glances, and then she'd catch him and give him the shy smile he loved so much.

After a quick lunch with Amy and Landon, Mitch asked her if she wanted to do a little sightseeing. Her eager response thrilled him. He didn't want to tire her out, but he appreciated seeing his favorite city through the fresh eyes of a first-time visitor. At Ellis Island, Cassie squealed when she spied her last name in a computer. "Look, Mitch! There are three names listed under Thorenson." Taking him by the hand, she tugged him closer.

"Frederick Thorenson arrived in 1917 at the age of twenty-eight, but it doesn't say from what country. Hans Ole Thorenson arrived in 1892 at age seventeen. From the name Gothenburg, I'd assume he was from Germany, wouldn't you?"

"Hmm," he murmured. "With the name Hans, it's a fair bet."

"Then there's Rolf Thorenson. That's an interesting name. Isn't that the first name of the telegram delivery boy in *The Sound of Music* that Liesl—the oldest von Trapp daughter—fell for, but then he betrayed her by literally blowing the whistle on them? It says he was from Agnes, Norway, and he arrived in 1924 at the age of nineteen."

"Hmm," he said again, nuzzling her cheek and enjoying her excited chatter. "You sure talk a lot, woman." She might as well be speaking German. He couldn't focus on anything other than having her near him. He hated the thought of letting her go again. . .all the way back to Texas.

"You're not paying attention, Mitch."

"Oh, I'm paying plenty of attention to you, Cassie. I can't help it. You're completely distracting me." He enjoyed her blush. The woman was beyond beautiful, and he'd started to seriously consider paying a visit to City Hall on Monday morning just to keep her in the city with him.

On the Staten Island Ferry, the wind whipped her long hair around her face and her blue eyes sparkled with excitement as the boat approached the Statue of Liberty. He snapped a photo. That was the one he'd frame for his office. They dodged the birds flocking around the base of the Statue and then toured the exhibits before sharing a waffle cone of homemade strawberry ice cream. Before leaving, Mitch bought her a green foam crown and fake plastic torch in the gift shop.

As the taxi driver drove them back into the city, Mitch asked him to stop at a jewelry store.

"What are we doing here?" Cassie asked, her voice sounding a little nervous.

He pointed to the sign above the door. "It's Free Appraisal Day. I saw it advertised on a billboard five miles back."

"What are we appraising? I'm surprised they're open on Sunday, and especially so late in the afternoon."

"It's a special event. They do this twice a year or something. I thought we'd see if they can appraise the ring set that angry jilted groom threw on the ground. Just so we'll know once and for all. You still have the rings in your purse, right?"

Cassie nodded. "Yes. I told you as part of the whole library caper story, didn't I?"

"You sure did." Mitch liked the fact she'd kept the rings and carried them with her at all times. Had to be some significance to that. He opened the door and led her inside. There were three tables set up and short lines for each one— one for rings, one for necklaces and one for miscellaneous pieces. "Do you mind waiting?"

"My time is yours," she said, already engaged in conversation with an older gentleman in the ring line. Cassie could charm anyone, anytime. He'd noticed how people reacted to her. That accent could soften anyone, and her gentle manner naturally drew others to her. A natural beauty, inside and out.

"Next!" The man sitting behind the table looked like he was ready to call it a day, and he darted a glance at the clock on the wall. "What do we have here?" He held out his hand with a bored expression.

"I have a ring we'd like appraised, sir." Cassie handed it to him.

After taking the ring, the man positioned the funky-looking magnifying glass he wore strapped around his head. "Where are you from, young lady?" He turned the engagement ring back and forth, twisting it this way and that. Bringing it closer, he studied it intently.

"Tuscaloosa originally. I live in Houston now."

"My dad was from near Tuscaloosa." He named a town and Cassie brightened.

"My mama was from there. Best catfish in the state."

He lowered the ring and smiled so wide Mitch thought his face might crack. "You got that right," he said. "Where'd you get this ring?"

Mitch's pulse raced. Why, he had no idea. Cassie was doing great, so he'd let her handle it.

"In Houston." Cassie shot him a look. Good answer. No sense in going into the explanation with a man who could probably care less.

"You got the matching wedding band, too?"

"Yes, sir."

The man pushed the apparatus back in place as he took the band she offered to him. "Young lady, you've got yourself a real fine set here." He nodded at Mitch. "And you've got a beautiful girl, son. Treat her right."

"I certainly will, sir." Mitch didn't want to ask for the estimated appraisal value, but he was itching to know.

"Can you tell us—" Cassie began before the man cut her off.

"I'll write down the appraisal amount, they'll input it into the computer and then give it to you over there." He pointed to a man and woman working together behind the counter. "Take one of these numbers," he said, giving her a wink. Either that or he had a serious twitch. "Say hi to Alabama for me next time you're there."

"I sure will. Thank you very much."

Mitch pulled off the number—fifteen—and showed it to Cassie. "I'd say that's significant."

"February fifteenth." Her eyes widened as she stared at the number and then up at him. "The date of the wedding ceremony in the park?"

"Right." They moved over to a less populated corner of the store while they waited for their number to be called. "Mr. Jeweler acted like the rings might actually be worth something."

"I know," she said. "The police officer might have guessed wrong. Maybe I should have had them appraised sooner." She giggled. "Who am I kidding? I've never had anything to appraise before in my entire life. It's not something I'd ever consider."

"Then all the more reason to be here now." Within another ten minutes, Mitch heard their number called. "Is there any cost?" he asked, reaching for his wallet.

"Not on free appraisal days." The woman handed an envelope to Cassie. "Your appraisal's in there. If you ever have any jewelry needs, I hope you'll come and see us. And may I say"—she glanced at Cassie—"that's a beautiful ring set. I wish you two the best."

"Thank you," Mitch said. Cassie added her thanks before they left the store.

"When should we open the envelope?" she asked as soon as the door closed behind them.

"I vote now. My curiosity's killing me."

"I agree." She handed him the foam crown and torch. After opening the back flap of the envelope, she quickly pulled out the appraisal. She moved beside him so he could read it at the same time. "Oh. My. Word. Mitch!" Cassie's fingers shook and the paper would have fluttered to the ground if he hadn't caught it.

His eyes widened as he spied the large amount written on the paper.

Wow, Lord, You knew all along, didn't You?

216

Chapter 38

Monday Morning ~ April 26, 2004

After a quick breakfast with Amy and Landon, Cassie stood on the front steps of their building while Louie carried her bags to the taxi. "Amy, I had such a great time this weekend. Thank you so much for everything." A light rain fell, and she scooted under the overhang before she got wet.

"You're more than welcome. It was a lot of fun." Amy gave her a warm, lingering hug. "I hope we'll see you again sooner than later. I'll be praying for you and Mitch. The Lord's hand is in this relationship, and I'm excited to see what He's going to do. We love you, sweetie."

"Love you, too." Cassie gave her another quick hug, reluctant to say good-bye. "Please tell Landon thanks again."

"I told Mom about the Lawrie sculpture, mainly because I wanted her to know the great pains you took to get it back for us. She's a bit perturbed with Mitch, but said to thank you."

"I'm glad my crazy plan that wasn't really a plan worked, but that might be the end of my detective career."

Amy smiled. "Call me when you get back to Houston so I'll know you're safe and sound. Beck's picking you up at the airport, right?" When Cassie nodded, she continued. "Please give everyone my love and give Chloe an extra kiss from her Aunt Amy."

"Will do."

"Winnie's bringing Chloe for their next weekend visit in June. You'll have to join us for one of our girls' weekends one of these days."

How she loved Amy's support and encouragement. "Sounds like a plan."

As Louie drove her through the bustling city streets—much busier again since it was the start of the new work week—Cassie replayed the events of the weekend through her mind. In retrospect, it had flown by quickly, but they'd managed to do so much. She smiled as she remembered their mutual shock over the appraisal for the rings. The round diamond was slightly more than two carats and worth thirty thousand dollars. Together with the matching band with six small diamonds, the set was appraised for an astounding forty thousand dollars. She shook her head, still amazed. Always amazed.

Mitch called it a God thing—the circumstances of how they'd come into possession of the rings. The whole thing seemed crazy, but she'd lived it and knew it to be true. Mitch told her how a guy traditionally wanted to be able to have his fiancée pick out the rings she wanted. Cassie suspected it was because of the money issue. What was it about men and money, anyway? Like it made a guy more of a man if he was the one to pay?

After asking her to put the diamond on her finger again, Mitch had held her hand. "The perfect fit is no mistake, you know. We couldn't have picked out more a more perfect ring if we'd tried." His smile, and the kiss that followed, were irresistible.

"I agree," she said in the quiet taxi. She still wore the ring, unable to remove it. Did this mean they were engaged? Oh, it was so confusing. Was it too soon? Were they crazy? Maybe, but did she care? She loved Mitch and hated the thought of leaving him again.

"What was that, Miss Cassie?" Louie called over his shoulder.

"Just thinking about a God thing, Louie. Lots of those going around these days." Light rain pelted the windows, a reflection of her mood.

"You can say that again. We'll be in front of Mr. Mitch's office building in two minutes. Be prepared to hop out. I'll be somewhere nearby. Give me a call ten minutes before you're ready to leave, but we should leave no later than noon in order to get you to LaGuardia on time to check in for your flight. By the way, the flight's on-time as scheduled."

"Thank you, Louie. You're the best." When he stopped for a light, Cassie opened her handbag and pulled out her gift for him. "Here," she said, handing him the box of Godiva chocolates through the window separating the backseat from the front of the taxi. "You won't let me tip you, so this is something to express my appreciation."

"Ah, my favorite. Thank you, Miss Cassie. You didn't have to do that."

"Yes, I did. I can't tell you how much your warm welcome meant to me when I first arrived. And then taking me downtown to the store. And picking me up this morning."

He chuckled as he pulled through the light. "Glad to do it for you. New York's not quite so scary, is it?"

"No, it's not. Not at all."

~

Mitch met Cassie in the lobby of his building, escorted her into the elevator and then up to his 33rd floor office. "I'm going to introduce you to a few people but then I need to jump in on a conference call with some Japanese clients. Sorry, but it can't be helped."

"Not a problem."

He introduced her to a handful of his close associates, and Cassie prayed she wouldn't be called upon to remember their names since it all happened so fast. Then he took her down the hallway and into the break room, asking her to wait. Giving her a quick kiss, Mitch told her he'd be back as soon as he could. "Do you want a magazine to read?"

"I'll be fine," she said. "Go on, and don't worry about me."

A pretty, dark-haired woman came into the room a few minutes later. "Want some coffee?"

"No, thanks." She'd already had more than her quota at Amy's. If she didn't want to spend the entire flight in the lavatory, she needed to refrain.

"Aren't you Cathy?" The woman gave her a curious look as she poured coffee into a mug and stirred in a packet of artificial sweetener.

"It's Cassie, actually."

"Oh, that's right. Forgive me. You're every bit as cute in person as you sound on the phone."

"When did—"

"Jen Goodrich. I'm Mitch's assistant."

"Nice to meet you, Jen." When she offered her hand, the other woman paused a moment before giving it a brief shake. Was that the wrong thing to do? Feeling like she was under a microscope, Cassie tried not to squirm. Could be the condescending way Jen had called her cute. She'd wanted to look nice for her visit to the office and—unlike most of America, apparently—she preferred to dress up for the plane flight home. In contrast to Jen's sophisticated dress— cut too low and revealing some serious cleavage—her own simple, classic pale pink dress could perhaps be considered *cute*. She bristled. Likewise, the word *sweet* was really starting to grate on her nerves all over again.

Mitch's assistant also wore a lot of makeup, enough so that Cassie had to wonder what she'd look like without it. Not that she looked cheap, but why did women feel the need to cover up their natural beauty? The way she saw it, God gave every woman unique features. They needed to accept and embrace them, not try to disguise them in some misguided attempt to look like everyone else.

Jen sat in a chair on the opposite side of the table, sipping her coffee. "Have you had a nice visit?"

"Yes, thanks. It's been great. New York's a fascinating city."

"I meant more in terms of your time with Mitch." Her eyes narrowed when she spied the ring on Cassie's finger. "Are you two engaged now? Seriously?"

"Well—" How to explain?

Jen spoke again first, thankfully sparing Cassie from having to formulate a feasible answer. "I'm surprised Mitch wants to settle down so soon. I mean, he's dated a lot, so maybe he finally worked the wanderlust out of his system and realized what a diamond in the rough he'd found in you."

"Excuse me?" Cassie tried to keep her anger in check, but this woman was blatantly egging her on. Like Sally Reynolds all those years ago but in a much more grownup way when she'd emphasized the wrong syllable in the word wanderlust. Why would Jen harbor such a strong dislike for her?

"Oops, look at the time." With a quick glance at her watch, Jen pushed back her chair and poured the rest of her coffee in the sink. "I need to get back now. Mitch asked me to sit in and take notes at the end of his important conference call. Congrats on your engagement or whatever, sweetie. Have a nice flight back home to Alabama or wherever you live."

"Texas," Cassie muttered. She sat and stewed for a few minutes, wondering how long Mitch's conference call would last. Glancing at the clock on the wall, she bit her lower lip.

"My, my. Mitch Jacobsen sure is a lucky man."

What now? Cassie blew out a breath, trying not to be obvious about it.

A dark-haired man came around to the side of the table and offered his hand. "Tony Marzetti. I heard there was a beautiful girl in the house, but the description didn't do you adequate justice."

"Cassie Thorenson. Nice to meet you."

He eyed her in a manner Grandma Thor would have called impudent, lacking respect and honor for a lady. *Thank you, Lord, that I'm sitting down.* She felt his gaze raking over as it was and crossed her arms over her chest. She gritted her teeth and forced a smile. "Nice to meet you."

"Mind if I join you for a few minutes?" Not waiting for her answer, he pulled out a chair and dropped into it.

"Not at all." Inside, her sense of unease mounted. What kind of place was this? Obviously, it was full of players. Maybe that was an unfair assessment, but the behavior of Jen and Tony would attest to that particular notion.

"Tell me, Cassie, what kinds of things do you like?"

What in the world? "I'm not sure what you mean. I like Mitch," she stammered. "He's kind and has a great sense of humor." Maybe that would put him in his place.

"A woman like you must be used to getting what she wants from a man." With a glint in his pale gray eyes, Tony leaned forward.

A woman like you? Inside, Cassie seethed and prayed Mitch would return soon. She couldn't take much more of these people and their rude, snide insinuations from what she wore to her personal life. She scooted her chair back a few inches, cringing at the sound when it scraped the break room floor. "I'm not interested in getting anything in the way you're implying, Mr. Marzetti."

"Are you really as innocent as you act? Is that possible?" Rising to his feet beside her, Tony reached for her hair. He dropped his hand when she stepped back a few paces, putting distance between them. "My, my. I do believe you are. Look at those big, clear blue eyes. How old are you?"

"Old enough to recognize when I need to walk away." Cassie prepared to leave, but she wasn't quick enough.

Touching her arm, Tony pulled her around to face him. "Sweetheart, all Jacobsen can offer you is a good head of hair, a trust fund courtesy of his famous grandfather and big dreams."

Cassie tried to slow her breathing. The unmitigated nerve of this guy! "Besides the fact we don't even know one another, neither my affections nor anything else can be bought for any amount of money." Pivoting to storm away,

Cassie stopped short when she spied Mitch. A sense of relief flooded through her. Judging by the fire in his eyes, he'd returned during her speech.

Mitch's piercing stare skewered the other man. "Tony, you have five seconds to get out of here." His voice was commanding, a low growl.

"Come on, Mitch. I'm only complimenting your lovely lady. I was telling her what a lucky man you are."

Mitch didn't answer and Tony's gaze moved back to her again. "Call me when he tires of you, sweetheart. He always does. Eventually." With that final parting shot, Tony stalked out of the room.

"What's up with that guy?" Mitch sounded outraged. "Are you okay? I'm sorry. I had no idea he'd come in here and act like that."

"I think I'm okay, considering the fact that in the span of ten minutes, I've been treated like a cute little nothing and a. . .well, a paid escort. . .or something." She shook her head. "I'm not even sure which was worse, to be honest."

"Shh," Mitch said, pulling her to him. "You're shaking. Who else came in here?"

"Never mind. It doesn't matter." She needed to leave. Get on a plane and return to her normal life in Houston. Shake off the effects of this strange morning and focus on the great time she'd had with Mitch. Figure out the next step.

A distinguished, gray-haired man appeared in the hallway. "Mitch, a word, please?"

"Sure, Gordon. I'll be right there."

The man gave her a curt nod and departed.

"That's one of our senior partners. I need to talk with him, Cassie. Forgive me for not introducing you. Some things transpired in the conference call a few minutes ago, and I know that's why he's sought me out." Mitch's sigh was deep and his countenance spoke of his weariness. "I advised the clients not to invest in a stock the firm's been pushing down our throats lately, so I'm pretty sure Gordon's not pleased with me. You don't balk the system. It's the first time I've ever done it, but I can't push something I consider a bad risk. I think they're wrong on this one, and I let it be known."

Cassie took his hand. "I'll say a prayer while you're in there. No matter what happens, God will take care of you. And so will I. Remember that."

"Thanks. I'll probably need your prayers. Your faith in me means everything, Cassie." For the first time since she'd known him, Mitch appeared genuinely worried. "I need to go. It can't be helped. Sorry. Wait for me, please." After brushing a quick kiss on her forehead, he walked down the hallway and didn't look back.

She glanced at the clock, disheartened. Unease settled inside her and she doubted she'd be able to shake it until she left the building. This office was starting to give her the creeps. "I'll wait," she said into the quiet of the hallway.

Rounding the corner to go sit in the reception area—an area she hoped would be safe—Cassie overheard raised voices. Without a doubt, one of them was Mitch. The door to the corner office stood open. Against her better judgment, she hesitated.

"Mitch, what are you saying? You want out?"

Cassie covered her mouth to muffle her gasp, unable to believe what she'd heard. Had she stepped into a realm of nightmarish proportions? Had the world suddenly gone completely crazy?

She closed her eyes. *Lord, what's happening?*

"I never wanted this, Gordon, but I have no choice. For the past couple of years, especially, I've been going through the motions. I've done a good job for you, made a lot of money for this firm and our clients, but I can't do it anymore. I used to be excited to come into the office every morning. Used to get pumped up when I made a good trade. But some things recently have highlighted the deficiencies in my life. The thrill of the hunt is gone. I miss the pure *joy* in loving what I do. You need someone young and hungry. Someone who will give you the 24/7 you want. I'm no longer that man and you deserve more than I can give. My heart's not in it."

A long pause ensued. Cassie opened her eyes and slumped against the wall, thankful no one else was around.

"What do you plan on doing? Where will you go?" The older man's tone had transitioned from anger to resigned acceptance.

"I'm not sure yet, but with God's help, I'll figure it out."

"You've managed to do it again, Mitch. Even in making what I consider a huge mistake professionally, you have my respect. You're an honorable man. If you need a reference, let me know."

"I'll keep that in mind. I'll give you another couple of weeks—a month, if you want—to get things wrapped up here."

Cassie held her breath while Gordon apparently considered Mitch's offer. "That's a good plan. I'd like to pick your brain on a few things and see if I can get you to spill your secrets. The way you can get millions out of old lady Donovan for one. I know it's more than sweet talk, but I can't figure it out. She's tighter than a drum with her money. And don't even get me started on Roger Parker. Whatever you choose to do, I know it'll be a worthy endeavor and you'll give it your all. I'm sorry to see you go, but thanks for everything you've done for us all these years, Mitch. If you change your mind, let me know."

"It's been my honor. Now, if you'll excuse me, I need to say good-bye to Cassie."

"Let's meet tomorrow morning to discuss your exit strategy."

"Thanks, Gordon."

When he strolled back into the hallway, hands in his pockets, Mitch spied her and frowned. "I guess you heard all that?" His voice held an edge she'd never heard before. She didn't like it, but she understood he was under stress. In that moment, she wished she could, in fact, wind back the clock and go through the door to the past.

"I didn't mean to eavesdrop, Mitch, but the door was open. It's my turn to ask—are you okay?"

He raked his fingers through his hair. "Yes. I don't know. Maybe. I didn't expect to go in there and give my notice. In some ways, maybe it was hasty, but in another way, I've wanted to do that for a long time. Most of all, I hate that you're leaving." He moved his hands to his hips. "I'm kind of a mess right now. Thanks for putting up with me."

"Anytime. Louie's waiting downstairs and I really need to get to the airport now."

"Sure. Please give Louie my best." Moving one hand around her waist, Mitch walked her to the elevator. "I'll pray for a safe flight and call you tonight."

"Okay," she said, trying not to be hurt by the fact that he didn't intend to ride in the elevator with her to the main lobby and then put her in the taxi.

"Moonbeam, I had a great time this weekend. I'm so happy you were here and my birthday surprise was the best ever. When I call you tonight, let's make plans for the next visit."

For some reason, she got the feeling he meant her coming to New York again. Did he ever plan on coming to Houston? Would he ever be able to step foot on a plane again? Cassie didn't want to feel like she was chasing a man, but if she was the one coming to him every time, that's exactly how she'd feel. Relationships were a two-way street. Two people meeting one another in the middle.

"Sure," she said.

When he kissed her, she broke it off with a small cry. "I have to go now."

"Cassie—"

"Good-bye, Mitch. We'll talk soon."

"Right."

The last thing she saw as the elevator doors closed was his handsome face, but he didn't look happy. Neither was she. Not the ending of the weekend she'd expected. Not at all.

Chapter 39

A KNOCK SOUNDED on his door. Mitch's heart skipped a few beats as he bounded to the door, hoping Cassie had come back for a last kiss. He hated the way they'd parted. Maybe he'd acted like a jerk, but his entire world had suddenly turned on its axis.

Jen stood in the doorway. Crossing her arms, emphasizing the low cut of her dress, she gave him a seductive smile. "I thought you might want some company."

"Why would you think that?"

"Let me count the ways. You more or less walked away from your high-profile, well-paying job. Not to mention your sweet and oh-so-innocent girlfriend got hit on by the lowest of the lowlifes around this place—"

"I'll call Becky in Human Resources right now if you so much as say one word against Cassie." Mitch bit his tongue not to lash out and tell Jen she'd never be half the woman Cassie was. Why was she hitting on him if she couldn't respect his decision to leave the firm? Nothing in his world made sense.

"Sorry." Walking further into the room, Jen kicked the door closed with her red, high-heeled shoe. What kind of shoe was that to wear to the office? Her outfit was more suited for a nightclub after-hours, not a professional work environment.

"Leave the door open, please." He moved to open the door when Jen stepped to her right, blocking his way. It didn't take much to read what was on her mind when she pressed up against him and raised her painted red lips. She must think it would entice him, but all it did was make him want to make a mad dash for the airport, haul Cassie out of that queue for her flight and take her home with him. Back to the townhouse. Permanently.

In one quick move, Mitch stepped around Jen and jerked open the door. "I'm asking you nicely to leave my office. For the next two weeks, I don't want to see you—or hear from you—except for business. Otherwise, stay clear. If I didn't already have one foot out the door, you'd be packing up your desk right now. Do I make myself perfectly clear?"

~

"Louie, can you please wait for me a few more minutes? Sorry, but I need to see Mitch one more time. I forgot to. . .tell him something." Cassie had never felt so unsettled. More than anything, she hated to leave with things so weird between them. If she hurried, she could talk with him for a few more minutes and still make it to the airport with plenty of time to spare.

224

Louie chuckled. "Go kiss the guy one more time. I'll be waiting when you get back. Go on. Give him my regards."

"Will do. Thanks. Be back in five minutes. Don't leave without me."

"I'll be waiting, Miss Cassie."

Shifting from foot to foot, she fought her frustration as she waited at the bank of elevators. Finally, she heard the ding of the elevator on the far left and hurried down to it. She returned the polite nods of several others entering the elevator and tried to quell her apprehensions. As soon as the doors slid open on the 33rd floor, she hurried out and opened the heavy glass door to the brokerage office. The receptionist wasn't behind her desk. What to do? After only a moment's hesitation, Cassie headed down the hallway toward Mitch's office. She stopped outside his door when she heard voices, one of them female.

Oh no, here we go again.

"Mitch, I understand why you're attracted to her. She's pretty and she's safe. You can take her home to Mom and not be embarrassed. She's the type of girl who'll cook your meals, do your laundry, keep your bed warm at night and give you adorable children. But she's not exciting. She's comfortable, but she's not what you really want long term."

Cassie moved her hand over her mouth. As much as she wanted to barge in his office, she needed to wait and hear Mitch's response first. *Lord, forgive me for eavesdropping.* Her life had apparently morphed into a soap opera. In the span of an hour, her life had gone from great, to good, to bad, then worse. Now, it seemed it had sunk to the lowest depths. Not much lower it could go.

"Jen, I've done nothing to encourage you or lead you to believe there's anything between us other than as professional colleagues."

Thank you, Mitch.

"Don't worry," Jen said. "I'll tell Becky myself that I need to be reassigned, but you wouldn't want me to imply there are personal—as in *intimate*—reasons for my request, would you?"

To his credit, Mitch snorted. Good man. *Throw her out on her ear.* She'd ask forgiveness for that one later, but Jen deserved what she had coming.

"You don't know when to quit, do you?" Mitch said. "Unbelievable. I'd suggest—if you don't want to find yourself unemployed as of today—you march back to your desk and let's both forget this ever happened."

"We don't have any witnesses. Mitch, you're an incredible man and I'm very attracted to you. I can't believe you're actually thinking of marrying that southern girl. Come on. All I'm asking is the opportunity to show you how great it could be—"

That's it. She'd heard enough. Pushing open the door, Cassie didn't say anything but she enjoyed the expression on Jen's face when she spied her.

Although the woman attempted to compose her features into a look of neutrality, it didn't work. "Cathy!" Jen had the decency to lower her gaze. "I thought you'd left."

"Obviously. As Mitch can attest, I like surprising people. I believe I heard him tell you to leave. I suggest you take your hands off his chest and heed that suggestion."

Smoothing a hand over her dress, Jen walked past her, elbowing her on the way to the door.

"Jen?"

The other woman turned, her eyes narrowed.

"It's Cassie, for the record, and yes, you *did* have a witness. Oh, and one more thing? Alabama girls ain't stupid." Cassie gave the door a firm push with one hand. Turning back to Mitch, she raised a brow and gave him a sheepish grin. "Did I actually use the word heed? And—Heaven forbid—ain't?"

Mitch nodded and the grin she loved emerged. "Yes, I believe you did. I'm so glad you came back, and you can't even begin to know how proud I am of you right now, Cassie. I'm going to miss you so much." Hauling her into his arms, he gave her a soul-dragging, heart-palpitating kiss the likes of which would keep a silly grin on her face all the way back to Houston. And then some.

Finally, Mitch pulled away. "When I first saw you standing in the doorway, I was afraid you were going to misinterpret what was happening and every bad cliché of the other woman scenario I could think of ran through my mind in the span of twenty seconds."

"I guess with me, you can expect the unexpected." Her eyes widened when Mitch slid to the floor on one knee.

"Cassie, I'll be unemployed in a few weeks and have no idea what my future holds, but I'm completely in love with you. I want you with me on my life's journey whether it's to darkest Africa or wherever the Lord leads." He ran his finger over the diamond. "The Lord's guiding hand has been in this relationship all along, and I want to marry you."

Rising to his feet, he kissed her fingers, first on her left hand below the ring and then on her right hand. "Cassandra Liane Thorenson, will you agree to wear this ring as my pledge to you of my love and the promise of all my tomorrows?"

She smiled through her tears. "Fine by me, Mitchell Ainsworth Jacobsen."

Chapter 40

Monday, July 12, 2004 ~ Mitch's Townhouse

*M*ITCH HESITATED, DARTING a glance at his laptop still open on the kitchen table. A new email had come in, but he was almost out of time or he'd be late getting over to Tam's Place. Thinking the email might be from Cassie, he crossed the kitchen with Sammie at his heels. Better check just in case.

He quickly scanned the list of emails. Josh Grant. Dropping into the chair, Mitch clicked on the message.

Hey Mitch,
Confirming your arrival at Bush Intercontinental
Friday, July 16, 2004
Delta Flight 1309 arriving at 4:20 p.m.
Will meet you at baggage claim.
Praying for you, brother. Read Sam's book on the flight.
That'll either put you to sleep or keep you calm.
Until His Nets Are Full,
Josh

Mitch hoped Lexa and Winnie would be able to keep his visit a secret. That might be tough since they worked so closely with Cassie. Knowing of Cassie's close relationship with Rebekah, he'd thought it best not to mention it to Kevin although they'd been in touch a few times. Maybe he didn't have a prayer of pulling this off, but he had to try. Every time he envisioned Cassie's face flushed with pleased surprise, it got his heart pumping hard and fast.

Almost three months without seeing her in person had been pure torture. If not for the wonders of modern technology, he'd have gone out of his mind. Thoughts of her preoccupied most of his waking thoughts. No woman had ever captured him like this. He'd never truly loved a woman until now—loved her heart, her mind, her spirit and deep faith. The promise of loving her in every way was sweet, but he prayed the Lord would take away those thoughts until she became his wife. Then he'd embrace the reality of loving her fully.

Focus. He rubbed a hand over his jaw. Dashing off a quick reply email to Josh, he confirmed the details of his flight, not bothering to check the itinerary since he'd memorized it. He needed to pray he didn't hyperventilate on that flight. If Cassie knew he was coming by plane, she'd worry. Another reason not to tell her. Why worry her when he was anxious enough for both of them? He'd long ago given up the idea the Lord would somehow be displeased with him for breaking the vow never to fly again. That was a rash decision made in the heat of the moment after the crash landing, compounded by losing Brad because of another aircraft. The plane that slammed into the South Tower wasn't evil, but a conduit of the twisted minds of those intent on threatening the security of a free nation.

This was something he needed to do for himself. Conquer his fears. God wouldn't want him to be fearful. *Be anxious for nothing.* He'd cling to that verse, as he always had in all respects of his life.

Lord, I'm still going to need Your help. Always.

~

That Same Morning ~ Houston, Texas

"Cassie, could you come into the office, please?"

That was odd. Lexa rarely used the intercom. Usually she called to her from the open door. She'd also caught a glimpse of Winnie scooting out of her office and into Lexa's a couple of minutes ago. Then she'd closed the door, something they never did.

No reason to be nervous. No way could the business be in any kind of serious financial trouble. Lexa was brilliant with bookkeeping and no one was better than Winnie at coordinating the catering jobs. Business was steady and they were in-demand to the point where they'd had to turn down a number of events. They were talking about hiring more part-time servers. As far as Cassie knew, she hadn't botched scheduling any events. Hadn't burned or otherwise ruined any batches of food, mainly because Winnie still kept her away from the food as a general rule. Standing beside her desk, Cassie smoothed her skirt with one hand and inhaled a quick breath.

Knocking on Lexa's door, she heard her call to come in.

"You wanted to speak with me?" Cassie stepped inside, glancing between her two bosses. They didn't look upset, so that was a relief. "Is everything okay? I haven't done anything egregiously wrong, have I?"

Lexa beckoned for her to come closer and have a seat. "Of course not. The opposite, as a matter of fact. We've both noticed how hard you've been working for us."

Winnie's lips upturned. "Did Chloe teach you that word? Egregious?"

"No, why?"

"Well, she taught it to *me* the other day. One of her ten words. That child is a walking dictionary. Now, back to the matter at hand," Winnie said, clearing her throat. "You've really thrown yourself into your work, especially during the last few months. Above and beyond with all the things you do for us outside of working hours—the babysitting, errands, and everything else. You're always running around on our behalf."

Lexa's smile was kind. "We've been selfish and hope we haven't taken advantage of your good nature and willingness to drop everything to help us whenever we need it."

"It's not like you have to twist my arm. I love helping all of you, and those children of yours are irresistible. Besides, you make it easy. I have no complaints."

Picking up a small, business-sized envelope sitting on the desk, Lexa offered it to her. "This is to say thank you for all you do, but it's also part of the job."

Her eyes wide, pulse beating hard, Cassie took the envelope.

"Go ahead and open it." The enthusiasm in Winnie's voice was infectious.

The flap on the back wasn't sealed and Cassie pulled out a colorful brochure. "What have you two done?"

"We're sending you to The Institute of Culinary Arts in New York for a week!" Winnie announced as Cassie stared at the front of the brochure. "They have all kinds of fabulous classes. We want you to take a week off—paid, of course—and enjoy it. Take a look at the list." Winnie ran her finger down the brochure. "Pastries, breads, Italian cooking, steak and meat preparation. It's not until the middle of August, but you'll have fun and come back with all kinds of new ideas for the business. Don't worry if those dates don't work for you. They're interchangeable since they're ongoing, weekly or bi-weekly classes."

"They'll work fine," Cassie murmured, feeling as though she was in shock. Was this real? She scanned the page, noting her name and reservation number at the top. The courses of study covered everything from appetizer preparation to sautéing, and a few involved making a full-scale gourmet dinner after which the students would discuss their experiences as they sampled the various dishes.

"You're paying me to go to New York?"

"For the job. We insist," Lexa said.

"You wouldn't want to disappoint your bosses now, would you?" Winnie's grin was so sweet that Cassie wanted to hug her.

She opened the brochure again. "Well, I suppose I could take time out of my hectic schedule and go to New York next month. For the good of Doyle-Clarke Catering, of course."

"Plane ticket included," Lexa added. "We might even spring for a private plane if you ask us nicely."

Jumping up from the chair, Cassie opened her arms. "I'm so blessed to have you in my life. Thank you." Both ladies embraced her, hugging her in turn.

"We realize by doing this we'll probably lose you," Lexa said. "But we want to see you happy."

"Yes, you've been pretty hard to take lately, mopey face." Winnie's coy grin belied her words. "Check out that brochure some more. Especially the *Cooking for Two* classes."

"I'll definitely do that."

Back at her desk again, Cassie stared out the front window, lost in thought. It'd been almost three months since she'd seen Mitch. Three *long* months. Keeping busy during the day kept her mind mercifully occupied, but it was in the quiet times and random moments when she ached most for Mitch's friendship as much as anything else. She missed laughing at something silly he'd said or done. Missed slipping her hand in his, resting her head on his shoulder and enjoying the emotional closeness. Never in her wildest imaginings would she have expected to miss a man this much. But Mitch wasn't just any man.

This is the man I love.

Since leaving his Wall Street brokerage firm in the first part of May, Mitch had traveled with the New York TeamWork group on two short-term missions—one week in Haiti and another most recently in the Dominican Republic. He'd assisted the medics with physical exams, shot clinics and the distribution of medical and food supplies. When she'd talked with him, he'd sounded happier than ever. The underlying edge of sarcasm in his voice—often present when she'd first gotten to know him—was still there but had softened. In its place, a more confident maturity had emerged.

Except for when he was on the missions, they'd burned up the phone wires, sent emails, texts throughout the day and talked via Skype most evenings. Once she finally confessed she loved lavender roses more than any other, she'd received a weekly bouquet. Every Monday like clockwork. Her gaze strayed to the lovely blooms on her desk now, and she breathed in deeply, enjoying the fresh fragrance, as sweet as the love blossoming in her heart.

Mitch often asked her to sing for him in the late evening, and although she felt silly, she'd sing a few verses of a new song she'd written. And before signing off, he always told her he loved her. What Mitch didn't realize—not that she'd ever say anything—was that he didn't have to say the actual words. She knew. He told her in everything he said and did.

~

Monday Evening ~ Rebekah and Kevin Moore's Home

Cassie stretched out on a deck chair, a glass of lemonade in her hand. "I don't know, Beck. Am I crazy to be madly in love with the man when I've only spent eight days total with him?"

Rebekah smiled. "Maybe I'm not the one to answer that question, but I think you need to consider how much you did together in those eight days. They were, shall we say, action packed. And you've been in constant communication every day. Sounds completely feasible to me."

"Did I tell you about his latest anniversary gift?"

"The fifteenth of the month gift, you mean? In addition to the *How to Use Chopsticks* instructional video and the gym membership?"

"This month it's a certificate for ten hours of private swimming lessons. He sent it early, but I have no idea why."

"I guess he figured the sooner you got started on the swim lessons, the better. Is he sending Celeste to teach you?"

She laughed. "No. Celeste emails me every now and then. She's back with Ashton, at least as of a week ago. I hope it works out for them. In the last message, she said she was praying for Mitch and me to work out our plans to be together sooner than later. It meant a lot, especially coming from her. I'm hoping to meet Mitch's mom when I go to New York next month for the cooking lessons."

Rebekah smiled. "That move was a stroke of genius. Again, leave it to Lexa—and Winnie, too—to come up with a valid excuse for a little more matchmaking."

"Beck, I'm feeling a little guilty about something."

"Oh?" Rebekah lowered her glass of iced tea after taking a drink. "What's that?"

"I more or less encouraged Mitch to consider leaving his job. I guess I never thought it would happen in the way it did. With me right there in his office, as a matter of fact. That morning was the strangest one of my life. Talk about roller coaster emotions."

"You have no reason to feel guilty, Cass. From what you've told me, Mitch is happier now than he's been in a long time. He wasn't asked to leave his job. Look at it this way: maybe you planted the seed in his mind and it gave him the push he needed to make it a reality. Mitch isn't the kind of man to do something that rash in terms of his professional career. He's worked hard to build his reputation and he wouldn't walk away from it unless he'd already been considering that move. It's also brought him one step closer to a permanent relationship with you."

Cassie eyed her curiously. "How do you figure that?"

"Do you ladies mind if I join you?" Kevin walked out onto the deck and gave Rebekah a quick kiss.

"Not at all," Cassie said after sipping her lemonade. "You can lend the male perspective."

Kevin laughed. "Maybe I should leave now."

"Oh no, you don't." Rebekah grabbed his hand and pulled him down into the chair beside hers. "Cassie's missing Mitch and she's wondering—since he's no longer working on Wall Street—why he's not down here visiting her."

"Your wife's putting words in my mouth." Cassie shook her head with a smile.

"Are you denying the truth of anything I just said?"

Both Kevin and Rebekah waited. "No. I cannot." She blew out a breath.

Kevin stretched out his legs and took a sip from Rebekah's iced tea. "Mitch is a go-getter, but—from my perspective—he's also the type who could easily become a workaholic. He's a man with an extremely strong work ethic. A commitment to excellence. Those qualities are admirable as long as it's not to the exclusion of other things."

"Such as a personal life?" Cassie traced a pattern in the sweat of her glass, pondering his words. She'd always trusted Kevin's judgment, almost as much as Sam's.

"Yes," Kevin said. "The way I see it, the Lord's bringing opportunities into his life. He's leading Mitch to where He wants him to be, in order to reach his full potential, both professionally and personally. Working a mission is one of the best ways to clear your head and get your priorities in order, so I'm glad he's been able to go on those short-term missions. Before he can fully commit to his future with you, I think he needs to find out for himself where he belongs."

"Putting his house in order," Rebekah said.

"That's one way to put it." Kevin took another sip of the tea. "By the way, Mitch read Sam's book. Sam gave it to him and suggested he read a chapter a night during that road trip back to New York in February. Rule Number 5 seems to apply to your current situation."

Both Rebekah and Cassie leaned forward. "Which is?" Cassie said.

"I don't know it verbatim, but the book's upstairs."

"Paraphrase please," Rebekah said, winking at her husband.

"Basically, it's the idea that a Christian man is the leader of his home. It's our God-given right and responsibility to take care of our wives and families and put them above ourselves. Once Mitch gets his house in order, I have no doubt he'll come for you, Cassie."

I hope he's right. I'm ready.

Rebekah squeezed her hand. "Mitch doesn't do anything half-heartedly. I'm sure he misses you as much, if not more, than you miss him, sweetie. And when he's ready, that man's going to come charging into Houston and sweep you off your feet. Then he'll carry you off into the sunset to live happily ever after."

"My prince," Cassie said with a small smile.

Maybe Chloe had the right idea, after all.

Chapter 41

Tuesday, July 13, 2004 ~ Sam and Lexa's Home

WOULD YOU TWO please try and focus? We need to get some real work done if we're going to be ready for Friday night."

Both Winnie and Lexa stopped and stared at Cassie.

Winnie cleared her throat. "We're sorry, boss." She made a big show of opening the oven door and pulling out a tray of quiche appetizers, one of her specialties. Always perfectly baked, never burned.

"My apologies," Lexa echoed. "We'll try to be better."

Their final plans and preparations for the sixtieth birthday party they were catering at a prestigious, historic downtown hotel were going well, but for the past twenty minutes, the other two ladies had been telegraphing silent signals to one another and now they were huddled together, laughing quietly. What was up with them? Still, they were her benefactors for the trip to see Mitch next month, so she couldn't ride them too hard.

An hour later, Joe came into the kitchen from where he'd been playing quietly in the family room. He sidled up next to Lexa and laid his head against her shoulder. "Mommy. Hannah cry."

"Oh, I completely forgot the monitor's in the family room." Lexa jumped up from her chair at the desk where she'd been working on the Doyle-Clarke accounting ledgers.

"Go," Cassie said. "Winnie and I can handle things here while you check on her."

"I've got her, Lexa." Sam walked into the kitchen with one small daughter cradled in each arm. Lexa pulled Leah into her arms and together they worked to strap the girls into their highchairs. Watching them, Cassie marveled at how well they'd adapted to the twin routine. Squirming in her seat, Leah started to bounce up and down and clap her hands, and Hannah soon followed.

"Snack time. Yum." Removing his suit jacket and hanging it on a hook by the side door, Sam took a chair at the table with his girls. "What are we having today, Leah?" He nuzzled his baby girl's cheek.

"Dada!" Leah giggled and clamped both hands on Sam's cheeks, squeezing them between her two small, chubby hands. When he blew a loud raspberry, both girls giggled like they'd never stop.

Hannah reached for Sam with both hands, wanting her turn.

"Of course, Hannah Banana." Sam obliged and she let out a belly laugh so loud that Cassie turned to stare at the blonde-haired tyke. So did Winnie.

"Now, those are some mighty impressive lungs," Cassie said. "To think we've always thought Hannah is the quiet one. I suggest you give that child vocal lessons in the near future. Channel all that power into something worthwhile."

"She didn't get it from me, that's for sure." Lexa put small bowls with pureed fruit on the table for the girls and then handed Sam a peach.

"Have any more of those apples or grapes?" Winnie asked. "Non-pureed, that is?" She patted her stomach. "Little Josh or Joshina is getting hungry."

Lexa laughed. "I keep forgetting you're pregnant since you're not showing yet, Winnie, but please don't name that poor child Joshina. You want some fruit, too, Cass?"

"Grapes sound good, thanks." Cassie started to rise from the counter stool. "Let me help you."

"You stay. I'll get them." Lexa reached for the bag of grapes.

"What are you writing now, Sam?" Cassie asked a minute later as she popped a seedless green grape into her mouth.

"I'm just getting started, but if I can convince her, Lexa's going to co-author this one with me. Advice for women in how to help their husbands become a better man and reach their full potential, that sort of thing. Tips for how a couple can work together toward a healthy, God-honoring marriage. What do you think?"

"If you're asking me, I think it's a fabulous idea," Winnie said. "I'm good for a few hints and tips. After all, I trained Josh and he turned out pretty well." She blew air kisses to the twins and then took a bite of an apple wedge.

Cassie's eyes widened. "Kevin mentioned the same thing last night—the part about helping a man reach his full potential."

"By the way, I heard from Max Thomas, the TeamWork director in New York, and he told me Mitch has been invaluable. He's been working behind the scenes with projects in the Bronx and Harlem."

"I didn't know that, but he's helping to build a screened-in porch at Tam's Place," Cassie said, stealing an apple wedge from Winnie. No big surprise Sam had picked up on the fact she'd inadvertently referred to Mitch.

"You and Mitch are keeping in touch every day?" Sam asked.

"Several times over. Once I finally agreed to start texting, the man hasn't been able to stop. He must be exhausted every night from all the texting he does."

"Is that what you kids are calling it these days?" Sam spooned pureed fruit into Hannah's eager mouth.

"Sam!" Lexa scolded although she couldn't stop her smile.

"Tell us more about these rules, suggestions, or whatever you're calling them for your new book," Cassie said.

"Sounds like you have a vested interest in this subject, Little One."

"I guess I do. For the future."

Sam winked at his wife. "For starters, offer your man his favorite fruit at least once a day and he'll love you forever." Taking a bite of his peach, he chewed it slowly. "I'm mulling over a few more. Mind you, these are in no particular order and subject to change."

"Enough with the public service disclaimer or whatever." Winnie waved her hand. "Get on with it already."

"Pregnancy must make some women a little slaphappy," Cassie teased, plopping another grape in her mouth. Winnie threatened to send a flying apple slice her way and she held up her hands as if to catch it. To think this woman was her boss. Ah, she was blessed.

Sam's smile lines appeared. "Okay, here goes. Stifle the first thing you start to say in the morning that you know you'll regret later on in the day. Don't worry so much about what you look like and focus on keeping your heart healthy and happy. If your heart's healthy, it will be reflected in the rest of you. Find one thing about your partner to praise each day and be gracious in accepting compliments when they're offered."

He paused for a minute to feed each of the girls a spoonful and then wiped their messy mouths.

"Be adventurous and willing to try one new thing each day. Focus on at least five small things that make your partner happy each week and work on fulfilling those needs. Have a date night once a week. And without fail, pray together every single day."

Sam took another bite of his peach. "That's what I've got so far."

"I think I'm still reading between the lines of some of those," Winnie said. "Still, really great material."

"Pway!" Hannah clapped her hands together. Cassie smiled as Hannah bowed her head and closed her eyes.

Mimicking her sister, Leah did the same. "Pway!"

Out of the mouths of babes.

Chapter 42

Friday, July 16, 2004

"WHAT TIME IS Josh getting here?" Cassie asked Winnie as they arranged appetizers on a tray.

"Don't worry. He's coming." Under normal circumstances, Winnie would be pacing the floor an hour before an event if her husband hadn't arrived. A pregnant Winnie should be even more agitated. Then there was the fact she'd been avoiding looking her in the eye. Something was amiss. What, she couldn't begin to fathom.

Cassie fisted her hands on her hips. "Forgive me for saying this, but the time might be coming when we don't recruit husbands to help out with these events. I mean, if they can't be on time—"

"Give it up already, Cass." Winnie winked at Lexa. "Our guys dress up the room, they have muscles we need, and—perhaps the biggest shocker—they don't mind helping us out."

"Don't forget they're cheap labor," Lexa said.

"I'll pretend I didn't hear that." Sam put his arm around Lexa and dipped his head for a kiss before heading back out the side door to bring in more trays from their cars.

"If it makes you feel better, I'll call Josh."

"It would, actually," Cassie said. "Thanks, Winnie."

"Yes, Little General."

Cassie made an effort not to roll her eyes. "Please don't tell me that's my new nickname."

"Nothing new about that one."

"Be right back." Needing to escape and focus on the task-at-hand, Cassie left the kitchen and went into the small ballroom to check on the servers. Everything seemed to be in order and the room looked beautiful. White linen tablecloths, fine china and good silver—all special requests of the relatives planning this special birthday party. The floral arrangements in shades of purple, lavender, pink and gray were elegant and a very nice touch. Gayle and Marta waved to her from across the room.

"We light the candles on the tables in twenty minutes," she told the head server. Next she checked the buffet line. The food was warming, the servers ready and waiting. She breathed a sigh of relief. All the details seemed to be in place.

"Gotta run. Love you." Winnie snapped her phone closed as Cassie entered the kitchen again. "Josh is five minutes away. Traffic is bad and he got a late start."

"Thanks for checking. We're all set now, and the guests should be arriving soon."

Winnie's eyes welled with tears. "Honey, you're so good at this. And you look prettier than ever tonight." She gave her a quick, fierce hug. "I'm so happy for you."

Cassie patted her friend on the back. "Everything okay, Winnie?"

"Fine," Winnie said, pulling away. "Just. . .pregnancy hormones kicking in. I predict this night is going to be"—she sniffled—"very special for you, sweetie."

For her career? Wow, those pregnancy hormones must be *really* strong.

~

Mitch started through the door of the hotel's side entrance, but Josh put a hand on his arm, stopping him. "Wait here a minute. I'd better run interference."

"What is this, spy games?"

"Shh. I don't want Cassie to hear you if she's in the kitchen," Josh whispered. "Our six-foot-five lookout is checking. He'll give us the all-clear soon."

Sure enough, Sam appeared in the doorway within the minute. "Great to see you again, Mitch," he said, first shaking his hand and then pulling him into a quick hug. "Glad you could make it. How was the flight?"

"I survived without a major panic attack, so that's a positive step in the right direction. A commercial jet doesn't seem to induce as much anxiety as a private plane."

"I told Mitch that working this event with us tonight is a rite of passage for TeamWork guys," Josh said.

Sam winked at Mitch. "Especially those in love with TeamWork women. Okay now, time to get on with it. The last penguin has arrived."

"Come back in now, you sappy boys. Mitch!" Lexa opened the door and tugged him inside the kitchen before wrapping her arms around him. "I can't tell you how happy I am that you're here. The guests have started to arrive and Cassie will be occupied for a while, so it's safe to come in the kitchen now." Pulling back but still holding onto his arms, Lexa gave him an approving once-over. "You look so handsome. Thanks for agreeing to help us out tonight. I know it's not exactly how you wanted to spend your first night here with Cassie."

Mitch opened his arms and smiled. "Whatever you need. I worked as a waiter in a tony restaurant in Cambridge during my undergrad years at Harvard. Might be a little rusty, but put me to work and I'll try not to do too much damage."

"You're a welcome addition to our group of servers, and I can't wait to see Cassie's reaction to having you here."

"That's the spirit," Winnie said, coming into the kitchen as Lexa departed with a small wave. "Cassie's working hard, but having you here will give her a second wind. And then some." Her breath caught and she moved one hand over her heart. "This will be the best surprise ever for that sweet girl." Following Lexa's example, Winnie enveloped him in a warm hug and then kissed his cheek. "Normally we don't allow the help to kiss our staff, but we'll cut you some slack in this case."

Mitch lifted a brow. *Pregnant?*

Josh gave him a thumbs-up sign and then raised two fingers while Winnie pulled a tissue from the pocket of her apron and dabbed it beneath her eyes. "As you can see, I'm over-the-top emotional these days and cry at the drop of a hat. What a mess."

"You're not a mess, sweetheart." Josh pulled his wife into his arms, giving her a light kiss. "Why don't you sit down for a few minutes?"

"I think I'll do that." Winnie said, hopping onto a counter stool by the stainless steel island in the middle of the kitchen. "I'll park myself right here and you can bring trays or whatever needs to be refilled. Just for a few minutes, though. That's all the time I need and then I'll be good as new."

Sam and Josh asked Mitch questions about his TeamWork experiences in Haiti and the Dominican Republic while they waited for the signal to go into the ballroom. Talking about it energized him and kept his mind occupied. Otherwise, he'd live up to Amy's nickname of Mitch the Itch and drive himself nuts.

Marta rushed into the kitchen a few minutes later. "Cassie's coming in here! Mitch, hey. Great to see you again, but you need to step outside for a minute, okay?"

Mitch chuckled. "Hi Marta, but why can't Cassie just come in here and discover me shooting the breeze with my homeboy fellow penguins?"

"Come with me, funny man."

"You TeamWork women sure do like to manhandle the help." Mitch pretended to grumble even as he allowed Marta to tug him back outside the building.

"Wait here. It'll be worth this silliness in a few minutes. Promise," she whispered, smoothing her apron before hurrying back inside.

Leaning his head against the wall, Mitch wondered how much longer he'd need to wait. He smelled cigarette smoke coming from a small group of hotel employees on their break. Hopefully, they'd call him back in soon.

"Josh and Sam, we're ready for you to come serve the appetizers."

Cassie. He'd know that voice anywhere, that great accent. Closing his eyes, Mitch steeled himself not to barge through the door in spite of their plans for the big surprise. Holding her in his arms again was the only thing on his brain.

Knowing she was so close and he couldn't make his presence known made him crazy.

A few seconds later, Gayle came out to summon him into the small ballroom. "Hi, Mitch. Thanks so much for helping us out tonight. Cassie's going to be so surprised. Now, come with me, please."

"My pleasure. Thanks." With a quick tug on his bow tie, Mitch squared his shoulders. "Houston, we're good to go."

~

Cassie couldn't believe what she'd witnessed. With a firm set to her jaw, she made a mental note of the server's nametag as she neared the buffet line. Stepping behind him, she leaned close and lowered her voice. "Please go wash your hands. Wash for a full minute with hot, soapy water. And when you come back out, don't return to the serving line. You've been reassigned to bus tables."

The man ducked his head, guilt written all over his expression. "Yes, ma'am."

Marta sidled up to her. "What's up, Cass? That guy giving you a hard time?"

"Um, no. I almost wish he had. Let's say he shouldn't be serving food. And he won't be tonight." She shook off a mock-shudder.

"Enough said. Listen, there's a cute new server tonight. Never seen him before."

"We have a few new ones tonight." What was this about?

"I'm not interested for myself," Marta said, "but I can see where a lot of women would take a walk around the block with this guy."

She smiled when Cassie slanted her a frown. "Only making an observation. The guests really like him. It's sort of cute—but also sort of strange, I guess—to hear all the comments from sixty and seventy-year-old women. They keep talking about how he looks like some old time movie star. . .or something like that."

Cassie's pulse sputtered at that comment. Could it be? No, of course not. Mitch would have told her if he planned on coming to see her. A wave of sadness threatened to overwhelm her, but she couldn't allow it. Raising her chin, she was determined to be a professional and not act like a lovesick woman. Even if she was. Glancing around the crowded room with the thought of spotting this new server, she couldn't find anyone she thought might be him. A number of guests were standing and milling about, and the room was abuzz with conversation.

Oh, Mitch, why won't you come see me? Practically every day and every evening, he told her how much he missed her. He was the one who didn't have a full-time job at the moment. But he was devoting his energies to very worthwhile causes. Still, if he didn't come soon—or if she didn't go to New York—she'd need to fabricate some mission called Operation Cassie and beg him to come. Okay, now she was losing it. She did have the trip scheduled in August to see him under the guise of the cooking lessons, after all.

"Cassie, honey? Where are you? Yoohoo." Marta waved a hand in front of her face.

"I'm here," she said, her tone a bit snappish. "Why are we even talking about this guy?"

"Sorry," Marta muttered. "I'll be moving on my way now. Guess someone's a little touchy."

"Marta, forgive me." Cassie bit her lower lip. "I'm in boss mode, I suppose. Do you all really call me Little General?"

"Only at events like tonight. But it's all good. You get the job done. Winnie's so overly emotional right now with her pregnancy hormones flying all over the place, so you help keep us straight. Someone's got to do it."

Cassie allowed a small smile. "At ease, Corporal."

Marta saluted. "Aye-aye." Her expression softened. "We know you're missing Mitch. Never fear. I have the feeling that situation will be remedied in the near future."

Right. *August can't come soon enough.* Moving slowly around the room, Cassie made sure the needs of their guests were being met and the empty plates were promptly cleared from the tables. A number of guests beckoned her over to their table to compliment the food or the service, sometimes both. Always good to hear.

Gayle walked over to her as Cassie checked to see whether the entrées in the buffet line needed replenishing. "We have a great new server tonight. Have you met him yet? Winnie said he came highly recommended."

Cassie kept her eyes on the buffet line or else she might snap at Gayle, too. All this fawning over some gorgeous new server needed to stop. Counting under her breath, she stepped aside so they didn't block the way of the guests. "Let me guess. He's handsome and getting the eye from a number of the ladies?" She darted a glance at Gayle. "Marta already told me. I'm glad he's working out so well. If you can get his name, I'll be sure and tell the temp agency to specifically request him for future events."

"That's why I mentioned him. He's a charmer who can schmooze with the best of them."

At the word schmooze, Cassie's heart skipped a beat. *Silly girl.* How lovesick was she that the mention of a word made her all mushy inside? Is this what yearning felt like?

"I'm afraid I won't remember what he looks like, Gayle." How ridiculous was she? It'd only been a few months, not years, since she'd last seen Mitch. Getting emotional while on the job definitely wasn't a good thing. She needed to regain control and get on with it or she'd drive herself crazy.

240

"What did you say?" Concern furrowed Gayle's brow as she stepped closer.

A tear slid down Cassie's cheek. "I'm sorry, Gayle. I'm being so unprofessional." She wiped away the tear with the back of her hand, praying more wouldn't follow.

"Honey, go take a break. You're working so hard. Step outside the side door for a minute and catch your breath, get some fresh air."

"Isn't that where the smokers are?"

"Oh, right. Well, then, go down the hallway or something. Take a little walk. I think I saw an alcove to the left of the ballroom. Why not go out there? It'd give you some privacy." Gayle patted her shoulder. "You might be surprised how much good a short break can do."

"Okay, now you're tempting me," Cassie said. "But only for five minutes."

Gayle tapped her watch. "Time's a ticking. Off with you."

"If you're sure. . ."

"Tick tock tick tock."

"Fine. I'm going." With every step toward the exit door, she felt guiltier. This wasn't a good idea. Still, she kept going. Turning left and spying the alcove, Cassie hurried over to the loveseat and sank into the soft cushions. *Ahhh. . .* Maybe she *should* take breaks more often.

Leaning her head back, Cassie closed her eyes. A couple of minutes later, she tried not to frown as someone sat down on the other end. The loveseat wasn't all that big. Couldn't she enjoy a few minutes in peace without being interrupted? *One stinking minute, people?* Maybe if she kept her eyes closed, they'd take the hint and leave. Anything but making small talk with a stranger. Not to be rude, but for once, she wasn't in the mood.

The scent of a masculine, heady aftershave filled her senses. The same fabulous aftershave Mitch always wore. Her eyes quickly fluttered open.

"Hi, Moonbeam. Sorry I'm a day late for our anniversary this month." Those green eyes, that sexy voice, that handsome face—tanned from the Dominican sun—that irresistible mouth.

She sighed, tracing the plane of his cheekbone, trailing a path down to his jaw. "What took you so long?"

"I never really left."

"I'm so very glad about that," Cassie whispered, wrapping her arms around him. Never wanting to let him go ever again in her lifetime.

Chapter 43

Later That Night

$\mathcal{C}$ASSIE LEANED HER head on Mitch's wide shoulder as they sat on counter stools in Sam and Lexa's kitchen. His shoulder seemed broader than before, his chest more firm, if that was even possible. He'd really buffed up in the three months since she'd last seen him. Must be from all the manual labor he'd done during the short-term missions and at Tam's Place. Not to mention that great tan he sported. So totally not fair. She could never tan and always had to slather on a high SPF whenever she spent an extended time in the sun.

"I need to go home, but I can't even move." She snuggled closer into the crook of his arm.

Mitch softly kissed her forehead. "Then don't. I can sleep sitting up. No problem."

Lexa worked at the sink, washing up a few dishes left by the babysitter. "Cassie, why don't you stay here tonight? When you're ready, go on upstairs and take the guest bedroom at the end of the hall on the right. The one by Joe's room."

"I don't know, Lexa," she said, not bothering to hide her wide yawn.

"Sweet girl, it's after one o'clock in the morning and you're exhausted. I'll put a new toothbrush on your bed and bring you some fresh towels. The sheets are clean, but help yourself to anything else you need."

"Don't need a toothbrush," Cassie said between yawns. "Always keep one in my purse."

"That's my girl. Dental hygiene is—" Mitch's laugh was muffled when she gently slapped her hand over his mouth. "Lexa's right," he said, capturing her hand in his. "I can't in good conscience allow you to drive home tonight. Come on." He helped Cassie to her feet. "Time to go upstairs. Night, Lexa."

"Good night. Sleep well," Lexa said. "See you in the morning."

"How is it you're so wide awake at this insanely late hour?" Cassie asked, thankful he was beside her again. Finally. Oh, how she'd missed him. Oh, how she'd *kissed* him.

Mitch slipped his arm around her waist as they climbed the front steps. "I managed a catnap on the plane. It's been a good day. I survived the trip without hyperventilating and being here with you is its own kind of adrenaline."

"Want to tuck me in?"

"Definitely tempting, but I don't think that's the best idea. Good night. I love you, Cassie." Mitch kissed her forehead and ran the back of his hand over her cheek. In its own way, it was as tender as the sweetest kiss.

242

"Love you, too, Cassie," she murmured. Wow, she was so exhausted she sounded tipsy.

"Crawl into bed, Moonbeam, and I'll see you in the morning."

"Good idea. Night." As soon as she closed the door behind her, she only stopped long enough to kick off her pumps and peel off her vest and skirt. She ran her tongue over her teeth. Her mouth felt cottony. She couldn't sleep with herself if she didn't brush. Grabbing her toothbrush out of her purse, she opened the door, looked both ways and then darted into the bathroom in the middle of the hallway.

Five minutes later, Cassie dropped into the bed.

"Thank you, Lord," she said into the quiet darkness of the room. Turning on her side, she hugged her pillow and closed her eyes. "Mitch is here now and all is right with the world."

~

Saturday Morning

"Come on, Cass, you can do it!" Lexa shouted. Chloe and Joe jumped up and down, clapping and cheering beside her. Hannah and Leah sat in their stroller beside Lexa, wide-eyed from all the excitement.

Sticking his fingers in his mouth, Mitch gave an ear-piercing whistle. Cassie smiled as he clapped and then pumped his fist into the air. "Show them how it's done, Alabama!"

Holding the bat in the proper position, Cassie kept her eyes trained on the ball. If she was going to miss, she might as well go out in style. This was her third year playing on the church softball league, and she'd steadily improved since the first year when she'd struck out almost every time at bat. Soon enough, the pitcher released the ball and it sailed toward her.

Focus. Keep your eye on the ball. On a swing and a prayer, Cassie gave it her all.

Crack! Such a beautiful sound. Tossing the bat on the ground, she ran for all she was worth toward first base. Seeing an outfielder scrambling for the ball, she rounded to second base before stopping. She might have been able to make it to third base, but it was safer to stop and count her blessings she'd made it this far.

"You've got a great swing." The second baseman smiled, his brown eyes warm with appreciation.

"Thanks." Trying to catch her breath, Cassie planted her hands on her knees.

"Want to go get something to eat after the game?"

She darted a glance his way. He was young, cute, and she'd seen him in the church singles group a few times. "I can't, sorry. I'm engaged." Other than sharing her news and the ring with the ladies at church and Bea Richardson, she hadn't said those words aloud before.

Disappointment surfaced in his expression as his gaze lowered to the diamond on her left hand. "I didn't notice the ring. My apologies."

"Don't worry about it. It's still nice to be asked." Keeping an eye on Sam up at bat next, Cassie tightened her pony tail sticking out of the back of her cap.

"Better get ready to run. This guy's gonna hammer it," he said.

True to expectations, Sam slammed the ball hard, grunting with the effort. The bat cracked in two and Cassie sprinted toward third base. "Out of the park!" several of the spectators yelled, giving one another high-fives. She passed third base and kept going as Lexa and the kids cheered her on. Sliding into home, Cassie jumped up again as the umpire pronounced her safe. Her uniform shorts would need a good soaking, but who cared? She darted out of the way seconds before Sam plowed toward home plate, stomping on it with a smile of triumph.

Lexa, Chloe and Joe jumped up and down and ran to greet him as he came off the field. Crouching, Sam positioned Leah on his shoulders as Joe stood proudly by his daddy's side. Lexa beamed and rocked a sleeping Hannah in her arms. How could the child sleep through all this commotion?

Waving and calling to her, Mitch bounded down from the stands where he'd been talking with some of the guys from their church. When he reached her, he lifted her off the ground and whirled her around. Laughing, she dislodged her cap.

"You were great out there, Moonbeam." He gave her a quick kiss and then retrieved her hat from the ground, tugging it back on her head.

"The second baseman told me I have a great swing."

Mitch's gaze narrowed as he looked out over the players on the field. "Number 12, huh?"

"You have nothing to worry about. He didn't see the ring, and I told him I'm engaged."

His grin emerged. "You'd better believe it. Speaking of which, I have another proposal for you."

"Oh? Bad timing. Sounds intriguing, but I have to scoot back into the rotation now since the inning's not over yet. Tell me later?"

"Count on it."

Sam joined her as they met the others lining up for their next turn at bat. "Mitch and I had a nice chat this morning," he said.

She hid her smile and dug the toe of her shoe in the ground. "Give it up, Mr. Lewis."

He laughed. "It's all good, Little One. He's thinking ahead. Making plans."

"Gonna give me a clue how far ahead we're talking?"

Sam shook his head and chuckled. "Far be it from me to spill his secrets. If I know Mitch at all, I can tell you with a reasonable degree of certainty he won't make you wait long."

If anyone should know, it was the man who married the love of his life within an hour or two of reuniting. Of course, their separation lasted an entire year. Sam's words sent little shivers of anticipation through her, especially with the knowledge that Mitch wanted to talk with her later.

"Sam, how were you able to wait an entire year?"

He leveled his gaze on her, his expression tender. Oh, how she loved this dear man. "Our circumstances were different, but He'll let you know when it's time."

Cassie nodded. "Seems to me you said something very similar back in mid-February."

Sam's chuckle warmed her heart, as it always did. "I'd say He's definitely answered that prayer."

Three innings later, their team emerged victorious after—shock of shocks—she'd hit another double. Sam hit a triple and they both scored runs again.

"You're my inspiration. I've never played so well," Cassie told Mitch as he helped her gather her things and then they walked off the field together. Grabbing her towel, she wiped the perspiration from her brow. The day was beautiful and not too hot.

"I can't take the credit, but I sure enjoyed watching you. That guy's right. You do have a great swing."

"Do you two want to join us at Richardson's?" Sam said. "Lexa ran into Bea at the grocery a couple of weeks ago. She complained she hasn't seen these kiddos of ours in a while. I'm sure she'd love to see you and Mitch." Hannah now sat on Sam's shoulders, tugging on his thick, dark hair like she was weeding in her garden. "Easy there, Hannah Banana. Daddy wants to keep his hair a few years longer."

"Sure. Richardson's sounds good," Cassie said.

"Lead the way." Mitch slipped his hand into hers.

"Cweam, Daddy! Ice cweam!" Hannah said, now using Sam's head to practice her drumming.

"Joe, can you get my bag, buddy?"

The bag was almost as big as Joe, but he didn't seem to mind as he retrieved and dragged it across the ground. "Thanks." Removing his cap, Sam put it on his son's head. "One of these days, you'll be playing on the team with me, too." The look on Joe's handsome little face was precious.

"Here, Lexa. Time for Hannah to go in the stroller." Sam carefully lowered her from his shoulders and transferred her into Lexa's arms.

"No, Daddy," Hannah said, wiggling and sliding down from her mother's arms. She wrapped herself around Sam's legs and looked up at him with pleading eyes. "Sip?"

"Leah? Come with Hannah and Daddy." Sam beckoned his dark-haired daughter closer. Holding each of his girls' hands, one on each side, he began to half-carry and half-skip with them across the field in the direction of their cars.

"I don't believe it." Cassie shook her head. "Papa Bear is skipping with his cubs."

"Or *sipping*, as Hannah would say." Mitch slid his arm around her waist. "Guaranteed, Sam's their hero." He exchanged a smile with Lexa.

Cassie pulled out her cell phone. "Let me call Winnie and see if she and Josh can join us. Beck and Kevin, too, if they're available. Make it a regular ice cream event."

Lexa scooted closer. "Josh and Winnie won't be joining us today, Cass. She's feeling a little overwhelmed, and we're keeping Chloe for the day so she and Josh can have some time alone."

"I hope everything's okay."

"It will be," Lexa said. "Beck and Kevin have Luke and they can probably meet us."

"Now this is a different kind of teamwork," Cassie said to Mitch a minute later. Acting silly, they crisscrossed their legs as they walked, and she cried out when he almost tripped her. "If I fall, you're going to answer for it and pay any medical bills."

"One way to make sure that doesn't happen." Laughing, Mitch swooped her off the ground and cradled her in his arms.

Right where she wanted to be now. . .and forever.

Chapter 44

"MARRY ME, CASSIE."

They sat beneath their special tree in the Houston park on Saturday evening. They'd come a long way since that day back in February. Giving him a flirty smile, Cassie inched her hands around his neck. "I think you're forgetting something. You already asked me that question." Her kiss was light, teasing. "Fool that I am, I agreed."

"Marry me today. Tomorrow. Whenever you say, but whatever you do, make it soon." Mitch tightened his already firm hold on her. "Why wait? If you know in your heart it's what you want, let's make this union official and get on with the rest of our lives." He nuzzled her neck, inhaling her scent, losing himself in the warmth, the softness of her skin.

"Cassie, I want you in every way," he whispered. "I can't wait to make you my wife. I was awake a long time last night, knowing you were sleeping in a room down the hall."

Her beautiful blue eyes rounded and her jaw dropped. "You're serious, aren't you?"

"Completely." To prove his point, he caressed her cheek and then gave her his best effort at a convincing kiss.

"It's not just your hormones talking?"

He chuckled. "That, too. I'm a red-blooded, living, breathing man who'll never stop wanting you in that way. I could get all cave man on you and drag you off by your hair, but I like to think I've evolved into a true gentleman. I want to do this the proper way and right in the eyes of the Lord. If you want a big church wedding, that's fine. As long as you can arrange it in the span of a few days. I'm not a patient man."

"I'm glad you told me now," she said, running one finger across his lower lip and driving him crazy. "Actually, I think I already knew that about you."

He rested his forehead on hers. "I talked with Sam last night and he's agreed to marry us."

"Where would we find a place on such short notice?"

His pulse tripled. He'd been planning to talk with her all day and her question implied she wasn't adverse to the idea. She hadn't flat-out told him no and he sensed a growing excitement on her part. Mitch knew she loved him, but she might need longer to prepare. He'd give her whatever she wanted, the time she needed, but he'd love nothing more than to fly back to New York with her as his wife. The thought sounded more appealing by the second. But the decision was hers.

"Well, we have our park," he said. "And I happen to know a man with a gazebo."

Cassie's eyes lit. "The gazebo's beautiful and holds up to eight people. What would you wear? More importantly, what would I wear?"

That made him smile. "Kevin's my size and height and owns a tux. You, sweetheart, can go shopping with Beck."

She stared at him, a lovely smile upturning her lips. "You've really thought this out, haven't you? Can you tell me what date we're talking about here?"

"You choose."

"You work out all the details but then leave the date to me?" She tapped her fingers on her chin and pretended to ponder the idea. "How about Tuesday?"

Covering her mouth with his, Mitch kissed her deeply, passionately. "Tuesday, July 20th it is," he said at length. "Cassie, before this can happen, I need to meet your father."

Dropping her arms, she turned aside, strangely quiet.

"Is there something wrong with my wanting to meet him?" Was she ashamed or embarrassed by him? "He's your dad. Call it a guy thing, a matter of honor and respect, but I need to ask your father for his blessing to marry you."

"You're an honorable man, Mitch, and I appreciate that more than you know. I haven't seen Daddy in a few months and I only pray he's. . ." A frown creased her lovely features. "Please don't misunderstand. It's not that I don't want to introduce you to him, and more than anything, I want to be your wife. Soon."

"Afraid I won't measure up in his eyes?"

She slowly shook her head. "No, it's not that at all. The opposite, actually."

"I don't follow."

She breathed out a heavy sigh. "Once he finds out you went to Harvard and are so accomplished, he'll probably wonder what on earth you're doing with me."

Ah, man. That was a tough one. How to answer? Usually self-confident, Cassie now seemed suddenly insecure. What kind of man would make his daughter feel unworthy in any way? If anything, he wasn't worthy of Cassie.

"*For I am confident of this very thing, that He who began a good work in you will perfect it until the day of Christ Jesus.* I think we should pray. Pray for direction in the next few days and ask the Lord to bless our plans for a future together."

The admiration in her eyes as she lifted her gaze to his made everything he'd gone through to get to this point worthwhile. He'd made so many mistakes, but he could offer her his heart, his mind, his body and soul. The thought that Cassie desired him as her husband satisfied his thirsty, weary soul and mended the holes in his heart. He'd spend the rest of his life making her happy.

~

Sunday, July 18, 2004 ~ Early Afternoon

Cassie's mind was spinning. Had they really decided to get married on Tuesday? Two *days* from now? *I'm getting married!* This was the most spontaneous thing she'd ever done in her life. The craziest, wildest, most exhilarating, fantastic adventure of her life.

The whole drive to Tuscaloosa—all nine hours of it—they discussed their plans. Thankfully, Landon agreed to bring the new plane. He and Amy would make the short flight up to Boston and get Natalie, Marc and Gracie. Then they'd swing down to Philly and pick up Mitch's mom and Celeste on their way down to Houston.

As Mitch drove them into the outskirts of Tuscaloosa, Cassie tried calling her father. "He's not answering." She stared out the window. "Something doesn't sit right with me. When I talked to Daddy last night, he promised he'd be listening for the phone."

"Let's swing by the house first and see if he's there," Mitch said. "If he is, we'll take him somewhere to eat and talk about our plans."

She directed him through the streets, darting glances his way to gauge his reaction. When they passed over the railroad tracks closest to her house, Cassie felt heartsick. The area was more rundown than ever. "Second street on the left and then the first right," she said, her voice quiet. Although she tried her best to sound upbeat and positive, this was so hard.

Pulling the car to a stop in front of the small, one-story white clapboard house, Mitch turned to her. "This doesn't have to be complicated." He tucked her hair behind her ear and, cupping her jaw with one gentle hand, kissed her. If only he knew the comfort that gesture gave her.

"My heart's beating so hard I think it might fly right out of my chest." Taking his hand, Cassie positioned it over her heart. "Don't get any big ideas," she said with a nervous laugh. She appreciated how careful he was as he splayed his fingers above the steady rhythm of her heartbeat.

"Your turn." Taking her hand, he placed it over his heart, pressing against his chest. "I think you're right. Yours is faster. This will be fine. Come on." Mitch helped her out of the car and they started up what remained of the front walkway.

Cassie rued every crack in the sidewalk—weeds sprouting between them— and every rotten board in the front porch. Being mindful of where she stepped, and thankful it was still in the light of day, she made her way to the front door. "I'm not sure if I should knock or use my key and go inside. I don't feel like I belong here anymore. It's not really my home." Her eyes filled with moisture, and she blinked hard to stem the tears.

"If you're looking for your daddy, Cleve's not here."

Cassie stepped to the side of the front porch. "Hi, Mr. King." Their elderly neighbor had lived next to them all her life. She couldn't ask Clarence the question. She *wouldn't* ask. Because she knew exactly what he'd say and she didn't want to hear it. How many times had her mother gotten the call telling them he was in jail again? He'd started calling it his second home, making a joke out of something that had brought her such shame.

How many times had she and Tagg huddled in his bedroom as they'd overheard Daddy pleading with Mama to give him just one more chance? How many times did she have to make excuses and explanations for either his absence or his negligence? And why, oh why, couldn't her father stay out of trouble long enough to meet Mitch? Did he even want to escort her down the aisle at her wedding?

"Hauled him in last night," the older man said.

Sucking in a quick breath, Cassie summoned the strength she'd need to get through this again. Mitch came over beside her and slipped his arm around her waist. "Mr. King, this is my fiancé, Mitch Jacobsen."

"Nice to meet ya." Clarence gave Mitch a nod. "I'd shake your hand, but as you can see, I've kinda got my hands full right now." He'd been working among the bushes at the side of his house and clutched weeds in both his hands. Somewhere there was a sweet irony in that picture.

"Honey, if I were you, I'd turn around and go straight back to Houston. Forget about your daddy. He ain't worth all that worry he causes you." His gaze moved to Mitch. "You look like a good man. Cassie's a fine woman, but she deserves better than her old man."

"He's still my daddy," she said. "We're getting married and I was hoping he'd want to be there."

Mitch laced his fingers with hers. "May I ask what the charge is against him?"

"Disorderly. Not drunk, but Cleve caused a ruckus down at Bernie's Bar last night. Got some out-of-towners all riled up by hurling stupid insults."

"Thanks, Clarence. It's nice to see you again."

"Best of luck. You make a real nice couple. Wish you a lot of happiness together."

"We should probably forget it and head back to Houston," Cassie said, her shoulders slumping.

"Nope." Mitch opened the passenger door and escorted her inside the car. "I didn't come all the way here only to turn around without meeting your father. At least he's not in the hospital. Point me in the direction of the jail and then we're off."

Cassie blew out a breath. She could give him the directions in her sleep. "Turn right at the end of the street."

~

The Deputy Sheriff's reaction when Mitch entered the jailhouse with Cassie was borderline comical. As soon as he glimpsed her coming inside the building, he whacked his knee on the desk in his haste to scramble to his feet. "Why, if it's not Cassandra Thorenson." A wide smile creased his lips. "I swear you get prettier every time I see you." He whistled under his breath.

"Unfortunately, we usually see each other here in this jailhouse." She squared her shoulders and attempted a brave smile. "How are you, Tyler?"

"Still pining away for you." Deputy Tyler eyed him up and down like he was bait for a bull. "Tyler Rainier." He stuck out his hand. "Nice to meet you."

"Same here. Mitch Jacobsen." The guy pumped his hand up and down a few times. "I'd like to post bail for Cassie's dad."

"Mitch and I are getting married," Cassie said. "I'm hoping we can keep Daddy out of jail long enough to walk me down the aisle." Although she sounded calm, he detected the tiniest hint of nerves.

Tyler's brown eyes narrowed and he grunted. "Seems congratulations are in order. Tell you what. Your dad's one of our regulars. Seeing as how he didn't cause any trouble since they brought him in last night, I'll give you and Rich here—"

"It's Mitch." Cassie's tone was quiet but firm.

"For you and *Mitch*, I'm gonna give your dad a *get out of jail free* card. Call it my wedding gift or whatever. You two gettin' married here in town?"

"In Houston. Sorry to be abrupt, Tyler, but would you mind releasing him now?"

"Oh, sure. Sorry. Give me a few minutes. Why don't you go down and see Wanda in the office and sign the paperwork while I go back and get him. I'll bring him out in about ten minutes."

Cassie nodded. "Thanks, Tyler. I appreciate it, and it's good to see you again."

He nodded and shot Mitch a look. "You're a lucky man. Take good care of our Cassie."

"I will," Mitch assured him. Cassie seemed to inspire loyalty in people everywhere. What a woman. *And she's all mine. Thank you, Lord.*

At least Cleveland Thorenson hadn't acted belligerent and seemed genuinely pleased to see his daughter when Deputy Tyler released him into Cassie's care. He shook his hand and made small pleasantries but was otherwise a quiet man.

And now, a few hours later, Mitch wasn't even sure where they were parked for the night. Somewhere off I-59 South in Mississippi. He glanced over at Cleve, sprawled across the width of a double bed in the motel room. He mumbled under his breath and smacked his jaws a few times. Hard to believe this man was Cassie's father. With his weathered face and etched lines around his eyes and mouth, Cleve's appearance evidenced he'd fought life's battles and come out on the losing end. A tall, lanky man, his thinning gray hair had once been red as he'd seen in the photos Cassie had shown him during their road trip to Tuscaloosa. Fully clothed, he wore a plain white T-shirt, stained black work pants and, curiously enough, steel-toed boots on his feet.

He'd been a factory worker for nearly thirty years, assembling parts for air conditioning units and appliances until he'd fallen on the job and taken a short-term disability leave which had extended from months into years. Surprisingly, before then, he'd somehow been able to keep his job in spite of frequent visits to the county lockup.

"You sleepin' with my daughter?"

Ah, he was finally awake. Mitch lowered his book from where he reclined on the other double bed. "No, sir, I'm not. If you'll recall our earlier conversation, I'm in love with your daughter and intend to marry her. Cassie and I are taking you back to Houston with us. We're hoping you'll walk her down the aisle and give her to me in marriage so then I *can* sleep with her." He probably shouldn't have stated it in such blunt terms, but he didn't seem to think this man would mind.

Cleve roared. "You've got a good sense of humor there, Mr. Jacobsen. I like that in a man. It'll get you through the bad times."

"I hope you'll call me Mitch, sir."

"Tell you what. You don't call me sir and I'll call you whatever you want."

Mitch eased into a smile. This man was more agreeable than he'd expected. Might as well bring up the painful subject of Tagg now. Get it out on the table. He wanted to know some things for his own satisfaction but also to help him understand Cassie a little more.

"Do you know that Cassie has blamed herself for Tagg's death all these years?"

That caught Cleve's full attention. "What are you saying?"

"She jumped into the water that day and called for Tagg's help. She's been riddled with guilt, thinking she's the reason he died and took him away from you and her mother."

The other man stared at him for a full minute. "I never blamed her, if that's what you're thinkin'."

"I'm not thinking anything, but I'm glad she told me about it so I could try and help her."

"Losing that boy and puttin' him in the ground was the hardest thing I ever done. You ever lost someone like that, Mitch?"

Mitch nodded and sat up to face Cleve, planting his feet on the floor. "I lost my best friend on 9/11. He worked in the South Tower of the World Trade Center. He'd invited me to breakfast, but I turned him down. If I'd gone with him, he might have been spared. I've blamed myself ever since."

Cleve whistled under his breath. "That's tough. I'm sorry, son."

Mitch warmed at the term. "I'm sorry for your loss, too. From everything Cassie's told me, Tagg was her world and a great big brother. She loved him very much."

"That's all you need, you know. Someone to love you and watch over you. Cassie's all the family I got left in this world. I ain't done right by her."

"Cassie loves you, and it's not too late to make things right. I know she'd like that. But it takes both of you willing to meet each other halfway. Love doesn't come with strings, doesn't come with demands. It's unconditional, the same as our heavenly Father's love for us."

Cleve nodded slowly. "I had faith a lifetime ago, you know. But when you get beaten down one too many times, a man can lose his focus, lose sight of what's most important."

"What's most important is in the next room and she's waiting to get reacquainted."

"You really love her, don't you?" Cassie's father met his gaze and held it steady.

"I wouldn't be here with you now if I didn't."

Cleve broke out in a wide smile. "I like a man who speaks his mind and gets to the point. You seem like a good man and I can see Cassie loves you."

In spite of his otherwise disheveled appearance, the man still had good teeth. He couldn't be much older than his early fifties, but he looked much older. But when he smiled, he seemed much younger. Years were erased in that smile.

"How about we get you cleaned up and then we'll all go get something to eat? Cassie and I will tell you all about it. It's quite the story, but it takes more than a few minutes."

"Sounds good." Pulling himself up to a sitting position, Cleve cleared his throat and rubbed a hand over his grizzled jaw. When he glanced his way, Mitch was struck by the intensity of his light blue eyes. Cassie had her father's eyes. From what he'd heard of Cassie's mother, Anna Thorenson had been a gentle, loving woman until her alcohol addiction had grown all-consuming. Cassie had inherited a number of her mother's better character traits, it seemed. Cleve's mother, Cassie's Grandma Thor, had been a godly woman and taught Cassie the value of finding her self-worth and confidence in a personal relationship with Christ.

Mitch needed to respect and honor this man. No matter what he'd done in the past, no matter how he'd treated Cassie, he needed to accept and forgive the man so they could move forward.

~

Cassie hadn't spent so much quality time with her father in years. Maybe she never had.

They hadn't bothered going back to the house after they'd left the jailhouse. Too many memories awaited her there, both good and bad. They'd bought her father new clothes, a suitcase and the toiletries he'd need for the trip to Houston. Coherent and alert, Daddy asked Mitch to tell him about himself and—as she'd predicted—his eyes about bulged out of his head when he'd heard her husband-to-be had a medical degree from Harvard.

"You mean that fancy university where presidents graduated?" Cleve choked out.

"The same, sir."

"Well, now, ain't that something? How come you're not a doctor then?" Her father nodded, listening to Mitch's brief explanation. Then Mitch told him about his career on Wall Street and the recent turn of events. Cassie held her breath, wondering how Daddy would react to that one.

"So, let me get this straight." Cleve finished the steak dinner and pushed aside his empty plate. His gaze zeroed in on Mitch. "You got an M.D., but you don't use it. Then you had a solid job on Wall Street and walked away from it. What are your plans to support my daughter?"

"That's a fair question, sir—Cleve." Mitch took her hand, squeezing it beneath the table. "Cassie and I haven't even discussed this yet, but what I'd like to do is work from home and set up a private investment practice. Bottom line, I enjoy helping people. By working independently, I'll be able to make a good living, but it would also give me the flexibility to continue my short-term mission projects with TeamWork. I'm able to put my medical training to good use on the missions."

Cleve nodded and drained his water glass. "What about your place? You got a mortgage to pay?"

"The townhouse where he lives was his grandfather's and he left it to the family in his will, Daddy. His grandfather was Eric Carlisle, the famous actor."

Cleve whistled under his breath. "No kidding? No wonder you looked a little familiar, Mitch. I reckon that's why. My mom, God rest her soul, loved his movies. Well, I'll be." His focus moved to her. "And what about you, Cassandra? You gonna start having babies?"

Mitch shifted in his chair and nudged her. She ignored him. "I might go back to school. I'd like to get a teaching degree. There's a counseling ministry for women called Tam's Place in Queens that Mitch and his sister and brother-in-law founded, and I think I could be of use there."

Tapping his fingers on the table, Cleve appeared to ponder his next words. "I have one more thing to say."

"Anything," Mitch said while Cassie straightened in her chair.

"Don't you ever treat my daughter wrong or walk away from her and any children you might have together. If you do, you'll have to answer to me. That might not sound like much of a threat, but I assure you it is. But more than me, you'll have to answer to God for everything you do, and you don't want to fight the Almighty." His eyes clouded and he lowered his gaze. "I've been fightin' Him too long and it's time to get straight. Seein' you two together and how happy you are does my old heart good."

"I fought the Almighty for a couple of years, but I'm done." Mitch's voice was firm, and he kissed her cheek. "You have my word I'll make your daughter deliriously happy, and I hope to give her many children." She blushed while Mitch turned back to her father. "I hope you'll give your blessing for our marriage, sir." It wasn't really a question, and how she loved the confidence in Mitch's voice.

Cleve chuckled, and what a great sound *it* was. Good for her heart. "I sure hope so, considerin' you've kidnapped me and you're takin' me to Texas. Welcome to the family, son."

Chapter 45

ℛETURNING TO HOUSTON, Cassie felt like she was floating in a fabulous but wildly fanciful dream. So much was happening all at once. Mitch and Daddy were getting along well, and much better than she could have hoped. She'd almost burst into tears the night before when he'd called Mitch "son."

Sam and Lexa welcomed her father into their home and helped him quickly feel at home. Giving him a guest bedroom and feeding him well didn't hurt. Winnie brought over some new creations she was testing and Cleve loved being her guinea pig and master taste tester.

Before she knew it, Daddy was bouncing the twins, one on each knee, and telling them exaggerated stories of life in the magical land called Alabama. They tried to pronounce the name Tuscaloosa and collapsed against him in giggles. Joe seemed wary of him at first, but as Cassie left to go bridal gown shopping with Rebekah, she spied Joe sitting next to Daddy in the family room and reading a Bible storybook together.

She tried on three dresses at a suburban bridal shop, modeling each one for Rebekah. None of them worked for her, and even though Rebekah was kind with her compliments, she could tell she agreed. "Maybe this is an impossible task," Cassie said at length, her frustration surfacing in her voice. "Trying to find a dress and planning a wedding in a couple of days is completely crazy. I'll just wear one of my pretty white dresses and that'll be the end of it. Mitch can wear a nice suit instead of Kevin's tux." She sniffled. "No need to be all fancy. Right?"

"Hold on a red-hot minute," Rebekah said as they sat in a deli eating a late lunch. A smile teased the corners of her mouth. "I can't believe I didn't think of it until now. I have a really great idea, as long as you agree."

"Can you give me a little hint?" Cassie said, stabbing a baby carrot in her salad.

"How tall are you? Five seven, right?" Rebekah's green eyes were positively sparkling.

"Last time I checked, yes, but I might have shr—"

"Come on, then," Rebekah said. "Let's finish quickly so we can go."

A half-hour later, they pulled up in front of Rebekah and Kevin's home. A party supply truck was parked in the driveway. Cassie laughed after she entered the house with Rebekah and spied Marta, Gayle and Winnie running around the backyard, carrying flower arrangements—silk, most likely—to workers who were affixing them to the outside of the gazebo.

256

"Beck, I never heard. Did Kevin get the approval for the patent of the Rebekah's Heart design?"

Rebekah's smile said it all. "Oh, I'm so happy!" Cassie embraced her friend, hugging her tight. "I told Kevin at the birthday party for the twins back in February that I knew he'd get the patent and it would be the start of something big."

"Thanks, but come with me. Speaking of something big, I'll show you why we're here. And I'm not talking about Winnie since she's not showing that much yet."

A minute later, Cassie sat wide-eyed on the bed in her friend's second bedroom as Rebekah pulled out a heavy plastic, zippered bag from the closet. "If you're willing, I want you to wear my gown."

Immediate tears sprang into her eyes—seemed to be a common occurrence with all the blessings of the last few days—and Cassie nodded, speechless.

Rebekah smiled. "Is that a yes?"

Swallowing hard, Cassie nodded. "It's definitely a yes. I'm overwhelmed. Your beautiful dress." Cassie watched as her friend removed it from the bag. She was almost afraid to touch the exquisite gown. White silk with beading and a lace overlay, column style, off the shoulder, three-quarter length sleeves and an empire waist. She only knew the terminology because she'd helped Lexa with the write-up for the local paper and the TeamWork Missions monthly newsletter after Rebekah and Kevin's wedding.

"Mitch hasn't seen the gown since he wasn't at our wedding," Rebekah said. "I think you'll look great in it since we have very similar figures."

"The only difference being a few inches in height. I'm afraid I'll need teeter-totter shoes."

Rebekah laughed. "Teeter-totter shoes? Never heard that term."

"Shoes I can't walk in very well. You know"—Cassie jumped to her feet and stretched her hands out on either side of her, trying to demonstrate by acting as though she was trying to balance—"playing dress up like you also mentioned on the day of the twins' birthday party. I'll feel like a little girl playing in her mama's shoes. Pretending to be a grownup."

"You're very much a grownup, and trust me, Mitch knows and appreciates that fact. What I find interesting is that several things you've said today all point back to the day you met Mitch. I'm not talking about Amy and Landon's wedding either."

"I know." Cassie couldn't stop her smile. "I feel the same way. The day Mitch walked into my life and completely captured my attention." Within a minute, she'd stepped into the bridal gown with Rebekah's help, breathing a grateful sigh of relief when her friend zipped it up all the way with no effort whatsoever.

"Wait a second." Pulling a box down from the closet, Rebekah brought out her beaded, mid-length veil. "This will complete the look. It'll look great with your hair down." She lightly anchored it in Cassie's hair and then opened the closet door with its full-length mirror. "You look gorgeous, Cass. Here, come and take a look."

With slow steps, Cassie approached the mirror. "Oh, Beck!" She raised her hands to her cheeks. The dress was absolute perfection, highlighting her neck and shoulders and falling over her curves. The gown looked like it had been tailored specifically for her, except for the length. "It's so beautiful, but I can't cry all over this gown. I'd better get out of it quick."

Moving close, Rebekah smoothed her thumbs under Cassie's eyes. "So you'll christen it a little. You don't have mascara on, so don't worry. I keep telling Kevin we should take stock in the tissue companies."

Cassie laughed a little. "I know a good stockbroker I can recommend." She sniffled and surveyed the length of the gown in the mirror. "I'm afraid I'll still need those teeter-totter shoes, though."

"Not necessarily. Winnie's become quite the seamstress." Rebekah glanced out the bedroom window. "She's also running around my backyard like a crazy pregnant woman. Let me go get her and see what she thinks. If anyone can give the gown a quick hem, it's my sister-in-law." She gave Cassie a quick hug. "We're going to make this work, sweetie, and tomorrow you're going to marry the handsome prince of your dreams."

Cassie could only nod as Rebekah darted out of the room.

Thank you, Lord, for making all things possible.

~

Mitch sat with Kevin, Josh, Landon, Marc and Sam at dinner. Their version of a bachelor party. Later, they were going back to the Lewis homestead and having a time of prayer. Cassie had gone out to dinner with all the ladies and then they planned on joining the men at the house. Not the way the rest of the world celebrated the night before their nuptials, but he wouldn't have it any other way.

The TeamWork way. *God's* way.

Gracious as always, his mom had been so good with Cassie. Together with Amy and Celeste, she'd met with Cassie in Sam's office earlier in the afternoon. The Lord only knew what they told her during that girl-talk session. He hoped Cassie would still want to marry him.

Earlier in the morning, they'd visited a jeweler Sam recommended and selected his platinum wedding band. He insisted on paying for it, and she'd reluctantly agreed. They wanted to have scripture verses engraved on their bands, but that would have to wait until they returned to Manhattan.

After leaving the jewelry store, Cassie marched him to a nearby store and made him model a few Stetsons. "My wedding gift to you." She'd given him a nod of approval when he chose a light brown one. "There's something irresistible about a man in a Stetson, you know," she said, giving him a coy grin. He'd definitely remember that for future reference. He'd also become an adopted, honorary Texan. Landon had schooled him in the dubious art known as *talking Texan*, slapping him on the back and telling him it worked like a charm. Considering how happy Amy was, Mitch figured anything was worth a try at least once.

Tucked in his suitcase was a diamond necklace he'd had especially designed for Cassie that would be a worthy complement for the ring and wedding band set. He'd present that to her tomorrow night. He could wear the Stetson and she could wear the necklace and. . .

"Where are you taking Cassie for your honeymoon?" Josh asked, interrupting his thoughts.

Mitch grinned and saluted Marc. "Our friend Marc has a superstar client who owns a luxury hotel downtown. Not sure how he did it, but we've got the bridal suite until Thursday and then we're flying back to Manhattan."

"Commercial?" Kevin asked.

"Yes. With Cassie beside me, I think I'll be fine."

"Great. Back to the honeymoon night," Josh said.

Marc laughed. "You *would* be the one to keep bringing that up."

Josh shot him a look. "Only because I want to offer to spring for a luxury ride to the hotel from the gazebo. Here's to Mitch and Cassie!" Josh raised his glass in a toast.

Sam was quiet, but Mitch could tell how pleased he was by their lively camaraderie. He'd told them the plans were falling into place for the mission outside Albuquerque for the following summer. "Sheila and Angelina are planning on joining us, and so is Dean. We haven't had him with us for a mission since the short-term mission to Montana, and it'll be good to catch up with him. I've already told Eliot to free up his schedule. And," Sam said, glancing around the table at each one of them in turn, "I'm hoping all of you can be there. We need each other. It'll be a good time to reinforce the bonds we've established, brother to brother. I'm looking forward to seeing what the Lord will do."

"To Albuquerque!" Josh, the self-appointed toastmaster said, and they all raised their glasses a second time in a rousing toast.

"To our brothers!" Kevin said, and they did it all over again.

"To marriage!" Marc added, winking at Sam.

By the end of their dinner, Mitch sighed with the deep personal contentment of a man immeasurably blessed with the best group of friends a guy could ever want. These men were solid and sought the Lord's will in their lives first and foremost.

For a last-minute wedding, the details were falling into place effortlessly. Their friends, true to their generous, giving natures, had rallied together to help them make it all work. Marta and Gayle were moving into Cassie's condo since both of their respective apartment leases were up at the end of the month. Gayle's old car had finally died, so Cassie happily signed over the title to Edwina to her and wouldn't think of accepting any money for it. Winnie, Rebekah and Lexa had volunteered to help pack Cassie's clothing and personal items to ship to her, and she was leaving all her furniture behind since she wouldn't need it in the townhouse.

Such good people. So many willing hearts. Incredible blessings.

Thank you, Lord, for making all things possible.

Chapter 46

Tuesday, July 20, 2004 ~ Cassie and Mitch's Wedding

$\mathcal{C}$ASSIE'S EYES MISTED as she walked toward her groom on the arm of her father. A white runner led the way to the gazebo where Mitch waited. Standing behind him, Sam held his Bible and Landon stood beside Mitch as his best man. Both her father and Landon wore dark suits and sported lavender roses on the lapels of their jackets like the gorgeous ones in her small but elegant wedding bouquet. Mitch wore a white rose on the lapel of the dark tuxedo. Rebekah waited as her matron of honor on the opposite side.

The day was lovely—almost perfect, really, with blue skies, a few white clouds and a gentle breeze. Moderately cool and not too humid for a mid-summer morning in Houston. Gathering the skirt of her gown, Cassie carefully made her way up the three short stairs with Daddy's assistance. Thankfully, miracle worker Winnie had been able to hem the dress.

Mitch stepped forward and offered his hand, helping her when she reached the last step. Oh my, he was the most handsome man in the world. His hair curled slightly on the ends, and his eyes lit with love as his gaze fell on her. After her father lifted the veil and kissed her cheek, he stepped aside and Mitch took his place beside her.

Looking at his gorgeous face, this face of the man she loved with everything in her, Cassie melted all over again.

"You are so beautiful, Moonbeam," he whispered as they faced Sam together.

"So are you," she whispered back, and they shared a smile.

Truly, at least for this one special day, she *was* a princess. With her prince right beside her.

During the ceremony, Cassie gazed at the faces of her friends gathered around the gazebo. How blessed she was to count these wonderful people as her friends. Her *family*.

When it came time for their vows, Mitch turned to her and repeated Sam's words in his quiet but resonant voice. How far they'd come since that ceremony in the Houston park in February. It might as well have been a lifetime ago. "I do," he said, squeezing her hands.

Cassie did the same when it came time to recite her vows. Pledging to love this man forever was the best thing she'd ever done. She might not have known him long in terms of the earthly measure of time, but in her heart, she'd known him her entire life.

When Mitch slid the platinum diamond wedding band on her finger, he kept his eyes trained on hers. So expressive, those eyes. Today they were a brilliant, deep mossy green color that shone with such a depth of love it stole her breath.

Sam announced them as husband and wife amidst claps and cheers, and Mitch didn't wait for Sam to tell him to kiss his bride. "Love you forever, Cassie."

"Love you longer, Mitch."

They waved to their friends as their Mercedes limousine waited at the curb. Their bags had already been transported to the hotel, and the others were planning to celebrate with a picnic supper in Sam and Lexa's backyard. Winnie promised to keep the top layer of the cake so they could celebrate on their first anniversary. Sam planned on taking her father back home the next day. She'd said her good-byes to her father, to Mitch's mother, and all her TeamWork friends. Everyone but one.

"Hold on just a minute," Cassie told Mitch, giving him a quick kiss as he waited by the limousine. Hurrying over to Sam, she leaned on her tiptoes and kissed his cheek. She heard his familiar, deep chuckle.

"Papa Bear, I love you. Thank you for everything, and especially for taking such good care of my Daddy."

"You're welcome, Little One." Cassie swallowed her sudden tears. In that moment, with those words, she knew he was there. *Tagg* was also there, in her heart, sharing her special day.

She glanced up at him through her tears. Happy tears, but tears all the same. "I'll miss you, Sam."

"We'll be seeing you. You're never far from our hearts."

Chapter 47

The Next Year ~ Friday, August 26, 2005

$\mathcal{M}$ITCH GLANCED AT the display on the home phone. A Houston number flashed on the screen. TeamWork Missions. He grabbed the receiver. "Mitch Jacobsen."

"Hey, Mitch. It's Josh."

"Good to hear from you. How are things in Houston?"

"I'll get to the point." Josh sounded as serious as Mitch had ever heard him. "I'm sure you've heard about Katrina, the Category 5 hurricane headed for the Gulf coast."

"I heard the words *unprecedented cataclysm* on the news this morning and caught wind of a potential mandatory evacuation."

"Right," Josh said. "It formed over the Bahamas on August 23rd and then crossed over southern Florida as a Category 1. Killed a few people and caused some flooding. It's strengthening rapidly and is projected to hit New Orleans hard by Monday. They're hoping it might weaken before it hits land, but FEMA's preparing for the worst. Some parts of the city are below sea level, and with the right front quadrant winds forecast to be twenty-eight feet, the emergency management officials fear the surge will go over the levees. So, potential flooding seems to be the biggest potential and immediate threat. They're going to use the Superdome for those who can't—or won't—leave the city, and refugee centers are being established at various points in the city. Mississippi just activated the National Guard and Louisiana Governor Blanco's in talks with President Bush. They expect a state of emergency to be declared by tomorrow at the latest."

"What can I do?" Mitch said. "Whatever you need, I'm there."

"We're organizing TeamWork groups to assist in the relief effort. Sam and I are in touch with FEMA and the local authorities. We're keeping a close watch on the situation, and we're gathering volunteers to head down there a week or two after it hits. Landon's going to fly in relief supplies of food and water. We've talked with the New York TeamWork leaders and they're lining up a caravan of trucks to bring lumber and building supplies, clothing, first aid, that kind of thing. We'll know better once we get there, but I'm sure your medical training might come in handy."

Mitch didn't need to think about it. "Count me in."

"Thanks, buddy. I'll be in touch with more details as we know them. In the meantime, pray."

"You've got it."

~

Later that Night

"What's wrong, Mitch? Talk to me." Cassie snuggled closer to him, running her finger in circles on his chest.

Mitch blew out a breath. Beautiful Cassie. She could always tell since she was such a part of him now.

Jumping out of the bed, she moved over to the closet. She loved wearing his shirts—opened a few buttons at the collar, the diamond necklace nestled against her bare skin. He admired her long, shapely legs and her tousled auburn hair which now reached almost to her waist. Rolling over on his side, Mitch drank in the sight of his gorgeous wife.

The past year had been the best one of his life. The laughing. The living. The loving.

Cassie had mastered the cooking classes Winnie and Lexa had arranged, and he'd gone with her for the *Cooking for Two* classes. They'd learned to work well together in their own kitchen, experimenting with new dishes and feeding one another. She'd developed into quite a good cook, and he'd learned to make some of the desserts. They listened to jazz and slow danced in their living room. When it was warm enough, they'd sit on the balcony and sip their morning coffee, wrapped in their robes and one another. The sleepy, morning-after gazes were the best, especially when Cassie gave him that shy little smile, even after a year of married life. How he loved this woman. More every day.

Sammie went on evening strolls with them every night except when it was pouring down rain, and even then sometimes. Made going home and getting out of their wet clothes that much more fun. Sammie liked to sleep at the foot of the bed and didn't like it when they kicked him out for some alone time.

Saturday mornings were a personal favorite. They'd enjoy the lazy morning together and then cook breakfast or go out for brunch before spending a few hours in the library. Arielle still worked there, and they spoke with her on occasion. As much as anything else, the librarian seemed grateful he hadn't filed charges against her. Every now and then, Cassie would invite Arielle to attend church with them. Bless her heart, she tried, and Mitch knew she'd keep on trying. Another reason to love his wife all the more.

What would a first year of marriage be like without a good, rousing fight or two? They'd only had one semi-serious disagreement over something so insignificant he wondered why they'd fought in the first place. He'd plied her with kisses and even bought a freaky Eddie-type bear and brought it home. That's all it took to break the ice. As soon as she'd seen that ugly bear, Cassie had thrown her arms around him and promised never to raise her voice again. Small chance of that happening, but he enjoyed the making up that followed.

He'd introduced Cassie to the orchestra, the opera and the ballet. They met Landon and Amy for weekly Tuesday night dinners, often at Café Eduardo. They'd met a number of their neighbors and got together with some of them on occasion. Louie had suffered a mild heart attack early in the year, but he was fine and enjoying a forced early retirement. Tam and Helena were busy as ever with Tam's Place and both he and Cassie helped with whatever needed to be done as often as they could.

His business was starting to pick up more clients. The income had been a little slow at first as he'd established and started to build a clientele, but now it was steady with the promise of an increase. Together, they'd gone on a short-term mission to Trinidad. He'd worked with the medical team and Cassie taught the school age children. She'd loved it, and he'd admired how well she worked with everyone. With his encouragement, Cassie planned on starting college courses full-time, but not until the following winter semester—one of the primary reasons being the mission to Albuquerque had been pushed back to early October due to scheduling issues.

Taking the Stetson down from the shelf in the closet, she perched it on her head and did a little dance as she moved back to the bed. "Talk to Cassie."

"When you do that, you know I'm not thinking of talking."

"Sorry." She scrunched her nose and blushed.

"No, you're not." As distracting as she was, he needed to focus and tell her about the call. "I got a call from Josh today. He's getting a TeamWork group together to head down to Louisiana to help in the aftermath of Katrina."

"I figured they'd be going down." Cassie's lovely smile faded as she climbed into the bed beside him. "I want to do something to help, too."

"I'm sure there's plenty you can do. Help collect food and clothing. I'm sure Lexa and Winnie can give you ideas from what Sam and Josh are telling them. Ever since Josh called today, I've been watching the news, listening to the predictions and forecasts. It doesn't sound good. Katrina's going to be a monster. God be with the people of New Orleans or wherever it hits. There's bound to be a lot of devastation in its path."

~

Wednesday, August 31, 2005

"Sam, I want to help with the Hurricane Katrina relief effort. When Mitch comes to New Orleans next week, I want to come with him." Cassie kept her tone steady although inside, she quaked. She wished she could see his face, do this in person, but a telephone conversation would have to do for now.

"I appreciate your willingness to help, Cassie, but I can't allow it. In my position as Director of Domestic Missions, I'm responsible for those under my watch."

"What do you mean?"

She could hear his deep sigh, even through the phone lines. "Little One, it's dangerous. Things are happening there that most people can't fathom. I won't sugar coat it. Women are being raped, homes are being ransacked, and children are neglected and running naked in the streets. Animals are being slaughtered for food. It's heartbreaking and not all that much different than a war zone."

Cassie flinched at his words. "I can handle it. I saw my own brother killed in front of my eyes. If I survived that, I'm sure I can be tough enough to face whatever's happening in New Orleans."

"I've seen how strong you can be, Cassie, but this isn't the time to assert your will or prove your independence. It's time to be smart and understand there are some things you can't do, as much as you want to help. Have you talked with Mitch? I can't imagine he'd agree for you to go."

She bit her lip. "No. I called you first."

"Hi, Cass," Lexa said.

Cassie's heart lifted, as it always did, when she heard Lexa's voice. "Honey, Mitch needs to do this for himself as much as anyone else. If you go along, he'll spend too much time worrying about you and trying to keep you safe. Trust me, I'd love to go with Sam, too, but we need to stay on the home front and be here when they need us."

"I know, and I have to let him go. Mitch needs to see how the inherent good in people can overpower evil. He saw that to a certain extent when he helped at Ground Zero, but I think he was still in shock at the time and going through the motions."

"This need is going to be ongoing for years, but we'll do what we can, when we can," Sam said. "When he comes back from this experience, Mitch will need you more than ever. Working the effort on the front lines, so to speak, is going to change him in some way. It's inevitable. It changes all of us. I've seen how it's changed Josh after working with hurricane relief efforts on a much smaller scale than this one."

"I can't lose my husband, Sam. In some ways, I've only just found him." Cassie stared at the TeamWork business cards in a holder on Mitch's desk with TeamWork's slogan and theme verse: *Rebuilding lives worldwide and binding souls for Christ.* Next to it were the business cards for his private practice.

"You won't lose him, Little One."

Sam's words gave her renewed hope. "Other than pray, what do you suggest I do while he's gone?"

"Call him, send him messages, whatever you can to let him know he's loved," Lexa said.

Cassie smiled as she remembered the postcards Mitch sent to her from all along his route between Houston and Manhattan. How precious they'd been for her heart.

"Letting him know you care and that you're praying for him will mean the world." Lexa's tone was so full of compassion that it swelled Cassie's heart with even more respect and love for this couple.

"And tell him you'll be waiting for him when he comes home," Sam said.

That I can definitely do.

Chapter 48

Thursday, September 8, 2005 ~ New Orleans, Louisiana

*M*ITCH WEPT. HE'D seen things no man should ever see. The evil men can do to one another indeed. He thought he'd be cleaning, building, feeding and clothing the homeless. Instead, he'd witnessed atrocities that wrenched him apart. Even the tragedy of 9/11 was instigated by those of foreign origin who hated America and the freedoms for which it'd always represented, but this? To think what horrible things one human being could do to another gutted his very soul. On his home soil, his own country. How could they have a conscience? Did they not believe one day they'd have to account for their wrongdoing?

The lack of hope and respect for others had brought him to his knees several times, dropping to the ground as if felled by a physical blow. He'd been sick at least three times in the last forty-eight hours and emptied the contents of his stomach so that all that remained was bile. And still *that* came up and out of him. He'd already lost several pounds evidenced by how loosely his clothing hung on him now.

Even in the midst of it all, the citizens of New Orleans worked alongside them, doing anything and everything they could to try and right—or at least mediate—what the natural disaster and resulting self-destruction had wrought on their city. Mitch had seen Josh sitting on what was left of the front steps of a home, his head bowed in prayer with a man and his son. Witnessed Kevin and Sam ministering to an overburdened young family, giving them words of comfort and giving them a Bible.

TeamWork. *Rebuilding lives worldwide and binding souls for Christ.*

Sitting on the front stoop of the church where they'd camped out for the past two nights, Mitch stared, unseeing, into the twilight. His eyes drawn to the moon, he stared at it, admiring the beams, like a shining beacon. "Wish you were here, Moonbeam, but how thankful I am that you're not."

At least the night was relatively quiet. The stench of something—he didn't want to think what—permeated the night air, but he'd gotten used to the smells. And the noise, making the lack of chaos a welcome relief.

"You got a piece of mail." Kevin gave his shoulder a gentle nudge and handed something to him.

Glancing down at what he held, Mitch spied Cassie's lovely cursive. "Moonbeam," he whispered, running his finger over the front of the card with its photo of the Manhattan skyline. Turning it over again, he read the words:

Hi Mitch,

I ate a Corner Dog today and thought of you. I walked Sammie and thought of you. I sat in the park on our

special bench and thought of you. God was there beside me
today. Just like He always is. It's almost like I could feel
His arms around me, giving me sweet comfort. As if He
was whispering in my heart, "Rest in Me, child. Mitch is
safe."
I'm praying for you. . . .and I'm waiting.
All My Love,
Cassie a/k/a Moonbeam

Kevin dropped onto the step beside him. "According to Pastor Evans, the card was delivered somewhere down the street. Cassie had the right address, but the mail carrier left it at the wrong place."

"I'm just thankful to get it at all." Maybe it was his overactive imagination, but the card held the faintest hint of her scent. Light, pretty, floral. *Cassie.*

Beside him, he heard Kevin's chuckle. They hadn't found much to laugh about since their arrival in "The Zone" as they'd taken to calling New Orleans.

"You've really got it bad, don't you?"

Mitch allowed a small smile. "Yeah. I love her so much I physically ache for her, Kevin."

"I know, buddy. You're still a newlywed. You can go home if you want. Everyone would understand."

"I'm not a quitter. I want to see this mission through. But when I get back to New York, I'm going to hole up with my wife for a week and love her. Like Sam's rule says. Just love her."

Kevin blew out a breath. "Tell me about it. I can't wait to get back home to Rebekah."

"I can't imagine a soldier sees much worse than what we've seen the past few days. Cassie's my first thought in the morning, my last thought at the end of the day and every waking thought in between. I can't stop thinking about her." He glanced over at his friend. "Not that I'd ever want to. Makes it hard to concentrate sometimes. Being around all this devastation makes me realize how much I've always taken for granted. I never wanted for anything like Cassie did when she was growing up. I probably shouldn't tell you this, but her dad was in jail a lot. In the last year, he's straightened himself out some. He's been doing some volunteer work and staying out of jail for the most part."

"Rebekah and Cassie are close and she's shared some things with her. You're not giving away any confidences you shouldn't."

"Did you know about her brother?"

"Tagg? Yeah. Cassie's been through a lot, but it shows how strong she is. I know she wanted to come with us and help in the relief effort, too, but I heard Sam and your New York TeamWork Director wouldn't allow it."

"She feels helpless being on the sidelines." Mitch waved his hand at their surroundings and breathed out a deep sigh. "Cassie would be the first person to tell me how she's lived like a queen compared to what we see here. How can this happen, Kevin? As crazy as it sounds, in some ways Katrina was the least of their problems. And it was the instigator for more hardship."

"It happens because people are lost, like they are everywhere else in the world." Kevin's voice was quiet, filled with deep emotion. "They don't have a center in their lives and no sense of what's right and wrong."

"No hope." Mitch rested his arms on his propped knees. "It's the only answer my mind can comprehend or accept. That's at the root of it, isn't it? And that's the saddest thing of all." A tear slipped down his cheek, and he didn't bother to wipe it away. "I've been on mission trips to some of the most desolate areas of the world, and yet what I'm seeing here—in our own country—breaks my heart." He'd shed more tears in the past seventy-two hours than he could ever remember. In some ways, he felt like he'd aged since their arrival.

"If it helps, you gave a glimmer of hope to one mother and her little girl today," Kevin said. "Don't think what you're doing here has no impact, Mitch."

Mitch raised his head and looked at his friend, focusing through glazed eyes. That little girl earlier tore his heart out with her big eyes brimming with hurt. "I want the kids, especially, to see that people can be good. Not all people are bad and want to hurt them or take something precious from them. But sometimes I feel like we're up against a brick wall."

"That's why we have to keep going. These people have lost it all and then some." Kevin paused a few moments before continuing. "Like God's word tells us, our job is to plant the seeds and sow righteousness. The world operates differently than we do. We know that, and it's all about cause and effect, Mitch. What they don't understand is that every action has consequences, and one day we'll have to stand before God and account for every one of our decisions."

"I remember my dad preaching from Galatians," Mitch said. "In chapter six, it talks about how God is not mocked. *For the one who sows to his own flesh will from the flesh reap corruption, but the one who sows to the Spirit will from the Spirit reap eternal life.*"

He dropped his head in shame. "I've lived both ways."

Kevin placed a hand on his shoulder. "But you're forgiven. A man of God. You're living for Him now and that's what matters. By the way, do you know the reason Marc's not here?"

"No."

"Natalie found out she's expecting and she's having a difficult time with the pregnancy."

Mitch nodded. "Praise God since they've been trying for a while now, and if anyone understands the importance of keeping your loved ones close, it's Marc. I'll pray everything's okay."

"I'm sure they will be, and I'm really glad you're here with us, buddy." Kevin nudged Mitch's shoulder.

"As difficult as it is to say now, I am too, Kevin. I am, too."

~

The Next Morning ~ Friday, September 9, 2005

The men—Mitch counted twenty-three—sat in a circle on chairs in the church basement. Even at seven in the morning, it was sticky and hot but still the coolest area of the building. His shower had been pointless since sweat already coated his brow and ran down his back. After singing a few hymns and a time of sharing, Sam began his short message before they headed outside to another day with its new challenges.

"I'd like to read from Second Timothy, Chapter 3, verses 1 and following. As it always does, God's Word speaks for all time. This particular passage spoke to my heart when I prayed what message I could give this morning that might encourage you."

With his glasses in place, Sam began to read. *"But realize this, that in the last days difficult times will come. For men will be lovers of self, lovers of money, boastful, arrogant, revilers, disobedient to parents, ungrateful, unholy, unloving, irreconcilable, malicious gossips, without self-control, brutal, haters of good, treacherous, reckless, conceited, lovers of pleasure rather than lovers of God, holding to a form of godliness, although they have denied its power; Avoid such men as these. For among them are those who enter into households and captivate weak women weighed down with sins, led on by various impulses, always learning and never come to the knowledge of the truth. . ."*

Mitch lowered his head and closed his eyes even as he absorbed the words that spoke to his very soul. He wished his father could sit beside him now. In some ways, perhaps he was. But if he could be here, Mitch knew he'd probably read that very same scripture Sam read.

Sam continued, *"Indeed, all who desire to live godly in Christ Jesus will be persecuted. But evil men and imposters will proceed from bad to worse, deceiving and being deceived. You, however, continue in the things you have learned and become convinced of, knowing from whom you have learned them, and that from childhood you have known the sacred writings which are able to give you the wisdom that leads to salvation through faith which is in Christ Jesus."*

Lowering his Bible to his lap, Sam glanced around the circle. Mitch liked how their TeamWork leader had a way of making every person in the room feel important and special. He accepted them. Among the group, they'd had a few squabbles. Tensions had been high, sleeping and showering in tight quarters, but—like soldiers in barracks—any one of these guys had his back. He'd do anything to watch out for each of them.

"I'm sure you all know the words of the next verse," Sam said. *"All Scripture is inspired by God and profitable for. . ."*

"*Teaching, for reproof,*" Mitch said under his breath, "*for correction, for training in righteousness; so that the man of God may be adequate, equipped for every good work.*" Reaching into his pocket, he pulled out the post card from Cassie, reading it for the hundredth time since Kevin gave it to him the night before.

"We've been put here for a reason, every one of us, each to his own purpose," Sam said, removing his glasses. The lines around his eyes were more prominent, the smile lines not seen much in recent days. He'd gotten little sleep each night. Mitch had seen him praying earlier that morning when he'd grabbed some cereal for breakfast. Sam still had his head bowed when he'd passed by him as he'd gone to get dressed.

Sam's words now interrupted his thoughts. "As always, the Lord's given us everything we need to accomplish His perfect will here in New Orleans. And He'll continue to do so. Keep the faith, brothers. Feel free to come to me, Josh or Kevin. We're here for you. Whatever you need."

Mitch rose with the other men as they discussed their projects for the day. Sam was right. He was here for a purpose. God had called him here.

A big hand clamped on his shoulder. "The postcard in your pocket is from Cassie, isn't it?"

He grinned. "How could you tell?"

Sam's deeply etched smile lines emerged again as they walked outside and stood on the front steps of the church. "The look on your face said it all. Being in circumstances like this can change how you perceive your everyday world. I'd say you're learning that firsthand." Raising his face to the sun, Sam squinted before lowering those piercing eyes on him. "Keep that postcard in your pocket."

"Will do, Sam. I'll see you sometime tonight."

"God go with you, brother."

Chapter 49

Saturday Morning ~ September 10, 2005

"CASSIE, MITCH IS missing." Sam's voice was low, anguish in his words.

Her breathing stopped. She sputtered, then coughed. "Missing? What. . .how?"

"We're doing everything we can to find him. Josh and Kevin are scouring the neighborhood, asking questions and getting some of the church members and neighbors to help. There's a lot of flooding in the area, and it's difficult to get around."

"When's the last time anyone saw him?"

"He was helping down in the 5th Ward."

Cassie swallowed her sobs. Wasn't that one of the Wards hardest hit? *Be strong.* "When was that?"

"Yesterday morning."

She sank into a chair. When Sammie padded over to her, she put her arm around him and hugged him close. "I'm assuming you've called his cell phone?"

"Multiple times, but he's not answering." That would explain why Mitch hadn't texted or answered her calls. She'd been worried, but convinced herself he was too busy and would call as soon as he could.

Cassie's pulse throbbed in her temples and her palms grew clammy. "What about the police?"

"They've been alerted, but they have too much to do down here. I'll call whenever I have an update. You do the same."

"Thanks, Sam." She heard him say he was praying, but she'd dropped the phone.

"Sammie boy, we've got to pray for Mitch. God, please, bring him home to us."

~

Mitch groaned. What happened? He scrubbed both hands over his face. Where was he, anyway? He glanced down at his body, sprawled on the hard floor of some dank smelling place. He patted himself down, thankful everything seemed to be in its proper place. To his left, a section of the floor was covered in sludge. . . or something. Not going to speculate on that one. His throat was dry and he felt like he'd been run over by a cement truck and left to die.

What have you gotten yourself into now, Jacobsen? This was one adventure he'd rather skip.

Moaning, he managed to reach a sitting position. His brain was fuzzy. Why couldn't he remember anything? When he heard voices, he turned his head in their direction. Male voices speaking in low tones. From the few words he heard, he knew these people weren't friends.

Grunting under his breath, he managed to lift himself to his knees. He swayed a bit and planted his palms flat on the ground to steady himself. Wow, this was worse than any hangover. He felt dizzy and not more than a little nauseous. Mitch clamped his arm over his abdomen and deep breathed. *Not the time for a panic attack.* Glancing around the room in its stark reality, his eyes focused a bit more. Current circumstances might warrant a few feelings of panic and more than a few fervent prayers.

He looked up when a man approached him. A big man covered in tattoos and sporting a full beard and an abundance of piercings. His jeans were dirty and torn, the expression on his face angry and defiant.

"Decide to finally wake up, did you?"

"Who are you and why am I here?"

The man spat at his feet. "None of your business."

Ignoring the man's choice curse word in that statement, Mitch struggled to his feet. "Well, it's been nice chatting, but if you'll excuse me, I'll just be moving on my way now."

"Think again." The man swung at him. Catching the movement, Mitch stuck out his arm and stopped the bruiser from making contact.

Feeling strangely weak, Mitch stumbled backward. "Hey, man," he mumbled. "Did you actually. . .actually. . .dr—drug m-m-me?" When he glanced up at the man, his outline was hazy.

"You could say that."

Mitch reached for his back pocket, groaning again. Empty. His ID and one credit card were missing. The one he'd loaded the day before coming to New Orleans. He reached for his other pocket. No cell phone.

"How long have I been here?"

"Long enough," the man snorted. "Lie down and go to sleep again like a good little boy and say your prayers that somebody finds you before you rot down here. Or someone wants your clothes. Or whatever else you've got left to give."

"Why'd you come back then, if you're not here to help me?" He'd rasped out the question but could barely keep his head up long enough to wait for an answer.

The guy stomped over to him and spat in his face. "For the satisfaction of seeing your eyes rolled back in your head and deader than a doorknob. Maybe I'll get lucky next time."

"Lord forgive them for they know not what they do." Mitch used the bottom of his T-shirt to wipe the man's saliva from his cheek.

With a derisive and bitter laugh, the man departed. In the recesses of his consciousness, Mitch heard a click. They'd locked him in this hole like a prisoner? At least he wasn't chained. He spied a small paper cup. Water? Half-crawling toward it, he seized it. Empty as his pockets.

Slumping to the hard cold floor, Mitch found comfort in its coolness, its peace.

A tear slid down his cheek. "I love you, Moonbeam. Please pray. Please. . .*pray.*"

Unable to keep his eyes open, he closed his eyelids. The blessed relief of sleep beckoned.

~

Later that Day

Cassie couldn't concentrate on anything. She'd cried until she had no more tears. The only thing she'd managed to do since Sam's call was to throw on sweats and walk Sammie. Amy came over and brought her lunch and stayed with her for a few hours. They'd prayed and been there for each other. Their mom and Celeste were on standby and Landon was fueling the plane in case they needed to pay a visit to New Orleans. Getting a private aircraft into the area was easier than a commercial jet right now, it seemed. Not that she wanted to find out firsthand, but the knowledge was good to have, in any case.

Lord, I can't lose him. I love my husband. Take me if You must, but please bring Mitch home.

She'd talked with Rebekah. She'd called Marc and Natalie and told them how happy she was to hear they were expecting. They understood why she was subdued and told her they'd been praying mightily for Mitch. People all over the country were praying. She'd let the phone calls pile up on the answering machine, let the emails go unanswered.

She set up a Skype call with Winnie and Lexa after Amy left the townhouse. Seeing and hearing her friends in Houston was such a soothing balm for her hurting heart. They'd set up a laptop computer on the kitchen counter at Josh and Winnie's house.

Cassie gave them a wan smile and watched her own laptop computer screen through vacant eyes. Winnie approached the screen and gave her a cyber-hug. "Not that it helps much, but I brought you something." Moving one hand from behind her back, she placed a cupcake in the middle of the screen. A pink, loaded with buttercream frosting cupcake.

She couldn't help herself as she burst into tears. Again. She'd lost count of how many times she'd erupted in the past few hours alone. "Oh, Winnie. That's the most beautiful thing I've ever seen. Thank you."

Winnie smiled. "Honey, besides my love, prayers and support, it's the best thing I can offer right now."

"It comes from your heart and that's what matters most." Cassie sniffled and then snatched a tissue from the box beside her on the kitchen table. "How's your new little one?"

"Emily's fine. Luke's fascinated by girl baby, as he calls her. Chloe's the little mother, as you might imagine. I suppose there's no word from the guys yet?"

"No." Cassie shook her head, biting her lower lip to stem the waterworks. "Nothing."

"I'm sure they'll find him, honey. Amy wanted to go down there, but like with you, Sam practically roared like a lion and demanded she stay home. I've started calling him *no way, no how* Sam."

That made Cassie smile a little. "I love your optimism, Winnie."

"Our guys are going to need some extra good loving when they come home, that's for sure. Maybe Mitch went off on his own for some project and forgot to check in?"

"I doubt that's true. You know how Mitch is conscientious about those things. If nothing else, he'd tell Sam or Josh. Or call me to let me know where he is, especially if he's gone overnight."

Lexa came into view on the computer screen. "Come on. I'm taking you to Richardson's. A dose of cyber ice cream and Bea will be good for you."

"But I've got my cupcake for all the cyber sugar overload a girl could possibly ever need." That statement came out more a half-wail.

"Bring it along," Winnie said. "It'll go great with the ice cream."

~

Mitch startled as he heard a loud banging. "Huh?" He sat up and tried to focus on the door, but it was too much effort for his muddled state of being. He closed his eyes again, willing sleep. The pounding started again. "Go away!" he said, smacking his jaws. Man, his throat burned. He hoped it wasn't Bruiser returning to knock him around some more or taunt him again. He opened his eyes. At least he remembered that guy, so it proved he wasn't completely losing his mind. Maybe this time it was someone who could help him.

The door burst open and a dark-haired man raced inside with Bruiser right behind him. Mitch watched as the two men exchanged punches. The first guy ducked and grabbed Bruiser around the knees, dropping him to the floor like he was a featherweight. Bruiser groaned from a few feet away. The other man stepped closer, and in a crouched position, clubbed him in the jaw. "There, that should do it. You're not going to feel good when you wake up."

"Am I in Heaven?" Mitch glanced over at his captor. "Guess not because I'm pretty sure that guy"—he gestured to Bruiser—"won't be there."

Glancing up at him, his rescuer reached out a hand to help him to a sitting position. "Here," he said, pulling a water bottle from a small pouch attached to his waist. "Drink this."

Mitch grabbed it like a dying man and guzzled the contents of the bottle. A few ounces of the liquid dribbled down the side of his mouth and dripped onto his clothes. The wetness seeping through his thin T-shirt and onto his skin felt so cool, so good. Wiping his mouth with the back of his hand, Mitch shot him a grateful glance. "Thanks, man. That's not water. What is it?"

"Vitamin-infused mineral water and a few nutrients to build your energy level. Totally natural and something to give you some sustenance until I can get you to a hospital."

Mitch stared at his health-conscious rescuer. "A hospital? Last time I checked, I was still intact. At least I hope so. Anything missing?" He patted himself down again.

The other man chuckled and regarded him through kind brown eyes. "You're gonna be fine buddy. Come on, let's get you out of here."

He hauled Mitch to his feet and put a supportive hand under one arm, the other around his waist. This man was almost as tall as Sam and stronger than a bull. Was he military? Whatever he was, the guy had his undying gratitude.

"Are you like some really cool angel? If you're going to hold me like this, don't you think you should at least tell me your name?" *Oh, oh.* "Hang on a minute. Gotta go. . ." Turning aside, falling to his knees, Mitch lost the contents of what he'd just downed. "Sorry," he muttered, gasping, staring at the floor. "I'm not myself today. Not sure I can get up on my own speed either." His head felt like it was going to explode and his mouth felt like cotton. The hospital didn't sound like such a bad idea.

Bruiser lifted up on one arm and pulled something out of his back pocket. "He's got a weapon," Mitch said. In seconds, his rescuer crossed the room and kicked whatever the man held in his hand—a knife?—and sent it sprawling across the cracked, uneven cement floor. As Mitch leaned his forehead against the cool ground, he heard Bruiser cry out in pain. When he raised his head to see what was happening, the dark-haired man pocketed the weapon and hurried back to him.

"Let's get you out of here." Without another word, the man hoisted him on his back.

"What about Bruiser over there?" Mitch nodded over his shoulder.

"He's not going anywhere soon. I'll turn in the knife. They'll run prints if you want to file charges. I went easy on him and only broke one of his legs before I knocked him out cold."

Darting a quick glance at the guy, Mitch noted Bruiser's left leg was positioned at an odd angle. "Wow. Remind me to never get on your bad side. Hang on a second." He slid down and reached into his front pocket. "The one thing they didn't take," he said, holding up a Christian tract. Tossing it on the inert man's chest, he grunted. "Hopefully he'll read it instead of blowing his nose with it."

"Sometimes you give them to the Lord, buddy. That's all you can do."

"Right," Mitch said, shaking his head.

"Need a lift, Mitch?"

"Nah, I think I can make it on my own speed now. Thanks again. I'm indebted." He offered his hand. "Seems you have the advantage in knowing who I am, but I didn't catch your name."

"Eliot Marchand." He shook Mitch's hand, pumping it up and down, nearly crushing his fingers with his hard grip. In the haze of his brain, Mitch thought he detected the faintest trace of an accent. Foreign. Maybe German or French? He must be delusional. Still, wasn't Marchand a French name?

"Quite a grip you've got there." Mitch opened his eyes wider as recognition slowly filtered into his brain. The name rang a bell. "Eliot," he repeated. "You mean as in *TeamWork* Eliot? That Eliot?"

"The same." Reaching into the bag around his waist, Eliot pulled out a second pair of sunglasses. "Do yourself a favor and put these on. We'll be outside in a few seconds and the sun will be brutal since you haven't seen it for a couple of days."

"*Merci beaucoup.*" Mitch put the sunglasses in place while Eliot did the same. "Let's go."

~

An Hour Later

Cassie seized her cell phone on the first ring tone. She'd left it on the kitchen counter. *Sam*. Her hand shook as she brought the phone to her ear. *Please, Lord, let it be good news.*

"They found him, Cassie. Mitch is dehydrated and a bit delusional, but he's finally agreed to stay in the hospital overnight for observation."

"Oh, thank you, Jesus." Cassie released her tears, holding tight to the phone with one hand, wiping under her eyes with the other. She listened as Sam relayed the story about Mitch being mugged and hauled to an abandoned building, robbed and left without food and water.

Winnie and Lexa looked at her expectantly from the computer screen. Cassie mouthed *he's okay*.

With a huge smile, Winnie gave her a thumbs-up. "They found Mr. Mitch," Cassie heard her whisper to Chloe. The little girl beamed and clapped. Scrambling down from her chair, Chloe made the announcement to the rest of Richardson's. Cheers and claps arose from the customers and Bea grabbed her teenage employee and hugged her tight, jumping up and down as best as her rather large frame would allow. Cassie turned down the volume on the computer screen to muffle the hoopla and hysteria.

"Are you having a party?" Sam said. "Where are you? Unless my ears deceive me, I heard Winnie and maybe even Chloe."

"You did," Cassie said, mopping her cheeks. "We're having a Skype session and they've taken me to Richardson's. Lexa and your kids are here, too. There. Wherever." She shook her head. "We're together in spirit."

"Wish I could be there, too." The weariness in Sam's voice surfaced.

Cassie's head pounded from the stress, but the heavy burden in her heart had lifted, replaced by a quiet joy. Maybe now she could breathe. Maybe now she could take a long, hot shower. Maybe now she could eat. "Sam, tell me more about what happened, if you know any details."

"I called Eliot, and he flew in from wherever in the world he's been most recently and he tracked Mitch down. Then he met up with Josh and Kevin and they transported Mitch to the hospital. They've got a rotation going to watch over him. Of course, the hospital personnel are getting irritated with all the visitors." Sam's chuckle was such a balm for her hurting heart.

"When are you all planning on going home?" Cassie asked.

"The Houston crew, by mid-week. Mitch might be flying home when he's released from the hospital."

Cassie sat up straighter. "Tomorrow?"

"Most likely, Little One. He's weakened from this and I don't want him overdoing it. Landon can fly him home, and I don't think he'll mind being on a private jet this time. Hang on a second. I have someone here who wants to speak with you."

"Hey, Moonbeam."

"Mitch!" Cassie clamped her hand over her mouth and more tears sprang into her eyes and streamed down her cheeks.

"Sam's calling from my room at the hospital. He seems to think I'm an invalid. He's going to start spouting Bible verses any minute so talk to me. Distract me." Sam's laughter could be heard in the background.

"I heard you met Eliot," she said, saying the first thing that popped into her mind. From the computer screen, she could tell Winnie was listening even though she turned aside to wipe strawberry ice cream from her son's mouth. Cassie leaned closer to the screen to get a glimpse of baby Emily in her carrier next to Winnie.

"Eliot's great. My hero. If you're in trouble, Eliot's the man to call. You should have seen him. He burst into that hole I'd reportedly called home for a day or so and knocked Bruiser out cold. Then he brought me out into the sunshine and among the land of the living again. It was pretty wild."

"Bruiser?"

"Some guy who apparently wanted to see me dead."

Cassie's pulse stopped cold. "Are you serious? Please don't say things like that, not even in jest."

"I'm not joking. He told me he hoped"—he hesitated—"never mind. Doesn't matter. I'm fine and can't wait to see you."

"Everyone's been calling, emailing and asking about you. People from all over the country have been praying. You gave us a scare. Don't ever do it again, okay?"

"Can't promise that, but the Lord watches over His own. Always. No matter what happens, Cassie, everything will be okay."

"Come back to me, Mitch."

"I never left."

Chapter 50

*C*ASSIE SNUGGLED CLOSER to Mitch, prepared to listen as he read to her.

"I want to read to you from Mark Twain's *Innocents Abroad*, another favorite of mine," Mitch said. "'*I began to feel that the old Venice of song and story had departed forever. But I was too hasty. In a few minutes, we swept gracefully out into the Grand Canal, and under the mellow moonlight, the Venice of poetry and romance stood revealed. Right from the water's edge rose long lines of stately palaces of marble; gondolas were gliding swiftly hither and thither and disappearing suddenly through unsuspected gates and alleys; ponderous stone bridges threw their shadows athwart glittering waves. There was life and motion everywhere, and yet everywhere there was a hush, a stealthy sort of stillness, that was suggestive of secret enterprises of bravos and of lovers; and clad half in moonbeams and half in mysterious shadows, the grim old mansions of the Republic seemed to have an expression about them of having an eye out for just such enterprises as these at that same moment. Music came floating over the waters—Venice was complete.*'"

"Cassie, you make *me* complete. Do you realize the significance of this day?"

"Besides being the day my husband came home to stay? At least for now?"

Mitch chuckled, and she felt the rumble beneath her cheek where she rested on his chest. Pulling up, she kissed him again. She couldn't seem to stop kissing him since he'd come home to her. He was sore and he'd endured a few beatings, and she'd lovingly pressed her lips over every bruise and place where he'd been hurt.

"It's September the eleventh," he said, his voice reverent. "A day I'm going to celebrate *life* from this day forward."

She pulled back, her eyes wide. "I can't believe I didn't even think about it. I've been so preoccupied with getting you home, it never crossed my mind."

"I've learned it's not our place to ask why things like 9/11 and Katrina happen. We need to trust in the Lord and know He's got it all under control. Yet we can never forget." Sitting up in the bed, he caressed her cheeks and drew her closer again. "We need to cherish our loved ones and treasure each day He gives us. And I'm so thankful He gave you to me."

"And you to me," she whispered. His kiss was exquisite, so filled with passion.

Much later, holding her in his arms, Mitch brushed his lips over hers and gazed at her through sleepy eyes.

"Rest now, my love," she said.

"God knows what He's doing," Mitch murmured as she rolled over on her side. Then her husband wrapped himself around her, spooning her in the way she loved. "We're a perfect fit in every way. I love you, Moonbeam."

"Yes, we are," Cassie breathed. "I love you, too, Mitch. Forever."

About the Author

JoAnn Durgin is the author of *The Lewis Legacy Series: Awakening*, *Second Time Around*, *Twin Hearts*, *Daydreams* and *Moonbeams* as well as a standalone novel, *Catching Serenity*. Her books with Pelican Book Group/White Rose Publishing include Christmas novellas, *Meet Me Under the Mistletoe* and its sequel, *Starlight, Star Bright* as well as the upcoming *Echoes of Edinburgh* in September 2014.

An estate administration paralegal in a Louisville, Kentucky law firm, JoAnn lives with her family in southern Indiana. A member of the American Christian Fiction Writers (National Chapter, ACFW Indiana, ACFW Kentucky) and the Louisville Christian Writers, JoAnn's prayer is that her contemporary romantic adventures will touch hearts and lives with the redeeming love of Jesus Christ.

WEBSITE: www.joanndurgin.com

BLOG: http://www.inspyromance.com/author/joann-durgin/

FACEBOOK: https://www.facebook.com/authorjoanndurgin

www.ingramcontent.com/pod-product-compliance
Lightning Source LLC
Chambersburg PA
CBHW020241180626
46810CB00006B/2301